NOD

Book One

Nothing Sacred, Nothing Harmed

Jason Chmielewski

Nothing Sacred, Nothing Harmed

The First Book in the NOD Series

Written by Jason Chmielewski
Edited by Stefani Manard
NOD logo and title by Josh Werner

Published by Scapegoat Press, Inc.
First Edition
Copyright © 2017 Jason Chmielewski

ISBN: 0-9981515-2-1
ISBN-13: 978-0-9981515-2-6

Scapegoat Press is an independent publishing
company located in southeast Michigan.

Facebook.com/ScapegoatPressInc
ScapegoatPress@Gmail.com

DEDICATION

This book is dedicated to my friend of a very, very, VERY long time, Stefani Manard. Without her prodding over the years, this book would likely never have seen the light of day.
I'm not saying it *should*, but, well...judge for yourself!

CONTENTS

INTRODUCTION

This has been a long time coming.

Work on this novel has taken place over the course of around a third of my entire life. I've been through some ups, a lot of downs, and spent months at a time without even typing a thing. Ultimately, it was the insistence of my friend (and publisher!) Stefani, and some drastic, unfortunate changes to my life that led me to finally finish. Art is pain, after all.

Although the basic story has remained the same this entire time, I've grown and changed, and hopefully maybe even matured a bit. There may be some relics here and there of when this book was a bit more childish and lewd (and there are some *very* outdated music references, although part of that's by design,) but overall I'm very proud of what I've created.

Otomo Katsuhiro's *AKIRA* was a huge part of my formative introduction to manga and anime, and I wanted to write something in a similar vein, but perhaps less bleak. It's been said that they are no actual good guys in *AKIRA*; it's just that the bad guys are worse. There are definite shout-outs to this work (among others) in my writing, but I like to think that my good guys are a *bit* likable, at least!

One point, though, in regards to references. The characters of Steve, Matthew, and Andrew are not an homage to *Chronicle*, having been already committed to paper long before that film's existence. However, as it's another story exploring psychics and relationships, which I like well enough, I'll consider it a happy accident.

In any case, I hope you enjoy reading this as much or more so than I did writing it. I have a lot of story to tell.

I'll let you get started.

Jason Chmielewski

May 20th, 2017

Prologue:
The World Shudders

Omaha was a decent kind of place to live. The roads were a little screwy, sure, the humidity in summer nothing short of awful, but the atmosphere was laid back, crime was low, and the water was clean. Suburban and rural ways of life collided and created a peaceful, neighborly environment, the sort of big-town-with-the-small-town-feel that vacationers are so keen on. And in the center of all that was nifty and swell in Omaha was the Gates Building, a shiny testament to the greatness of mankind. Nary a soul walked by without glancing over and smiling. For it was due to the Gates Building, due to public services and donations, that Omaha was such a perfect place to live.

Almost perfect.

For Omaha was torn flesh, and the Gates Building was a scab resting on it. The promise of new skin was an empty one, for once the healing was over and the scab fell away, a horrible scar would be revealed. Most people were oblivious to this fact; they walked by in a daze of soulless bliss. Their problems were insignificant compared to the disease that laid beneath the scab, though they were too naive to know it.

There were those who lurked in the shadows, huddled in alleyways and underpasses like rats and cockroaches. They had escaped the deluding. They knew the truth; they still remembered. They gibbered on and on about this and that, and if one listened to the words between the words maybe, just maybe, one could discover what had really happened. They spoke of angels and demons, of life and death. They told of a cataclysm that had shaken Omaha, and maybe the world, to its core. A cataclysm so immense in its power and its meaning, that most could not comprehend it. Most had been quick to forget it, with help, of course.

Not they.

Like lunatics they were, equal parts madness and genius springing forth as they wrung their hands over their burn barrels and shot paranoid glances in every direction. Omaha was diseased; right at this moment, an upwelling of puss and rot and pestilence threatened to blow away the scab, threatened to tear wide open the wound and spread its vile, infectious illness to every corner of the world. It was an illness of depravity and greed and inhumanity disguised as knowledge and good intentions. It promised a new era in mankind's legacy, but gave no mention of the strife it would cause.

They were the only ones who knew this.

Most shied away from these crazies, as people generally do to those who remind them of humanity's dark, desperate side. Those few that listened thought them daft; thought them to be babbling loonies. Their stories couldn't be true, mustn't be true, they were an affront to logic and decency. They were the product of each and every bum's own particular brand of insanity.

Lunacy aside, one nagging problem would have led credence to their stories, had anyone bothered to look for it.

All of their stories were the same.

As for those working the abominations, feeding this new pestilence, they justified their actions with the scientist's standby:

The greater good outweighs the suffering of the few.

But where do you draw the line?

Part One
Two Paths

One:
White Room

Mina looked around. She hated this room with a passion, or at least as much of a passion as she was capable of feeling; but even so, it always gave her a feeling of awe. It was so huge that even though the ground level around her was fairly well lit, she could barely see the far wall and could not make out the ceiling at all. The wall curved all about like a great, white, graceful sphere, but the curve was so grand it seemed almost flat close up.

In truth, the wall wasn't technically white. It seemed to be, at a glance, but up close one could see that it was really made up of a myriad of patches in soft hues of pink and blue and green that flickered about and switched colors with each other. The result was that from a distance, the patches seemed to blend into a solid color but the flickering was still visible as a sort of wiggle that disoriented and nauseated Mina.

Maybe that was the idea.

Around her on the floor was a series of concentric rings of the same glowing colors as the wall (only their hues were more pronounced) spaced about three yards apart.

A voice filtered down from above. "We would like you to move to the center of the circles, if you please."

Hanging her head in a shameful way, Mina obliged the voice. Her hospital gown rustled as she walked. Reaching the center of the rings, she stood straight up, trying not to cringe at what she knew would come next. When the floodlights hit her face, she instinctively tried to block the light with her hands, but the shackles that connected her wrists to her ankles by way of a steel chain prohibited this movement. Apparently someone saw her attempt because the voice from above said, "Sorry. They're for your own protection; you know that." Mina nodded.

An older man, perhaps in his late fifties judging by the color and thickness (or lack thereof) of his hair, leaned back from the microphone he had just spoken into. There was one other person with him, a younger man of Hispanic descent, sitting beside him in the control room. There were several monitors on the wall in front of them, all showing closed-circuit video of Mina from different angles.

The older man spoke. "Begin the activation sequence of the otomo particle generator." The Hispanic man nodded, and fiddled with several dials and sliders on a panel next to him.

"Initial output stabilized at point-oh-five maximum capacity."

"Raise to three-point-five and begin flooding the subject."

Mina felt a slight tingling on the surface of her skin. There was a dull ache beginning in the base of her skull, and as the tingling became more pronounced the headache spread forward and up. Several minutes passed.

"Psychoactive radiation levels are now at twenty percent capacity," spoke the Hispanic man. "Should I begin the sync process?"

The older man nodded. He watched one of the monitors eagerly. It showed a distorted image of Mina, surrounded by a yellowish glow that pulsed more and more quickly as the radiation bathing her intensified. A greenish glow surrounded the yellowish one, pulsing much more quickly than the yellow one, and in a more orderly manner, however, as time passed, the yellow one seemed to be trying to match the actions of the green.

"Yes! The subject's aura is resonating with the artificial pattern! Raise the output to thirty-five percent!"

The pain in Mina's head was intense. Her balance was spinning away from her and she began to wobble. Her eyes were wrenched shut but her inner vision was bathed in a seething foam of dark green and black that made her want to throw up. The tingling on her skin had proceeded through stages of itchiness and pain, and was now starting to burn.

The output had barely passed twenty-one. The older man watched with the blank dissatisfaction of someone who didn't like what was happening but had expected it all along.

"Sir, the resonance is breaking down. The subject's aura is varying wildly and the interference has become destructive."

Mina was on her hands and knees, rocking side-to-side.

The older man spoke. "Up to thirty-five."

Mina's eyelids snapped open, revealing the veiny whiteness of her rolled-back eyes. She fell to the floor, twitching and convulsing, and vomited searing hot bile. Her gown burst into flames and her shackles started to melt. The pain was great, although Mina wasn't conscious to feel it. Despite the fire and the melting metal, her skin remained unscarred, the same pale white hue it had always had.

In the control booth, the older man squinted his eyes as he looked into the monitors. He pushed in the button on his recording device.

"In prior tests, subject has shown a definite reaction to seizure-inducing conditions. Psychoactivity has been confirmed, *again*, via otomo particle test three. Pattern cohesion was not attained, combustion reaction occurred, leaving no wounds visible at this time. Subject appears to be unconscious." *So much power that she can't tap properly!* He thought with disgust.

He turned to face the other operator.

The younger man looked at his superior and spoke hesitantly. "What happened?"

The older operator looked at the monitor, seeing the twitching, naked girl lying amidst gently smoking embers. Then, with neither malice nor care in his voice, he calmly answered.

"Neural misfire failure. Let's try it again."

Two:
Hallucination 1

Raven brushed her auburn locks out of her face and lit another cigarette. She wiped some tears out of her eyes.

Fuck her. She isn't worth it. She couldn't fool herself, though.

She looked over at the picture of her and her girlfriend Crow that was on her dresser. It was taken last Halloween; she was supposed to be a witch and Crow was supposed to be a dominatrix, but in truth both costumes had wound up looking very similar.

Dissatisfied with the cigarette, Raven put it out. Leaning over the edge of her bed, she pulled out a small tin. Opening it, she pulled out a joint and lit it up. She edged towards her nightstand and hit the play button on her CD player. The song that came on was an ethereal one about a dead, colorless world and the loss of emotions. It made Raven think of death and computers and cyborg movies. She laid there, waiting for the mellowness to kick in, thinking.

She had been going out with Crow for several months now. She had come into Raven's life at a time when she needed companionship most, while she was still mourning a bad breakup and her family life was spiraling downward, when she had to look forward to her senior year without her best friend, who had graduated already. There was an instant connection between them the first time they saw each other. They completed each other's sentences and laughed at jokes no one else even understood. That was how it was supposed to be, wasn't it?

Then, last night, everything had fallen apart again. It had been a bad night from the beginning; her dick-weed brother had gotten her in trouble over something she couldn't remember anymore, and her mother had bitched her out for what felt like forever. Once she had finally left, Raven met up with Crow and they went to a house party. Then everything really went to shit.

For a while now, Raven had been experiencing occasional audiovisual hallucinations. They were fairly rare, and thankfully, some were minor. Most weren't. Sometimes it was like memories played out in front of her; sometimes it was a confused alteration of what was actually going on around her; and, sometimes, it was so indescribable she would sit as still as a rock, letting it wash over her, praying for it to end.

She had been sitting across from Crow, her in a chair and Crow on a couch with some boy they didn't know sitting next to her, talking her ear off as she rolled her eyes. The music was so loud neither of them could hear him, anyway.

To Raven, the music dropped away entirely, and was replaced with a low-key hum. There was a man floating in the air with a fuzzy crowd standing around him in a sphere, and glowing orbs shot out of his hands and cut off everyone's head, but they all grew back. Raven looked next to herself and she was holding her mom's hand, but her mom was ten feet taller than her and when she looked back in front of her there was Crow, fucking someone. Their faces kept changing but Raven got it into her head that what she was seeing was real and couldn't let go of it. She got up and left in a hurry, not hearing or seeing Crow get up and call to her. All the way home, she kicked little pale, sickly children out of her way as blood rained on her head. All night long a siren blazed in her mind and even now she wasn't feeling quite right yet. (Not that the pot was exactly helping.)

Blissfully, in the midst of circling through this memory over and over, she managed to pass out as the pot smoldered away.

Three:
Orange

There was a sudden *whoosh* as the fluid around Mina was drained., a scraping as the tube was pulled out of her throat. She gagged. A thin crack of light slit the darkness ahead vertically. The slit expanded abruptly and the light forced Mina to shut her eyes as she exited the large, womb-shaped cell. She put one sloppy foot on the ground, then the other. Disoriented and nauseous, she wavered to the right, then the left, before falling to her hands and knees.

Mina's arms gave out and she collapsed to the ground, rolling over onto her side. She retched up a syrupy, orange liquid that dribbled down the side of her face and hit the floor with a soft *pat, pat.* Groggily, she stared over at the womb—"Sensory deprivation float chamber"—and immediately hurled up more of the breathing liquid. She wiped off her mouth, happy for the feeling of air entering her lungs.

She looked at the liquid—"Para-amniotic fluid"—and changed her focus so that she was looking through it, to something beyond. The puddle began coalescing into little orange beads, which jittered around on the floor. She focused harder, trying to command them. They combined into little ringlets that started rotating in midair. Mina had three under her control, then four, then five, but as the sixth formed, her eyes rolled back. She fell unconscious, her head smacking against the floor as the orange rings fell all around her.

Four:
Hallucination 2

That damn siren!

Raven sat up and instantly she wished she hadn't. A rush of intense pressure filled her head and green and black patterns flooded her vision. She turned towards her phone, and, as her vision returned, she discovered that it was pulsing red with each blare of the siren.

"Raven, dear, can you get that?"

Raven thought that maybe the voice was her mother's (the voice *looked* like her mother) but she wasn't sure where it was coming from. It might be coming from behind her. She rolled over to check and stared back at herself. The siren blared again and the voice spoke again, and the extra Raven washed away.

"Raven, can you get the phone?"

Raven tapped her head because she thought maybe she could make the voice fall out. Then the siren made her wince with pain.

"Fine. Don't answer."

She heard a series of booms, each louder then the next. Later, she would realize her mother had been speaking to her from the basement through the heating ducts, and that the booming was her rushing up the stairs. For now, though, she was dazed and confused.

Raven looked over at her clock and after the numbers had stopped wiggling, she saw that it said 4:48 pm. Luckily, the siren had stopped and the disorientation had left, but the slow realization that she was hallucinating again began to bother Raven.

For the past couple of years, she'd also begun experiencing blackouts. They had been few and far between but had slowly been increasing in frequency. She told no one, other than Crow, about either problem. She was afraid she was going crazy, or worse, and was afraid to find out if that was true.

Crow desperately wanted her to see a doctor. Raven refused.

Crow. Ugh.

There was a knock on the door.

"Raven, dear, the phone's for you."

"Who is it, ma?"

"It's Crow."

"Ugh. Tell her I'm sick and I'll talk to her at school tomorrow."

"Can I get you anything?"

"No. Thanks."

She heard her mom walk away, talking into the phone. She didn't know Crow was her girlfriend. Raven had never discussed her sexuality with her mother and she figured that she just assumed she was straight. She preferred it that way—not just because it meant that her mother would let her "best friend" Crow spend the night, but because her mother would have a heart attack if she knew the truth. Because the truth would involve a conversation she couldn't get into, Raven had told her mom to lie and just say she was sick. Not that it was really that much of a lie; she felt terrible.

Raven's mother wasn't exactly a bigot—she would never turn anyone away —but she was a "born-again Christian," and that rubbed Raven the wrong way. Raven wasn't aware of any facet of Christianity that wouldn't have considered her a sinner just for loving someone, so she wasn't terribly fond of the whole idea.

Sometimes Crow felt like the only real family she had. How could she have a good relationship with her mother? They had nothing in common, and Raven couldn't even tell her who she really was, couldn't introduce her girlfriend AS her girlfriend. A major part of her life—her relationship—she was afraid to talk about.

Raven was a bit of a troublemaker, smoking cigarettes and weed, and sneaking off to parties, but her brother was worse. He fancied himself a thug and spent most of his time getting high in the suburbs with his loser friends and in general being a local nuisance. They had never had a good relationship but her conversations with him had degenerated to "move" or the more forceful "get the fuck out of my way."

Raven had no grandparents, aunts, or uncles on her mother's side, and all she really knew of her father was that he was a scientist and he lived in another state. She had vague memories of him, rectangular framed glasses and short, jet black hair, but her parents had divorced when she was so young, she couldn't remember much more. Her mother refused to talk about him and she had stopped asking questions years ago as a result. The most contact she had with him was a hundred dollar check she received each birthday and Christmas.

In moments of clarity and compassion, Raven appreciated her mother. Raven wasn't really too bad herself, but she was in that non-communicative teenage phase, so she had to give her mom credit for putting up with two fairly difficult children with only God and child support to fall back on. Really, given the hell her brother raised, Raven had to admit her mother was a strong person. It was no surprise, though, that her mother was so religious. She had to have *something* to pull her through the tough times—which were most of the time.

Raven looked again at the clock and realized she had been unconscious for several hours. A good chunk of the day was gone, but she didn't feel up to doing anything anyway. She picked her compact up off of her nightstand and grimaced when she saw what was staring back at her. She looked as bad as she felt.

She was, generally speaking though, confident in her looks, unlike so many girls her age. She stood at just under five and a half feet, petite, with a well-proportioned though in no way voluptuous figure. She had inherited most of her looks from the Japanese side of her family, although her hair was auburn, like her mother's. She had an oval face and well-defined, if not plump lips, and rich brown eyes that were more rounded along the top then beneath. She had a low-bridged, cute nose. Her skin tone was light and even, but darker than her mother's rosy-pale complexion.

Outside of a few bad habits, Raven took good care of herself. Except for avoiding the doctor....

She got up, and—with some difficulty—grabbed some clothing from her dresser and went to take a shower.

Five:
Others

Mina stacked the blue "A" block on top of the red "Q" block, and looked across the play table at Danny, who smiled at her. They rarely spoke to each other (there really wasn't much talking at all in this room,) but he was the closest thing she had to a friend in this godforsaken place. She glanced over at the mirrored window that ran the length of the room, knowing that on the other side was a room full of scientists waving clipboards around.

Danny levitated one block on top of another, and Mina realized he had spelled her name out vertically. She smiled and leaned back. Danny had shown her that the simple act of play could help ease the migraines brought about by The Tests, though blocks and such were of course extremely boring to her (not that the concept of *fun* was something she knew very well.) But where Mina played with her hands, Danny often played with his mind.

He had told her once that he was eight years old when he had arrived here, and that had been many years ago. In appearance, he still seemed no older than eight except that he was wrinkled, his hair was white, and his skin was so pale it was almost blue. It was "The Process" that had done this to him and to the others; Mina still looked healthy, but she hadn't been here as long as the others. Not as far as she could remember, which wasn't really much.

Danny spoke into her head. *They're not happy with the way you're proceeding. You know that, don't you?* She nodded yes.

I know telepathy is painful and difficult for you, Mina, he continued, *so I'll try to make the questions yes-or-no, but I have some very important stuff to tell you and I think it's best if we don't talk out loud.*

It's...okay, she sent back, a dull ache entering her mind. She absent-mindedly fingered the series of lines tattooed on her right palm. All of the children had one.

Mina, Keiko and Johnny know things. They hear things without ears. I think they know more than the doctors think they do. They hear...the secrets. Why this is. What we're for. They won't explain but they said it...we...haven't always been like this.

The Process, Mina painfully returned. "The Process" was the term used for whatever it was that made people like her and Danny come to this place.

Yes, but there's more to it than that. They said we all had a...a...before.

That idea confused Mina and added to her headache. One of the doctors came into the room now, and the mental conversation paused as the doctor passed out little plastic cups of pills and water to everyone in the room. Mina and Danny took theirs, and handed the cups back. The doctor said, "Remember, Mina, your weekly shot is tomorrow morning." She nodded. Once the man had left the room, Danny continued.

You know you're different than all of us. We look like kids. You look like an adult. Mina's appearance was of someone in her mid to late teens. *Everyone here is like us, always has been. Keiko and Johnny said, the doctors think you have so much trouble with the Power because you were changed after poob... pub....* He struggled with the word. *...Puberty. They might do bad stuff to you. Tests. Other stuff.*

Every day was a daze of bad "stuff." A slanted, hazy outlook kept everyone in line so from the inside of the system, all of the test subjects had difficulty grasping concepts like "outside," "before," and ideas of day-to-day growth and change. They were prisoners to a lifestyle they thought was natural because they were conditioned to accept what was put in front of them. Each day blended into the one before and the one after. Get up. Tests. Relax. Tests. Lessons. Tests. Go to sleep. The pain and stress some of the experiments caused were never forgotten but quickly rendered irrelevant, in their drugged minds. They asked no questions because they had none.

At least...most of them didn't. It was a few...like Keiko and Johnny...who seemed to exist both inside and outside the system. Whether this was known or unknown to the doctors, purposely created or not, they kept even more to themselves than most did. They knew things and had concepts that hurt the mind and caused confusion. Occasionally, they shared these ideas with the others, like they apparently had with Danny. Why they did this was unknown except to them but "why" was a question only they asked.

Acceptance was the cornerstone of the system. The system was the world. The world was acceptance. The children were like the proverbial wolf boy... deep down, they knew there was more to them than just this, but they had neither the means nor the will to express such a thing.

However...that wasn't exactly true anymore. Through Keiko and Johnny, through the network of the children, a sort of collective consciousness was beginning to form, the result of individuals being presented questions and concepts and information that somehow countered the dulling effects of the medications and the conditioning. Questions, concepts, and information they kept alive by constant sharing.

What were they preparing for? Was there a threat to counter, or were they to be the threat?

Mina ran a hand through her soft blond hair. It reached to her mid-back.. It was trimmed regularly. Her legs were shaved more often, but not every day. She thought maybe it was once a week. Her teeth were cleaned at distant intervals.

She had been receiving reading lessons, and was quite capable, but those were terminated recently.

In the morning she got up. She took a shower, read her daily schedule, and went to breakfast. Halfway through the day she would eat lunch. At the end of the day she would eat dinner and go to bed. Drugs were administered regularly. At intermittent intervals, she would be allowed to relax here. Often, there was a large amount of such time after dinner.

Dormitory-hallway-cafeteria-hallway-playroom. When appropriate, hallway-elevator-hallway-test room. That was her world.

Mina stopped mentally reciting her routine, and wondered about something. There were several dormitories occupied by many subjects of both genders. The lavatories had shower stalls, and were connected to each dormitory: one for girls, one for boys. Mina was the only one with her own room, her own shower. They were yellow.

Why didn't the others have their own rooms? Maybe it was because she was different. She was "older"... sort of.

Her room was yellow, on the walls. The ceiling was white. The floor was a rug, soft and a deeper shade of yellow than the walls. Her bed had a yellow comforter. Her nightstand had a lamp. It was yellow.

Everything was yellow.

She had a small bookcase filled with picture books and silly stories. She had a small dresser with clothes in it. Underwear, socks, shirts, pants, gowns that tied up in the back. They felt kind of like paper.

Her bathroom had a toilet, a sink, soap, toothbrush, and toothpaste. Her shower had another bar of soap and a bottle of shampoo, and a special kind of soap just for her face.

She had a teddy bear. It had a camera in its eyes.

This was her world.

Mina stared at one of the blocks on the table, and she made it wiggle a little. Even such a tiny movement hurt her head. She looked at a table across the room, where a boy and a girl were making rubber balls circle around each other in the air. She couldn't do that. Out of the corner of her eye she noticed Anna sitting by herself, playing with building blocks.

She was very pale, but not as pale as the other subjects. Her eyes were sunken in and had a vacant look to them. She was bald, with scars crisscrossing the top of her head. The same doctor who had come in before now re-entered the room. He went over to Anna and injected her arm with a greenish liquid. Anna seemed not to notice. She received injections very often, as evidenced by the marks on her arms. Green equaled sedative.

Anna did not talk. Anna did not take tests. Anna sat in the playroom drawing and building all day. The story was that Anna had once attacked several doctors by starting fires. Mina had heard this from some of the other subjects. Anna was "pyrokinetic." This had happened before Mina had arrived here, though.

Mina thought about that. "Before." She had no memory of "before," or "outside." She had seen pictures of "outside" in books, but not pictures of other real people, just of trees and flowers and mountains and birds. *Nature.* She never saw any people from outside.

She had dreams, though. Dreams that would wake her up at night and make her look for the blood she thought was on her hands and face. She never told anyone about these dreams, not even during counseling. She would be "outside," and there would be people, people that would cry and scream. People that would get hurt, somehow. Then she would run up to them, and open her mouth, and then....

Mina looked over at Anna again. There was something to her, some sort of genius lurking deep inside, for everything she built was maddeningly complex, but geometrically, both fascinating and elegant. Her drawings were the same way. It was as though she was trying to depict more than three dimensions on the two-dimensional paper. Everything she created was geometric in nature, and there was a striking similarity between them all even though Mina could never quite figure out what it was. She felt like Anna was peering into something amazing, something unexplainable, and evidently the doctors shared a similar opinion. They were immensely interested in Anna's creations, much more so than they were in Anna herself. Although this girl seemed unable to think for herself, it was as though her mind churned ahead at light-speed by itself.

This was not very far from the fact.

Six:
Bedtime

Raven had been sitting in her room since her shower, reading. Perhaps that was her healthiest habit: she thoroughly enjoyed a good book and had read a great many over the course of her life. Unfortunately, she was currently quite preoccupied and barely retained any of what she was reading.

She looked at her clock and it was after nine pm. Her mother hadn't spoke to her since earlier and was probably in bed now. Raven got out of bed and looked out the window: it was gently snowing and the ground was covered in a light blanket of white. It was pretty, and she smiled.

She left her room and walked down through the darkened hallway to the kitchen. Her brother Jake was nowhere to be found, but that wasn't at all surprising. She got some food out of the refrigerator and made a sandwich. She poured a glass of milk and went back to her room.

The sandwich was good but the milk was starting to turn. Raven grimaced and spit her sip back into the cup, and sat it on her nightstand, as far away from her nose as she could manage without actually getting up. She had been feeling better but now the milk had made her nauseous again and she laid down. She started to think about Crow, and a little anger started building up again. She closed her eyes but only saw the image of Crow fucking someone. Again, both people kept changing, and she was unsure about things, and....

Her head started to hurt and she was cognizant enough to know *it* was going to happen again. Images and sounds and tastes and smells and touches assailed her senses, and any train of thought she might have had was lost. She shuddered, muscular twitches passing through her body, and the world became black once again.

Seven:
Monday Morning

Raven's eyes popped open, and she stared off into an unfocused, blurry mess of lights and colors and shadows. She was lying on her stomach, on the floor, with her right arm trapped beneath her and her other limbs at awkward angles. Something reeked and she was lying in something crusty yet sticky and it took her a second to figure out it was her own vomit.

"My mom's gonna kill me," she grumbled with a raspy voice. Worrying about that, it didn't occur to her just how much danger she had actually been in by throwing up while unconscious.

She got up and wiped herself off as best as she could, and went over to her window. She opened the blinds and saw that it was still snowing. It looked very peaceful outside, and for a moment that was all she thought about. Then she remembered what had happened and she frowned. An idea started forming, one of vengeance, although something in her head was trying to tell her no.

Her clock showed that it was still early, but if she wanted to do this right she wouldn't have time to clean up now. Or, regrettably, time to take a shower.

She went to the hall closet and grabbed a towel and disinfectant. She generously sprayed the puke and dumped the towel on it. Then she went to the bathroom and cleaned herself up a little. Her head hurt so she took some aspirin. She went back into her room and got dressed: A tight, long-sleeved black top, blue jeans, and steeled-toed boots she had spray-painted black. She put on her makeup and pulled on a green hooded sweatshirt. It had gotten cold early this year and stayed that way, but she wasn't one for heavy coats. Grabbing her backpack, she left her room and closed the door.

Raven went down the hall to her brother's room. Unfortunately he was there, but he was asleep. She crept up to his bed and reached under it. She knocked over a stack of what was very likely either marijuana magazines, or porno. With no computer of his own, the kid had to take what he could get. Afraid of what else she might touch, she sighed in relief as the next thing she found felt like a familiar, wooden box. She pulled it out, and was glad to see it was just what she was looking for.

"What the hell do you think you're doing?"

"Uh," said Raven, looking up from the floor to see her brother Jake looking down at her. He yawned and scratched himself.

"Stealing your pot," she said, taking the honest, blunt approach. She smirked as she thought that.

"Why?" he asked, not amused.

"I'm out."

"Why the fuck is that my problem?" He ran a hand through his spiky, brown hair and stretched his eyes wide open, trying to focus.

She scoffed. "I'll get you more. I'm good for it."

Jake was exhausted and really just wanted to go back to sleep. "Fine, bitch, whatever, just leave me enough to smoke when I get up."

"Thanks, hun," she said, punching him in the shoulder. "Bye," she said, leaving the room.

Jake mumbled, "Bitch," again and then pulled his covers back up and rolled over.

When Raven got to school, the doors were still locked, but the track team was running laps through the halls. She knocked on the door and a girl she knew from math class broke off from the pack and let her in. She said thanks and walked over to the stairs. Upstairs, there were a couple kids sitting in front of their open lockers, reading and doing homework, but no teachers were around.

She almost turned back when her head started to hurt again, but she pressed on. She walked over to one of the lockers and opened it, and was greeted by a picture of herself. There were lots of pictures, pictures of her and Crow, pictures of their friends, pictures of various actresses and musicians. At the sight of all this, her heart softened a little, but she still carried out her plan. Opening her backpack, she discretely removed the bag of marijuana she'd taken from Jake and shoved it under some of Crow's stuff.

Raven closed the locker and went back downstairs, leaving through the same door. After a brisk walk to a nearby parking lot, she leaned against a building and alternately exhaled cigarette smoke and winter breath. She turned around and viewed the school from across its athletic field, which fit against the L-shaped building like an inverse L of a similar size. She felt kind of bad as she watched other students slowly trickling into the building; a feeling of doubt spread through her, but she pushed it away, thinking that she'd put up with enough crap in her life to let anything pass anymore. She had to take a stand, and now was the perfect time, because her revenge would be perfect, and Crow would know it had been her but wouldn't be able to do a thing.

It was freezing outside but Raven didn't realize it until it began to snow again as she walked back towards the building. Despite the amount of time snow had been falling over the last day, the ground was only lightly covered. She watched her breath mingle with the falling flakes and thought of how positively fucked Crow would be.

Once in the building, she took an envelope out of her bag and quickly slipped it under the vice principal's office door. Then, she headed off to homeroom, smiling the whole way.

Eight:
Matthew

Mina awoke slowly as the soft caresses of artificial sunlight brushed against her cheek. She hugged her teddy bear (the one with the camera) closely and yawned. She came to life gradually and after a while opened her eyes and looked around. She yawned again and got up, stretching. She reached over to her nightstand, grabbing the note she knew would be there.

Mina-
Today we will be running a lot of tests. Breakfast will be served in cafeteria A today at 9:45. Today's experiments will not interfere with your eating or drinking. Report to laboratory room 36 DF-2 at 10:20 to receive today's full schedule. Please wear a hospital gown today.
-Dr. Jacobson

The note was from Emma Jacobson, one of the nicer and more personable of the doctors here. "Nice" and "personable" were of course relative terms, as the lot of them was cold and distant. Once in a while, Dr. Jacobson would seem just a tad more humane than the others, and Mina would appreciate that. The end result wouldn't change, though, no matter what. Mina was still the guinea pig, and Emma was still the scientist. To Mina, though, this situation was normal. She was emotionally and mentally capable of appreciating Emma's methods, but the end result of almost every test was some sort of pain.

The clock on the nightstand said 9:13 so Mina had time to take a shower. She walked over to her dresser and pulled out a pair of panties, a sports bra, a hospital gown, and a pair of socks. All of her clothes were chosen for practicality, but there was a darker side to that choice that she was only half-aware of.

Of all the test subjects, only Mina was physically mature past a child-like state. Though she didn't quite grasp sexuality (though she knew the biology of intercourse), Mina was a looker and quite developed and was aware that her body drew attention. The scientists and guards already viewed her as a thing, just as much as much as the other test subjects, but as a result of this they made almost no effort at all to conceal their stares. Naïve as she was, it still made her uncomfortable.

After getting a towel and a washcloth, Mina walked over to the bathroom. It was the only place she could get any privacy because the door to her room did not close, although a curtain did block the view of her bed from the hallway. She didn't exactly crave privacy, not knowing much better, but it was nice. Had she known she was under constant surveillance (as were all the rooms in the area) she might have felt a little different. She knew about the camera in her teddy bear, but not about the multitude of others.

Despite having plenty of time, Mina took a quick shower. When she was done, she stepped out of the stall and grabbed the towel from off the toilet, where she had set it. After drying off, she wrapped the towel around her hair and reached for her deodorant but it wasn't on the shelf like she thought. She glanced out the bathroom door towards her bed and sure enough, the deodorant was sitting on her nightstand. She walked out to get it, shivering a little.

"Damn, good-lookin'. I knew I sensed something fun about you."

Startled, Mina reflexively folded her arms across her naked breasts as she turned to face her intruder. He was a young man, maybe a little older than her (at least in appearance) but not by much. he was easily half a foot taller than Mina, or more, with a trim, athletic build. His brown hair was spiked, and he was clean-shaven. He wore dark blue jeans and a white T-shirt. His eyes glowed with a frightening, unearthly green hue. He might have been handsome, even, but Mina couldn't easily quantify that idea, and wouldn't have entertained it now anyway, as the threat from him seemed to ooze off in palpable waves.

"Wh-who a-are you?" stuttered Mina as she stepped back. "W-What do you want?"

"My name is Matthew," he answered, and added, simply, "I'm going to rape you."

Nine:
Oops

Raven drummed her fingers against her desk. She was nervous; third period was half over and she hadn't seen Crow or heard anything about her yet today. Did the bust already happen? She heard some giggling off to her right and slowly turned over to see a couple of boys glancing at her and laughing quietly. One of them pointed at her, and then faced his buddy. He held up his first two fingers in a "V," and put his tongue between them. Then he pointed back at Raven. Both boys started giggling again.

Raven's eyes narrowed as she gave both boys a disgusted gaze. She gave them the finger. The first boy mouthed out "please do" and then they both started laughing yet again.

Ugh. High school boys.

Raven turned to face forward again. It wasn't fair. Her head still hurt and her thoughts felt screwed up. The teacher was talking about some shitty tribe in Australia and some "dream time" crap. Raven looked at the clock, and put her head down as the teacher turned out the lights and started a video....

Raven sunk through the desk and the floor into the room she'd been in the other night. She went through the motions of lighting a cigarette, and immediately saw Crow sitting on a couch across from her. She came over to her, sat on her lap, and leaned against her. They both watched as an unknown woman started making out with a faceless man, sitting right where Crow had been sitting. Crow looked Raven in the eyes and said, "memories," and then kissed her briefly. When they turned back to the other couple, the faceless man was lunging against the woman. A man's voice began to speak....

"Okay, Crow, thanks. You can sit down."

"Thanks."

Raven jolted upright in her seat, wiping a bit of the drool of sleep off her face. She saw the teacher, walking back to his desk while reading a tardy slip. She looked over at Crow, who was walking towards her seat....

Time stopped, and all Raven could see was Crow. She was fucking gorgeous. Her long, red hair (that perfect kind of red, fake as hell, like an apple) swayed gently as she walked, her lithe, athletic body practically poured into the short tank top and tight jeans she was wearing. Raven fixated on Crow's stomach, staring at her perfect navel, and...and she ran her vision up the girl's gentle form to look at her face...such a face, more cute than beautiful, with perfect little ears and pouty lips and orange-green eyes that gave her a almost an exotic look, and....

And she was crying. Her mascara had run a little and her eyes were red.

She looked at Raven with a desperate kind of look, and Raven's heart completely melted and she knew that she had made a horrible mistake, that her mind had played one too many tricks on her and that she needed some sort of help and....

Oh, shit.

Raven immediately got up and walked towards Crow, who was standing still in the middle of the darkened room.

"Raven? Please return to your..." began the teacher, but he stopped in mid sentence when the door opened slightly and a hand gestured him over.

"I'm sorry," Raven whispered to Crow. Crow nodded, smiling in that sad way when a newfound comfort doesn't completely wash away the old sorrow. She bit her lower lip, but then Raven reached over and hugged her.

Just then, the light came on, and the teacher stepped back into the room. "Crow, would you go out into the hall with Mr. Kingsley for a moment? He needs to speak with you."

Raven and Crow ended their embrace. Still looking at Raven, Crow hesitantly agreed. "Um, yes. O-of course."

The melancholy look on Raven's face worsened. She whispered, "I'm sorry," to Crow as she herself began to cry. Crow looked briefly concerned and confused, and then slowly walked towards the door and left. Raven was still standing dumbstruck as the teacher closed the door. She was brought out of her trance when she realized at least half of the class was facing her, laughing.

"Fuck—you—all," she said as she returned to her chair.

"Raven! Watch your language!" ordered the teacher. "I don't want to hear a word out of any of you!" He rewound the video to before the interruption, and then turned the lights back off.

Raven was a mess inside. All sorts of conflicting thoughts and feelings played war in her skull. She put her head back down and tried to sort things out. A minute or two later, she heard barking. Drug dogs. Crow was severely fucked, and it was all her fault.

The video ended soon and the teacher started another one. It was now forth period but of course everyone had to stay where he or she was while the school was searched. Raven screwed her eyes shut as the pounding in her head became fierce, but a sudden noise broke her from her thoughts and her pain.

"Miss Raven Yamada, please report to the vice-principal's office. Thank you."

The PA shut off and Raven slowly got out of her seat, grabbing her backpack. Every snickering face was turned towards her as she left the room.

"Oh, shit."

Ten:
Lesson in Sexuality

Mina tried to scream, but couldn't, not with Matthew's left hand over her mouth. He was straddling her, trapping her right arm beneath her while his right held down her left. She tried to kick but her feet flailed uselessly.

She honestly felt as though she had the physical strength to throw him off, but it was as though his *will* wouldn't allow it. She looked down and saw that his pants were unzipped, a growing terror between his legs.

He put his mouth to her chest and sucked with all the grace and skill of an angry, desperate vacuum cleaner. When she recoiled as best she could, and he struck her face, she cried out, but even with her mouth momentarily free, she could manage no more than that.

Even that respite was over quickly, as he moved his face up and forcefully began kissing her, invading her mouth with his squirming, disgusting tongue. She felt a touch between her legs and tensed up; her pubic muscles tightened in horrific anticipation. And, in a moment, it was in, and he began rocking.

It was though he played at sex in the guise of rape; clumsy, immature attempts at normal techniques made awful through violent aggression. And yet, there was a quality to his touch, where Mina wished it wasn't real, that in some way, it actually wasn't, despite all the pain and anguish it brought her.

Her face, free, turned to the side, tears streaming down her cheeks, tears that carried a complex set of emotions, of pain; physical, mental, and emotional; of a basic understanding that what was happening was wrong, so wrong, but without any real experiences or useful knowledge to root it in any kind of context.

Instinct set in, her mind drifting, trying to numb itself, even as every savage lunge pushed her head up along the bed sheets and burned like a fire on her dry insides.

"You're going to thank me after this, you know. You have no idea what you're going to become, what we're going to become...."

Her mind drifted, drifted, into blackness, and her eyes began to roll back. She could see—or sense, she wasn't sure—warm red blood running up the walls, and across the ceiling, where it darkened into a foul, black ichor, and poured onto Matthew, covering him in its disease-ridden filth as he continued to thrust at her. The last thing she noticed before he was completely covered was a series of black parallel lines on his right palm, held up before her, and then he exploded, a fountain of blood and pus that threatened the world and colored everything Mina had ever seen or known, every emotion and memory, in a sea of death.

Mina saw herself, a child, bloody-handed, blood dripping from her mouth as she chewed, her filthy hair matted to her head, her torn clothes stained with dirt and death. She shivered like someone who had never felt warmth.

"Help...."

Eleven:
Lesson in Responsibility

Raven was no stranger to the vice principal's office. Though a fair student, she had been caught smoking a number of times, had been suspected of smoking pot a few times, had, over the years, been caught in a handful of minor PDA's that went against policy, and was involved in or the cause of any number of other minor infractions. She was used to the whole procedure. Usually, she'd greet Mr. Kingsley with a cheeky, "Yo, Vice P.!" She'd hand over her backpack for inspection, he'd have a brief conversation with her (basically, the same one every time, about integrity and school honor and becoming a fine adult,) and he'd hand her her detention slip and she'd be on her merry way.

Today was different. She walked into his room, solemnly, with her head hanging. "Let me see that," he said as she neared his desk. He reached out and she handed him her backpack. She glanced over at Crow, who was in a chair, sitting on her hands on one side of the room. She looked up at Raven with an expression of sadness and fear. Raven looked back, starting to cry again.

Mr. Kingsley had dumped the contents of Raven's backpack onto his desk and was in the process of sorting through them. Without looking up, he motioned Raven over to a seat across from Crow's. "Over there, please. Thanks." He spoke dispassionately.

Raven and Crow stared at him as he separated the pile before him into two groups. In one, he put everything that was clearly school-related: pens, pencils, books (once he had flipped through them,) et cetera. The other group was made up of everything else, things Raven guessed might be considered personal in nature: folders, papers, and notebooks. Placing the last item, a box of tampons, into this latter group, Kingsley looked up. He folded his hands together and gave the girls a sobering look.

"See girls, we have a bit of a problem here. We found a bag of marijuana inside Crow's locker, and she insists it isn't hers and that she has no idea where it came from."

He looked at Raven. "Now, Raven, Mr. Henderson says that he saw you opening a locker in the general area of Crow's quite early this morning."

Crow turned to look at Raven, literally gape-jawed with disbelief. *So this was what the second "I'm sorry," was about?*

Meeting Crow's astonished gaze with her timid one made Raven feel lower than a worm. She had been a complete and utter jerk.

"Now, I tend to believe Maria's—Crow's—story," Kingsley said, using her preferred name. "Mr. Henderson's story corroborates hers, and, other than her dalliances with you, she has a relatively clean record."

"Let's see here—" He opened up his desk and pulled two sheets of paper out, and, pushing one of the piles of Raven's belongings aside, he placed the pages in front of him and looked down at them.

"Maria Fischer—seventeen?" He looked up at her without moving his head. She nodded.

"Raven Yamada—recently eighteen, I believe?" He looked at her the same way and she nodded as well.

"I'll be honest with you, if I turn you over to the police, the worst that will happen is that one or both of you will have to pay a fine for a first offense. Luckily for you both and your surely bright, bright futures, this isn't a zero tolerance school so expulsion is not a choice I am willing to make right now nor do I have to." There was a hint of sarcasm when he said "bright, bright futures."

Mr. Kingsley leaned back in his chair and sighed. "Effectively immediately, you are both suspended until further notice. I will contact both of your parents and decide how to proceed from there."

He waved his hand at Raven. "Go on, Raven, get your stuff. You're an adult, you can leave as you see fit. Crow, you can have the secretary call for a ride, but a part of me doubts you'll bother."

Raven hastily scooped up her belongings. Relieved that the punishment seemingly wouldn't be that severe (at least from the school,) she muttered a "Thank you, sir," as they left.

Mr. Kingsley watched the two young girls leave, and then walked over to his door, locked it, and closed the blinds. Returning to his desk, he pressed the call button on his intercom.

"Miss Janney, hold my calls, please."

"Yes, Mr. Kingsley."

He reached into a cabinet behind him and pulled out a pack of smokes and a bottle of whiskey. He lit up a cigarette and took a long drag, then poured himself two fingers of whiskey into a lowball glass. He took a swig.

The school superintendent was retiring at the end of this year and he was gunning for the position. He had the credentials and he'd done impressive work, but it was far from a done deal. Two things were on his mind as far as motives. One was the constant stress of dealing with the kids face-to-face. The other— well, he was very aware of how intently he'd watched Ms. Fischer and Ms. Yamada leave his office, and was duly ashamed of it.

*These high school girls—they don't **look** like kids these days.*

Wordlessly, fearfully, Raven followed Crow to her locker where she got her hoodie and her backpack. The entire time, Raven was one nudge away from bawling.

They walked out into the cold, aimlessly at first, their hands jammed into their hoodie pockets, just trying to get away from the school, Crow in the lead, Raven several steps behind. Their breath twirled noiselessly into the air above.

Finally, after almost a block, Raven spoke.

"Crow, I....." But that was all she got out.

Crow twirled around, her hair getting in her face. She took a hand out and pushed it away. She looked more worried than mad.

"Let's put aside what you just did for a moment. You know, you just stormed out the other night. I tried to call you ever since. What the hell happened?"

Raven started to cry as she began to try and explain. "I..." She wiped away a tear and sniffled. "I...When we...when we were at that party, I saw...I thought I saw...you were kissing him, and then...." She burst into tears. Crow was very mad, but her love and concern came first.

"You were hallucinating, again?"

Raven meekly nodded.

"You know I love you, right? That I wouldn't do that?"

Raven nodded again and embraced Crow, crying against her chest. Crow put one hand on her back and one on the back of her head.

"This...things like this are happening...a lot. You need to see someone, Raven. Before anything worse happens. You could have epilepsy, and be schizophrenic, or something." She held Raven's face up to face hers. "I don't want anything bad to happen! To you, or...to us!" She let go of Raven's face and held her arms.

"I'm so scared," said Raven.

"What I'm really worried about," said Crow, choked up, "is exactly what happened today. Look what you did today! These—episodes—are screwing with your sense of reality!"

"I know! I'm so, so sorry!"

"You have to try and separate reality from what goes on in your head."

Raven nodded rapidly.

"Look. I love you, okay? You know that, right?" She said it matter-of-factly.

Raven nodded again and sniffled, her tears finally stopping.

"I'm not going to cheat on you. Maybe we *won't* be together forever, but I'll never, ever do that. I'm not...Michelle." Normally, invoking *that name* would have pissed Raven off, but here it drove the point home.

"You need to see a doctor," Crow said finally.

"Yes. Definitely," Raven responded with her final sniffle. Anything to keep Crow, to keep this from happening again.

"Okay then. I'm not going to hold this against you. But you need help."
She pulled Raven in for a kiss, then a hug. Raven could have held her forever.
She breathed in deeply, the comforting scent of cucumber and melons emanating
from Crow's hair. Raven was not fond of most perfumes and flowers, finding
their odors cloying and heavy. What she did like, however, was fruit, and this
scent especially. No doubt Crow had washed her hair this morning with it on
purpose, as a means of apology, when she didn't know what had caused Raven
to storm out.

"You smell amazing."

"Thanks." It was the biggest smile Crow had had all day.

They gently separated, and realized simultaneously that it was too cold for
just hoodies.

"Do you want to go to Steve's to warm up?" Raven inquired.

"Sure."

And so the girls walked off, doing their best to hold each other in the
winter cold.

Twelve:
Physical Rape is Psychological Murder

She felt her mind floating, floating through a void of ether. Mists that felt —not looked, mind you, but *felt*—purple swirled past her diaphanous form. She turned—or rather shifted her perceptions—towards an object, an eddy in the mists that seemed to have no cause. For as an eddy in a river must have a rock as its cause, so to must an eddy in the ether have a cause. This one did not—at least not in this particular realm of existence.

The eddy shifted around, wobbling rather like a top, as it swirled in on itself endlessly.

Your time is now. My time is now. We shall achieve perfection together, as I become you and you become lost.

It moved toward her. It engulfed her.

"Wake up! Mina, wake up!"

"Ehhh?" Mina bolted upright.

"Mina, what happened?" asked Dr. Jacobson, who was standing next to her.

"I...." Mina looked around; she was in a hospital room lying in a bed. As the memories of what had just happened to her came flooding back, she instinctively reached towards her groin. The fact that it was unharmed only added to her disorientation and confusion. "I'm...I'm not...."

"You're not what? What happened, Mina? I came in to see you and found you unconscious on the floor!" The truth was, she had been alerted when surveillance saw Mina appearing to have a seizure on her bed.

"I was...." She struggled; there was a word for it. Where had she heard it? It wasn't her word. "Raped.... I was raped.... Didn't you see the blood? It was all over...." She started to cry.

Dr. Jacobson, taken aback, sat down on the bed next to her. "Mina, there was no blood. There were no signs at all of—"

"But there was blood everywhere!" cut in Mina, exasperated. "I was in the shower...and I needed my...and I walked out and he was there! He...grabbed me...and he...." She broke down into sobs. The veins in her forehead were pulsing, and she was gripping the sheets so tightly that little holes were beginning to form where her nails were.

"Who raped you, Mina? Was it...someone you knew? Was it one of the guards?" Emma knew nothing physical had happened, but she needed to know what Mina believed she'd been through.

"His name was Matthew," Mina quietly said, sniffling now instead of actively bawling. She gripped the sheets very tightly again, and Dr. Jacobson was worried. She reached into the pocket of her lab coat and pulled out a syringe filled with a pale, sea green fluid.

"Mina, I'm going to inject you with this. It'll help you calm down, and then we can get to the bottom of this." She lifted Mina's gown to expose the poor, fragile girl's hip. She seemed whiter than usual. She pulled the stopper off the needle, and as she went to inject the liquid, Mina stared very intently at it.

Green equals sedative. She knew that. *He* knew that, also.

Mina slapped the syringe out of the doctor's hands. "I don't need to calm down," she said, her veins now drawing a violent pattern of blue and purple snakes around her skull, "I... will **not** be... ***contained***!"

The doctor scrambled for the needle, and as her hand closed around it, it shattered into a million shards of glass and drops of liquid that drew ragged gashes across her hand. She stared at the bloody mess, raw tissue bleeding profusely, specked with glass and bits of the sedative. The wound, far too grievous for the cause, burned worse than any pain she could remember, but then...she felt surprisingly peaceful, and the urge to sleep was great. She knew it was because the sedative, which was particularly strong, was right now coursing into her open bloodstream.

I'll just lie down here, she thought. *Someone else will take care of Mina; I'll just rest now....*

Thirteen:
Sanctuary

Raven knocked on the door in front of her, as Crow glanced around the decidedly run-down neighborhood they had come to. Both girls shivered; they were starting to lose feeling in their fingers and ears.

"He's just *gotta* be home! He never *does* anything!" After a moment, the door opened.

"H-hi Mrs. Ph-phillips," said Raven, her teeth chattering.

"Quickly girls, inside! You two must be freezing!"

"Thanks," they both said, as they came inside.

"Steve's upstairs," said the always likable Mrs. Phillips. "If you girls want anything, maybe some hot cocoa or a blanket, you be sure to let me know, okay?"

"Actually, a blanket sounds like a great idea," said Crow.

Mrs. Phillips smiled. "Sure thing," she said, and left the room.

The girls were in the living room, directly in front of the staircase. Across the room they could see into the kitchen. In the middle of the floor was a baby in a highchair eating some sort of baby goop, watching something on TV that sounded like it could have been any of half a dozen children's shows about grown men singing ridiculous shit. Although the living room was spacious and had a couple of nice couches and a fairly decent entertainment system, that didn't hide the fact that it was still a run-down house. Paint was missing all over, the carpet was thick with pet hair, and plaster was missing from the walls in fist-sized chunks. Still, the Phillips were pretty decent, as people go.

Less than a minute later, Crow and Raven were making their way up the stairs wrapped in huge, fluffy blankets. They passed through a short but suffocatingly narrow hallway. Steve's room was wide open, and the blankets turned out to be a good idea because his window was open and a bitingly cold gust of wind was coming in through it.

Steve smiled as soon as he saw Raven. He was a decent looking guy, tall, with a long face and short brown hair, caught somewhere between ruggedly handsome and ruggedly pimpled. His nails were painted a sparkling blue and he was wearing a pair of blue jeans and a T-shirt for an industrial band so niche even Raven had never heard of. He had a lit joint and was listening to something guitar-heavy, but mellow. "Hey, come on in, sit down!" He mentally shifted gears. "Aren't you two supposed to be in school?"

"We're...kind of suspended," Raven answered. Crow waved hello, although it looked more like a funny wiggle because her hand was wrapped in the blanket. The two girls flopped down on his threadbare couch and looked around.

Steve's room was comfortably familiar to Raven, as they'd been friends for years, but it was messy, run down, and practically *tasted* like pot. The bed he was sitting on was unmade as always. Clothes and CD's were scattered all over the floor, peppered here and there with dirty paper plates and silverware. An old TV sat in a corner on top of a tray that was buckling under the weight.

Steve was anything but neat.

He took a hit from his joint, and then held it out towards the girls, but they both declined with a wave of their hands. "So what did you do?" he asked.

Raven and Crow both sighed deeply. Raven spoke.

"I...had a...moment. I thought Crow had hurt me, and I put marijuana in her locker to get her in trouble."

Steve had a look of deep confusion on his face. "What?" was all he could muster.

Raven and Crow looked into each other's eyes, and a wordless agreement was made between them.

"I've been seeing things," Raven admitted. "I've been confused by them, and I've made bad decisions based on them."

"Seeing...things?" Steve asked skeptically. He didn't notice the joint burning down in his hand.

"Hallucinations," Crow elaborated.

Steve felt the heat on his fingers and shook them, accidentally ashing on the floor. He took one last hit and put out the rest on a TV tray next to his bed. "How long."

"A couple years," Raven replied.

"And you never told me!?"

"I was afraid of what they meant." Raven could feel sadness and guilt welling up, but willed herself not to cry again—she felt she'd done that enough for one day. "They were rare enough that I ignored them, until recently."

"That's pretty fucked up. So—doctor?"

"Yeah. It's time. I have to tell my mom."

Crow put her blanketed arm clumsily around Raven and rubbed her back. She leaned over and kissed her forehead. "It's gonna be okay. Whatever it is."

After a time, Steve switched gears again. "Okay, question? Off topic"

"Shoot," Raven said.

"The bird names. Been bugging me for awhile. What's up with that? Raven's Raven, but—Crow?"

"Oh!" Crow smiled. "My first name is Maria. My middle name is Crowell, after my grandfather. One of my friends started calling me 'Crow' in elementary school, and it stuck."

"Ah. Okay."

"You're such a bonehead, Steve," Raven said, laughing.

Crow leaned against Raven. For a time, the three of them sat there, shooting the shit. Steve asked about school—he was graduated (barely,) being a year older than Raven. Raven talked about her mom a bit, about how she felt bad about being so distant from her. Crow was mostly silent outside of responses.

Eventually, having warmed up and beginning to feel hungry for the first time in awhile, Raven asked Crow if she wanted to leave and get some food. Crow answered with a kiss. They got up, dropping their blankets on the couch.

"We're gonna take off," Raven said.

"Yeah. You—take care? Go see that doctor."

Raven nodded, and Crow waved good bye. They let themselves out.

Steve laid back on his bed and let his emotions wash over him. He considered Raven his best friend, and she considered him the same. But the greater feelings he had for her were not reciprocated. He had hidden them for—God—years, now. Of course she was aware of them, but he didn't know that and she wouldn't bring it up.

He might have told her, at one point. There was a brief time when he thought they might be a couple. But then, she had started dating a girl, and those hopes were dashed.

He sat up, and set about rolling another joint.

Fourteen:
A Demon Possessed

Mina stared into the guard's open but lifeless eyes and mouthed out his words.

"No, sir, my gun misfired. There's a damage team on their way right now to check things out. Over."

"Roger, then," spoke his radio. "Be careful, private, there's something going on and I've just been informed surveillance is out in your sector due to a damaged relay. Over."

"Yes sir. Over and out, sir."

The dead guard's torso slid back to the ground to become reacquainted with what was left of its lower half. Mina thought how lucky she was not to have punctured his lungs, or else he wouldn't have been able to talk. The other guard wasn't of any use, mostly because Mina wasn't exactly sure where his head was.

The guard's bloody card key floated up into Mina's hands. It was a little worse for wear; in fact, the magnetic strip looked burnt and she wasn't sure if it would work. She floated over the fresh corpses to the file room door and slid the card through the reader.

CARD READ ERROR
2 TRIES UNTIL SECURITY NOTIFICATION

She slid the card again.

CARD READ ERROR
SECURITY CALLED IF NEXT ATTEMPT FAILS

Fuck it, she thought, and tore through the door with her mind. She ducked in through the hole she'd made and levitated towards the central desk in the room, her bare toes an inch from the floor. There was a feeling of being cramped in here, despite the fact that it was a mostly open room. It was just that there were so many file cabinets and computers and desks and papers lying around...it was just...well, it was just a fucking mess.

And, had Mina been in a state of mind to think about it, this would have confused her quite a bit. This was a top-secret room, far off the beaten path through this building, along a maze of corridors and almost duct-like tunnels. There must have been a simpler way to get to it then the way she'd used. The actual hallway around this room looked much like the halls she had been in before, just with a slightly different decor. Probably, it was just that a single regular door from her section led to this section, a high-security door that she hadn't passed. Not that she knew how she'd found her way here anyway.

In fact, Mina didn't really "know" much of anything right now; she was just doing what her body made her do, and most of it was stuff she wouldn't have been able to understand anyway. She could think, in a low-level sort of way, and most of her thoughts left her confused.

Especially when her mind answered back.

The first guard Mina had seen when she rounded a corner had seemed to explode from the chest up as he reached for his gun.

AK-47, her mind said.

What?

Never mind. I'll tell you later.

Okay.

Mina grunted as her levitation failed her and she fell to the floor. For a moment, she was herself again, and rather than worry about what the hell she was doing, she briefly wondered about the guards.

For the first time she wondered why they were there and why they had weapons. Guns and grenades and...

Tasers.

...and looked like, what was the word, "military," and....

"Ahhhg!" She screamed. Her head felt like it was on fire. She thought of the people she had massacred just minutes earlier. She could almost taste their blood, almost wanted to go back and eat...

The computers were on and some of the cabinets were open and papers were scattered around. There was a file open out on a table nearby. She floated over and looked at it.

```
Form AD-X12
*****ABOVE TOP SECRET LEV12+ EYES ONLY!*****
Subject: Hummel, Anja
Registry: 0-00000-03248-NULL
Gender: Fem
Date of Birth: Classified
Date of Acquisition: Classified
Primary type: PhotoKin S++
```

Mina paused here because something in her head that wasn't her was immensely interested in what this document had to say.

"-Kin" meant "kinetic." The scientists used it as a shorthand suffix;

"TeleKin" meant "telekinetic," for example. The letter part, S++, referred to the strength of the ability listed before it. "E" was the weakest of these such classes, and generally referred to someone naturally born with an ability; such abilities were almost, but not quite, invariably weak.

Mina did not know any of this, but her head did. She also didn't know what "PhotoKin" meant; her head did but it wasn't telling. It seemed very interested in this.

Classes went E-A, then S, in increasing order of strength. Pluses marked subdivisions between classes. Mina knew that Anna, (if this was THE Anna, the one she knew,) was pyrokinetic. She looked further down the form and sure enough, she found the word "PyroKin," but it was listed only as a sub-type of class C+.

The next couple pages of the file were all numbers marked "DataRef" and "SysSec," except for one paragraph that referenced other files. She looked around and found two other pamphlets, one very thick, lying nearby. She checked the file IDs' and they matched two of the referenced ones.

The thicker paper was titled, "The Effects of Diazepam-based Sedatives on Test Subjects in Liquid, Gaseous, and Solid Forms."

Scientists are so fucking pretentious.

Yeah, Mina absent-mindedly agreed.

The other pamphlet was titled, "Studies of The Process and its Affects on Subjects of Various Ages Through Childhood to Post Pubescence." She started thumbing through it. Most of it was jargon but one paragraph caught her eye. It spoke of how The Process affected undeveloped, younger minds by placing more emphasis on the mental development of a child than on physical growth or even maintenance, whereas on older subjects (those who had passed through puberty) it was already ingrained into the mind to spend more resources on the physical self than on the mental self. This was why, it said, that the bodies of those changed before puberty stopped growing and actually seemed to wither and waste away, but the bodies of those changed after puberty grew normally.

This was all well and good, but the reason it caught her eye was that both she and Matthew were mentioned by name.

Fifteen:
Deadly Force

"If you find her, you must not be afraid to exercise deadly force. Do you understand?"

"Aye, sir." Private Brito knew better than to question his orders, but come on! Not be afraid to use deadly force on a kid? Kids killed and all, but he was *military*! Was this kid some kind of fucking ninja master?

"There was a disturbance by room 48-042, so head over there first. One of the guards radioed that everything was fine, but check there anyway."

"Roger. Any recon data?"

"Negative. Radio contact has not been made since the aforementioned communication. Also, surveillance is out in the whole sector. Be on your guard."

Brito crept down the hallway, his acute, army-honed senses functioning at their peak. He detected nothing. This area, due to the fact that most of the rooms in it were off-limits to low-level personnel, was notoriously quiet and empty of people. If someone were making any noise anywhere nearby, he would have heard it.

He walked by a pair of bathrooms, and around a corner. A ways down the hall was a corner, and past that a ways was room 48-042. To the best of his knowledge, there wasn't any other rooms of note nearby.

"…The fuck?"

Blood was splattered on the walls around the corner ahead. A fleshy red chunk of something was on the ground.

It was a head.

Sixteen:
Sex

Raven stared into Crow's eyes; hazel, by name, but in actuality, orange in the centers but green at the edges. She leaned forward, gently shutting her own eyes, and kissed her girlfriend, taking in her scent. Slowly, they undressed each other. As time passed, the intensity of their pleasuring grew, and Raven had the distinct feeling that all was right with the world.

Seventeen:
Kamikaze

"…the head…it's…on the ground, sir. One of the guards."

"Are you sure?"

"It has a helmet on."

"Do you have a location verified for the target?"

"Not verified, sir, but I believe the target is in or near room 48-042." There was a pause before the reply came.

"I expected as much. Listen, private, under normal circumstances, you would never be allowed to enter that room, do you understand?"

"Yes…"

"However, no other military personnel are in your sector, and unfortunately, there isn't time to regroup. You must enter room 48-042, and recover the target through any means necessary, killing her if need be. Anything you see in that room is classified and may not be discussed. Do you copy?"

This was crazy! "Lieutenant Colonel, I…."

"She killed the guard, private! She beheaded him!"

Brito was feeling weak in the knees. *A child did that!?* He was scared and uncertain. What was going on? "Sir, requesting permission to speak with the captain of my unit."

"Your captain is no longer in charge of your unit, private, at least not for the time being," came the reply. In truth, the captain was dead, but Private Brito did not need to be burdened with that knowledge right now.

"I understand, sir. Over and out." Brito knew his role. He received orders, and then he carried them out. He stepped forward, unsure of what might be ahead. This wasn't the first strange thing that had made him wonder what *exactly* was going on in this building, but it was by far the worst.

Standing next to the radio, Lieutenant Colonel Joshua Richardson tried to suppress the feelings of guilt he had about sending this man to his death. It was a soldier's duty to carry out his mission. Things like this were inevitable.

But this wasn't a war, wasn't an ordinary combat mission. This was a suicide run against a child who had the power of an atomic bomb churning around in her head. Private Brito wasn't equipped to handle this. None of the guards were. They were equipped to fight terrorists and the like, not bulletproof monsters that could behead a grown man without touching him.

Being assigned to the Gates Building was supposed to be a cushy job for a military grunt: boring, but safe, and still "paramount to national security." It wasn't supposed to get anyone killed.

Not that it hadn't happened before.

He thought of the prototype laser gun in the next room over. That was the scientists' answer to situations like this: a weapon that moved so quickly, even the strongest psychic would not have a reaction window. Nothing moved faster than light, right? Unfortunately, it was under-performing, and decreased funding had stalled work on the unit and, until now, the need for such a thing had not seemed so pressing.

Too bad it was too late to change that now.

Eighteen:
Motivation

Mina concentrated on the card key reader in front of her. It let out a cloud of noxious smoke, and with a grinding of gears the attached file cabinet popped open. She went through the files, found a folder, and pulled it out. She looked closely at the first couple of lines that were on its cover.

```
Files D-128b to F-113a
Subject: Personal History of Ingraham,
    Wilhelmina
```

"Is this me?" she said aloud. She wasn't sure why she had felt the urge to look through the files, let alone how she came to find this one almost immediately. She had, momentarily, rested control away from the voice in her head, but its goals were still coloring her actions.

So, this is what you want, said the voice in her head. *You were using me to find this!*

Who's using who? Mina answered.

I must know! I've waited years to find out who I am! What I am!

Then you can wait a little longer.

Mina dropped the folder, its contents scattering. She grabbed her head, which felt like it was splitting in half. Her control was slipping.

Pain is the single greatest motivator, said the voice. *Haven't the scientists taught you that yet? That's what they taught me.*

Mina tried not to cry out. A new word came to mind, or at least one she had never had felt motivated to use before.

"Fuck you…" she muttered.

*Fuck you, **Matthew**,* the voice corrected.

Nineteen:
Last Rites

It was Evans. He was splattered all the fuck over.

"Oh, fuck."

There was a moment where Private Brito thought he was going to throw up. He had killed; he had seen the dead. Killing wasn't like this. The dead he had seen were either fresh, and tidy, or well along their path of returning to the soil. This was fresh and raw and visceral. He had seen some difficult things in his field days, but nothing like this. Nothing so savage and animalistic.

He got his gun ready, and continued on down the hallway. He passed the rest of Evans along the way. There was another body nearby. Except for the missing head, it was completely, eerily intact.

In this hallway, lights flickered and the buzz of electricity could be heard; blood stained the walls and bullet holes and dents were everywhere. One such dent was red with chunks of flesh and blood. It had a body beneath it—or two halves of a body, to be exact. The lower half was sitting against the wall, a mess of red with the spinal column jutting up from its back. Swathes of redness led up from the body to a splatter above it at the heart of the dent, as though it had slid slowly down the wall after it had been split from its top half. The other half of the body lay on the floor next to it, a pool of blood still spreading from it. While the head of this one was intact, his entire front was stained with death starting from his mouth and going down. The look on the face was frozen into one of unimaginable terror, a look probably mirrored on Brito's own face.

He gulped, and walked on. Just ahead, an alcove on the left would lead to room 48-042 by way of a narrow door. As he understood it, 48-042 was a file room like any other; however, it contained several items of very high security. As such, guards were always posted outside it; Brito knew Evans but did not know the others.

Leaning against the wall at the edge of the alcove, he peaked around and looked towards the door. A person-sized hole had been blown out of it, and it was still smoking at the edges. Inside, he could see a desk and a computer. He sneaked around the corner and sidled up next to the door. He took a better look inside.

A reddish-purple glow surrounded her. She floated two, maybe three inches off the ground, her slender, pale legs bent slightly at the knees, her feet angled with her toes pointing down. She bobbed up and down slightly, and although her long blond hair blocked his view down to the middle of her back, he could tell she was completely naked. Though he made no noise, she knew he was there. He somehow knew this as well, and began to quietly say his final prayers.

She turned just enough so that he could see both of her green, pupil-less eyes. Save for them, she had the face of an angel. She had the body of a goddess.

But she was a demon, and he was going to die.

Twenty:
Lavatory Interlude

Fuck, thought the doctor, washing off his hands. *What a fucking time to have the squirts!* He had been busy getting a couple of files for his research when the feeling hit him like a kick in the gut. He didn't want to get in trouble; he had left the files out on the table. Though he had told the guards not to let lower security personnel in before he got back, they couldn't really stop authorized people. Though normally he was annoyed by it, today he was glad that this particular file room was in a mostly-unused wing. It meant no one was likely to wander by.

He went to the bathroom door, opened it, and stepped out. Out in the hallway, he walked towards the corner that would lead him back to the file room.

Twenty-One:
Chemistry Lesson

Brito felt his entire body shaking at what felt to him, crazily enough, like the subatomic level, as an odd warmness came over him. The gun slid out of his hand and clattered to the floor as the girl floated towards him in all her evil nakedness. She spoke to him in a voice that was deep and unearthly, both female and male.

"WHAT WE PERCEIVE AS 'HEAT' IS THE MOVEMENT OF MOLECULES. ADDING ENERGY TO A MOLECULE INCREASES THIS HEAT BY EXCITING THE MOLECULES INTO A FRENZY OF MOVEMENT. INFRARED RAYS CAN CAUSE THIS; SO CAN FRICTION. AS THIS MOVEMENT INCREASES, THE MOLECULES MOVE AWAY FROM EACH OTHER AND ESCAPE THEIR ATTRACTION. THOUGH THEY HAVE NOT CHANGED, THIS IS WHAT WE PERCEIVE AS..."

She paused, as if waiting for an answer. He felt obliged to give one as he slid to the ground, sweating from his rising temperature. "...evaporation."

"BUT DURING THE PROCESS OF 'BURNING,' WHICH IS THE REASSOCIATION OF MOLECULAR BONDS DUE TO THIS ADDED ENERGY, CHEMICAL CHANGES OCCUR. THIS IS..."

"...fire." Brito's mind was scattering, his whole body jittering as his flesh turned red.

"BUT WHEN FIRE OCCURS IN A PERSON, WITHOUT AN OUTSIDE ENERGY SOURCE, WITH SEEMINGLY NO REASON, WHAT IS IT? IT IS CALLED BY ONE NAME..."

"...spontaneous...human...combustion...." Private Brito's body burst into flames and he screamed holy hell as his flesh burnt and melted away from his bone, as his sinews and tendons charred and snapped and curled, as his organs deflated and roasted.

"Human?" said Mina. "Am I...?"

Quickly! Said the voice. *Get the file!*

Mina looked around, confused. The file? What just happened? What file?

"What am I?" At this, the pain re-entered her head and she screamed.

Don't worry about your 'humanity.' It is an outdated concept and you, we, are far beyond that phase.

Mina grabbed her head as the pain grew intense. She almost lost balance and fell. She wondered momentarily how much suffering he was going through.

Suffering?

"Did you really rape me? Are you real?"

Don't worry about that! Don't worry about 'me' anymore! 'I am you and you are...'

    "Get out of my head!"

Twenty-Two:
Biology Lesson

The doctor stood in dumbfounded silence.

"What in god's fucking name happened here?" he finally managed to get out, after overcoming both his inability to speak and the urge to vomit. He reached for the radio at his waist, and then he had a quick image of it sitting on the table back in the file room. "Shit!"

Despite knowing better (much, *much* better, as a matter of fact,) he walked along past the first dead guard and saw the second and third up ahead a little further. He'd done a few autopsies in his day, so he had a pretty strong stomach, but he still felt queasy. He was ill, of course, which was part of it, but these grievous wounds were just so…*unnatural*. The headache he'd had all day seemed to get worse with every step forward he took.

He came to the second guard, who had been violently torn in half, and stooped a bit to examine. Despite an overwhelming urge to be smart and turn back, he continued towards the door to room 48-042. He had an idea about what was going on, and despite the certain danger to himself, he felt that he *must* find out if he was right.

At the door, there was the smoking, charred body of yet another guard (some help they seemed to be) and, oh yes…the general lack of an actual door. Feeling somewhat flippant despite his overturned stomach and headache (and the overall situation itself,) the doctor bent down by the card reader to examine a piece of charred plastic that was lying there. One hand was on his nose, trying to plug out the acrid smell of burnt flesh; the other hand he used to pick up the object. It was in fact a security card, but it probably belonged to one of the guards and as such its security clearance would have been too low to open the door. Not that that had been an issue, apparently.

He walked in. "H-hello? Th-this is D-doctor Benton. Is anyone here?" He moved over to the table he'd been working at. There was his radio, just as he had thought. But the files he had been going through, as well as some others he hadn't, were scattered all over the table and floor. Even the computer had been messed with, because it was on an ID check screen that wasn't the same as when he had left.

One of the file cabinets in the room was opened and the files were dumped in front of it. The doctor was just about to go over to it, when he doubled over in pain as his stomach cramped. He thought for a second that he was going to mess his pants, but the feeling passed…only to be replaced by another.

"Hmm?" The hairs on the back of his neck began to feel weird like they were standing up, and the ache in his head grew. He wasn't sure if he *felt* it, or *heard* it, but a low, ambient hum seemed to fill the room. He felt static electricity all around him. "...the hell?" he muttered. He turned around to face the doorway, and she glimmered into view from around a series of cabinets.

"AUTONOMIC NERVE FAILURE." She held up a hand, and a sensation seemed to pass from it through the doctor's neck. It didn't hurt in the front so much as in the back, near his brain stem.

He was dazed for a moment, and then started to panic as he realized he was no longer breathing. His lungs simply weren't doing anything. He tried to inhale, to force them to start working again, but then....

"THE HEART IS ALSO AUTONOMIC."

The doctor felt his pulse suddenly leap from that of a scared man to something utterly off the charts. It hurt like hell, and the fact that he wasn't breathing anymore, made it infinitely worse. His stomach was knotted in severe anguish. There was no death ray, no "force bolts," just a delicate, girl's hand, but he knew instinctively that that was where the condition was coming from. The girl mentally pushed him up against the wall, and actually lifted him a couple of inches off the floor. Every nerve in his body began misfiring, and he twitched uncontrollably, his chest literally feeling like it was going to explode.

"Uuuhhhruhrhhhur...."

There was a noise like "pok-pok-pok" and the girl spasmed violently as a dozen or more bullets pierced her from behind. Several seemed to glance off but most hit their mark. A couple blasted through her stomach and several more blew out through her face. She dropped to the ground in a curled, twitching, bloody heap, and her grip on the doctor was lost. He too fell to the ground, at which point his bowels emptied themselves.

"Shit," he managed to mutter, as his heartbeat remained frantic but his breathing resumed. He looked past the naked body and spreading pool of blood to the hallway beyond. His vision was blurred, but he could make out the image of the burned guard collapsing, a machine gun falling from his blackened, desecrated grasp.

"Fuck," said the doctor as he lost consciousness.

Twenty-Three:
After Sex

Crow stretched her toes out and sighed out of contentment. Raven gave her a quick peck on the cheek and began rubbing her back with one hand while she fiddled with the TV remote with the other. On one of the local channels, a news story caught her eye. A cute, Hispanic anchorwoman was speaking in front of a video image of downtown Omaha.

"...Remarkably, no one was injured when the 48th floor of downtown Omaha's Gates Research Center was extensively damaged due to an internal explosion. Apparently caused by a laboratory experiment, those in charge were hesitant to comment further, but readily offered to fund the cleanup and repair necessary to fix the street below. Of course, it was the businesses of the Gates Building that provided a great service to the people of Omaha, by donating much of the money used for restoration after the domestic terrorist group R.O.F. attacked the city eleven years ago this coming May. Now to you, Chuck..."

"Wow," said Crow, turning at least part of her focus towards the TV. "That's like, less than half a mile from here. I'm surprised we didn't hear it." A moment passed, and she smiled. "Actually, I'm not."

"I thought they just did medical stuff there," said Raven. "I wonder what they were doing that could cause an explosion?"

"Well, it's a big building. There has to be more than one company working there, I guess."

"Makes sense," offered Raven. Then: "I'm beat."

"Me too."

Twenty-Four:
Stable Condition

Dr. Jacobson stared down at the body of the girl, lying on the table in front of her, dressed in a papery white hospital gown. She showed no signs of any damage of any sort. She was breathing shallowly and her heart rate was low, but that was to be expected. The machines hooked up to her gave back signs of "stable."

Emma looked down at Mina's arm. She had tried repeatedly to get an IV in to administer sedatives, but it had just come out each time, leaving no marks. She had been manually injecting her instead, although given what she now knew, finding a proper dosage rate was basically impossible.

Emma sighed and brushed some stray curly hairs out of her face as a tall black man, Carl Redford, entered the room. "He's dead," he said.

"Benton?"

"Yeah. Cardiac arrest. About ten minutes ago."

Emma muttered something to herself, then turned to face the monitors that were next to Mina's body.

"When they found her, they said she was laying in a pool of blood. There were bullets on the floor as well, and the body had minor puncture wounds."

"And?" questioned the other doctor, knowing something more was coming.

"And now there's nothing. No wounds. None of her surgery scars are there, either. Her entire body looks completely untouched by anything. Her bar code's gone too."

"A healer, then? Any bullets left in her?"

"None. Her body expressed *all* of them. But there's more." She pointed over to a steel surgical tray that had three small, bloody objects on it. "These were found on her bed."

"Heart monitor...RFID...what's the third one?" Carl pointed at the largest one, a T-shaped object. "Is that...?"

"It's a copper IUD," Emma answered. "And just like the rest of these, it was pushed out by her body. Judging from the amount of blood and tissue on it, it wasn't pushed out the easy way, either. It was probably expressed *through* her torso."

"Okay, give me a sec here. An IUD? Why?"

Emma had a shameful look on her face. "Look, Carl, Mina is post-pubescent. She is an intact female. This place is crawling with doctors and guards, and there is plenty of time when the test subjects are alone.

"She wouldn't have a relationship, though, the medication keeps emotions low and libido almost non-existent."

Emma stared at him crossly. The shame was not from the precaution itself, but the admission that it was in place because, sooner or later, inevitably, something would happen, and it would be needed. That was a defeatist attitude, but in Emma's experience, those who could disappoint, often did.

"Oh," he said quietly, finally understanding. "It's in case someone forces himself on her."

"Which is exactly what she claimed happened, although nothing corroborates that. But yes, the last thing we need is a pregnant psychic, and the copper IUD doesn't add hormones, so it doesn't affect test results."

Carl spoke uncomfortably, changing the subject, "Anyway, so it's not phasing."

"Nope. The amount of blood and some tissue attached to the implants points to the fact that they were definitely *pushed* out through her body, out through her innards and her skin. She bled a lot while they were emerging, but the wounds probably closed up instantly." She looked again at the tray. "I'm sure it was awful."

"Shit."

"Oh yeah," added Emma, "she has a full supply of blood. Completely normal pressure. Whatever bled out has already been replenished."

After a slight pause, the other doctor spoke. "The board room is a complete fucking mess. I'm just glad we got the hole in the building covered up before the damn news chopper showed up. God, though—it looks like a war zone in there! Blood fuckin'...urp..." He put his hand to his mouth and gagged, but he was okay after a second. "With Benton dead and the conference room massacre, that means the entire senior staff is gone. They'll probably promote you to lead, now, Emma."

"They'll probably pull in someone from another post."

"Not after this," said Carl. "They're going to want to keep this quiet—even among themselves."

"This isn't the first time something like this has happened, Carl."

"No, but this is the first in a long time. This was a major fuck-up."

"I just want to know what happened. Mina was never—well, she couldn't do that! Never before, anyway."

"Yeah," agreed Emma, absentmindedly. Then she asked, "Did you hear where they found her?"

"Yeah, 48-042. File room."

"Do you know what kind of files they keep there?"

"No," answered Carl.

"Histories," explained Emma. "Histories of each and every test subject that's ever been to this facility."

"She was trying to find her past?"

"I guess."

"Do you," began Carl, but Emma cut him off.

"No. My clearance is too low."

They stood there for a minute, gazing off into space. Then Emma spoke again.

"I want to see if there are any scars on the inside, mainly her uterus. There should be degrees to healing. Umm, prep the operating room for some exploratory surgery."

"Uh, shouldn't we check with…" began Carl, before he realized that there wasn't anyone to check with. "Uh, okay. Twenty minutes."

"Great."

With that, Carl left. Emma glanced down at Mina, and then turned her mind's eye in on herself. She didn't want to cut Mina open—she had a gut feeling there would be nothing to find. But she had to check anyway. It was her job. On the off chance that something would be learned. No scars, no cuts. Where had this power come from? Tests had shown Mina to be mildly telekinetic; she was capable of telepathy and according to hearsay she had actually burst into flame during some of the tests above Emma's clearance, but she had never been hurt by it.

But this was different. She had literally destroyed people. She had been shot nearly a dozen times and showed no sign of wounds. There had to be a cause or a catalyst. Something weird had happened to Mina this morning, whether she had actually been physically assaulted or not, if something weirder even had happened. It had to be connected. There were too many forces at work here, many that Emma didn't know about and many more that probably no one did. And it was all her fault. Well, it was the facility's fault at least, the scientist's fault. Anyone who might have known everything that was going on here, that had their hands in the middle of it, was dead now.

Her thoughts trailed off. She was a scientist. Sacrifices had to be made for the greater good. She looked down at her heavily bandaged hand, which still stung quite a bit. It wasn't Mina's fault, really…. It was a sacrifice.

Just what *was* the greater good?

Emma looked again at Mina. She knew the girl was sedated, but still…she felt that her mind must be racing along. Emma wondered if she would feel the scalpel.

Twenty-Five:
Spheres

Here was nothing. There was something. That's what drove him.

A burned out head and a missing body. He wanted power. Revenge was a possibility. But mostly he wanted to know why. And who. And what.

What was he?

They said it didn't matter. *They* said everything here moved in big spheres that endlessly curved back on themselves. Beginning and end weren't just irrelevant; they were nonexistent.

They said *can't you feel it? Feel the energy surging around you? It moves in cycles that never end, never weaken. We are the eddies in this river. We absorb and redirect the energy. But it never lessens.*

Oh, but it did. It lessened through a space that he felt familiar with; a space he would peek through, and sometimes, when the stars were right, he'd pass through it, and into someone else.

Someone like Mina.

Oh, *they* said he shouldn't. Said it wasn't right, that that world was gone to him and should be left alone. Whatever wrongs it had caused were over.

But the wrongs here keep cycling, he had argued. *Everything is spheres.*

He didn't want spheres. He wanted lines. Nice, straight lines with a beginning and an end. He wanted structures, not loops. Structure here was a myth. There…at least there, it was a possibility.

There was a city here, but it too was a sphere. It was built and destroyed at the same time, forever and ever.

But the spheres meant one thing that was good. They meant he could wait, because it really wasn't waiting. Another chance would come by soon, far too soon to notice the wait. And then he would succeed.

Twenty-Six:
Reflections

Raven was leaning on her elbow, in her bed. She watched the steady rise and fall of Crow's back as the girl slept. She seemed so angelic, and Raven felt like utter shit. How could she have distrusted her? She knew she was forgiven but that didn't make it any easier. Raven was not one to forgive herself so easily. Plenty of things were a mess now (she didn't even want to think about the school situation) and they were all her fault, all because of her stupid head that saw things that weren't there and believed in them.

She brushed her hand through Crow's hair and smiled. Crow was too good for her. Dammit, Crow didn't even smoke pot until she had met Raven.

She lay down and snuggled up next to her girlfriend. She tried to go to sleep but couldn't. She was so lucky her mom and Crow's dad didn't know they were going out; neither was the type that would allow sleepovers with opposite-sex friends, regardless of the relationship. Hell no. So when Raven's mom would remind her that all boys had to be out of the house by ten o'clock, both girls would secretly smirk. How little she knew.

But what it all boiled down to was that one way or another, Raven almost always had someone to sleep next to, and that was comfort to her. Nothing else matched the peace of that shared space, that warmth, that feeling of someone's heart next to yours.

Drugs and sex were escapes. But sex was brief and drugs were ugly. Sleep —that was escape from the dead reality of every day life. She was plagued by nightmares, but Crow...Crow made it all right.

Raven's mind wandered back to the other girls she'd dated. No one had made Raven as happy as Crow did except Natalie, but in retrospect, that was because it was new, not because it was especially good. Michelle had cheated on her. Twice. And Kelly was simply, a possessive bitch.

Crow was not something she could afford to lose, whatever the cost of keeping her would be.

Raven thought of her past. There were things she didn't remember much of, like her father. She remembered crying once, after he left, when she realized he wasn't coming back. He never said good-bye.

She reached over to her lamp and turned it off. She knew that before long, she might start seeing things in the darkness, but she was safe. She grasped Crow tightly and shut her eyes. Love was something she craved in life.

At least she had that.

Twenty-Seven:
O.R.

"This is a waste of time," exclaimed Carl with frustration. "I've cut her so many times I'm starting to feel like a goddamn butcher," complained Carl. "I can't get to the right spots and even if I could these sensors are just gonna get pushed right back out." He threw a small electronic device on the floor, shattering it. Tensions were very high. He grabbed a scalpel.

A miss-cut. Blood spurted, then stopped. On a normal person, it could have been a deadly mistake. On Mina…it healed almost instantly. No one said a thing about it.

They had used a scope on Mina and hadn't found any scars inside her uterus. Emma had decided to try and fit her with a few sensors to monitor nervous activity. She didn't have high hopes, but she was hoping some of the newer ones they had wouldn't be rejected. The problem was that they couldn't *get* to where they needed to be implanted.

"The sedatives are thinning out, Emma," said a third doctor. "Heart rate is rising."

Thanks for pointing out the obvious, Jameson, thought Emma. They had to inject Mina manually because her body kept pushing out any IV's they put in. Emma grabbed a needle and injected her. Again. She too was starting to feel like a butcher.

Mina's eyes were rolled back. She had a gas mask on and the oxygenated atmosphere she was breathing was entering her at a very slow rate. Her heart was slowly beating because of the tranquilizers, but despite the sluggish circulation the chemicals still drained rapidly from her blood.

Emma was leery, of course, of letting Mina come to before they had some idea of what the hell was going on with her. Danger was an issue, after what had happened…. If worse came to worse, Mina could be put into cryo-stasis temporarily, but then, chances were, whoever took over the project would have her put into storage instead of studied and dealt with. But the surgery was going nowhere, and it wasn't even going nowhere fast…it was going there *very* slowly. However, there was another possibility. It wouldn't provide the same results as this would, but it would keep Mina sedated while allowing some data to be acquired.

"We'll use the SDF," said Emma suddenly. The sensory deprivation float chamber had always proved to have a calming effect on its occupant. Perhaps that was because it created a womb-like environment. The warm liquid, the darkness, the breathing fluid…of course, the ability to administer drugs through the fluid would be the most "calming" effect it could provide in this situation. A wide variety of non-intrusive bio-sensors would let them gather information.

"Eh, we'll have to go to 44 then," mentioned Carl.

"I wonder what's going on out there right now?" asked Jameson. Emma had isolated the room they were in from the rest of the facility when they had begun the operation. She told herself it was to protect anyone outside should Mina awaken, but, given what she had already done, that was clearly nonsense.

In truth, her scientific curiosity had been piqued. Mina was an anomaly among anomalies. Science was supposed to be unselfish but Emma wanted this. Her morals had been eroding ever since she had started working here, what with the horrible, horrible things they did to *children* and she could be told it was for "the greater good" as often as she was and she still had trouble sleeping some nights. Finally, in the middle of all of this death and destruction and ongoing human experimentation, was something interesting and exciting.

Of course, the isolation denied communication with the outside, not a good thing in an emergency. "Halls could be swarming with military," Jameson conjectured.

"That's not really a problem, though," said Emma. "What if there are reporters?"

"There won't be if the building's under lockdown…which it probably is."

"Spencer's right," agreed Carl. "Media clearance wouldn't be allowed up here anyway, not without at least a day to cover-up. Still, though, we should turn on the intercom. We might be in trouble for cutting off."

Emma nodded and walked over to the control panel for the room. She reactivated the intercom and deactivated the emergency barrier, which slipped away, revealing the room's doors.

"—nyone copy me? Hello? 42-021!"

"Hello? This is Dr. Redford…." Began Carl, who was closest to the intercom itself.

The voice cut him off. "This is Lieutenant Colonel Richardson! Is Dr. Jacobson there?"

"Yes, I'm here," said Emma, coming near. "We have the test subject."

"Thank God. Emma, you're in charge of this operation now. I need to meet with you immediately."

"Ah, lieutenant colonel, that'll have to wait a while. We need to get her to 44 and put her in an SDF."

"Negative, doctor. I have a disposal team on standby."

Emma had expected this but was no less taken aback. It wasn't right, regardless of what happened. She took a chance and argued; the whole series of events, while unfortunate, were fascinating.

"With all due respect sir, I can't condone that. Regardless of what may have happened, Test Subject Mina has undergone an unprecedented change in abilities. Without any prior signs, she has shown amazing telekinetic and healing powers. We could learn a lot from her."

Richardson paused for a moment, considering, and then spoke. "You make a good point. Very well. But are you certain you can contain her?"

"Yes," said Emma. *No*, she thought.

"You do realize, of course, that if control is lost you could very well wind up like the senior staff?"

"Yes, sir." Was that a precautionary statement, or a threat?

"Agreed, then. But see me as soon as you are able. I'll be in my office." The intercom went silent. From the other end of the room, there was a loud yawn. Emma and Carl turned to look towards Jameson.

"Sorry. I just realized how late it was."

Twenty-Eight:
Solace

Raven slept, at last. Morning would come soon, but it wouldn't wake her. She was exhausted.

Twenty-Nine:
Run!

As soon as they got the okay from Richardson, Emma had told Jameson to inject Mina again before they moved her. He had objected, saying they'd already given her enough to kill a whale.

"She'll be fine," Emma had said. She went on to explain. "It's obvious the girl has extraordinary healing powers. Her body perceives the sedatives as toxins —and rightly so—so even while they're working, her body is diluting them and breaking them down. I don't think they can hurt her."

Carl agreed, stating, " I sure as hell don't want her to wake up."

Right now, they were running with the gurney towards an elevator. "Out of the way!" screamed Dr. Redford at the people that seemed almost to be purposely cluttering the hallway. "Oh, shit!" he exclaimed, looking at Mina's face.

"What is it?" asked Emma, and then she looked down. "Already?" Mina's eyes appeared to be moving under her lids, and she seemed to be clearing her throat.

"Jameson! The last syringe! Give it to her!" They had started rushing once they realized that they only had enough drugs left for one more dose, but apparently they didn't rush enough.

Spencer Jameson let go of the gurney and started fumbling for the needle. All three of them watched in horror as it slipped out of his grasp, flying through the air....

Crash! Emma winced as she remembered her earlier mishap with a needle.

"Fuck! Jameson!" Emma looked at Carl, and he looked at Spencer with pure hatred on his face. Jameson had a tendency to choke at crunch time.

They got to the elevator, and Carl pressed the button. The light indicated that the elevator was already in use—and that it was going away from them. "Why are all these fucking people here at this time of night?"

Jameson looked at his watch. "Actually, it's already morning." He received two dirty looks.

Emma glanced down at Mina. She was strapped to the gurney and covered with a tightly wrapped sheet. Only her head was free, and she seemed to be unconscious still. "We might still have enough time...."

Mina twitched, and a rasping noise came from her throat. "...Or maybe not...." She watched in shocked silence as Carl Redford clocked the girl in the face. She groaned slightly and stopped moving.

"Now we do," he said, rubbing his fist.

Ding.

"Here's our ride."

Thirty:
That Darn Cat

"Raven. Raven. *Raven!* Wake up! You're going to be late for school!"

"Huh...?" moaned Crow, stirring briefly. Raven shushed her.

"Ma, I...." She faked a cough. "I feel like crap today.... I don't think I can go...."

"Raven, dear, do you want me to stay at home with you today then?" She was genuinely concerned.

"No Ma, thanks, you go to work. I'll be okay."

"Well," came the voice through the bedroom door, "you're old enough now, make sure you call yourself in."

"Okay mom." She put her arm around Crow, kissed her, and started falling back to sleep.

"Oh, one more thing."

"What?" asked an exasperated Raven.

"I cleaned up the cat puke in your room yesterday while you were at school. Next time, let me know right away, okay?"

"Okay, mom."

Thirty-One:
Emma

"Um, colloid or liquid setting?"

" Colloid for now. Safer, I think." There were two settings for the SDF chamber's contents. "Liquid" created three layers of fluid of different densities, the idea being that the occupant would float in the middle layer without contacting the top or bottom of the chamber. "Colloid" used the same fluids but mixed an agent that gelled them. The occupant would float in it like fruit cocktail in gelatin.

Mina was already in the tube. She'd been injected with more sedatives as soon as they had arrived in the room. The bruise from Carl's punch was already long gone. The sensors were fitted and the face-mask was in place; she was already breathing the orange para-amniotic fluid. The first, most dense layer of liquid was entering the chamber through the bottom. Mina began to get buoyed up by it as it rose.

"I've got the tissue sample entered into the sequencer," said Jameson. "But, it's going to be a long time before it's completely read and compared her current DNA with that on file."

The second layer of fluid was almost done. Mina was floating in it, upside down. They had chosen an opaque tube to put her in but the video from inside was crystal clear.

"Why do you want to test her DNA?" asked Redford. "Are you expecting a change?"

"I'm not sure," said Emma, "but I don't want to miss anything."

"Granted, there have been some—ahem—*major* changes to her," spoke Spencer, "but I think they're all in her mind, not in her DNA."

"Look at her, Jameson," said Emma, turning to face him with her arms crossed. "What do you see?"

Spencer Jameson had a puzzled look on his face. What did she want him to say? A naked chick in a tube? "A girl? Sorry, a woman?" His standard approach and methodology towards women was both crude and unsuccessful. He had no desire to be judged at the workplace, however, and was often overcareful.

Carl and Emma just shook their heads. He was getting on their nerves. Carl noticed something, though, looking at her back on the monitor. Carl gasped. "Her birthmark's gone."

"Yes," Emma responded. "I want the sensors to take all of her measurements and compare them with her last physical. What I was going to say, though, is that she doesn't have any moles."

"So?" said Jameson.

"Everyone's got moles," said Carl. He wanted to add, *numb-nuts*, but didn't. "I didn't even notice!" He glanced at the monitors. "Damn, that's weird."

"Yes," said Emma, looking Mina up and down on the monitors to double-check her hypothesis. "She doesn't have any stretch marks anymore either. There are tiny little imperfections on everyone's body, and I'd wager a month's salary she doesn't have a single one anywhere. But there's something else that puzzles me, too. Other than the obvious." *Why she went on a rampage*, she thought. That was the obvious question. The other one....

"The medicine represses libido and sexuality. She has been taught reproduction so that she understands her period, but there is no reason she should even have a concept of 'rape.' So I don't understand how or why she could claim a man raped her today. Surveillance reported she was having a seizure, and I went to check on her. There was never any rape."

"She is different than the others," said Carl. "It's possible the medicine does not work properly. And it could have been some kind of mental effect, a hallucination."

"Still though, she would have needed some way of obtaining that concept to hallucinate it. And... Her body perceives our sedatives as toxins, and disposes of them. It's entirely possible she perceives the medicine the same way. It may not have affected her today, or...."

"It may not have affected her at all," finished Carl. It was a horrible thought. "But, all our data, all along, showed that she reacted normally to all of the drugs we gave her."

"It's unlikely," said Emma, "but depending on the level of control she has over her body and her healing abilities, we can't rule out the fact that she was just going along with everything the whole time, waiting for her chance to act. Still, I tend to believe that the drugs were, until now, effective."

"You mean, she could have been unaffected by the drugs, and was faking the effects?" questioned Jameson, who just now seemed to be catching on.

"I guess it's possible," Carl said absentmindedly, as he turned to face the SDF. Then: "Oops. Almost forgot." He went to the controls and initiated the gelling sequence. "I've got steady readouts."

"Great. Have the reports come in yet on the other subjects?"

"Yeah, Emma," Carl answered as he accessed a monitor. "Let's see, most are accounted for; several are seeing counselors, and...okay, they found the last two."

"Good. I'm going to go see Richardson now, call me if anything happens."

"You betcha."

Emma left the room and began the trek to his office. Lieutenant Colonel Joshua Richardson. The two of them didn't have much in the way of casual contact but at a work level they knew each other well enough. He was essentially the head of the facility, at least as far as Emma knew, although being an army officer, he probably answered to someone. It seemed an odd position for someone at his rank to have, but she didn't really know much about those matters.

He was a handsome man, tall and powerful in stature with pale blue eyes and short, shiny black hair he always kept perfectly parted and combed. He was clean shaved, with an oblong face and a chiseled jaw line. He was stern, but he had a good sense of humor and a strong, determined voice. There were times she could swear he was flirting with her....

Her stomach dropped suddenly; she felt guilty thinking about such a thing given all that was going-on right now...still it was nice (and necessary) to take pleasure in *something* in the middle of all the stress that had been dumped upon her in the past hours.

No, she'd seen him look at her before. She was sure of it.

Emma smiled. She knew she wasn't a supermodel, but she was happy with the way she looked. She took full advantage of the company gym and had a toned, fit physique. She had naturally curly, mahogany hair that she kept highlights in and usually wore in a loose ponytail with a few free strands in the front. Her narrow eyes were a light shade of brown and she wore smart-looking wire-frame glasses that gave her pretty face a sense of seriousness. Her favorite quality about her appearance, however, was her mouth: she was blessed (or cursed, given the rude things that had been said to her from time to time) with full, pouty, naturally pink lips.

Emma was pulled out of this tangent when the elevator she was in front of opened and she was greeted by three men covered in blood-stained hazmat suits. As she got into the elevator, one of the men said, as if to explain, "We did the clean up on 48."

"Oh," she said. "Bad?"

"Horrifying. Bestial violence."

"Jesus...."

"You're the doctor in charge, right?"

"Yes."

"One of them was my brother."

The door opened on floor 45 and the men got out, leaving Emma with a sick stomach and a guilt complex as she rode up another floor and walked the hallway to Richardson's office. Any flights of fancy that had temporarily raised her spirits were dashed to pieces.

Thirty-Two:
Richardson

"Yes, I gave the order... A shame, I know... Good soldier." The man in the chair fidgeted. Some people just didn't understand *orders*. "Yes, *highest* honors. Peacetime... Look, he died completing his mission. Burned to death. I want full benefits for his family...." A woman entered the room.

"Please, Emma, sit down." She did. "Push it through... I don't care... B-R-I-T-O... Thanks." He slammed the phone down in disgust. "Jesus Christ, some people."

His dark hair, was perfectly cut and parted, as always.

"Lieutenant Colonel Rich—"

"Please, call me Joshua now," Richardson said. "We're going to be talking a lot from now on and it'll just make things easier." He reached his hand across his desk, past a model of the *USS Nimitz* and shook her hand.

"Of course."

"Is the girl safely secured?"

"Yes." She almost said, *for now*, but stopped herself.

"Any theories yet on what caused this?"

None she wanted to tell him about, for fear it would put things—studying Mina, in particular—in jeopardy. "None yet, but we're working on it."

Richardson glanced down at the papers on his desk, and turned his vision towards Emma without moving his head upright. "It says here that you have a Level 8 security clearance." He paused for a moment, and Emma felt nervous. "That's high for someone of your former station."

Emma began to explain. "Drs. Utsugi and Hanin trusted me greatly. They would have me do research for them when they were very busy."

"That's good," said Richardson, placing his elbows on the table and locking his hands together in front of him, "that means that there is less you have to catch up on." Emma sighed in relief.

"From now on your clearance is Level 14. You need to become acquainted with the information you were previously not privy to. I am authorizing you to temporarily remove files and take them home with you to read, as there is a lot of ground for you to cover, and as the new head of staff, you need to quickly reach the level of knowledge that Dr. Hanin had. You are now running this project. You must understand it fully ASAP. You live alone, correct?"

"Yes."

"Boyfriend?"

"None." She swore she saw a glint in his eye when she said that.

"Good," he said. "Nondisclosure shouldn't be a problem." Of course, the line taps and surveillance team would ensure that.

"Now," he continued, placing the top few sheets on his desk beneath the others, "we are not bringing any scientists into this project from the outside, at least not at this time. What this means is that only the former junior staff will be working for you, and as such, you will need to determine on a need-to-know basis who should have their security level raised."

"What exactly happened to the senior staff?" Emma quickly worked in.

"Well, Dr. Benton had a close encounter with your girl Mina and died of cardiac arrest. The rest of the senior staff was in the conference room on 48 when she walked by. She dropped the whole damn ceiling on them, collapsed the walls, blew out the windows. The street below was damaged."

Emma didn't know what to say to this but luckily Joshua didn't give her a chance to reply. He pointed to a narrow brown attaché case sitting in the chair next to her. "The information about what I've told you, among other things, is in the briefcase."

He leaned forward "I will have to authorize any and all changes you make, but rest assured that I have good faith in you and will cooperate with your needs."

She felt herself blush a bit when he said *needs*. Then she felt stupid; like a damn schoolgirl with a crush. Why was she letting her mind wander so foolishly? Was it stress? Fatigue?

A defense mechanism of some sort?

"Hanin's office on 43 is yours if you want it."

"Certainly," Emma said. It was a very nice office.

"Once you are fully settled in, I expect a full report on the current situation in the laboratory and of our progress in general."

"Definitely."

"Now, once everything is all set with the girl, I want you to take some files and go home. Read them, and rest for a couple of days. This has been quite an ordeal."

"Yes." After a pause, she added, "May I ask you a question sir—Joshua?"

"Of course."

"Why *was* I chosen? Why *not* bring in someone more qualified?"

Richardson tapped his fingers on a stack of papers lying face-down on his desk. "I've been going over your record here at NOD. You haven't done much —that's understandable, given your previous station—but what you have done is top-notch. You are, obviously, a little under qualified for this position, but the fact is, there isn't anyone more qualified *left*. Based on everything I've read about you, I have no reason to doubt your abilities, Emma. You *can* do the work. And, given the nature of the work we do here, even the lowliest lab tech on your team is more qualified than anyone we could bring in from the outside. You're going to be running a small staff for now; eventually, we will bring in more doctors, but they will fill the ranks from the bottom, not the top."

"Understood." She felt very proud of herself; that had been a glowing appraisal of her work.

"Good, good. Emma, for too long now this organization has sat mired in aimless *research.*" He said "research" almost as though he loathed such a lowly concept. "You are going to be in charge of moving things forward. Once you have read the contents of those files, come and see me and I will give you my plan."

"Of course. Well then, if that's all, I'll be going," said Emma. Richardson nodded, and she got out of the chair and picked up the briefcase. As she was leaving, Richardson spoke.

"One last thing—I am now the only person you have to answer to. Within reason, you have total control. Prove me right, Emma."

"I will," she said, and left.

Richardson watched her leave and continued to leaf through his papers for a bit without actually doing anything useful. He had so much to worry about now. The project, in complete shambles, was being placed into the care of a person who knew virtually nothing about it, putting it in severe jeopardy. He knew how many files there were. Would Emma be able to absorb it all in time? Things like this called for quick action, something utterly unavailable.

Richardson liked Emma. She was a smart girl—she knew how to get things done. She could do the job—but would she, once she found out exactly what it was? Most scientists—most of the ones he'd known, anyway—had a very specific mentality. They believed themselves above, or at least detached from, the objects of their study. Whether their goal was knowledge, money, or both, they did not hesitate to do anything that was necessary to accomplish these goals. It wasn't ruthlessness—it was devotion.

Emma had shown signs of being—different. Just a little, not much, but it was there nonetheless. She wasn't quite as hard as the other scientists. The subjects of the project were living human beings—an idea that made Richardson queasy at times, but that didn't bother him morally. Would Emma's scientific scruples break down when she confronted some of the more atrocious facets of her job? Finding out the answer would take time, and if the answer was yes, everything would be back at square one.

Richardson knew his own perch was precarious, as well. One of his predecessors had been relieved of his position after a catastrophe similar to this one. It had been less destructive, perhaps, but far more public. The true goal of the project had been put on the back burner at that point, and it had languished there for years while the scientists "acquired data." The best way to make his superiors happy was to get results, and fast. Speaking of his superiors....

Richardson pushed a button on his desk. A female voice came out of the intercom. "Yes, Lieutenant Colonel Richardson?"

Richardson cleared his throat, and then spoke.

"Get me General Kresge."

Thirty-Three:
NOD

Emma sat in Dr. Hanin's chair. She was about to open the briefcase when she noticed a framed photograph on the desk.

It was his family—him, a wife, two sons, and a big, bushy dog. She fought back tears. Did they even know yet? She wondered a few things, things that led to a train of thoughts that eventually made her question her current position again. Regardless of what Richardson had said, the question begged to be asked: What was she doing taking over a project when her former position in it was nothing more than a glorified lab assistant? She understood a lot of the basics, but several, very important things were unknown to her. She did not understand "The Process" that turned helpless children into powerful psychics; she did not know what the actual goal of "The Project" was; and last but not least, she had no idea where "The Project" had come from or who was in charge above Richardson.

The facility was called "NOD." N-O-D, all capitals, and when she had asked what they stood for, she had been told, "nothing really." Originally she had been told she would be working on genetic studies regarding mental disabilities. Fresh out of school, she had earned a job based on her academic proficiency. It was a job that paid damn well and she hadn't looked back even when she found out how unsavory some of the work really was. She had top of the line benefits, an expense account, and her taxes were even done for her, free of charge. The Gates Building, where NOD was located, was an impressive structure with state of the art facilities, most of which were advanced beyond anything the public was even aware of. There were of course nondisclosure agreements, and she assumed she was under surveillance. But life was good, and she understood it.

Except for the nights she couldn't sleep. But that seemed to be a lessening problem, whether that was a good or bad thing, she couldn't say.

But the things she didn't know, she needed to learn, and quickly. She was going to take at least two days off, she decided, so she had to set up a schedule for people to take care of Mina and the other subjects. She pulled up a scheduling program on the computer that was on the desk. It startled her a bit when she went to cross-reference abilities with availability, to see the word DECEASED next to so many of the doctors' names. Within ten minutes, though, she had worked out a suitable schedule, and she emailed it to the staff— her staff.

Once that was finished, Emma went to check if any experiments were in progress and needed someone to watch over them…something that had just dawned on her as very important. Luckily, there were none. She sent out another email saying that she would be gone for a couple of days and that until her return, maintenance and routine lab work were to be the subjects of everyone's duties.

Remembering the briefcase, Emma opened it. A folder titled "Assigning Rank to Staff Members" was on top. She set that aside, deciding she would look at it later. Under that, she found a letter. The cover letter was plain white, with the NOD logo in the center. It was a black shield—a square with a half-circle attached to the bottom. At the top of the square, in large, white capital letters, was the word "NOD." Beneath it, reaching down into the half-circle was a black-and-white (mostly white) drawing of a branch with a bird on it. A dove, maybe? Going around the half-circle on the outside were black letters that read, "Nothing Sacred, Nothing Harmed."

That was weird. She hadn't thought about it before but she wondered what it meant. She turned the page, and began to read.

To Whom It May Concern:

This letter has been prepared by Dr. Mahir Hanin and Dr. Setsuna Utsugi, in the case of an emergency of the sort wherein they are no longer able to continue their work as heads of the NOD Project. In it, you, the new head of NOD, will find information referencing top- and above top-secret files, including a suggested order of reading said files, to help you better become acquainted with your job and to bring you up to speed regarding information you previously may not have been privy to.

The letter rambled on for a while, explaining basic duties (preparing schedules, sanctioning lab space,) and included tips on dividing up duties and taking care of test subjects. What caught Emma's eye was the line that described her main duty:

"To work in conjunction with the military and black ops to work towards a happier, better world through NOD's ultimate goal of providing unlimited energy to Earth through the production of the perfect psychic."

That was certainly a noble goal, but how would psychics bring unlimited energy to earth? And what were black ops? She read on—no answers yet, nothing important, really, for the next couple of pages until she came across the list of files. They were grouped under headings, sorted first by sub-headings, then by classification, and finally, by the actual file numbers. The first few headings were: "History of NOD," "Ley Lines," "Psychic

Transformation Process," "Nod," and "Working Discretely with the 'Black Army'." History and transformation she understood. They should give her some background on her job and what exactly it was. Probably, "Black Army" was the same thing as "Black Ops" because "Ops" probably stood for "Operations." That should clear that one up.

But the other two didn't make sense. "Nod," seemed to be used as a noun in several titles where it wasn't spelled in capitals. The only "Nod" Emma remembered was a land of dreams from a nursery rhyme or poem. And ley lines? They were some occult thing, some mumbo-jumbo druid thing about energy fields that surrounded the earth.

Emma almost laughed aloud at her use of the phrase "mumbo-jumbo." After all, before she had started working at NOD, the word "psychic" meant late night phone calls to your fortune-telling "miss" and street corner demonstrations from spoon-bending charlatans. Now it meant something entirely different. Psychic phenomena were real, and they had scientific explanations. Not all recorded manifestations had been explained, yet, but Emma was certain that in time, they would be. All were rooted in biology, genetics, and particle physics.

The human body was surrounded by a field of particles held in place by forces that were exerted subconsciously. This was the "aura" some people were able to see—or at least claimed to be able to see. Telekinesis occurred when a person consciously manipulated their aura to affect other objects' positioning or structure. Pyrokinesis was the ability to localize heat at a specific point in the aura, and in some cases, it included the ability to affect outside heat sources and even the combustion process itself. They were many other abilities as well.

So, maybe ley lines were just something she didn't know about yet.

Emma turned to the next page. The next file listed for her to read caught her off-guard. It was titled, simply, "MATTHEW." The ID was blacked out, however. Redacted.

So, Matthew was a real person—a real something, at least. It could be a coincidence, but Emma was intrigued now. She decided she would do this calmly, rationally, and in order. She didn't want to miss something important. She gathered up the papers, shut them in the briefcase, and headed for a file room.

Thirty-Four:
More Sex

Raven felt the world of the living calling to her, and she took a deep breath. Slowly, her eyes fluttered open, and she rolled over onto her side. Crow was leaning on her elbow and smiling at her, her beautiful face surrounded by messy, vibrantly red hair.

"Huh, how long have you been staring at me?"

"Just a couple minutes. I woke up when your mom left for work," Crow answered.

Raven grinned. "I'd think it was creepy if you weren't so pretty." Crow started to move closer. "No no no," Raven refused. "Don't kiss me, dork, my mouth tastes like butthole."

"Fine, I won't kiss your mouth," Crow said slyly. She smiled broadly and pulled the covers over her head.

Awhile later, the girls laid side-by-side, staring at the ceiling, holding hands beneath the covers. "We have all day together," Raven said. "On a weekday! What do you want to do today?"

"I could probably get a little money from my dad, but not that much," Crow offered.

"I might be able to scrounge up enough for the matinée…but I don't think there's anything good playing. I'd like to go shopping, but I don't have nearly enough for that."

"You know," Crow said, "it isn't often we have either of our houses all to our selves. We could stay in...find stuff to do."

"Sounds good to me," Raven said. She leaned over and pecked Crow on the cheek. "Sounds fun."

It was going to be a good day.

Thirty-Five:
Black Ops

"Over there! Over there!"

Marcus said thanks and put the man out of his misery. "Hey Carlos! You doin' okay?"

"Yeah, the bleeding stopped. Let's go."

Amidst the gunfire, Marcus Graley and Carlos Gonzalez, buddies as well as teammates, made haste through an open room towards their goal. The room looked like a typical boiler room, but something about it was weird.

"Blood...and pus. It smells like blood and pus!"

"Aw, put your damn gas mask on if you're going to be a pussy!" yelled Carlos.

"Look! Jackpot! I hope the boys at the other terminal have finished cracking the codes." They walked over to a large computer terminal that stood before a vast cylindrical cell, with all manners of hoses and pipes attached to it. "I think it's cool, but I can't read Portuguese," said Marcus.

"Yeah, it's cool, I'll get it from here." After a pause and some keystrokes, Carlos continued. "All right, everything's all set! I'm going to shunt the field to the backup system and open the cell."

There was a yell into the room, something foreign but too garbled to be understood anyway, followed by an explosion.

"We've reached the target, keep us covered," Marcus said into his headset. Just then, noises of decompression and escaping gases began emanating from the cylinder, and it started to rise up. Water vapor began pouring out of it, and when that had cleared, Marcus and Carlos looked in awe at the biggest one of *these* they'd seen yet.

"That's gotta be more jade than in all of feudal China. And the crystal's still perfect, even at that size!"

"Well, almost perfect...there's something in it," said Marcus, pointing near its base. "Wait...that's not..."

They walked forward. There, in the front of the jade crystal and a couple feet down from where it began to taper off, was a human fetus, afterbirth intact. It was big enough to be fully developed, but it had gills, long, feathery gills like a baby newt's or a tadpole's, but much bigger.

"...a baby...."

"This shit gets weirder every mission. Well, if you'll place the charges and the resonators, I'll go set up the computer to restore the field."

"Yeah...." agreed Marcus, still staring at the baby.

"Now man! Come on!"

"Sorry...." Marcus took off his backpack and removed several cylinders from it. Half of them were sonic resonators that could crack the jade by vibrating at a certain frequency, and the rest were standard C-4 charges. He began placing them on the facets near the base of the crystal, all the while unable to pull his vision away from the fetus. When he had moved around to the side of it, he could see through the jade what appeared to be small, leathery wings on its back and a tiny triangular tail.

"We're standing in it right now, you know," said Carlos from in front of the computer.

"In what?" asked Marcus, placing a charge.

"The ley line," answered Carlos.

"How do you know? You shunted it. It could be anywhere."

Carlos inhaled deeply, and in a very satisfied voice, said, "I can feel it."

Marcus placed the last charge and walked over to his backpack, shaking his head. "You are so full of shit."

"You all set?" asked Carlos, all business again.

"Yeah. You?"

"Yup. Give the warning and set the timers!"

"Attention all operatives—the device is ready. Secure the jewel room and prepare to evacuate. Five minutes starting...now!" Marcus ran out from under the descending cylinder.

"Okay, Marco, buddy, the field is locked into a countdown, four-forty-five from the start until it's in place, with only a fifteen second window for anyone to stop it before the charges go. And even *I* couldn't do it in less than eighteen. Dillons, maybe. So...."

"So let's get the hell out of here!"

They made their way back through the base amidst gunfire and the dying screams of Portuguese guards. The yard opened up before them through a large cargo door. Three black, unmarked helicopters sat before them. Within minutes, they and the rest of their company were airborne and fleeing.

Carlos counted down. "...Four...three...two...one!"

An explosion spread out from the base, and two ripples passed through the air out towards the horizon. Out in the sea, a faint explosion was visible at the end of one of the ripples.

"Let me just get a secure line and I'll report...." Marcus mumbled as he tapped on his laptop. "Hey, I got an email from command...."

```
<ENCRYPTED MESSAGE>
TO: GraMar021@TheBiz.xfr <Marcus Graley>
FR: ESno256^7*~hgP;( <ENCRYPTED>
```

```
CC:  ------
BC:  ------
BODY:
```
    Attn. Marcus Graley
Yo Marcus, some shit went down at the Gates
building. Ops say one of the psychs went crazy and
killed off half the scientists in the building and
some of our men too. No cover lost, but probably some
shake-ups with work… maybe. I dunno. Anyway I'll tell
ya more back at base. Tell Carlos he's a pussy.
    --Leonard

"Hey Carlos, Dillons emailed. Check this out."

Carlos scanned the message. "Shit. Hope this doesn't fuck up this deal. Bonus last check was *sweet*."

"Shit, yeah."

They looked out over the ocean for a few minutes, and then Carlos spoke again. "Hey, you and Jackie want to go out to dinner tonight?"

"Sure. How's Carrie doing?"

"Eh, pregnancy's hell, but she's doing great. If we go out to dinner, though, it'll probably have to be Chinese."

Marcus grinned. "Fine with me. She's a sweetheart."

"Yeah. So's yours."

"Lucky men."

"Yup, we're lucky men."

Thirty-Six:
Files

Emma rolled over and turned on her lamp. She could sense it.

Read me. Read me. I can't possibly wait any longer.

The damn files seemed to be calling to her; she couldn't put them out of her mind; the prospect of the knowledge they contained was very exciting, but at the same time the reading promised to provide unparalleled amounts of tedium.

She couldn't sleep, anyway. She'd laid down at least an hour ago and still felt wired up. She got out of bed and walked over to her drapes and peered out. It was midday, but she felt like keeping them closed anyway. She looked across the street at a car that the same man had been sitting in since she'd gotten home.

She laughed. Did they really think she didn't know she was being watched?

Emma decided she'd read for an hour, two at the most, and then try to go to sleep again. She felt exhausted, but too shook up.

She put on her robe (it was powder blue, with a hint of gray) and her glasses. She took the files off of her nightstand and went into the kitchen. Dumping the papers on the table, she turned on her laptop and went about making tea while it booted up.

A "ba-ding!" sound indicated email. She checked it while the water was heating up. In the middle of all of the garbage was one from Carl.

```
Emma:
    Mina's completely stable now, and I'm going home
to get some rest for a few hours and let Spencer keep
an eye on things until I get back. No need for you to
respond, (cause I'm assuming you'll be asleep by the
time I send this,) I just wanted you to know what was
up.
Carl Redford
```

Spencer Jameson? Emma hoped he wouldn't screw anything else up. There were some mannerisms even a PhD couldn't change, and Jameson's sloppy lab work was apparently one of them.

As much as Emma tried to play nice and keep an open mind, she couldn't stand Jameson, and she was by far from the only one on the junior staff who felt that way. He had a rat-like, scurrying demeanor, a tendency to talk with his hands and watch over his shoulder. What was absurd, what seemed to make him almost a caricature of a man, was that he also *looked* like a rat. He was tall and gaunt, with a long face, a long nose, a thin mustache, and greasy black hair. His dark, almost black eyes seemed to be scheming no matter the expression he wore.

Emma shivered a bit.

The tea kettle started whistling so Emma went to go grab it off the stove. Pouring some of the water into a mug, she added a tea bag and sat down. She looked in disdain at the size of the stack of papers before her. She could have gotten it all on disk, (not that that would have made it any less to read,) but from her experience, all the hyperlinks would have driven her crazy, leading her around in circles.

She started reading. The first files were about the history of NOD, which, as this paper would eventually confirm, wasn't short for anything. The top paragraph read:

OVERVIEW: BRIEF HISTORY OF NOD

The origin of the NOD project is unfortunately steeped in mystery and best guesses. What is known as fact is that it grew from a department known as SPECTRE, which was formed by President Abraham Lincoln shortly after his re-election in 1864. It was given access to however much funding its heads decided was necessary to pursue their interests, and they were required to answer only to the president. It is important to note that this occurred during the latter part of the Civil War, so it must be assumed that President Lincoln considered SPECTRE to be of utmost importance to set up a limitless fund at that time.

One event that may have led to Lincoln's assertion that the "unknown" was worth earnest study happened in October of 1862, when Caleb Smith, President Abraham Lincoln's secretary of the interior reported to the president a sighting he had made of a ghostly apparition. Several friends of Caleb confirmed the appearance of the apparition, over the course of several sightings. Many of these people were held with high regard in the community. According to Caleb, the apparition had been of a late friend who had dabbled in the occult.

Additionally, in 1863, the Lincolns held a séance in the White House. Spiritualism and table reading were popular at the time, and it is colloquially believed that this was essentially, a public relations stunt for the Lincoln presidency.

However, given the fervent beliefs of the first lady, Mary Todd Lincoln, in the occult (and her subsequent mental decline following the president's death and her continued dabbling in spiritualism,) this belief is suspect.

Thus in 1864 Lincoln formed a department, *Spiritual and Paranormal Energies Communication Team for Research and Explanation*, or SPECTRE, to investigate spiritualism, ghost sightings, unexplained events, and paranormal phenomena. Often referred to as Project S, their exact work is mostly unknown as most records from that era have been lost, or were never written down in the first place.

Following Lincoln's untimely death, Project S became an organization understood fully only by its members, who transformed it into a nearly autonomous part of the government answerable to essentially no one. When in the early 1900s it was determined that most paranormal phenomena were actually caused by psychic projection, the focus of SPECTRE was aimed towards the power of the mind. Following research and the classification of psychic abilities, SPECTRE was officially rechristened *NOD*, after one of the names for the mythical "plane of the mind" that has since become the target of this organization.

Today NOD exists as a black ops organization dealing with matters not disclosed to the public due to legal, moral, and national security reasons, for the good of the American people. It operates under unparalleled secrecy. All information is on a need-to-know basis. The physical headquarters of NOD is located in Groom Lake, Nevada. *[Further information including the unedited Nod history appears later in sections 21j-a1 through 21m-b3.]*

She had no idea that it all went back so far. Another paper briefly described the current leadership setup for NOD. Richardson was the vocal head of the Omaha location; a man named Nicholas Kresge served as the liaison between NOD itself and a group called the "advisory board" that oversaw all projects. Presumably, they were high-ranking government officials, though this was not expressly stated. Neither were their names.

Richardson apparently *was* from the army, though he didn't seem to take active part within it. Much of NOD's funding came from the military; it occurred to Emma then that they must have a vested interest in the work performed there. Of course the "unlimited energy" mentioned in the letter she had received would be of interest to the military, but she wondered if there wasn't more. Certainly, some of the test subjects had very destructive powers, but this opened up an unpleasant train of thought she didn't want to continue. The thought had crossed her mind before, but now she had evidence to back it up.

The files also mentioned a group called the "Black Army." The Black Army was a specialized, highly-trained, top secret army branch that performed "secret missions" for NOD, and although they received regular, (probably quite handsome) pay, each mission was handled contractually and they were paid additionally for each completed contract.

Members of the Black Army were hand-picked (the document did not say by whom,) not just for skill, but also to make sure they were ethnically diverse. They even posed as a mercenary army from time to time, offering their services to nations and powerful individuals, for a fee. These precautions were taken to obfuscate their overall goals and their country of origin, so that targeted foes would not be able to point at the United States as the culprit. It was safer than using an actual mercenary army, and plausibly deniable, which using the regular army wasn't.

The file said that they were contracted by NOD to perform industrial and government espionage and sabotage, and to "occasionally acquire test subjects discretely." This bothered Emma a little, for she was under the impression that all test subjects were orphans, and this hinted that they weren't. The same Nicholas Kresge that controlled NOD was also in charge of communicating with the Black Army; this gave him quite a bit of power in Emma's eyes.

The next several pages had very large sections that were entirely blacked out. Emma flipped to the "unedited" history in sections 21j-a1 through 21m-b3 and saw that they were, in fact, heavily edited. This did not surprise Emma much; many documents she technically had clearance for before her promotion had similarly blacked-out elements. This was typical among government documents; even Freedom of Information Act requests, when accepted, sometimes had redactions. Of course, the file in her hand was probably not under the Act's jurisdiction, since apparently NOD wasn't under the government's jurisdiction.

She set the papers down and smiled. It was always the parts you couldn't see that were the most intriguing. It was the blacked-out text that kept ufologists and conspiracy buffs busy, not the parts they could actually read. Emma had once read a book by a Mr. Stanton Friedman that had presented a very compelling case for UFOs built from research into declassified government files. It was as though the unedited parts were left as teasers for people like Mr. Friedman; they gave just enough information to let the researcher know something was going on without really saying anything specific.

Emma ended this mental tangent and glanced at the clock on the wall. She was annoyed because it was past midday and she wasn't feeling tired anymore. She wished she did because she knew she needed the sleep.

Her hand was throbbing a little and she went to the bathroom to redress the wound. She turned the light on and looked in the mirror, sighing at the bags under her eyes. She unwrapped the gauze and stared at her palm. She would definitely have a scar. A series of stitches ran perpendicular to her lifeline where the biggest piece had slashed into her. Several more stitches had been applied to smaller cuts, and those that didn't require stitches had scabbed a bit.

She threw away the blood-speckled gauze, and grabbed a roll from the cabinet behind the mirror. When she closed it, she thought she saw something behind her in the mirror and jumped, dropping the fresh gauze into the sink where it became moist as it rolled down the inside. She cursed to herself for not staying in bed, suddenly feeling all jittery and nerved up. Removing the wet layer, Emma applied a protective wrap of gauze around her hand and left, setting the roll on the toilet tank. She made sure not to look in the mirror, not wanting to give her tired mind a chance to play another trick on her.

Going back into the kitchen, Emma decided to gather up the files and try and force herself to sleep. As she gathered up the papers, she noticed something out of the corner of her eye. It was a timeline of major events in NOD's recent past. Next to one date, several years ago, was a line that read: ANDREW Incident. Following: Research Staff discharged except for Hanin, Mahir, and Utsugi, Setsuna. Richardson, Joshua, takes over as head of NOD.

Emma didn't know what the "Andrew Incident" was. That was before she had started working for NOD. Apparently, that was before most people had started working for NOD, she realized, because it looked like everyone except Dr. Hanin and Dr. Utsugi had been replaced following it.

She knew that Richardson was in his early forties, though, despite his smoking habit, he could have easily passed for someone in his early thirties. He was a lieutenant colonel, though she vaguely remembered hearing that he had been a major when he was first appointed to NOD.

Emma knew what the "Anna Incident" was. That was the term she'd heard used for when Anna, a test subject, had caused the death of several doctors. It had occurred earlier than the "Andrew Incident." Emma looked up the sheet and found nearly all of the information was blacked out, however, it seemed to have not been done properly because several short groups of letters were still visible between edited sections, including the letters MAT.

Matthew? There was something she wasn't being told.

Thirty-Seven:
After Sex (again)

Crow turned and smiled at Raven. "Your turn." It had been a very good day. Both girls were in high spirits.

The school hadn't called, which was good. Crow doubted they would, but still she wanted to know what the outcome of her suspension would be. Her dad had called, worried because she never went home last night, but she had smoothed that one out. Whether due to her decent marks in school, or the difficult balancing act that was being a single father to a teenage daughter, he tended to give her quite a bit of leeway.

No one was home, and neither girl had bothered to get completely dressed yet; Raven wore a pink tank top with red trim, Crow, a light green tee shirt. Each girl was sheathed in a fluffy blanket; Raven's was covered with cows, Crow's with antelopes and gnus. ("Water buffoons" Crow had absentmindedly called them.)

They were playing a game of chess. Neither Raven nor Crow knew all the rules of chess, so they'd made several up as they went along. It was mainly a distraction for their hands as they talked.

Raven sighed contentedly. "We haven't had a day like this in a long time. I needed it. I wanted to maybe go somewhere...but I'm glad we stayed in."

"Me too," Crow said, smiling deeply. It was a graceful, charming smile. "When I—," She chuckled briefly, "—when I was getting ready to wake you up, I was excited to see you. To talk to you. It was—I don't know. It was almost like, when you first get to know someone? It was a rush hearing you wake up."

"It was a rush for me, too, obviously!" said Raven, laughing. "Seriously, though, I know what you mean. I feel revitalized. Oh, hey, how do the little ball-headed guys move?"

"Um, three steps forward, or two steps back. Uh, I guess one left or right too, or that wouldn't be fair. So...."

Crow didn't want to ruin the moment (or the day) but in this moment of pure love and honesty, she would be remiss not to broach the subject.

"I was thinking, um...." She didn't want to say it. "Maybe...you should make a doctor's appointment for today or something."

Raven was holding a bishop and put it down neatly. She frowned. Crow sighed.

"I know it scares you, but it scares me to. You're my girl and I don't want anything to happen to you."

"I know...." Said Raven, looking down at the ground.

"You know I'll go with you," said Crow, inching over to Raven around the chess set and putting an arm around her, blanket and all. "And when they look inside your head I'll be able to see what you really think of me."

Raven looked up, confused, but Crow attacked her with a surprise peck before she continued speaking.

"That you really love me and wouldn't want me to have to worry about you."

It wasn't really a guilt trip because it was all too true. Raven smiled, and it was a real smile because Crow could see it in her eyes.

"I know you're right. But it *is* really scary. You're the only one I've ever told about this because you're the only one I've ever been this close to."

"I can't pretend to understand it. But I can understand that you're scared." She grasped Raven's hand. "I'm just afraid you could get worse."

"What if they lock me up in an institution? What could I do?" Raven wasn't so much arguing as she was explaining her fear.

"They won't do that. You're obviously not crazy. You just see things."

"What I saw the other night, when…you know…I think it was a memory."

"A memory of me having s—" Crow began, very skeptically.

"No! No. I saw you, *thought* it was you, but... it wasn't about you. It wasn't even about the girl, whoever she really was."

"How so?"

Raven thought very hard, a look of determination on her face.

"I remember my father…He was sad."

"I didn't know him very well. He worked a lot. No—he wasn't sad. He was *happy*. Happy to see me, happy to see my brother, happy to see my mom. God, I can *almost* remember what it felt like then, what life felt like. When he *was* home. It was...joyous."

It was incredibly rare for Raven to talk about her past, especially her childhood. Crow didn't dare interrupt.

"He changed. It was at our old house, I had to be eight...no, probably seven." There was a wistful, melancholy look to her eyes as she stared into the distance, remembering. A single tear slid down her face.

She could almost see them. He wasn't very tall (though he was much taller than she was at the time, of course,) or imposing, but he had a presence that could not be denied, even though she couldn't put a finger on exactly *what* kind of presence it was. Raven could remember glasses. Short black hair.

Her mother, all she could remember from then—a pretty face, her curly hair auburn, like her own.

They fought. She was too young then to realize it, and too old now to remember it, but insincerity of forced anger bred sincerity and a bitter taste in the mouth. What did they have to fight about?

"I don't remember the day he left and never came back, because it was just like any other day up to that point. Maybe my mom saw him again after that. I guess she would've had to, so they could get divorced." Ravens eyes were glazed as she stared off into the distance, the tears freely flowing without sobs. She wasn't aware of it, but Crow was holding her hands tightly, trying to hold back her own tears.

"Mommy brought me home one day." She never said *mommy* anymore. "Daddy should have been at work."

She told me to go to my room, but I didn't." her voice had no tone, no inflection, as she gently wept, quietly. Her eyes seemed glassy, and Crow was getting worried.

It was all so vivid now, like she could see it, hear it. Like she was *there*.

Raven walked down the hallway. Her teddy bear was dragging on the floor. She had her finger in her mouth. She could hear Mommy crying. Why was Mommy crying?

Mommy was standing in the doorway of hers and Daddy's room, leaning on the frame, crying. Raven lifted her teddy bear to her chest and hugged it tightly, and sneaked into the space beneath her mother, on the side she was leaning towards.

"And there was a naked woman on top of Daddy. I didn't know who she was. I think Daddy was naked too."

"She wasn't supposed to be here! Raven! Go to your room! Right now!"
"Don't yell at her!"
Mommy why is Daddy yelling at me Mommy why are you crying?
A third voice. The woman. "Aw, what the fuck is this?"
"Raven, please, go to your room. Molly, quick, take the picture."
"I'm leaving, you weird fuck."
"This is what I'm paying you for! Molly, we didn't do anything, okay? We planned this!"
Fumbling with a flip phone. Camera flash. Click. The woman rushes by, half-naked, putting her clothes on as she ran for the door, pushing past Mommy.
Raven was still there.
She had dropped her teddy bear. Mommy leaned against the door frame, phone in hand, sobbing.
Down the hall, little Jacob began wailing, the screaming and sobbing having woke him abruptly from his nap.

"I can't...I can't remember quite...it was my Daddy. That's what I was remembering. We came home and he was having...*sex*...with someone. I didn't know that then. Mommy was crying. Finally, I dropped my teddy bear and ran into Jake's room and shut the door. I could hear them yelling and mommy was crying. I cried too and so did Jake."

"It must have been not long after this that...he left. And then we moved here. And mommy changed when...when...." *When what? What was it? It wasn't just daddy...we met....*

In actuality, the front door opened and closed now, but neither girl heard it. "And daddy left!" Raven bawled, and, snapping out of her trance, she looked directly at Crow, who was now unable to hold back tears of empathy. "It wasn't you, it was a memory, I don't even know who she was. It was my father. I'm so, so sorry."

Crow tossed off her blanket so she could more comfortably hold Raven to her chest as she sobbed. In the process the blanket fell away completely, exposing Crow's unclothed lower torso and rear.

As Raven's sobbing continued, her breathing began to sound labored. A clammy mask seemed to cover her face as her eyes lost focus.

"Raven? Raven? Sweetie?" Crow held Raven away from her by the shoulders, so she could see her face.

Raven started groaning, her eyelids fluttering. All Crow could see under them was whiteness.

"Honey?" Panic was entering her voice. She had been present for a number of Raven's seizures. How she had never had one in public was unbelievable, but other than school, they were usually in one of their bedrooms hanging out. So, only Crow had ever seen one.

Raven's body tightened, and then went limp. Crow carefully released her onto the floor. Usually, these episodes appeared as fairly gentle affairs, though that didn't scare Crow any less. Raven would shudder and twitch, coming to after a couple of minutes in a dazed state, her faculties slowly returning to her.

This was different. The convulsions were violent, thrashing; terrifying Crow.

From out in the hall, Raven's mother's voice could be heard. "Raven? Are you home?"

Panicking as Raven's seizure worsened, Crow yelled out for help. "Mrs. Yamada! Call 911! Hurry!"

"What?" asked Raven's mom as she pushed open the door to see her daughter having a seizure as her half-naked "best friend" sat next to her, crying.

"Oh my god," she said, and meant it on so many different levels.

Thirty-Eight:
Sleep

Emma was fighting to stay awake, but still she kept reading, hoping to come across another reference to Matthew or a description of the Andrew incident. There was something more to everything that had been occurring, she was sure of it. But she had yet to find anything remotely interesting. Most of the last dozen or so files had dealt with mundane details of protocol and duties. She had skipped around a little, but for the most part had been reading them in order.

A lot of what she'd been reading her mind hadn't absorbed because she was so tired. Still, she got the general gist of most of it but didn't know her job goals any better than when she had started reading. She was head of research, but nothing had explained what, specifically, she was supposed to research. The term "perfect psychic" had come up several times but was infinitely vague.

Emma rolled over onto her back and looked at the ceiling.

Her bed was nice and comfy. *I should move the papers off my bed before I fall asleep.*

Too late.

Thirty-Nine:
Mother

Raven's mother looked over at Crow, who was sitting two cushions away in the waiting room, rubbing her hands together in nervous anticipation. Mrs. Yamada was not a fool; she could put two and two together. The fact that Crow and her daughter had been naked from the waist down pretty much spelled out what was going on between them.

She'd actually been suspecting something like this for awhile now. She was no fool; she knew her daughter didn't share the majority of her adolescent life with her, but she only ever seemed to hang out with a couple of boys, and she rarely seemed to be on the phone with anyone other than girls.

Looking back, Raven's male friends had been more or less constant, but her female ones had come and gone.

It wasn't...she didn't want to say the word...it wasn't something she had a problem with, per se, but it was shocking thinking about it in terms of her own daughter. Of course, there were more pressing matters with Raven's health, but she may as well break the silence while they waited.

"Maria?" Raven's mother corrected herself. "Crow." Crow looked up at her as she slid one seat closer on the big couch they were on. "We've never talked much."

"No, we haven't."

"I'll be honest with you; I don't talk much to my own daughter."

Crow nodded in silent understanding.

"I will say, though, that out of all of her friends, you've been the most polite. You've never given me any grief. Until...." Her voice trailed off, as she tried to decide how best to say what she wanted to, without actually having to say it. "Be honest with me. What I saw...there are certain conclusions I could draw from it, and I want to know if they're correct because I'm pretty sure we're both thinking of the same thing."

Crow nodded.

"Do you love my daughter?"

"Very much, Mrs. Yamada."

"Look at me." Crow looked up at her. She saw a face, prematurely aged, but that had once been beautiful, and still could be, framed in graying brunette curls. "I'm not entirely happy. But...what my daughter needs now are the people who care about her, and since you're at the top of her list I'm certainly not going to push you away." Mrs. Yamada almost laughed as she continued, feeling a little better in spite of herself. "Though, I doubt I could if I tried."

Crow smiled, feeling a little better, too.

Forty:
Doctor

"So, how long have you been hallucinating?"

Raven scratched her right shoulder. The hospital gown felt like paper and it was making her itchy.

"Umm, I probably had my first one when I was thirteen or fourteen, but I don't think I recognized it at the time. Most happened within the last two years."

The doctor scribbled a few notes, and then looked up. "And you say you act on these hallucinations as though they're real?"

"Yes. Sometimes." She hung her head and folded her hands, ashamed as she again thought of what she had done to Crow. "Sometimes...sometimes they feel so real, or rather, it's like they're telling me something real, even when I know they aren't literally real."

"Mm-hmm." The pencil scribbled. *Scratch scratch scratch.* "Do you take any drugs?"

"I smoke pot...marijuana. I'm...not going to, anymore."

"Okay. And the black-outs and seizures?"

"I think they're the same thing. I didn't realize I was having seizures until my girlfriend saw one."

"And when did these start?"

"About two years ago, I think. When the hallucinations got worse."

"Mm-hmm." *Scratch-scratch.* "And, do the hallucinations and seizures seem linked?"

"Um, sometimes I have a black out awhile after hallucinating, but not usually."

"Uh-huh," said the doctor, scribbling some more notes. He folded his clipboard under his arms. "Raven, the blood work and some of the test results are going to take a couple days, but I can tell you that most of what you've been experiencing are classic symptoms." He didn't say of what. "I'm going to give you a referral, but I'd like you to stay overnight for observation." Raven's expression changed; she obviously didn't like this idea. The doctor leaned towards her and she instinctively looked up at him.

"Now, you told me that you've recently decided to quit taking drugs. That's a very wise choice, but whatever happens, the important thing is not to quit quitting. Mental conditions and drug use often go hand-in-hand, and in some cases one is caused by the other. But regardless of the cause, drug use can make a mental condition worse. I don't want to see you hurt yourself, and I don't think that's what you want to do either, now is it?"

It was just fucking pot. Raven averted her vision from his eyes and said,

"No. I don't."

"Good," said the doctor, straightening up. "It's just your luck that there happens to be a facility right here in town that specializes in mental conditions that involve symptoms such as those you've been experiencing. I'll have to get your mother's approval, and yours, of course, but I think if you go there your chances for a full recovery *without* surgery are excellent. Now, do you have any questions?"

Raven, more terrified then before now that the word *surgery* had been used, had only one. "Can I see my mom and my girlfriend now?"

"Certainly," said the doctor, unaware (or not caring) that he had committed a sort of Hippocratic faux pas by unnecessarily scaring his patient, "just go out through that door and the nurse can call them in for you."

Raven got up silently and left the room. She was wearing underwear but still felt uncomfortable with the opening down the back of her gown, so she put her hands over her butt. The doctor made it a conscious choice not to watch her as she left. Once she was gone, he grabbed his cell phone from his waist and speed-dialed a number he hadn't gotten a chance to use before. After several rings, a man's voice answered.

"Hello, this is Dr. Richardson. Can I help you?"

"Ah, yes, this is Dr. Pensfield over at County General. I, ah, I have a patient that fits the description given out by your institute. Mid-to-late teens, eighteen to be exact, with two plus years of seizures and hallucinations. Some minor drug use, I'm afraid, but it doesn't appear to have been the cause of the symptoms. I'm going to keep her overnight."

"Good," came the reply. "Keeping her won't be necessary, though. That sounds perfect for our research. I'm sure we can help this—," he paused.

"Girl," Dr. Pensfield filled in.

"This—girl—with her problems. We've made exciting advances recently, you know."

"Good, good. So…"

"Give me your email address and I'll send you our basic proposal. Please share it with the parent or guardian, and if it's approved, give us a call back and we'll set up a meeting between our people and the family. If the teenager is signed on to our program, you will of course receive the $50,000 finder's fee."

The doctor happily gave all the necessary information before hanging up. He was just as happy for the girl as for himself. This was a great opportunity for her. Well, maybe he was a little happier for himself, but who would've blamed him? $50,000 was a lot of money for nearly anyone to receive all at once.

On the other end, "Dr." Richardson smiled as he put down the phone. This was perfect timing. As long as this one didn't turn out like Mina. Of course,

Mina had had more problems than just seizures....

Forty-One:
Arty

Emma woke with a start, the remnants of some disturbing dream quickly retreating to her subconscious. She suspected she'd be having a lot of those for quite some time. She pulled several crumpled papers from beneath her and set them next to the file folders on her nightstand. Looking at her clock, she saw that it was already late morning, but she still felt fairly tired despite having slept for well over twelve hours. She looked disgustedly at the files, knowing not only that she'd only read a fraction of the total, but also that she'd have to reread many of them because nothing from the last few had sunk in.

She got up, wanting to take a shower. She decided she would go into work today. She had several things she wanted to speak to Richardson about, several questions she wanted answered before she continued her reading—and her work. She took a leisurely shower and ate the most normal breakfast she'd had time for in—well, as long as she could remember. Eggs and cereal and toast, slightly burnt—just the way she liked it. Too bad it was well past lunchtime.

She got to the Gates building at quarter to two, and made straight for Richardson's office. He smiled as she entered.

"Didn't expect you back yet. You haven't finished reading the files yet, have you?" he asked with a sly look on his face.

"Oh, god no," she laughed, "there must be hundreds. I read for hours yesterday and I've barely started. There are just a few things I wanted to ask you."

"Of course, of course," he said. "There's something I want to show you first. Catch." He tossed a key at her and she nearly missed it. "This one too." The second key she did miss, and she had to pick it up off the floor. "I want you to see the generator."

"The generator?" she asked.

"You don't think we get all our power from the city, do you?"

"Well, I guess not, but that's not—"

He cut her off. "We're connected to the city's power grid, of course, but we're very nearly self-sufficient. Come, this way." He led her out of his office towards a freight elevator. "He's really something to see."

"He?"

"The generator," Richardson answered in a no-nonsense sort of way, turning aside to hide his smirk. Emma smirked as well, thinking Richardson a bit peculiar since men, especially military men, tended to refer to everything remotely mechanical as "she."

They stepped onto the elevator, and Joshua pushed the button for the third subbasement. The white room was on the second, and the third was a maintenance level, though Emma had never personally been there.

Richardson motioned towards a standing closet. "We should put on environmental suits before we get there."

"Why?" asked Emma.

"Well, it's just fairly uncomfortable in Arty's room. The air is humid and highly oxygenated, and the temperature is almost a hundred-Fahrenheit. We'd sweat like pigs and pass out, believe you me."

"Arty?" Nothing was making sense to Emma. Why would a generator room be humid? "Like the name?"

"Yes. Well, the letters 'R. T.' really. They stand for 'retarded transformation' and are the last part of some abbreviation of which I forget the beginning of. Dr. Utsugi got to calling him 'Arty' so it kind of stuck."

Emma just shrugged. Everything Joshua was saying sounded like nonsensical gibberish, mostly because he was saying it in a way that implied she should know what he was talking about, even though he knew she didn't. She began to put on the environmental suit, but left the zipper down and the helmet off, seeing that he did the same. As the elevator slowed to a stop on the third subbasement, she moved towards the door but Richardson stopped her. "Go over there," he said, gesturing towards a monitor on a stand. "Protocol dictates two enter at a time, just to be safe. It can be—intense—the first time. At the count of three, turn that key I gave you in the lock by the screen."

Emma fumbled for the key and pushed it into the slot. The monitor clicked on. Joshua counted to three, and they both turned their keys. Both monitors said, "WELCOME."

"Lieutenant Colonel Joshua Richardson," Joshua said in a clear voice.

"VOICE RECOGNITION CHECK..." said the monitor. "... CONFIRMED. HELLO, JOSH." The greeting in the end was spoken in an annoying, computer-generated "friendly" voice.

"Okay, you go," said Joshua to Emma.

"Dr. Emma Jacobson," Emma said tentatively.

"VOICE RECOGNITION CHECK...CONFIRMED. HELLO, DOCTOR."

The elevator started moving down again. "We're going to the seventh sub-floor," said Richardson. He seemed unprofessionally eager to Emma. It wasn't bothersome; it just wasn't his usual demeanor.

This is it, he thought. *The real test. All our atrocities and goals will be shown at once. If she can see it right, see that the goals outweigh...* His thoughts trailed off. Joshua tapped the screen in front of him.

"Yes, lieutenant colonel? What can I do for you," came a voice.

"Begin the shutdown sequence for Arty," answered Richardson.

"Aye, sir," was the response.

"I didn't know there was seven sub-floors," mused Emma, zipping up her environmental suit.

"There's actually nine or ten; I forget exactly, this building's so damn big."

As they passed the boundary between the fourth and fifth subbasements, the freight elevator gave a slight shudder and Emma noticed the shaft's walls change to a distinct blue color. Richardson caught her semi-puzzled gaze and answered her unasked question. "Sound-absorbing baffles. That's why I had Arty deactivated; further down, the sonic vibrations from the distortion chamber are very bothersome and up close, they'd shatter our bones." She looked startled. "On particularly productive days, low-level tremors will even pass above this floor."

Emma remembered a couple of occasions when she was working in the white room and it had shook a little. She had passed it off as a minor quake at the time.

Before long, the elevator stopped, and they both got off, fully dressed in their environmental suits. They entered a large room that was completely covered, floor included, in blue, sound-absorbing pyramids. It was tricky to walk on but almost fun. A door opened in the wall and they continued into a small grayish room with two doors, a counter, and a mirror that was probably see-through from the other side. A heavily armed guard opened one of the doors for them and spoke as they passed through.

"Hello, Doctor. Congratulations on your promotion. And by the way, good choice on that GAINAX stock. I certainly wouldn't have guessed a turnaround like that. Good afternoon, lieutenant colonel. Sorry to hear about Max."

Emma just walked by, stunned, but Joshua nodded politely. They walked down a long, baffled corridor, and the equally baffled doctor spoke.

"I've never seen that man before in my life. How—" That was the easy part. "Why—did he know that?"

"It's a psychological trick. It's a military thing. Intimidation through information—not only does he know our names, but he knew something else about each of us that he shouldn't have. It puts people off guard—you have to ask yourself, 'Why does he know me? What else does he know?'"

"Is it really necessary?"

"With us?" He shook his head, smiling. "Of course not. But it gives the guards something to do down here."

Satisfied with the answer, but still a little disturbed, Emma walked along silently. After a while, she asked, "Max?"

"My dog," replied Richardson, averting his gaze to the floor. "He got hit by a car last week."

"Oh…I'm sorry."

"These things happen," he said, and sighed.

They passed through two more small rooms and corridors. In each successive area, Emma saw that her environmental suit registered higher temperatures, higher humidity, and higher oxygen content.

"Here we are," said Joshua, as they came to a door. Warnings covered it, written in at least a dozen languages. They used their keys to open it, and went in.

A faint buzzing of electricity straddled the borders of their hearing. A hundred TVs, all set to different stations, with some changing repeatedly, covered the wall to the sides and above the door. They continued along both walls, but despite their soft, flickering glow, an inky blackness crept up only a few feet ahead of the two people. Emma perceived the room as being huge, but could see no further than her outstretched hand.

Looking around, she became aware of a dull ache in her temples that slowly spread to the front and back of her head and clamped like a vice. It wasn't a migraine but it was certainly painful. She glanced at Joshua, and he was grimacing slightly.

"Arty, I'm going to turn on the lights."

At this statement from Richardson, a faint mumbling of many voices that Emma had until now taken to be the TVs stopped all together. Then it began again, more narrow in focus but still unintelligible.

Richardson pushed a switch on the door. Emma looked straight ahead and a light flickered on in the distance, a haze softening its glow. Then another turned on closer, and closer, until the entire room was bathed in a dazzling fluorescence. Emma had to squint for a second, but then what she saw made her forget any discomfort her eyes might be having.

The room was a curve, circular in design and spreading off in the rear as a corridor. Starting in front of her and going as far as she could see, the floor was covered in what appeared to be a thick, slimy red liquid. Thick, sinuous, wormy brown and yellow coils undulated sporadically in the liquid. They crept up the walls and were coated by a thick shield of yellow jelly that looked like fat. Directly in front of her were several curtains of grayish-blue sheets laced with wheezing tubules and pulsing veins. They wavered as though caught in a slight breeze.

Emma followed them upwards towards their source, tentatively, afraid of what she might see.

Horrors! She dropped to the ground, unable to breathe, unable to move. The Lovecraftian beast clung like a great mildew in the corner. Like some Great Old One it crouched, staring at her with its hundreds, no, thousands of eyes, ready to tear into her soul—or worse.

Abject terror kept her still. This was a monster—a real, live, monster—and she was just a little girl who wanted her mommy. Nothing in any movie, any comic book, any nightmare, could have prepared her for this sight. Her vision blurred, her thoughts distorted, and her head pounded. She fainted.

An emergency shock deployed by her suit brought her back to consciousness. One of the great eyes hung directly in front of her, its visible surface as big as a football, the entirety of its orb encased in some green, moist sphere the size of a basketball. A gray cord like wound wires ran upwards from it, veins visible on either side of it. Slowly, the inquisitive scientist cam back in Emma, and she postulated that the gray cord was the optic nerve, but why was it exposed?

The eye blinked at her, and she realized how human it looked, save that its iris was orange. The pain in her head subsided a bit and she had a notion that the orb was peering into her mind. Suddenly, the eye leapt upward back to the mass, though Emma dared not look at it again so soon. Two-dozen more eyes-on-cords of varying sizes dropped down, the nearest being four or five feet away. They looked from her to the corridor and back, beckoning her onward. A feeling of calm overtook Emma, and she got up and slowly ambled forward. The eyes retreated to the ceiling as she walked between the curtains. She realized that they were the creature's lungs, oxygenated blood rushing away from their surface to be replaced with depleted blood. The room was so warm and humid because "Arty's" organs were *external*. And the oxygen content was so high because were it any lower, a being as big as this one would suffocate.

The length of the corridor was great, and a mist blocked the view beyond ten or twenty feet. The further Emma walked, the thicker the coils got and the thicker the wall-fat got. At the end of the hallway, the mist broke and she saw the beast in its den, a circular room like the previous, but smaller. The walls were coated in coils and other manners of organ-like growths, all stemming from a gradually pulsing blob in the back. It stretched to the center of the room and slightly beyond, a huge pink cylinder of flesh. As it pulsed, its constantly changing bumps and indentations gave Emma the impression of a giant, squirming baby from time to time. A thrumming noise emanated from it, accompanied by the same quiet chatter she had heard earlier.

She reached out to touch it, to comfort it. She was the mother, it, her child....

Her hand went straight through it.

She was on the other side, the inside, which was somehow larger than the outside. She watched ripples spread out from her otherwise invisible point of entry. Everything seemed pink, and was lit by a soft white glow. It slowly became brilliantly bright before fading again in an endless cycle of soft-harsh-soft-harsh. Emma stepped forward, each step a sharp noise in the thrumming ambiance of the great worm. Yellowish spheres danced on her fingertips, and she thought, *This is special. This is just for me.*

She saw what he—Joshua—had wanted her to see, she surmised. The eyes, the coils, the fat; the upended pillar of flesh, like someone's idea of the ultimate phallus. That this thing was apparently some sort of generator did not concern her now; all she was interested in was what *it* wanted her to see.

A thousand voices combined in her head and coalesced into one strangely hypnotic image. A great green crystal, facets tapered to a single sharp point, spun before her. Each flat surface glinted white as it passed through the plane of greatest reflection. Bands of energy like a coiled light glided around it, occasionally passing through the jewel, only to be eaten up by a suckered maw on the end of some fleshy tendril.

It was strangely beautiful in some deranged way she now accepted all too easily. But then—could it be? No, it was too egregious to believe!

She saw herself—naked, gloriously aglow—trapped *inside* the crystal, pounding on the facets, mouthing out some strange nonsense visible as bubbles escaping the mouth. The flesh was tinged with green, the hair long mats, like kelp. Her—its—legs bobbed up behind it, pointing upwards with no resistance to buoyancy consciously applied. As it pounded, Emma became aware of the yard-long tendrils floating daintily where it should have had gills—but it shouldn't have had gills...and it pounded...she pounded...and...and...her head pounded...

...and....

It was like being drunk, and something moves quickly by, leaving traced-out afterimages of itself for what seems like an eternal second. The same smallness of vision existed, too, where every direction except forward supplied only blackness.

"Are you all right?"

"What?" Emma felt groggy, and the pain in her head had not gone away. She looked around; it seemed she was in some sort of waiting room, with chairs, ferns, and magazines. Her environmental suit had been removed, and she was covered in sweat. Joshua looked down at her, his suit still on but his helmet off.

"I'm sorry, I said it can be extraordinary, but it's different for everyone. I just figured, what with everything you've seen here, it wouldn't have bothered you so much."

"Wha, bottha me?" she slurred, shaking her head side to side in stubborn pride. This hurt greatly and she stopped it immediately. "Wha happen?"

"Arty...you fell down, and after you got up, you went into the back room.

You came back with a glazed look in your eyes, and then passed out. Oh, did you have a vision!? Some people say they do, their first time, but I never...."

He helped her up. "I think so," she said. Something about a green girl with seaweed hair, and lightning?

"Anyway," continued Richardson, as he helped her to a chair, "I was going to walk into the back with you after you returned from your trip, but that can wait for another time." Emma nodded slightly, her head between her knees as she fought off a wave of nausea. A noise like a vending machine came from behind her, and presently, Joshua reappeared in front of her with a bottle of water. She gladly took it.

After several seconds of drinking, she spoke to him, "What on earth was it? How is it a generator?" She looked around. "Where are we?"

"We took a service elevator to 5BF. Just a waiting room that isn't used for much anymore."

"How long was I out?"

"About six minutes."

"Oh." *Was he carrying me?*

"Anyway, Arty is the culmination of several—failed—experiments into the realm of 'biomorphism.'"

"I don't believe I've read that far."

"Well, I'll be honest, neither have I, but I know a few things. You see, it was discovered quite some time ago that some psychics could heal their bodies by mentally altering them."

Like Mina, thought Emma.

"Well, some of the scientists thought that perhaps, this concept could be taken a step further. So, they laid the groundwork for *biomorphism*—in layman's terms, shape changing. Theoretically, it seems possible, but Arty is the only fruit of those experiments."

"What was it you said 'Arty' stood for again?"

"R.T. stands for 'Retarded Transformation.' The subjects involved in the biomorph experiments achieved reasonably successful levels of controlled cellular, organ, and bodily changes, but were without exception unable to revert to a stable form."

Emma had a crazy vision of people changing into animals, then into puddles of green goo as they tried to change back. "So, what happened? How did—it—happen?"

"Arty? Well, you'd be surprised at the resiliency of life." Richardson shook his head, thinking to himself. *Emma is a poor substitute for Hanin, but still, she's our best chance. My best chance.* He knew that her reaction to what he was about to tell her would be a major factor in determining if he could trust her—and ultimately, whether she lived or died. It was a sad fact, but dead men —women—don't tell secrets. Would she accept the truth with a scientist's detached resolve? Or would she prove to be too—human—to continue?

"Imagine, if you will," he cringed at the thought himself, "a sort of large, 'vat' filled with protoplasm, neural fibers, organs, other 'leftovers' of these experiments. Imagine that those remnants were not only still alive, but *healthy* on a cellular level." Emma turned a bit green.

"On the whole, you see, many of the subjects were able to function as a sort of complete organism. So out of this soup, they kind of joined together and there you go, there's Arty. That's a drastic oversimplification, of course, but the *ahem* exhaustive nine-hundred and thirty-two page document is simply beyond my comprehension. Though, you're welcome to read it if you like."

Emma was repulsed, horrified, and a bit fascinated, though she kept her resolve. That was a lot to take in. *Still,* thought Emma, *there's more, isn't there?*

"You said he was a generator. How so?"

"Well, it was known at that point that Nod—I'll get to that—was a source of great energy, but there wasn't any ideas about how—or if—we could tap into it. Then one day, Arty was accidentally exposed to a portal, and he started generating a measurable electric current. So, after many, *many* tests, Dr. Utsugi proposed we try using him as a generator by keeping a portal permanently open, so now it's...." He looked at the puzzled look on Emma's face. "How far have you read, truthfully?"

Emma took a sip of her water and shrugged. "Tuesday is meatball day in the cafeteria?"

Richardson laughed. "I don't know how much help I can be, then. I won't claim to understand any of it."

"Just give me the general scoop, if you can. I'll fill in the 'science' later. I'm not sure yet exactly what I'm even supposed to be doing, so any information will help."

"Well," began Joshua, walking a few feet from her, "all this..." His back was to her, and he looked up and held his arms out, as if to say "this institute," but somehow Emma knew he meant more.

"All this is for one purpose. Everything we have, everything we make— it's supposed to better us. Further humanity. Make us better people—better beings." An arguable point. "But, what is the one thing that holds humanity back?" He turned to face her, and she was about to begin a long list, starting with "wars," "poverty," "disease," but Joshua kept going.

"Energy. We don't have enough. Why do we fight over things? Resources. *Energy.* Why is the air polluted? *Energy.* We're running out of it, and what we do have is dangerous, dirty, expensive. That's the point of NOD, Emma..." He sounded a bit like a preacher now, "The point of NOD is to create *a happier, better world through the ultimate goal…*"

Here Emma joined in, "…*of providing unlimited energy to Earth through the production of the perfect psychic.*" It was almost verbatim from the letter she'd read.

"So, you have been doing your homework," said Joshua.

"I must have read that line ten times in the first few dozen pages. What does it mean?"

Joshua quickly sat down next to her, a hyperactive glint in his eyes. "There's a place, Emma, a place, right here," he gestured to convey the notion *all around us*, "but…not here. It's like—we move *next* to it all the time, like—shit." Explanations like this were not his forte.

"Like a parallel dimension?" Emma questioned. Science fiction, in general, was more prophetic sometimes than most people would care to know.

"Yes. Like a parallel dimension that coexists with ours, but that the average person can't access. It's absolutely overflowing with energy. But it's a mental plane, we can't physically move between it and our own."

"Dreamtime…" muttered Emma.

"You know about that?" asked a startled Joshua.

"Yeah. I took some anthropology in college. I think it was the aboriginal tribes of Australia or New Zealand, they believed that their ancestors lived in a world of thoughts they called 'dreamtime' while they formed the earth? Something like that?"

"They called it *altjeringa*," said Joshua. "That's what we call Nod…not with all caps, spelled big-N small-O small-D."

A small spark lit Emma's mind and she tried hard to remember something her mother used to recite to her at bedtime. It was such a weird coincidence that she knew this.

"For breakfast on through all the day, At home among my friends I stay; But every night I go abroad, Afar into the land of Nod.

"All by myself I have to go. With none to tell me what to do—All alone beside the streams, And up the mountain-side of dreams.

"The strangest things are there for me, Both things to eat and things to see, And many frightening sights abroad, Till morning in the land of Nod.

"Try as I like to find the way, I never can get back by day, Nor can I remember plain and clear, The curious music that I hear."

Richardson smiled. "Robert Louis Stevenson. Very impressive, Emma."

Emma smiled also, then said, "Okay, so there's this plane of immense energy we call 'Nod.' So how do we throw a psychic into the mix and use it to run appliances?" She could still muster a bit of humorous sarcasm, even in the middle of this onslaught of ideas.

"Very funny. The energy is in a form that a psychic is easily attuned to, because it—I don't know how else to say it—it works the same way their minds do. So, theoretically, a powerful psychic mind, if given a conduit to Nod, can absorb this energy and re-emit it in our universe."

"Okay," said Emma, skeptically, "So I guess that makes—sense—but how do we get a conduit to Nod? How did we even find this place originally?"

"Well, NOD—this organization, I mean—was initially running several projects in this building. One, of course, was the human psychic project, which at the time was headed by Dr. Utsugi and was devoted mostly to Biomorphism research."

Dr. Setsuna Utsugi, now deceased, had been Dr. Hanin's second. Even when Emma had started working at NOD, the little Japanese lady had seemed ancient.

"One of the other projects involved contact with a higher energy form the scientists were calling *Nod*." Joshua paused at this. "You know, Emma, there really is a lot to go over here. This was before my time, even."

"I've got the time," Emma said nonchalantly.

"Good." He put his forehead in his left hand. Where to begin?

"You know, I don't know how the scientists got to this point. All of you seem to have this knack for putting two and two together and getting five. Anyway, they'd been doing research into jade crystals and earth-energy."

Emma remembered something else from anthropology class. "The Chinese believed jade was a source of energy, and that it was attuned to the human mind."

"So did the Mayans," added Joshua. "It acts as some sort of capacitor for mental energy, and with the right energy fields—or whatever—it can focus them. Something like that. And the greenstone jade of the Maori was said to be a gift from the gods. It's…" He was obviously trying to remember something he wasn't too well informed of. Probably to his station, these were minor details. "…two different kinds of minerals actually, but both silicates I think?"

"You mentioned earth energy. You're talking about ley lines, right?"

"Yes. They're just one of the many, many things we can't explain but still go ahead and fiddle around with. They are rings of energy that circle the earth. Normally, they aren't powerful enough to effect much, but when they cross…"

"They get amplified if the interference is constructive?"

"Yeah. You know, I'm really not the person to be telling you all this."

Emma felt like saying, *Yeah, well they're all dead*, but felt that was too harsh. Instead, she said, "Go on. You're doing fine." All of this information was bizarre, and fascinating.

"Sure. Anyway, it was discovered—partly through modern experimentation, and partly through anthropology, believe it or not, that jade can tap into these ley lines, and can serve as a connection between them and people's minds. Of course, this doesn't work for everyone."

Now Emma was really starting to get it. Some of it, anyway. "But a psychic, whose mental powers are much stronger than the average person, can interface with a ley line through a jade crystal. But what does this do?"

"Not much by itself, really. I think it's supposed to broaden perception. The real good stuff happens when enough ley lines cross at the same spot to cause…constructive interference, I think you said. When the overall energy potential at this point is high enough, a tear can be made in our reality that leads to Nod."

"So," said Emma, putting it all together, "you use jade crystal to focus these crossing ley lines, and then a hole opens to Nod, and you can use a psychic to draw energy out."

"A drastic simplification, but yes."

"But, they can't cross in groups that often, I would imagine."

"No, they don't. That's when we have to change their orientation in regards to the earth."

Forty-Two:
Road Trip

Emma and Joshua were nearly out of Omaha, heading towards Papillion in Sarpy county, when Emma started talking again. "Okay, so I get the general gist of all this. But how did Arty come into it?"

"Arty," explained Joshua as he flicked on the turn signal, "was accidentally exposed to an open portal during an experiment. Remember me mentioning sound vibrations? Well, this accident proved to be very damaging. However, once the dust settled, so to speak, the readings showed that energy output from the portal dropped sharply, while at the same time Arty began giving off large amounts of heat and some electricity."

"Now, if you'll kindly let me skip all the in-between stuff, by now we have a pretty concrete theory on how all this works, and what exactly the connection is between Nod, earth energy, and mind energy."

"And this perfect psychic concept?"

"Arty is enormous, yet he barely provides enough energy to run the laboratory. His efficiency is very low. Theoretically, the 'perfect psychic' would have an efficiency several hundred times Arty's."

Emma had a ridiculous image of a hundred children, standing in a field, attached to power lines. It all sounded...so ludicrous.

"Certainly we're not planning to use people as dynamos in a power plant?"

"Oh, certainly not. The idea is to use beings with no conscious minds. Arty is at best an accidental prototype, so he's a special case."

Emma didn't understand. Psychic power without a mind behind it? How would it be controlled?

At last, they pulled up to a stop by a large, gray building in the middle of nowhere. It was marked "RESERVOIR 5" and was surrounded by a barbed wire fence and armed guards. It had a cluster of satellite dishes on its roof.

As the two of them walked towards the building, Richardson turned to Emma and spoke. "One last gap I should fill in—See, once the generator ability was discovered, the Biomorphism project was terminated in favor of the Nod Energy Project, as it was called. Dr. Hanin took over as lead and NOD's whole focus since then has been research into psionics, with the goal of..."

"I know, I know, making the perfect psychic." She shivered from the cold, thinking. This was weird, and convoluted. She would have to do a *lot* of reading to fill in the gaps in Joshua's explanation. "What is the developmental status of the project right now?"

"Unfortunately," said Richardson, showing his ID to a guard, "it's technically suspended indefinitely. There was a...setback some time ago, and research since then has focused strictly on psionic research of a general nature. But that's where you come in, Emma. I have great faith in you."

Forty-Three:
Going Home

Mrs. Yamada glanced up at her rear view mirror as she pulled out of the hospital parking lot. The two girls were sitting next to each other in the back seat. She and Crow had stayed up all night at the hospital; right now, Raven had her arm around Crow, who was leaning against her with an exhausted look on her face. Raven's face looked tired as well, although at least she had gotten some sleep.

Raven's mother thought to herself, *They really do look right together*. She could sense the quiet affirmation of their love for one another. She smiled; maybe it was okay after all....

Despite years of pain and disappointments, she was a large-hearted woman. It was hard for her to think ill of a love so obvious. She was a Christian woman but she belonged to no particular denomination; she had just found hope in God, plain and simply. Though some sects spoke ill of a love like her daughter's, in truth, it wasn't hers to judge.

She hadn't always made the best choices herself. But, this wasn't a choice. She believed that much, at least. She remembered young love, the excitement, the thrill, the butterflies. First and foremost, she wanted her children to have a better, happier life than she, so how was it any right of hers to stand between love? It wasn't as though she hadn't suspected it from time to time, and it never really gave her pause then, so why should it now?

Her children. *Shoot*, she thought. *Jake*. She had left so fast she hadn't even taken time to leave him a note. Still, he didn't even come home most nights until very late. It was not that she didn't care what he did with his time, far from it, in fact. It was that with two difficult children, her ability to manage her home as a single parent had become stretched so thin she had to pick her battles. Raven and she connected now and then, at least—Jake was a different story.

She wanted to talk to her daughter now, wanted to tell her everything would be all right. She wanted to tell her that a man was going to be coming over to talk with her tomorrow, and he might be able to help her out. She also wanted to scold her for not saying anything about the seizures earlier, because goodness knows what could have happened. She wanted to say, *I'm your mother, you could have talked to me about you and Crow and I would've understood*, but she wasn't sure if this would have been true until she saw it with her own eyes. She wanted...

"Mom?"

"Yes, dear?"

"I love you."

She smiled. "I love you too." She glanced out the window at the flurries of snow falling gently outside, glistening white and pure as they fell onto the dirty black snow piled up over the curbs. Raven and Crow looked at the flurries also, but as they drifted off to sleep, all they saw was the clean, fragile snow, not the dirt underneath.

Forty-Four:
Substation

Emma looked up at the huge sign above her that said RESERVOIR 5. She laughed on the inside. Of course, something like this was top-secret, so one couldn't say, just put a huge sign on it that said EXPENSIVE TOP SECRET GOVERNMENT ENERGY PROJECT and expect people to just walk by. But, with the grounds swarming with guards, it was silly to think anyone would believe it was just a reservoir.

Then again, maybe it wasn't. She'd driven by in the past and hadn't given the building a second glance.

Inside, Joshua asked Emma to wait in one room while he went to speak with someone in another. She sat down on the only surface in the entire room, a black bench with white cushions. The whole room was painted a bright white, except for the floor, which was tiled in black. After a couple moments, he returned wearing a clean suit, with another in his arms.

"Here, put this on," he said, his voice muffled by the ventilator on the helmet.

"A clean suit? Is this thing organic also?"

He shook his head no, but said, "Shh. The walls have ears, you know."

"Sorry," apologized Emma as she got into the suit. Joshua helped her get the helmet on and close the seals before they passed into the next room, where they were blasted by air currents to remove dust. They walked through a corridor with gratings on the floor and ceiling that replaced the room's air via a constant current. The door at the end of the corridor was labeled "Control Room."

They walked in and arrived inside a long room (also white,) with all sorts of computer equipment running along the opposite wall beneath a huge window that looked out into a darkened room. A single door was on the narrow wall to the right. It looked like an airlock; it was a couple inches above the ground, surrounded by a metal edging covered in rivets. The corners of the door were curved, and in the center was a large valve handle. A couple of men were in the room by the computers. They were also dressed in clean suits, but Emma wondered why it was necessary in a control room.

One of the men turned around. "Lieutenant colonel?" he said, questioningly.

"Turn the lights on, please," asked Joshua. The man flipped a large switch, and the darkness in the room ahead was replaced with a bright white light. There was a *whoosh* as the air replacement system in the room activated, but Emma didn't notice it.

It was so familiar.

She walked towards the long window, and looked into the now-lit room. A giant green crystal sat in the center, slowly rotating. The upper and frontal facets glinted white as they passed by her.

"That," said Joshua, "is an artificial, perfect jade crystal." It was surrounded by several clusters of antennae, dishes, and other electronic equipment. Emma knew untold quantities of energy were coursing through it right now, even though she couldn't see any.

Why was it so familiar?

"This is how we manipulate the ley lines," explained Richardson. "There's one passing right through the crystal now, but we can't see it, of course. The thing is, at least with our current technology, we can't change the path of a line by more than a few degrees at any place. So, we have a whole network of these substations, each one altering its line by a few degrees so that in the end, they cross where we want them to."

"Where do they cross?" asked Emma.

"Where do you think?" questioned Joshua.

Of course, thought Emma. *By Arty.*

Arty. Now she remembered. He'd shown her a vision of a crystal like this, and…. She tried to see the base, to see if there was something, *someone*, inside, but the view was blocked by mechanisms.

"Never mind. I got it," she said to Richardson.

"What happens if this thing gets turned off?" asked Emma.

"Doctor?" said Richardson to one of the other men in the room. He turned around, his muffled voice sounding excited. Probably because he didn't get much chance to talk about his work.

"Ah, before I get to that, I'd like to clarify a point. There are two types of jade: nephrite and jadeite. Both are commonly referred to simply as jade. Perhaps because they are both silicates, they have similar properties in regards to our work here. This crystal is in fact a laboriously grown combination of the two which includes in its structure—" He caught a glance from Richardson and cleared his throat.

"Ahem—anyway, a ley line is very particular about its shape. They move slowly, over time, but always maintain a ring shape. If we shut down all related substations at once, the line just snaps back to its preferred shape, no problem. But if only one goes down…"

"Boom!" yelled the other man, stealing his partner's thunder. Emma jumped a little.

"Yeah. Boom," Continued the first man, sounding annoyed. "If one substation goes down, the line is momentarily deformed without the stability provided by the machines. If the angle of deformity is greater than the remaining substations can accommodate, the ley line snaps free of their mechanisms so it can achieve a stable shape again. When it does this, it gives off a large amount of energy which results in a major explosion at each substation it pulls away from."

"Why does it cause an explosion?" asked Emma.

"We're not entirely certain," said the first scientist. "In simple terms, we believe the energy drags through the remaining activated crystals, hyper-compressing their atomic structure and supersaturating them with energy, which is obviously not a stable state. The end result is a fairly powerful explosion."

The second scientist looked up at Joshua, but his expression wasn't clearly visible through the helmet. "The ideal setup involves each substation moving its line at a smaller degree than technically possible. Within the arc defined by the maximum possible change, we'd like to keep a backup mechanism, so, if anything happens to the main one, the secondary one can "catch" the line and hold it within a stable degree of deformity." He sounded a bit annoyed now. "Of course, our budget isn't exactly what I'd call adequate for that kind of arrangement."

"Anyway," Richardson began, trying to change the subject. Emma beat him to the punch with a question.

"Has this ever happened before?"

"To us? No." answered the man sitting on the left. "Have you ever heard of Tunguska?" he asked.

"It sounds familiar."

"In June of 1908 an explosion occurred in Tunguska, Siberia, that flattened a thousand square kilometers of woodland. The current 'theory' is that a stony asteroid exploded about eight km above the forest." He paused.

"You're not saying that, in 1908, a system like this one malfunctioned and exploded? In 1908?"

"Well, not like this one, exactly," replied the man on the right. "It was infinitely cruder. Natural crystals were probably used. I can't even speculate on what sort of mechanisms they could even have been able to create that long ago."

Richardson, ever the military man, used this point to advance one of his own opinions. "You know the Russians, Emma. Always trying to keep up with the US of A. Unfortunately, they've always had a tendency to take the cheap route, which has more than once backfired on them."

The man on the right turned back around, and started working with one of the computers. "People have been manipulating ley lines for centuries. Haven't you ever wondered what Stonehenge was for?"

Emma just stood there, silent.

Forty-Five:
At Home

"I called the school," said Raven's mother. She was greeted with wide-open eyes and anxious expressions. "What?" Neither girl answered. "Anyway, dear, the principal says that he'll have your teachers set your assignments aside for you. There's a man coming over tomorrow to discuss possible treatments with me, and I want you at home at least until then."

"Okay," said Raven, slightly confused. *What about the suspensions?*

Mrs. Yamada walked over to the table and sat mugs of hot cocoa down in front of her daughter and her...girlfriend.

Mrs. Yamada prepared a third mug and sat down across from the girls. "Raven, this is a difficult situation...your condition, I mean...and I want you to know I'll be here for anything you need." She took a sip, burning her tongue a bit. "We have a lot to talk about. Right now, I want you to make sure you rest, and take the medicine the doctor gave you."

"Now Crow, I've spoken to your father." Crow looked alarmed, wondering what exactly Raven's mother had spoken to him about. "I told him what had happened to Raven and explained that you were at the hospital all night. He was very worried."

"I never even thought to call him last night," said Crow. That was two days in a row she had forgotten to tell him she'd be out. That wasn't like her.

"Yes...well...he would like you to call him in a bit." Crow nodded, and then Mrs. Yamada continued. "I think there are some things to discuss. I'm going to have to lay down some new rules." She looked off into the distance, remembering a happier time, a time when she had been in love, and there hadn't been restrictions or worries.

"You can't stop some things once they get started...." Her voice trailed off. After a moment, she took a big sip of her drink, got up, and walked over to the sink with her mug. With her back to the girls as she started to wash the dishes, she said, "Crow, you have my permission to stay with Raven tonight, if she wants the company. But no...you know.... I have some thinking to do...about a lot of things."

Just then, the side door opened and Jake walked in. He took off his backpack and threw his coat on the landing. "So where the hell were you all last night?"

"At the hospital," said Crow.

"I might have epilepsy," said Raven, her fear momentarily changing to anger at the sight of her brother. She wanted to avoid a confrontation and hoped maybe he could show a little human decency after news like that and just go away.

Jake walked straight to his room, and opened the door. He was still furious about the pot. "I think the word you're looking for is *lesbian*," he said just as he was closing the door to his room. He said the last word very loudly, wanting to make sure his mother heard it clearly. She just sighed, and Crow and Raven quickly left the room.

They went straight to Raven's room. Raven sat down on the bed, and as Crow closed the door she said, "Your mom's being really nice."

Raven's eyes were pointing downward. "She's really worried about me."

Crow came and sat down across from Raven. There was an uneasy silence for a minute or two as neither girl looked at the other. Finally, Crow spoke. "I'm sorry. I know this isn't how you wanted this to happen. Any of this."

Raven, still looking down, said, "It's not your fault." She looked up. "I was thinking, maybe it's okay this way." She reached her hand out, and Crow grasped it. "You were right. I needed to see a doctor. But still...I didn't want to. I don't know when I would have, if not for the other night. That was the worst it's ever been. I'm glad you were here." She smiled at Crow, who smiled back.

"Do you think your mom's going to be okay with us as a couple?"

"Well, she really doesn't have a choice. I mean, her knowing isn't gonna change anything between us, so even if she had a problem with it.... Still, I think she'll be okay."

"Your mom has a lot to worry about. With Jake, and..." She didn't want to finish, but Raven did it for her.

"With me. I guess really, I don't give her enough credit."

"You've never really been bad to her," said Crow, trying to make up for bringing this up.

"I suppose. But I've been distant. And I've lied." She couldn't help but grin as she squeezed Crow's hand lightly at that thought. "I never listen to her. I'm not as bad as Jake, not by far—I don't think he even has a conscience—but I've never been very good, either. Maybe it's time to change that, y'know? Maybe this happened for a reason."

"Now you sound like your mom," said Crow, giggling. "Still, you could be right. Maybe it's time we both changed."

"There's nothing wrong with you, dummy," Raven said, playfulness in her voice. Both girls grinned at each other. "The worst you've done is smoke pot with me. Ah, I'd love a cigarette, though. Nope nope nope!"

"Will power!" exclaimed Crow. "It's like a test of character."

Raven giggled. "Now *you* sound like my mom."

"Yeah, well, I guess she's smarter than we thought." Crow giggled too. "So what do you think's up with school? I was kind of hoping we wouldn't have any schoolwork."

Raven was a bit flabbergasted. "That's...not how it works. Haven't you ever been suspended?"

"No."

"Ha, like I said, there's nothing wrong with you." Raven thought for a moment. "God, so much has happened in the last two days."

"Hey, maybe this is the start of something. Something good." The girls leaned together and hugged. "I love you," said Crow.

"I love you too," said Raven.

"I feel pretty good, too," said Crow. "Things are going to get better."

"What if there's nothing they can do for me?"

"We'll cross that bridge when we come to it."

Forty-Six:
Questions

Emma stood across from Joshua in his office. "So, any clearer on anything now?"

"Sort of," was Emma's response. "You know, when I started here, I was told I would be doing research to prevent intellectual disability at the fetal stage of development. I guess, really, that my real job isn't any less noble. Still, I think of Arty, and I can't help but feel uneasy."

"Arty was a mistake. Science is full of them, Emma. But usually, it's the mistakes that lead us onto the right path. Once we find something that doesn't work, that gives us a better idea of what *will* work."

"I know."

"Hanin's ultimate goal was a psychic without a conscious mind, one that could be electronically controlled. Technically it would be alive, but it would be unable to have any thoughts or feelings. Really, that's a pretty humane plan. Sure, there's suffering along the way, but what major accomplishment has come without suffering? Human history is littered with it. If we succeed—if you succeed, Emma—your work can help end much of that suffering."

"I have to agree," Emma said. And she did. Children had already suffered under her hand and she felt guilty. But human research was a catch-22 situation —it was rarely possible to improve humanity without hurting some people in the process. She was not so naive to think that this facility—NOD—was the only one in the world experimenting on people. Still, now that the scope of her work had begun to be realized, she had reservations, and was beginning to think of Joshua in a different way. His hands were so dirty in the atrocities of NOD; what kind of man was he really?

"I still have so much to study," she said, "so much to try and understand. An alternate dimension, energy fields I've never believed in that my ancestors could probably screw around with. Mental energy converted into electricity? I never even thought of such a reaction."

"I have faith in you, Emma. We hired you for a reason. Top marks in your class, groundbreaking genetic study done in your graduate years while still at University. So far, you've done great work here."

She sighed. "It's just a lot to swallow. The main thing is, I have to figure out what direction Hanin was going with all of our experiments, and go from there."

"Like I mentioned, the actual project has been suspended for quite some time." Richardson opened a drawer in his desk, and pulled out a very thick folder. He handed it to Emma.

"More files?"

"These are Hanin's personal notes. Hopefully, they should help you fit the pieces together."

"Great," said Emma, sarcastically. *I'll be reading clear through next month.*

"Emma, I want you to know something. Hanin had always said that Mina was very important to the direction he planned on going with his work. I know I expressed concern about keeping her alive, but—maybe those will explain why he felt that way"

"Well, I'm going to check in on Mina, then I'm going home," said Emma. "More reading, you know."

"Okay," said Richardson. "Let me know as soon as you can what staff arrangements you have in mind."

"Definitely," answered Emma. *As soon as I know what kind of arrangements I'll even need.*

Emma turned to leave, but Richardson stopped her. "Just one more thing," he said. "I'd like for Jameson to be your personal assistant."

That putz? thought Emma. "I was thinking of Carl Redford."

"I think it would be good for him."

"Yes sir," she sighed, and left. Richardson got up and locked the door to his office.

"All clear," he said loudly. A side door in the office opened, and a man stepped through.

"How'd it go?"

"I'm not entirely sure, Spence."

Spencer Jameson looked at Richardson, and tentatively spoke. "Can she be trusted?"

"I think so. I'm not entirely certain. This is messy work and—consciences can get in the way of it. Still, I know she can do the work and I think she will want to as long as she's pointed along the 'noble' path. Keep a close eye on her, though. Let me know if anything seems fishy. I told her you were going to be her personal assistant, so you'll always be close by."

"How'd she like that idea?"

"She didn't."

"I'm not surprised."

"I'm not either," said Joshua. "You need to be more professional."

"Sure. No problem."

"This could have been your project, you know, if you'd worked harder. Don't let me down, Spence." *Or else...*

"I won't. Don't you worry. Hey, did you tell her about the new test subject?"

"No. I'll worry about that once she's acquired."

Spencer laughed. "Yeah, tell me again how you're going to do that?"

Richardson sighed. "The child is having seizures and blackouts. Officially, we're a mental health institute. I'll explain our program to the mother."

"Yeah, our breakthrough program where she doesn't get to see her daughter for five years. No mother would do that."

"You'd be surprised what some people will do when the price is right," said Joshua, smiling.

"You're incorrigible."

After Jameson left, Richardson thought very deeply on the matter, and spoke aloud his thoughts.

"Of course you're right, Spence. No mother would do that. But I have to try it first. Before anything *else* is tried."

What have we become? He thought. *What is the worth of a person these days?*

Such thoughts were counterproductive. He pushed them away.

A soldier follows orders. But what happens when there aren't any orders to give?

Joshua was very afraid, probably for the first time in his life. If Emma had to be removed, there was no one else with her skill to fall back on.

What then?

Forty-Seven:
HQ

"Dillons," said Marcus Graley, in a poor Austrian accent. "You sunnuva bitch."

They slapped their hands together, a big meaty slap, and rather than a handshake, it was as though they were arm wrestling in mid-air.

"Geez," Carlos laughed, "don't you guys ever get sick of *Predator*?"

"Nope," Leonard Dillons and Marcus Graley said in unison.

Carlos looked around at his friends—Dillons and Marcus were, and had been for quite some time, his best friends, and they were usually teamed up during missions. Although all Black Army personnel were trained in multiple areas, they all had their specialties as well. Dillons' was munitions and explosives, Marcus' was tactics, and Carlos' was stealth, sabotage, and wet works.

The Black Army promoted ethnic diversity under the guise of making it difficult for targets to determine their country of origin. Carlos thought this silly; only the United States realistically had the diversity the Black Army represented. The three of them alone represented "diverse" backgrounds.

Leonard was a huge beast of a man, with dark black skin and an enormous, completely shaved head. Marcus worked out frequently and it showed, though he was physically smaller than Dillons, with a clean-shaven face, a slight tan, and a blond crew cut, looking for all the world like a Midwestern farm boy straight off of the bus.

Carlos was Hispanic and smaller than both of them, both by height by bulk, but while he was wiry, he was agile, making up for in speed and dexterity what he lacked in strength. He had a healthy head of short black hair and perpetual five o'clock shadow.

"So how'd this one go?" asked Dillons.

"Not as painlessly as the last couple," answered Carlos.

"It's 'cause of me," said Dillons. "You boys just can't get by without me." He slapped his right leg. "Almost done with therapy, was fantastic to get that damn cast off. As soon as I'm combat-certified again, I'll—"

"Probably get it broken again?" cut in Marcus. He laughed.

"Hey, but my arms are just fine," said Dillons, throwing a few punches in the air. He almost fell when he tried to do this without leaning on the wall behind him.

"Now, now," Carlos said. "You don't want to aggravate the injury. Doctor's orders."

Leonard Dillons smiled. "Yeah, your the one gonna be aggravated when

I'm better."

"I'd like to see you try," came the response from Carlos, who laughed.

"Watch it," said Dillons, still smiling, "I'll be standing firm before you know it."

They walked down the hallway that led from the helipad to the main elevator. It was slow going because of Dillons. He was still using crutches to walk and wasn't very good with them, probably because he was too proud to let himself rely on them. By and by, they arrived at the meeting room. It didn't look very high-tech, especially when compared to the rest of headquarters. It was a plain gray room filled with combination desk-and-chairs like those found in a college classroom. There was a podium, a whiteboard, a screen, and an overhead projector at the front of the room.

The three men took their seats amidst the other men and women in the room.

"Glad you could make it," said the woman at the front of the room. She was in her early fifties, and had short, light-colored hair. She was wearing a white lab coat.

"Now that you're all here," she said, specifically looking at Dillons, Graley, and Gonzalez, "I can give you an update on our position."

She walked over to the podium. "The situation at the Omaha site appears to be stabilizing. Our men have replaced approximately thirty-five percent of the guards stationed there, working as undercover agents in the US military.

"Some of you have been chosen to take part in this operation sooner than others. Those involved will be briefed shortly.

"The recent incidents in Omaha have pushed our scheduling back quite a bit. No decisive action shall be taken until business returns to normal. Until then, we shall continue operation as usual in regards to our contracts with Lieutenant Colonel Joshua Richardson, head of NOD-Omaha. Any questions?"

There weren't any, which was not entirely surprising. Still, as a special operations team, they worked more openly then traditional army corps. In most situations, questions were encouraged, though of course, loyalty was still the number one concern.

"Mr. Graley, I'd like to see you for a moment. The rest of you are dismissed."

Marcus Graley walked up to the front of the room as everyone else vacated.

He stood at attention. "Yes, sir?" he said once everyone had left.

"At ease, soldier," said the woman. Marcus took on a more comfortable stance, with his hands together behind his back and his feet side-by-side. "Pretty impressive job you've been doing as squad leader since Dillons was hurt."

"Thank you, sir."

"So impressive, in fact, that I want you to continue leading the squad once Dillons is better."

"Sir?" He looked worried.

"Don't worry about Leonard. He's going to be stationed in Omaha. I want you here, to lead the strike against NOD, should such a situation become necessary."

"Permission to speak freely?" asked Marcus.

"Granted," said the woman.

"This isn't because...." He didn't want to say it.

"Have I ever acted out of favoritism before?"

"No, sir." Then: "Once the change is complete, will you still be in charge of this division?"

"Yes. Once Richardson is removed, our agent will be in line to assume command, but he will have no real authority. He will be there to keep our cover in regards to the government, and nothing else."

"So how does the final arrangement look?"

"NOD will continue to provide research to the US Army and government. We will also have access to that research, and our agent will receive kickbacks from our contracted missions in exchange for the research. He will essentially be taking orders from our superiors. Any further questions?"

"No, sir."

"Dismissed."

Marcus turned to leave, but the woman stopped him. "By the way, soldier, how is my daughter-in-law doing?"

"Great," answered Marcus. "She wanted to know if you wanted to come over for dinner on Sunday."

"I'd love to. That'll be all."

Marcus nodded, and turned back away from his mother and left the room.

Forty-Eight:
Subjects

Emma walked down the hallway towards an elevator, eerily aware of how quiet and empty the building was. Granted, it was a very large building, and much of it *was* empty (at least as far as she knew,) but this area was normally bustling with activity. She *did* notice that there seemed to be many more guards than before the incident, but that made sense.

"Miss Jacobson?"

The sudden noise startled Emma, and she nearly dropped the folder she was carrying. She looked behind her to see Benny, one of the test subjects. His hair and facial features were that of a young black child, but his skin was as light as any of the other children. It amazed Emma how pale all of the test subjects were; "The Process" (or some other all inclusive happening) removed nearly all the pigment from their skin.

Except for Mina, thought Emma. She was pale, but not nearly as pale as the rest.

Emma placed her belongings on the floor and leaned forward, placing her hands on her knees. "What can I do for you, Benny?"

"I was looking for you. Everyone wants to know how Mina is."

"Actually, I was just going to check on her myself. How are you doing?"

"I'm okay. Everyone has extra time now 'cause no one has to do any 'speriments right now. I been playing a lot."

"Sounds like fun, Benny. Do you want me to walk with you back to the playroom?"

"No, that's okay. Just let us know how Mina is, okay?"

"You got it."

Benny nodded and floated down through the floor. No matter how many times Emma saw that, it always caught her off guard.

Benny could phase—he could subtly alter the properties of his constituent atoms so that he could pass through solid objects. It was a good thing that he was a good kid, with a power like that…. But they were all good kids, more or less. They had to be. It was in the drugs.

But Mina was the glaring difference. Mina was post-pubescent; all of the other children seemed to age without growing. Mina had much more pigment in her skin. Mina had…Mina had gone berserk and killed people.

Emma quickly ran to the elevator and headed for the lab where Mina was. However, she stopped on the way, getting off on the 45th floor instead of the 44th. She made her way to room 45-314, slid her security card through the reader, and went inside.

45-314 was dark. She could see a light flickering on the other side of the room; the light was enough for her to avoid bumping into the occasional toy, book, or other object scattered on the floor.

Emma knew what the light was. Out of all the test subjects, only *they* were allowed to watch TV.

"Keiko? Johnny?"

She made her way around a large, pink, bubble-shaped object. The other side of it was open; there was a couch (or possibly a bed) inside. Sitting on the floor in front of it was a small girl and a small boy, watching a news program on TV.

"Can I talk to you two?" Emma asked. She received no reply. She tried to sit down and wait for a commercial in the couch-thing, but the curved bubble-top came down too far for her to fit, so she got back up. It was an odd piece of furniture, clearly intended just for children, but it was baffling in design and she'd never seen anything like it elsewhere.

"Ahh!" She jumped, alarmed; both children were standing now, staring at her. "Sorry, I was startled."

"Come," said the boy, Johnny, in a monotone voice as he held his hand out. They always spoke that way; very expressionless, always sounding like each word was carefully thought out.

They led Emma through a door in the wall behind the TV. Both children floated a couple of inches above the ground; Keiko was in the lead, followed by Johnny, who was holding Emma's hand. The door closed behind them, and a soft glow illuminated the room, slowly getting brighter.

It was a fairly large room. Or maybe it just looked that way, because there was nothing in it. In any case, the feature that made it stand out from the others was the beautiful mural that ran all the way around the room. It was painted but looked like mosaic; it featured fantasy and fairy tale themes, running the gamut from princes and princesses to trolls and dragons.

Keiko and Johnny sat cross-legged in the center of the room, facing each other with their eyes closed.

"You want to know about Matthew," said Keiko.

"Yes," agreed Emma.

"The Man was involved."

Emma thought for a moment. "Richardson?"

"The Man that you are now," corrected Johnny.

Emma thought that one over for a bit. "Hanin?" Apparently she was right, because they didn't correct her again.

"Matthew was the first," said Keiko.

"First what?" asked Emma, trying not to sound exasperated.

"The first to cross back," answered Johnny.

"Once you go, you're not supposed to come back," explained Keiko.

From where? thought Emma, but she didn't say it aloud. Not that it mattered.

"The other place. Inside."

Nod? thought Emma. Again, their lack of correction was an affirmative answer.

"You have to stop him from coming back. Or it will just happen again."

"How?"

Johnny spoke now. "The Man knows."

Emma thought for a moment. "Hanin! It's in this folder, isn't it?"

"Hurry," both children responded at the same time. Emma left. Quickly.

She rushed to the SDF room. She would see Mina, and then go home and read—

"Emma!"

Emma had just gotten out of the elevator on floor 44. Carl was sitting on a bench at the side of the hall. It was white, but stained red where his hands were. He had red on his scrubs, too. Emma sat down next to him, noticing the distant look in his eyes. "What happened?" she asked, a severe note of concern in her voice.

"You know," began Carl, staring off into the distance, "given what goes on, you'd think medicine would be the most intimate of the sciences. But it isn't. It's the most detached, most emotionally sterile study." He put his head in his hands, smearing blood on his temples. He sounded like he was trying not to cry.

"I never thought of it before," he continued. "Remember Anatomy? Those were real people, Emma. And people like us cut 'em open, took their insides out and studied them like they were rocks or minerals or any other thing that never breathed or ate or lived or died."

He looked at her, his eyes red and teary. "I wanted to save people, Emma. I wanted to make the world a better place. Not this." He looked down again. "Never this."

"Carl, what happened?"

"Nothing, really. Your buddy Josh up there"—he pointed upwards —"wanted Mina fitted with some sensors. They wouldn't stay in, Emma. I told him, but he wouldnt have it. Soon as I tried to sew her up, they'd come pushing out through the skin. Then she'd close up like I never touched her."

"Carl, I think you should go home. You need more rest."

"Why bother? I just have to come back sooner or later."

"If it hurts you this much, Carl, you don't. You're an accomplished doctor; you could get a job anywhere."

He laughed, a sarcastic, sad laugh. "'That really what you think? You think any of us could quit? After what we've seen? It's a tough choice, Emma. Live in hell every day or get killed and probably go there anyway."

"No one's going to kill anyone, Carl. Where's Mina?"

He pointed at the SDF room. "Did the operation in there. Tried to."

"By yourself?" Emma asked.

He just nodded. She knew better than to lecture protocol right now.

"Just stay here, okay? I'll be back in a sec."

Carl nodded again. Emma tentatively walked to the room, and entered. In front of her were rows of SDF wombs and monitoring devices. Underneath a large lamp was an operating table. It was covered in blood, some of which had gotten onto the floor. Next to the table was an instrument tray; it was completely red.

A trail of blood ran across the floor, away from the table, and around to the other side of a wall of machinery. Emma slowly followed it.

In the farthest corner of the room, Mina was sitting in a bloodstained hospital gown. She had her knees up against her chest in a sort of fetal position. Her eyes had a glassy look to them, and she was rocking back and forth on her rear. Emma didn't sense any threat from her, only fear.

"Mina?"

Mina looked over at Emma, and a yellowish, clear wall appeared between the girl and the doctor.

An aurakinetic shield? Emma wondered. After a few seconds, it faded.

"I'm not going to hurt you, Mina." The shield reappeared, but faded much more quickly this time. "Mina, you're going to wear yourself out if you keep doing that." Slowly, she moved towards the girl, who at first backed further against the wall, but finally let Emma take her hand. "Come on. I'm going to take you to your room. You can get some rest, okay? You can talk to me tomorrow, if you want."

Mina nodded. They left the room. "Carl?" called Emma.

He was gone.

Forty-Nine:
Astral Interlude

There! He could feel her again! But so weak, so weak…. He was impatient; all the looping was endlessly making him wait.

Then they came. He had wandered too close to the shroud. They didn't like him; he tried to move outside the spheres and they wouldn't stand for that. They attacked and he moved away, the piercing of the Yellow Things slowly petering off.

Let them have their damn light. The City of Luminescence was nothing to him. He wished for the dark rain that would wash away the shroud and expose them for the nothings they are. He focused on the myriad gray pillars, at the edge of space and time, their raw, insane fury scaring even him. They could bring that rain.

But that was a wish, not a true need.

He needed to *know*. He would wait, until she was stronger. He had no choice.

Little one. Please. Stop your foolishness.

You are the fool! You move in circles, chasing your own tail, for what gain? I choose a line, a line that leads somewhere.

But you move in circles as well. You leave and come back, leave and come back. You should choose a better circle.

Leave me. I want nothing to do with your kind.

He hoped he would not have to wait much longer.

Fifty:
Nicholas Kresge

The gray-haired man watched the person on the monitor slowly walk out of the building. "I don't trust him, Joshua. Take care of him."

"Carl Redford has always been a productive member of the staff."

"He won't be any longer. You heard what he said. He's unpredictable. Remove him."

"Yeah." Richardson looked up. "So what did you want to see me for?"

The older man walked over to look at some models on a shelf. His back was to Richardson as he spoke.

"Joshua, the advisory board is waiting for a full report. We need to know the cause of this incident and what needs to be done to prevent it from happening again."

Richardson sighed. "Trust me, Nicholas, that as soon as *I* know, *they'll* know."

The other man, Nicholas Kresge, turned around. "You know that won't satisfy them."

"So what am I supposed to say? Look, Nick, this is a very volatile situation we're working with. These things are bound to happen from time to time. The incident with Anna claimed several lives inside this facility. The outside knew nothing. Same with this one."

"Yes, but the 'Andrew Incident' was extremely public. There were heavy civilian casualties."

"But nobody remembers it," offered Richardson. "As far as the public is concerned, it was a terrorist attack. Nothing more."

Kresge walked over. "They remember it, Joshua. Maybe not in here," he said, tapping his head, "but they remember it in here." He tapped his heart.

"That's rubbish. Keiko and Johnny are very powerful; the deluding was all-inclusive."

"How can you be sure?"

Richardson said nothing.

"Immediately afterward, homeless population in this fine city sky-rocketed. So did mental illness cases."

"Acceptable losses. Side effects were predicted. Anyway, the difference here is that Mina is a natural-born human."

"So is Anna."

"But," explained Richardson, "she was being dominated by Matthew. Both Matthew and Andrew were artificially created. That could explain their behavior."

"I read the preliminary on Mina," said Kresge. "She claimed to have been raped by a 'Matthew' prior to the incident. Any ideas what that could mean?"

"There's a lot we still don't understand."

"I don't see why Mina wasn't disposed of immediately."

"Dr. Hanin expressly stated that he felt we could move ahead much faster by gathering data from a natural psychic rather than just with the ones we created. At the moment, Mina is the only natural psychic we have available."

"I thought she was considered a failure, at least until now."

"She was," conceded Richardson. "But the information gathered from experiments on her should allow the scientists better luck when attempting to enhance another natural psychic. And, it just so happens that we may have found one: a girl named Raven Yamada who lives not far from here."

"Yamada? We had a Yamada working here before you arrived. No matter. Are you sure this is necessary?"

"Absolutely. Dr. Hanin believed quite definitely that the children were too limited, that in order to complete the project a mature psychic had to be studied. By that, he meant one whose *brain* has fully matured. At present, the Process seems to work only on children. Unfortunately, while it encourages mental growth, it halts physical maturation. The human brain continues to change through puberty, so we can't get truly accurate results from subjects who never grow that far."

"Didn't Hanin create mature psychics?" asked Kresge.

"You're thinking of Matthew and Andrew," answered Joshua. "Both were problematic, of course. Matthew was severely underdeveloped psionically except in regards to the singular Anna incident, and Andrew, in the end, was simply uncontrollable. The third prototype, Angel, was frozen as soon as the Andrew Incident occurred."

"All right then. Well, in any case, the Nod Energy Project is officially reopened. Just out of curiosity, what makes this girl Raven so special?"

"She has a mental condition that has been linked to latent psychic powers. We're not really sure what to expect, but she seems to have potential. Plus, she's eighteen so she's nearly done growing. It's really a long shot, but a very worthwhile one."

"Get her, then," said Kresge. "By any means necessary."

"Any means?"

"*Any* means."

Nicholas Kresge looked deep in thought for a moment. "What of the new head scientist?"

"Emma? I have her under constant surveillance."

"Can you trust her?"

"I don't have much of a choice," answered Richardson, shirking the question. "I will tell you I've gone to great lengths concealing Matthew and Andrew from her. I don't need her preoccupied with their failings, and I don't want her prying into things."

"So you can't trust her."

"I didn't say that."

"Look Josh, the advisory board is unhappy. The military sank lots of money into the biomorph program with zero return. So far, the energy project has been the same. They want results; they're breathing down my neck."

"What are you saying?" asked Richardson, defensively.

"Isn't it obvious? Your position is in jeopardy. I'm sorry, it's not my choice."

Richardson sighed. "I suppose then that they won't be very responsive to my request for more funding, then."

"What do you need it for?"

"The development for the PLF has stalled."

"PLF?" asked Kresge. "Oh, the laser weapon."

"Yes. The Personal LASER Firearm."

"Why is it so important?"

Richardson explained. "When a psychic uses one of his or her powers, the effect is nearly instantaneous. A regular gun leaves too big of a reaction window."

"A reaction window for what?"

"Well, some of these psychics are able to create shields. Or, one might be able to redirect the bullets or even fire an energy projectile at the offending soldier."

"And," hazarded Kresge, "you want your guards to have lasers because they are, for all purposes, instantaneous as well?"

"Exactly," answered Richardson. "Zero reaction window. The problem is, the prototypes aren't up to snuff. We haven't gotten the power supply smaller than a backpack, it's heavy, and it's still only good for a few shots. The trade-off in battery size is that the LASER itself is fairly weak, and the nature of it is that it cauterizes any wound it creates. It's incredibly painful but useless outside of a perfectly-aimed vital shot."

"What do you propose?" inquired Kresge.

"This is a shot in the dark, but I've seen very promising small-scale rail guns. Civilian designed, and on the internet, no less. There's gauss rifles, too, though they seem less promising."

"Well, I'm sure you know we have been developing both rail and coil guns for years. I'm not involved in that directly so I don't know how far the tech has come."

Richardson was adamant. "I strongly believe casualties could've been much lower regarding the Mina incident, if we had sufficiently fast firearms."

"Well, I'll see what I can do," said Kresge. "But the committee isn't too happy. Anything else?"

"No."

"Well, bye then." Nicholas Kresge started to leave.

"Good bye."

Kresge had reached the door when he turned around and spoke. "Oh, Josh?"

"Yes?"

"Get rid of Mr. Redford."

Kresge left the building with a lot on his mind; he didn't even remember the walk to his car afterward. He got inside, and without looking next to him, began to speak. "Dr. Gra—"

The woman sitting in the passenger seat interrupted him. "Don't say my name. Start driving." He did, following her directions, and it wasn't until they were driving along a lonely country road that any real conversation began.

"What is the status of the facility?" asked the middle-aged woman.

"I'd say unstable. The new lead doctor seems like the questioning type. I want to get rid of her."

"Don't. We can't afford to jeopardize this operation any further."

Kresge changed the subject. "Is the integration going well?"

"Yes."

"You might be asked to do an acquisition shortly."

"Not a problem."

"There is also the situation of one Dr. Carl Redford. He is highly unstable and needs to be dealt with."

"By your command?" asked the woman.

"No," answered Kresge. "Wait for Richardson's order."

"Understood."

"Anything else?"

"No. I will contact you shortly. Take me to my pickup point."

Kresge did a U-turn and after a bit of backtracking, turned right into a large field. After a bit of silence, he remembered something.

"It depends on what the higher-ups say, of course, but I may have some interesting research for your people in the near future."

"What kind of research?"

"High-speed firearms. Nothing certain, but we do have prototypes."

"Interesting," said the woman, smiling.

Fifty-One:
Project M

Emma looked out her kitchen window at the car across the street. The man sitting in it had his head leaning back and appeared to be sleeping. *What a great surveillance job they're doing*, she thought.

She sat back down and sipped her coffee. She looked at the pile of paper to her left. They were the files she had originally taken to read. She had decided to wait on those; she wanted to read Hanin's personal files first, especially after what Keiko and Johnny had said.

Out of all the test subjects in the lab, Keiko and Johnny were the most aloof, the most bizarre. They were never separated, by their choice or by the choice of others. Their abilities were among the most poorly understood of all known psychic phenomena. They knew things they shouldn't know, even given the possibilities allowed by telepathy and ESP. They seemed to be "Metacognitive." They showed very clear signs of retro- and pre-cognition, the abilities to see the past and future.

Neither of the abilities was considered possible. No reasonable theory had been put forward to explain them. None of the children had ever shown signs of such powers.

Except Keiko and Johnny. They were different, and no one could explain why. But they were always right.

Emma set aside one paper she had just read. It had been titled, *"Neotenous Traits Brought About Through Application of the Psychic Transformation Process."* It had explained some things Emma had wondered about, and pretty much confirmed her theories.

"Neoteny" was a term used to describe a situation wherein an adult member of a species retains traits commonly associated with the young. Some newts, for instance, retained external gills even after passing through the juvenile phase of their development. Apparently, the Process, when performed on a prepubescent child, had a similar effect. The child would continue to age, in as far as the gradual deterioration of bodily tissue and functions were concerned. However, the child's physical growth would stop, and puberty would not occur.

It seemed the cause for this was that the Process redirected the body's energy towards mental development at the cost of physical development, or even upkeep. Most of the children were sickly with weak immune systems, and had lost most of their pigmentation.

Apparently, Dr. Hanin had believed that getting around this fact would be the first step towards creating the "perfect psychic." The onset of puberty marked the body's dedication of its energies to physical growth and upkeep. The

Process, when performed on a subject at or beyond this point, did not affect bodily processes at all. However, any psychic abilities unlocked at this point were generally very weak. Emma guessed this was the case with Mina, but as for what had just happened, perhaps Hanin's theory was flawed.

The next paper was an exhaustive study on the electrical glands of eels. It discussed biomorphic attempts to recreate similar structures within human subjects; apparently, this had been an early attempt at harnessing energy from Nod.

Emma wondered for a second if any of the files she had were about biomorphism. Joshua had piqued her interest in it, for better or for worse, but she hadn't run across much in her readings other than vague references. She flipped through the large stack of files, but found nothing promising. She started to do the same with Hanin's files, but the very next paper she looked at caught her eye. It was titled, *"Project M Generator Prototype II."* Richardson hadn't mentioned another generator.

The file said that a test subject, listed only as M, had died during experimental use of his psychic powers. His body was kept on life support and subjected to various experiments and tests which the paper did not provide details of. Although being consciously brain dead, his body was apparently able to draw energy from Nod much more efficiently than Arty. However, the small size of the body meant it had a very low capacity, so it was used for experimentation and not as a reliable source of power. The system was linked in with NOD's power grid, though, and apparently shared the same portal that Arty used.

The man knows, thought Emma. She decided to have a look at this "M" tomorrow.

Fifty-Two:
Wednesday Morning

"I wish you weren't going."

"Me too. But I should, you know? They revoked my suspension." Crow looked down at Raven, still in bed with her covers pulled up to her neck.

"I'll come back as soon as school's over. You just get some rest, okay?"

"I'm the same Raven I was before all this."

"I know," said Crow, sitting down on the bed. "Just do it for your mom's sake, okay? I'm gonna be thinking of you all day long."

"Okay," Raven conceded. "Me too." Crow leaned down and kissed her good-bye. "I love you."

"I love you, too."

"Bye."

"Bye."

Crow left, closing the door behind her. Raven sat still for a few moments, wondering what exciting tedium she would experience today. She turned on the TV, found nothing good on it, but watched anyway.

It would be a long day.

Fifty-Three:
Suicide

Emma was startled awake by the ringing of her phone. Just as her half-sleeping brain registered what the noise was, her alarm clock started whining. Still in sleep mode, she was unable to deal well with the sudden onslaught of noise, so she pounded her fist against the snooze button, picked up the phone, and gruffly said, "What?"

"Emma?" It was Joshua. He had a serious tone to his voice that woke her up pretty fast.

"Joshua?"

"Emma, You need to get here."

"Where?"

"Carl's."

"What happened?"

"He's dead, Emma. He committed suicide."

Emma pulled the phone away from her ear for a minute, and stared off into the distance. Her head was swarming with different thoughts, many of them conflicting. Carl had seemed severely depressed yesterday, but what had he said?

You think any of us could quit? After what we've seen? It's a tough choice, Emma. Live in hell every day or get killed and probably go there anyway.

Emma put the phone back to her ear.

"Emma? Are you there?"

"I'm here."

"Do you have the address?"

"No, hold on a sec…" She reached for a piece of paper and a pen. Richardson gave her the address, and she hung up. She reached over to her alarm and properly turned it off, then got up, got dressed in a rush, and left.

Fifty-Four:
Acclimation

Mina sat in her bed, curled up, rocking back and forth. She stared at the bathroom, not wanting to go in there again. That's how it all started.

She was naked, with the covers off, shivering from cold and fear and confusion.

Who am I? The question had never mattered before.

What am I? She could still smell the blood, and it made her hungry in a deep, instinctual way.

She looked down at herself. Her body was different; her skin, pure, smooth, and unblemished. She felt sexy, and that thought confused her even more because it wasn't something she'd ever considered before and it was connected with feelings of revulsion, guilt, and terror.

What did I do? But it hadn't been her, right?

After a pause in her thoughts, a new idea struck her.

*What **can** I do?*

She looked over at her teddy bear, and knew someone was staring back at her through its eyes. That thought no longer seemed all right to her. It just wasn't right. She concentrated on the bear's eyes and there was a tiny *crunch* as they cracked.

She watched the bear as she floated it up over her bed and above the floor. Its face ripped off, and a small, damaged camera fell onto the ground. Mina replaced the torn teddy onto her bed, and got up and stepped on the camera. It crunched under her foot, but a part of it cut her. She sat back down and held her foot up. There was a tiny spot of blood on it. She watched in fascination as the blood ran back into her body and the cut closed up.

She smiled, and got up to take a shower.

Fifty-Five:
Asphyxiation

Emma rubbed her hands together as she shivered. She was grateful that Joshua had brought an umbrella because it had started sleeting as soon as she'd gotten into her car.

She looked at the scene before her: a pleasant, well-maintained bungalow, surrounded by yellow police tape and absolutely crawling with cops. The ugly gray sky felt intrusive to her, seeming too low for her liking as it sloshed its freezing rain onto the gray, drenched snow beneath. A biting wind waxed and waned every couple minutes.

Joshua took one last puff from his cigarette, and then flicked it off to the side. He was wearing a long black coat, but no hat, and although his skin was red from the cold he wasn't shivering. Actually, he didn't look in the least bit uncomfortable. He had a distant look in his eyes, though.

A police officer came up to him, a chubby man in his late forties. "This looks pretty cut-and-dry; the detective will let you know in a bit when it's all right for you to go in."

"Thanks."

The cop walked back towards the house. "So," began Emma, speaking for the first time since she's said "Hello" to Richardson, "How'd it happen?"

Joshua handed the umbrella to her as he lit up another cigarette. He took the umbrella back as he started to speak, and they nestled under it, Emma drenched in the stale tobacco smell. "He was found hanging from the top of his basement steps. He tied a rope to the banister so that it rested against one of the vertical supports. Then, I guess he just put it around his neck and jumped off."

Emma had never seen Carl's house, so her mind momentarily tried to construct an image of how that worked, until she decided she didn't really want to think about it. "How did they find him?"

Joshua took a drag, and then answered. "Carl's always an early riser; I guess he goes to the gym before coming to work. He has one of the neighborhood kids come over and let his dog outside while he's gone; the dog wouldn't come outside today and the kid went looking for it. She found it lying under his feet, whining."

Emma had her doubts. Carl's words the other day had been double sided; he had sounded depressed but also in fear for his life. "It's so damn cold," she muttered, shivering like mad. "Why the hell is it raining?"

Richardson answered as the umbrella tried to rest itself from his grip. "It's not really that cold; it's the damn wind."

A couple of cops came out of the house, followed by two EMS workers carrying a covered stretcher. The rain splattered against the sheet, leaving translucent gray areas. As the men put the stretcher into the ambulance, a man in a trench coat and hat walked over to Emma and Joshua. "Morning," he said, tipping his hat to Emma. Then, to Joshua: "We can't rule out foul play just yet, but it seems to be your standard suicide."

Emma thought, *Regardless of if it's a suicide or not, there's nothing standard about it.*

"We'd like to go through his belongings, but my boss said I had to get the O-K from you."

"Yes, well, I'm afraid I can't allow that yet," said Richardson. The other man looked flummoxed. "My team will go in and do a thorough check. We'll contact you as soon as we're done, or if we find anything."

"Whatever," said the man, throwing his arms up. He sighed. "It's all yours, then."

Richardson threw his second cigarette onto the ground. "We're done here, Emma, I've got an investigation team on the way. There's nothing we can do. If you please?" he held his arm out forward.

"Of course," she said. He walked her to her car, then went to his. They both left by different routes, both of them silent the whole drive, but for different reasons.

Not too far from there, Carlos Gonzalez sat in a diner picking at his ham and eggs. He was silent, too, but because of disappointment.

He liked to stand with the gawkers whenever he did one of these. It gave him a rush. He looked out at the freezing rain slapping against the window. *Not today,* he thought.

Fifty-Six:
Sexual Harassment

Crow stepped into the school, drenched and frozen from the sleet she hadn't been expecting. She wiped the ice flakes off of her coat and backpack as she made her way to her locker on the second floor. She sighed, knowing she looked awful; her wet hair was glued to her face and when she touched it, it seemed to be covered in a thin layer of crystals.

She wasn't used to being alone in school anymore, and didn't realize ahead of time how much it would bother her. She didn't have very many friends. The girls she used to hang out with had been kind of cliquey, and when she started going out with Raven they started shunning her. When that had made her openly gay, most of the boys who used to talk to her ignored her, realizing she was pretty much permanently off limits.

She had no regrets about any of that, but just knowing Raven wasn't somewhere in the building made her lonely. High school was a shitty place filled with shitty people, and she missed holding Raven's hand as she walked, missed having her there to brighten her mood.

As she proceeded down the hall towards the stairs, she began to have the distinct feeling that people were talking about her behind her back. Everyone was avoiding eye contact with her, and if she did chance to look someone in the eyes, that person immediately turned away. Either she was paranoid or the incident the other day was still the freshest news on campus.

The second floor was crowded but the vibe was different; she didn't feel any eyes on her, and the students seemed more rushed, more caught up in conversations about their own issues to pay her any heed. Things changed as she neared her locker. The area around it was vacant, except for a crowd of mostly juniors across the hall, standing around a certain senior with short, curly dark hair. They were avoiding her eyes and she could hear stifled laughter. Something was about to happen. She sighed, and opened her locker....

"A blow-up doll?" The space behind her filled with laughter. Crow looked in disgust at the plastic mockery of life. It had brown hair, and someone had drawn slanted lines over its existing eyes in an attempt to make it look vaguely Asian. It stared at her, gape-mouthed and soulless.

She grabbed it by the neck and turned around.

"Tom Delfranco, you curly-haired fuck," she said, shoving the doll into the face of the shorter boy as he and his group guffawed like hyenas, "you're an asshole AND you're racist."

He pulled his arms back and stretched nonchalantly. "You know, we could have been something, you and me." His posse went silent, waiting for the response.

Crow dropped the doll at his feet. "I wouldn't have dated you even if I was straight. You're disgusting."

They started laughing again, and the bell rang.

"And now I'm late," she muttered, turning back to her locker.

It was going to be a long day.

Crow didn't pay attention to any of her lessons, and she even fell asleep in class at one point, which was totally unlike her. She was worried about Raven, and later thought back to the moment they had become a couple.

This was the day she was going to finally going to take a chance. Regardless of the outcome, she knew she would feel better for doing it.

"Excuse me," she said, getting up from her lunch table. The gaggle of giggling girls didn't even seem to hear her. She walked over to *her* table; she was sitting with two boys, Steve and...Sam, was it?

"Um, would you guys mind...giving me a moment?"

Steve looked at Raven and smirked. "C'mon, dork." Sam and him stood up with their lunch trays in hand and walked away. Crow sat down.

"Hi," she said.

"Hi. Crow, right?"

"Well, it's Maria, but my middle name is Crowell, after my grandfather, so everyone calls me Crow, yeah." It was obvious she was nervous, she was fidgeting and having trouble keeping eye contact.

She was silent for a bit too long. "Anything I can do for you?" Raven asked, her tone soft.

"Listen, um, I think you're really pretty, and I don't really know you, but I think you're cool and..."

"Holy shit, are you asking me out?"

Crow looked Raven right in the eyes. "Yes."

Raven looked back at the cluster of "it" girls a few tables away. "Aren't you like, Aubrey's third banana? You're gay?" She whispered the last part.

"Yes."

"Well, why the hell not! I'm single right now. I'm gonna go ahead and guess this is your first time asking someone out, let alone another girl?"

Crow nodded.

Raven smiled. "Don't worry, I'll go easy on you."

They had gone on an actual first date date, dinner and a night on the town. It had been wonderful, and Crow had never looked back.

Only one more class and she could go see her.

Fifty-Seven:
Flowers

There was a knock on Raven's door. She looked up from the well-worn book she was reading and muted the TV show she was barely watching and said, "Yes?" The voice of her mother answered back.

"Dear, you have a visitor."

Raven said, "Just a sec!" and grabbed some pajama pants and pulled them on. She went over to the door and opened it.

"Hey, you."

"Hey, those for me?" She grinned.

Steve Phillips was standing in the doorway, wearing a huge black coat. He had a bouquet of mixed flowers in his hand.

"Yeah," he said, following her into her room. They both sat on the bed.

"They're lovely," said Raven happily. *They smell awful, but so do all flowers!* "Thanks!" She leaned forward and gave Steve a big hug and a peck on the cheek, and then leaned back and set the flowers down.

"So how you doing?"

"I'm doing better, now. Sorry I didn't call you yet; it's a lot to take in and I've been avoiding people." A thought came to her and a puzzled look came over her face. "How'd you find out?"

"Actually, your mom called me. Said maybe it would cheer you up if I came by."

"Really," said Raven in a shocked voice. That wasn't exactly like her mother, who didn't really like Steve that much. It was, however, rather thoughtful of her.

"There a problem with that?" asked Steve, somewhat confused.

"No," said Raven. "No problem at all. It's just not like my mom."

"Well, I know I'm not exactly on her A-list of your friends."

"She doesn't have one," said Raven resignedly. Then: "Why don't you take your coat off?"

"Actually, I can't stay long," said Steve with a tone of disappointment in his voice. Then, his face brightened at what he was about to say. "I have to go enroll today."

"For what?"

"Duh, for college."

Again, Raven threw her arms around him. "I knew you weren't a dummy, dummy! That's so cool! How'd you decide that?"

"Well, when you and Crow were over the other day, you seemed so ready to move forward, you know? To be honest with your mom, see a doctor? I looked around my room and it was disgusting. I need to do *something*, anything, do better by myself and make some money and live better."

"So where are you going to go?"

"Just to the community college. Found out I can get almost a free ride, being dirt poor and all, even though my grades are crap." He looked at his watch. "Shit. All this time talking about me and it was *you* who went to the hospital."

"That's okay," said Raven. "I don't really have much to say anyway; they still don't know much about it."

"Well, keep me posted," he said, getting up. He pointed to the flowers. "You want me to get a vase for those on my way out?"

"Nah. I'll see you out and get one on the way back." She picked up the bouquet and followed Steve down the hallway. He ducked his head into the kitchen on the way.

"Thanks, Mrs. Yamada."

"You're welcome Steve."

At the front landing, Raven could feel the chill from the outside trying to press through the door. She and Steve hugged, and he kissed her on the forehead.

"I love you, girl."

"I know," she answered. "I love you too."

He held her for a second longer, thinking, *You don't really know. But... maybe you do.* Then he opened the door. "Bye."

"Bye. Thanks again for the flowers."

"No problem," Steve said as he left.

Raven closed and locked the door, shivering. She went into the kitchen to grab a vase, smiling all the way.

Fifty-Eight:
Meeting

Emma called for a staff meeting that morning. It was the first time she had done so, since her promotion, and she didn't know exactly how to handle it yet.

All of the staff had been notified about Carl, so there was a bit of somber talk about that for a while. Emma kept her opinions to herself. After a bit, she called order to the half-empty meeting room (it was really an unused lab; the main meeting room was still being repaired.)

She stood up, glancing down at Jameson, who had a smug grin on his face. Emma was still pissed he was her second.

"We all have an uphill climb," she began tentatively. "There's a lot of responsibility we have to assume now, many of it for things we don't even know about yet."

This isn't so bad, she thought.

"Shortly, all of you will be given new assignments, and some of you will be given new clearance levels and job titles. We have a specific goal, one that I will explain as soon as I am fully versed in it myself. For now, though, we need to maintain order among the test subjects and the facility in general." She paused for a moment. "Has the data concerning Mina been analyzed yet?"

A woman across the table to the left stood up. "I can have the report on your desk within the hour, doctor."

"Good. Off hand, did you happen to see the results of the DNA test?"

The woman paused. "There was only a slight change in base pair sequence between samples," said the woman. "Nothing definitive."

"Thank you." The woman sat down, looking around nervously.

"That'll be all for now," said Emma. Everyone started getting up, but then Jameson, who was still sitting, spoke.

"Wait," he said snidely. "The good doctor here hasn't really told us anything." Everyone had stopped moving and was staring at Emma.

"When I have more to tell you," said Emma, displeasure distinctly present in her voice, "I will." She was looking at Jameson the whole time.

Once everyone else had left, Emma confronted Jameson. "You have a way about you I don't like." He shrugged. "If it wasn't for Richardson, you wouldn't be my assistant."

"If it wasn't for Carl," he began, but he stopped at the look on Emma's face.

"As long as you are my assistant, you will do as I tell you. Is that clear?"

"Yes." He tried really hard not to sound mocking. Playing a part was another talent he did not excel at.

"Good. Now leave."

Jameson left. Emma felt pretty good, considering. She got up, and headed towards a file room.

Some time later she sat in her office, drumming her fingers against the desk. She glanced down at the report on Mina that was sitting there. She had skimmed through it; it had been mostly inconclusive.

The files Emma had hoped to find about biomorphism had to be above her clearance level, because she had found nothing in the files she was allowed to read. She was getting frustrated. Her curiosity was giving way to paranoia and moral dilemmas. She also felt like someone was purposely keeping her away from certain things. Joshua had this grandiose vision he wanted her to fulfill, but every time she went to look at something that might shed some light either on Mina or on the past of this project, she found it to be unobtainable.

Honestly, she thought. *How am I supposed to do my job when all the details of it are classified?*

She thought of trying to find project M, but figured it would probably be off-limits as well. Probably, she would just go see Mina.

Emma picked up the picture of the Hanin family that was still on the desk. "You're the *man*," she said. "What *do* you know?" The backing on the frame was poking her hand and she turned it over with the intention of fixing it. There, in the lower left corner where the paper backing had worked its way out of the frame, was a tiny, exposed piece of metal. She pulled on it, dislodging more of the backing as she did so.

It was a key with a three-digit number on it. A safe deposit box key.

The universe had, in its infinitely unlikely machinations, literally handed her a key.

Emma removed the backing entirely. It was black on the inside as well as the outside. She set it aside, reaching for the picture, when a glint on the backing caught her eye.

At most angles, the inside of the backing looked to be flat black felt. But if she held it at an angle so the light would glint off it, Emma could see an address written in pencil on it. It was hard to make out but she did the best that she could, scribbling it onto a piece of paper. Afterwards, she dropped the picture, the key, the paper, and the backing into her purse, and got up. She had some investigating to do.

Fifty-Nine:
Dr. Richardson

There was a knock at the front door. Mrs. Yamada went to open it. There was a man standing there, wearing a long black coat and holding a closed-up umbrella and a briefcase. "Mrs. Yamada? I'm Dr. Richardson. We spoke on the phone earlier."

"Yes, come in, come in." Mrs. Yamada motioned for him to come in and took his coat and umbrella from him. He was a handsome man, with perfectly cut, dark hair.

She led him into the kitchen and motioned for him to sit down. She walked over to the coffee pot.

"Coffee?"

"If it's not any trouble."

Soon, they were both sitting down, two mugs of coffee on the table in front of them. Dr. Richardson had his briefcase on the table as well. "Mrs. Yamada," he began.

"Please, call me Molly."

"All right. Molly, There's a lot we feel we can do for your daughter but it may not sound good at first. I just ask that you give me the benefit of the doubt and allow me to fully explain it before you make your decision."

"Sounds fair," she said.

"Now Molly, your daughter Raven has a form of epilepsy. It is a neurological condition wherein, either on its own or in reaction to certain stimuli...well, let me put this in layman's terms. Her brain 'shorts out' and causes her seizures." He sipped his coffee. "We'll get to the hallucinations in a bit, that's a separate issue. I'd like to discuss this first."

"The problem with this is that quite obviously, your daughter has no control over herself when she is seizing. She could fall and hit her head; she could collapse while crossing the street; she could...well, any number of unpleasant things could happen. Often, the symptoms can be lessened through the use of various medicines, but not stopped completely."

He leaned forward and looked Mrs. Yamada straight in the eyes. "That is of course an option. However, the hospital would suggest an alternative, which would very likely cure the condition, but is somewhat, ah, extreme...." He let his voice trail off.

"What is this alternative?" asked Mrs. Yamada once it had become clear that Dr. Richardson was waiting for her to ask before continuing.

"Well, it seems that the seizures originate in a very localized section of your daughter's brain. The quickest cure would be to remove the offending section...."

"Absolutely not," spluttered Mrs. Yamada. Richardson smiled slightly; so far, so good.

"I thought not.... My organization has a procedure they believe will attain the same results, without surgery, although it takes much longer." He patted the briefcase. "I have our statistics, if you'd like to look at them. They're very promising, I assure you." He took another sip of coffee.

"We have a non-invasive method, Molly, involving state-of-the-art medication and therapy that sort of 're-teaches' the brain how to work. Eventually, it should completely eliminate any and all symptoms your daughter has."

"How long does it take?"

"The time-frame is three to five years."

Mrs. Yamada looked at him skeptically.

"I'm going to be honest with you, Molly. There is a severe downside to our method, one that we take very seriously and offer generous compensation for."

Mrs. Yamada finished her coffee. "And it is?"

"The patient may not be visited during the treatment." Mrs. Yamada began shaking her head no. "It's a sad fact, I know, but the treatment requires an absolutely structured environment, and introducing—sorry to put it this way—variables, has in all cases delayed or negated a successful outcome."

This is ridiculous, thought Mrs. Yamada. Sarcastically, she asked, "Well, you said there was compensation. What is it?"

"During the time that your daughter would be with us, we will administer college-level studies to her. By the time she has completed the treatment, Molly, your daughter may well have a bachelor's degree."

"And how much will this wonderful treatment cost me?"

"That's the beauty of it," said Richardson excitedly. "This is all government-funded research. *We pay you* for the opportunity. Fifty-thousand dollars!"

Mrs. Yamada stood up and pointed to the door. "Get out."

Dr. Richardson stammered. "I know it seems like a lot to give up, but please, if you take the time to consider—"

"You should be ashamed, doctor, to work for a company that would steal a child from her mother for five years in the name of government research. Please leave now."

Maybe I should be ashamed, Richardson momentarily thought as he got up. As he was handed his coat, he said, "Well, I thank you for your time. Let me give you my card, should you change your mind." He reached into his pocket.

"That won't be necessary. Good-bye."

Joshua lit up a cigarette as he walked to his car. Of course the idea *seemed* ridiculous, but some people were pretty hard up for cash. And certainly, he couldn't be accused of not trying the non-violent route.

Oh well, he thought. *Time for plan B*

Sixty:
The Truth

Emma kept glancing nervously over her shoulder, afraid she was being followed. She looked again at the address. It wasn't even in Omaha, she had determined; it was in Bellevue, to the southeast. After some wrong turns and some meandering, she found it.

"It" was a doughnut shop.

She looked around, and right across from it was a bank. *I guess that "5" was a "6,"* she thought. She got out of her car and looked around before heading inside. At the desk, she showed the teller the key, and she was directed towards the safe deposit boxes. She'd never had one and didn't know what standard procedure was, but she was surprised that she hadn't been asked for her ID.

She sat down at a table and opened the box. A small stack of neatly folded papers was the only contents; she quickly shoved them into her briefcase, replaced the box, and left.

Emma drove around for another ten or twenty minutes, before pulling into a parking lot to examine the papers. She opened her briefcase, unfolded the first paper, and smiled when she saw what it was about.

How prophetic.

It was a case study of a biomorph experiment, or at least an excerpt from one. It appeared to be a poor copy; photographs that were supposed to be of an autopsy looked like nothing more than smudgy black marks. She looked at the first few lines of the page beneath the identification number.

```
Subject: Kirge, Randall
Cause of Death: Asphyxiation
Desired Anatomy: Working gill structures
```

She read the short amount of text below. Apparently, this Randall Kirge had successfully grown working gill slits on either side of his neck. He had died because during the growth of these gills, his lungs were absorbed into the surrounding tissue, and he was unable to reproduce them after closing the gills.

He had died of asphyxiation because he had nothing to breathe *with*.

The next sheet was another biomorphism case. Cause of death was listed as "Tissue ossification." The desired anatomy was a "calciferous exo-skeletal plating." Emma read to learn that what this meant was that during an attempt to grow what was essentially armor made of bone, all of the subject's soft tissues had changed into bone as well.

Paper after paper showed ever-more horrible atrocities. One boy was supposed to grow bony spurs out of his wrists; he had literally been cut apart from the inside as spurs started growing from all over his skeleton. A girl had attempted to thicken her skull; her brain had been crushed.

Most of the attempts seemed very bizarre. Emma could understand the ones that involved improving the subject's senses or physical abilities, but the other ones…if they were just experiments to see what could be done rather than to see if something useful could be done, it all made a little more sense. But even then, they were weird. Exo-skeletons? Bony helmets? Sharp bone spars? Emma began to make a mental picture of what all of these attributes would look like together, and then it hit her….

The biomorphism project was funded by the military for a reason; it was a purely military project. She turned to the next page and saw Hanin's quickly scrabbled words, echoing her own thoughts.

Super-soldiers

Biomorph project is military

Want to create quick, armored, killing machine

FAILURE

All right, if that was the case, then the current energy project….

She thought back to when Richardson had given her the speech about the world's problems going away once everyone had unlimited energy.

"You bastard," she said aloud. Then again, maybe he was just a pawn. It didn't matter. Whether it had always been that way or not, NOD now worked for the military. If the United States, especially the United States military, controlled a source of limitless power, then they could pretty much rule the world.

"You idiot," she said, referring to Richardson again. "This won't help stop wars, it'll only make them worse."

Emma suddenly realized she couldn't trust anyone. Except maybe Hanin here, but of course, he was dead. She unfolded the next page. It was a copy of a newspaper article from several years back. It concerned a terrorist attack that had occurred in Omaha some years back, before Emma had started working there.

The word "LIES" was written across it in red magic marker.

The next few sheets appeared to be the same timeline of NOD that she had received in her files, only this one wasn't edited but in fact had extra writing scribbled into the margins. Not long before the Anna incident was a line that read, "NOD Energy project leads to creation of

artificially sequenced DNA used to create Perfect
Psychic Prototype-I Matthew."

Scribbled to the side, it said:

Matthew was created to duplicate a natural psychic and was quickly matured to a post-pubescent age. Much of his learning was done quickly but he had little real-world knowledge.

Matthew was defective. He had weak psionic activity and seemed not to have any specific powers.

Matthew was kept for the sake of study. He did not experience normal reactions to medication, maintaining a strong interest in his past, which was never revealed to him. He was never told he was artificial.

Matthew took an interest in Anna, a new subject that was shown to be capable of strong photokinetic effects. Anna never spoke or interacted with others on her own behalf.

Anna one day headed of her own accord towards the history file room on 48. When confronted, she killed all those before her through the use of pyrokinesis.

During this event, Matthew was AWOL.

Once Anna had begun to make serious use of her powers, she appeared to be under great stress. She cried "I can't break the connection" and then she collapsed.

Matthew's body was later found inside a duct near where Anna was when she began acting strangely. All higher brain functions had ceased, although his body was alive. Tests on both his and Anna's brains showed high quantities of particles and markers associated with telepathy and mental domination, especially in the damaged areas of Matthew's mind.

My belief is that Matthew possessed the skill of mental domination, and, sensing a great power in Anna, attempted to overtake her. Perhaps his/her foray into the history room was his attempt to discover his past?

I believe Matthew exhausted and damaged himself either due to prolonged uses of his power or through an unsuccessful attempt to completely take over Anna's mind.

All this has been submitted in a report.

Following these events, Matthew's body was submitted to stimuli used during the biomorph program. His body was converted into a form that was able to draw energy from Nod much like RT, though on a smaller scale. This was known as Prototype or Project M.

Emma looked down the list to the "Andrew Incident." It, too, had writing next to it.

Perfect Psychic Prototype-2 ANDREW and 3 ANGEL were developed simultaneously although ANGEL required a much longer maturation time. Both involved different theories into the proper direction of this program; both were sequenced artificially.

Andrew was matured in the same manner as Matthew and seemed much more promising in regards to abilities and control via medication. Inexplicably, he revolted one day and violently removed himself from the building. He killed many in downtown Omaha within a few short minutes and was only stopped by the combined efforts of many soldiers.

Interviews with surviving witnesses pointed to the conclusion that Andrew was severely unstable, unable to speak full sentences at some points and essentially, killing at random.

This event was covered up through the very powerful mental abilities of subjects Keiko and Johnny. It was publicly explained as a terrorist attack. This usage of mental abilities is called "deluding," and does not affect all targets equally.

Following this event all scientists save for Dr. Utsugi and myself were replaced. Major Joshua Richardson was brought in as the head of NOD. During this event I successfully motioned for the temporary discontinuation of this program. I froze ANGEL, which had barely passed a fetal stage of development. It is stored in the cryonics lab. I have my fears.

The autopsy of Andrew showed high amounts of the same particles and chemicals found in Anna 's and Matthew's brains, and with the same characteristic signature. Additionally, the output of M decreased during the period of Andrew's revolt, though RT's output did not. I do not know how it is possible but I believe that Matthew's consciousness somehow rests inside his old body, and is still capable of dominating other psychics. I never published these ideas as they are too speculative.

I motioned for the destruction of M but was denied on the grounds that I could provide no good reason, for although I had quite a good reason I could not afford to put it forth.

ANGEL must not be thawed. It has no conscious mind. I believe that would make it very easy to dominate. Were its powers to be even half as strong as Andrew's, I fear Matthew would use it for his own purposes.

Emma thought about this. It seemed like insanity! And to think that the citizens of Omaha, who believed they had been the target of a terrorist attack, had implanted memories of the whole thing?

She noticed another line on the sheet that dated the acquisition of Mina. Mina was apparently a natural psychic; she had been aged in stasis until she was past puberty, and then subjected to the Process. Only after that was she integrated into the facility.

Emma knew she had to find Project M. She had to find out if its output had dropped during Mina's escapade. She had to check the report, to see what particle activity was present in Mina's brain during the event.

She had to stop this before it happened again. But she couldn't tell anyone, least of all Richardson. Whether he was aware of all this or not was beside the point—she couldn't risk telling him either way, just in case.

Emma remembered something, something that had confused her before but that made perfect sense now. The NOD logo—which she had seen nowhere else except in the first file she read, had contained the phrase "Nothing sacred, nothing harmed." It had made no sense before, but taken in the context of an organization that would go to any lengths to reach its goal, it made perfect sense. "Nothing sacred"—if nothing, not even life, held any true meaning, then no damage could be done to anything. Accountability did not exist—"Nothing harmed."

She was sure of it now. Carl had been murdered. And with that, she'd lost her only chance of having somebody else on her side. She was alone. And for the first time in her life, Emma Jacobson was truly terrified.

Sixty-One:
Alibi

"Yes, I have some new recruits for you, although one won't be there for a couple of days; he broke his leg, but he's almost done with therapy. Oh, and good news—the army has its own personal laser firearm that it recently developed, and they've cleared it for use by NOD soldiers. It's a shame both programs weren't combined, we would have saved time and funding. It's stronger and more light-weight than your prototypes."

"Great. Anything else?"

"No. That's it. Bye."

"Good-bye, Nick." Richardson put the phone down. "Sorry."

"Anyway, like I said, she just left," said Jameson.

"Who left?" asked Emma as she nonchalantly entered the office. She threw a bright box onto the desk.

"You guys want any donuts?"

Sixty-Two:
Homecoming

There was a knock on Raven's door.

"Come in."

The door opened. "Hi, sweetie."

"Hi!" Raven walked over to Crow and gave her a big kiss and hug that lasted for a minute or so longer than either had anticipated.

"So, how was school?"

"Oh, you're gonna love this," said Crow, taking off her backpack. She noticed the vase on the nightstand. "Hey, nice flowers."

"Thanks. Steve brought them over."

"You know, I think he's got a crush on you," she said sardonically.

"Can you believe he thinks I don't know he has feelings for me?"

"Poor guy," said Crow, and they kissed again before they both sat down on the bed. Crow set a folder down near Raven. "I picked up your homework for you."

"Thanks," said Raven, a mixture of honesty and sarcasm present in her voice. "Anyway, so what happened today?"

"Okay, so I get there, and Tom Delfranco and his fucking posse is all giggly and stuff, so I open my locker and a freaking *blow-up doll* falls out." She left out the part about the drawn-on slanted eyes; it just felt mean. Raven's mouth dropped open; she was incredulous.

"That's the guy that used to bug you all the time to go out with him, right?"

"Yeah, even after we started going out, he kept it up for awhile. The rest of the day wasn't that bad, but it *draaagged.* Oh, good news," Crow said, remembering. "I talked to Kingsley for a bit later in the day. Apparently, your mom called the school and told them...something, he couldn't tell me, but he did ask me to tell you you're no longer suspended."

"Weird and lame." Raven grabbed the folder with her homework in it and tossed it on the floor. "This can wait, then."

"Sorry. Well, that's pretty much all worth mentioning. How was your day?"

"Eh, I tried reading and watching TV but I just couldn't get into it. Steve came over, but that was like, only for five minutes. He's going to college."

"Not bad."

"Oh, and this guy from some experimental institute came by to talk to my mom, she said he wanted to keep me locked in there for five years for treatment! What a dick."

Now it was Crow's turn to look incredulous. "That's ridiculous!"

"I know, right?" Raven winced and put her hand to her forehead.

"You all right?"

"The medicine makes me a little woozy, that's all."

"So," said Crow, after a bit. "Boring day, huh?"

"Yeah."

"No black outs or anything?"

"Nope."

"Good." Crow smiled. "I've been thinking about you all day. I missed you."

"I missed you too."

Raven brushed a lock of hair out of Crow's face. "What the hell did you do to your hair?" she said, laughing.

"Ugh, it was sleeting when I got to school. I never even bothered brushing it. How bad is it?"

"Pretty fucking bad," Raven answered, smiling. She rustled her hand through it, making it worse on purpose.

"Same to you, then," said Crow, returning the gesture.

"I don't think so," said Raven. She grabbed Crow's shoulders and pushed her down to the bed and got on top of her, pinning her down. She smiled devilishly. "Try something now, I dare you." Crow grabbed Raven and pulled her in for a kiss.

"This was your evil plan all along, wasn't it?" Raven asked playfully.

"I have to work with what I get!"

The two girls went on to have the greatest, sweetest, most fulfilling sex they had ever had with each other. This was fitting, since it was the last time they would be together like that ever again.

Sixty-Three:
Wondering

Mina had been sitting on her bed for hours, looking through her books. She was confused. On one side she had a book called *Nature's Beauty*. On the other side, she had a book called *The Lorax*. Both had pictures of "outside" but the storybook, which had been written by a man named Dr. Seuss, looked very different from the other book.

Most of the pictures Mina had seen of outside looked like *Nature's Beauty*. But, she also had lots of Dr. Seuss books, the pictures in them looking vaguely similar at best to the pictures in the other books. So which was real? How *did* "outside" look? Also, her storybooks had pictures of people in them, but none of her nature books did. Did the people outside look like the people in *The Lorax*?

Actually, many things were confusing Mina. She had gone into her shower this morning with a weird sense of confidence, but having to face a tile wall for ten minutes made her start thinking more. She hadn't received a schedule today. In fact, only a couple of times did she see anyone else. Twice a doctor brought her a meal. Whenever she looked out of her room, she saw the hall swarming with more guards than she had ever seen in one place at once.

Was it because of what she had done?

Mina never really grasped the concept behind the guards before. They made her uncomfortable from time to time, but they were just there, like walls and lights and her bathroom. They had guns, and Mina knew guns made you hurt.

Mina had been hurt by a gun.

She never knew why they had guns. Now she thought she did.

To stop people like me. She gently touched a hand to her face. A gun had destroyed it, but now it was fine.

But she hadn't done anything, at least not on purpose. The voice in her head, Matthew, had made her do things she didn't want to. She was pretty sure he was gone now, but she was a little scared still. Plus, now she could do things like the other children....

Mina made all of the books on her bed fly up above her head. She watched them spin in a wide circle just below the ceiling, until her thoughts changed direction and she set the books back down.

She could vividly remember every second of her imprisonment. She had felt sort of detached, like she was watching herself, only in a mental sense (if that even made any sense.) The killing bothered her but had felt oddly familiar.

Matthew had changed her. She didn't used to think of some things that she was thinking about now, like who she was and where she had come from.

Matthew had wanted to know who his parents were. Mina understood the biology of parenting but had never really thought about it before. Who were her parents?

Matthew was mean; she wasn't. She didn't want to hurt people, but he made her.

Mina was glad she hadn't gotten a schedule today. Before, the tests had always bothered her, but she willingly did as she was told without hesitation. Now, she wasn't sure what she would do the next time there was a test.

She wanted to know something, though, that maybe the tests could tell her: she wanted to know the extent of her powers, what all she could *do*. She was fascinated with them.

There was, however, one element of self-discovery that completely befuddled her. While she had been in the shower, she had felt an odd tingle between her legs, and she had touched herself there, and it had felt....

She didn't want to think about that now.

There was something else   there was something far below her, a power, that called out to all those who would listen...

Kill me...

It was like ten thousand voices all at once, each one less than a whisper, and they all spoke slightly out of sync. It was enough to cause a dull ache in her head if she concentrated on it for very long. There was something beneath it, too. Something...indefinable. Something surging forth with power that didn't belong in this world.

And next to that, she could sense something else...it was like the opposite of the voices. It was a negative space that should have been occupied, but it wasn't. It felt so familiar, and it gave Mina the shivers if she thought about it too much.

What was it?

Sixty-Four:
Decision

Emma took the longest way back to her office that she could to afford herself time to think. She had several options open to her, none of which were completely without drawbacks.

The problem Emma was dealing with was one of conscience. As a scientist, she had always believed that her job was to remain emotionally unattached to her area of study. For some fields of study this obviously wasn't a problem. Geology, for one, didn't usually involve moral dilemmas and ethical gray areas.

But, Emma was in the profession of medical experimentation. It was a necessary field; without it, very few (if any) advances in the health profession would have been possible. But it brought with it a host of problems, for the single reason that the objects of the experimentation were living creatures. For most people, the only way for them to deal with this situation was to try and view the animals as no different from any other piece of laboratory equipment. The doctor had to distance him or herself from them, had to stop thinking of them as dogs or rabbits or mice but as Subject 1, Subject 2, and so on.

That was a lot harder to do when Subject 1 could carry out a full conversation.

There was always an element of human experimentation in medical advances; obviously, the first time any specific treatment was tried on a human being, it was technically experimental. But if the goal was to help people, then it was okay.

Right?

But Emma wasn't in the business of helping people, not as she looked at it. If the goal of NOD truly was militaristic in nature, then it could only hurt, not help. Truly, something…sinister…was going on here, but she had to toe the line. All she had to go on was her own suspicions and the scribbled fears of a man she in truth had barely known.

But the children! Keiko and Johnny were nothing less than an enigma. They had told her to trust in Hanin. And for some reason, Emma felt she could trust them far more than anyone else. So the only logical next step for her to take was to follow Hanin's lead. But, she had to do it in a way that wouldn't draw attention, because now more than ever, she knew the prices that would be paid.

It was time to see Project M.

Sixty-Five:
Date of Acquisition

A man's voice came through the receiver. "Yes, tomorrow. I believe she will be attending school."

Dr. Graley held her hand over the lower part of the telephone and motioned for a nearby subordinate to leave the room. "Go get Carlos," she said in a hushed voice.

"Yes, of course," she said. "And the fee—"

"Will be transferred to your account upon successful delivery of the subject."

"Good. Who is our contact at the institute?"

"A man named Jameson. He will contact you later with the drop point. Any questions?"

"No."

"Good."

Dr. Graley listened for the *click* on the other end of the line before she hung up her phone. Just at that moment, the door to her office opened and Leonard Dillons reentered with Carlos Gonzalez. They stood at attention.

"At ease."

"Carlos, I have an acquisition for you tomorrow. It will occur in residential Omaha, between three and four local time. I'll give you the details in a moment." She saw a glint in his eyes as he smiled. Not many others understood his thirst for missions like this one.

"As for you," she said, turning to face Dillons, "tomorrow will mark the inception of your squad into NOD as security guards. In a short time, all military personnel there will have been replaced by our operatives and we will be able to begin the final stage of the take-over. How's the leg?"

"Feeling much better, ma'am."

"Will you be able to function on it?"

"You betcha, ma'am."

There was a bit more to this conversation, mostly regarding the behavior and responsibilities Dillons must take care of to keep his cover, as well as the location and target information for Carlos' acquisition. When the three of them were through conversing, Dr. Graley dismissed both men, asking them to send in Marcus. Waiting, she passed the time in thought.

The beauty of the Black Army, the reason it worked so well, was its openness. In most military organizations, plans and decisions were made behind closed doors among a select few whose careers would profit at the expense of the grunts who carried out these plans. Rarely, if ever, did the grunts have any say in the planning of the missions they took part in, and rarely were they told the ultimate goals of such missions.

The Black Army was different. There were no grunts. Every soldier was highly trained—the best in whatever unit, organization, or cell that he or she had originated in. Every soldier taking part in a mission was encouraged to provide input during the planning portion. When a mission was successful, all those involved profited richly from it. That was the key to the success of Black Army missions and the loyalty of its operatives—the incentives were involvement and monetary rewards, rather than unexplained orders and the threat of punishments. Although, disloyalty did carry a steep price.

Ever since operatives had infiltrated the NOD infrastructure and learned of the goings on there, the leaders of the Black Army had been eager to gain control of the facility. The weapons, genetics, and energy research already in progress at the institute would be invaluable to a secretive group that was destined to play key roles in the high-tech wars of the twenty-first century. For the better part of a year a devious plan had been in effect wherein military officers that completed assignments as NOD security guards were replaced with Black Army operatives instead of US Army officers. The takeover would commence once all personnel had been replaced, which would be relatively soon.

The subversion of Nicholas Kresge had been instrumental in this plot. His brand of patriotism was different, to say the least, and he agreed with Dr. Graley as she did with her superiors. It wasn't really a coup, just a redistribution of profit and responsibility. Once the research at NOD was fully weaponized and ready to deploy, the advisory committee was likely to waffle on their usage, being that it would be, of course, technically illegal. Worse yet, they might spin off a shadow unit to take control.

Why take that risk when the Black Army was already in a position to do just that?

And, the Black Army could pay better than the US government proper; quite a bit better if necessary, in fact. NOD was such a stand-alone organization that it was incredibly easy to pull off such a stunt without anyone in power realizing what was going on until it was too late. If everything went as planned, no one would know what had happened even then.

Kresge was Richardson's boss, and everything Richardson was informed of came directly through Kresge. Kresge handpicked the officers to be posted as guards at NOD. Neither Richardson himself nor Kresge's superiors questioned his choices from their opposite sides of the system. As far as Richardson knew, every guard coming in was an army officer. And, Kresge's superiors were above being bothered by the specifics of his soldier assignments.

Everything was normal.

The takeover itself should cause no harm; it was a takeover in the loosest sense of the term, as the military would still have the same access and opportunities that they already did. Everything would operate normally on the surface. Richardson would be removed, leaving Kresge to take "command" of the facility. Any of its faculty that had a problem with this arrangement would be hushed up, one way or another.

The US military knew only two things about NOD: the money they put into it, and the reports they got out of it. As long as everything seemed normal, and money and reports kept flowing, they would never know that they were paying to finance and improve their own secret force. And when the moment inevitably came, when the underhanded, dirty tactics of the oppressed, insane, and ideologically monstrous became too much for the standard military, the Black Army would emerge as the only answer.

It was going to be a glorious, violent, and profitable future.

NOD was technically controlled by an advisory board; even "autonomous" organizations had bureaucratic red tape. But this board, even with military men sitting on it, technically answered to no one, and could easily be subverted, if it came to it.

Everyone in the Black Army knew of this goal, its benefits, and how they, as a whole and as individuals, would benefit from it. It was this kind of openness of knowledge and personal gain that made them much more loyal and successful than much larger, standard military organizations.

Of course, they had had plenty of chances to acquire useful technology during NOD-financed attacks on similar institutes in competing nations, and in some cases, they had. But nowhere else was as advanced as NOD.

There was a knock on the door and Dr. Graley stood as her son entered the room. He stood at attention in front of her desk.

"At ease, soldier." Marcus took a more comfortable stance. "I wanted you to know that Leonard is transferring to NOD tomorrow. Everything should be fine, but if a time for action arrives, it will be soon, and I want you at the front line."

"Yes, sir," was the eager reply.

Sixty-Six:
Egad

Emma clicked away at the keyboard in front of her. She found it almost amusing that although she had found no mention of the nature of NOD's generators among the files she had access to, all output data for them was very lowly classified. She pulled up a graph of energy output for the last two weeks and found that reactor "M" had indeed suffered a drastic drop in output during the period of Mina's attack, whereas reactor "RT" had not. Frowning, she read through the detailed analysis of output and noticed something very damning. During the period of M's lowered output, it had begun emitting otomo particles.

Otomo particles were a sort of calling card for psychic activity. They were named after the author of an anime movie and manga series from the 1980's that had been so dead-on about many facets of psychic phenomena that there was an ongoing debate among NOD staff members as to what the author may have truly known. Had he been trying to publicize knowledge he wasn't supposed to, or had he just guessed well?

In any case, otomo particles were important in detecting psychic forces. Although they were not always present during such instances, no other natural event had been shown to generate them. Highly specialized equipment was necessary to detect them, and as the readouts for M did not include levels for other, much more easily detected particles, Emma felt very sure that Hanin had personally set up the equipment to confirm his beliefs.

Also included among the information she was viewing was a detailed analysis of the facility's power consumption and production. The biggest consumers seemed to be the cryonics lab and the substations that maintained the portal to Nod. Emma thought it odd that they should be listed on the report, but guessed that since they were under the institute's control, it sort of made sense. Electricity and engineering certainly weren't her areas of expertise, but she could easily make a few key inferences. Arty was big but of course not nearly as big as a regular power plant; yet, according to the information she was looking at, it provided nearly enough energy to run the entire building. Just as the one file mentioning it had said, M provided much less power than Arty did, but when Emma looked at the figures listing the efficiency of the two beings she was awestruck. It only reinforced the idea that such a source of energy could be the cause of war, because nothing else on earth held this kind of potential.

Emma yawned and looked at her watch. It was getting late. She decided that tomorrow, for sure, she definitely wanted to examine M firsthand. It would be perfectly reasonable for her to want to do such a thing, given her job goal; she just had to think of a good reason to tell Richardson for why she knew about it. The one file that had mentioned it was so lacking in details it seemed a poor excuse.

She thought of Joshua—Richardson—for a moment. With all the hunches, suspicions, and ideas she had been having, he was starting to seem a lot less attractive.

Emma shut down her computer and put on her coat. She turned the lights off and left her office, locking the door behind her. As she walked down the hall, she thought that tomorrow she must also visit with Mina. The girl shouldn't be left alone to her own devices, and she might even provide some help to Emma now that there was credence to her story about Matthew.

In another room, on another floor, the very girl Emma was thinking of was having a difficult time getting to sleep, although she desperately wanted to. The cries and images of the dying simply would not leave her head, and she shivered from the terror of it all. Over and over again she was forced to replay the death scenes of the people she'd killed, and as horrible as they had been in the first place, her guilt made them worse. There was a murmur that ached in the back of her skull and she kept glancing around, paranoid, maybe rightly so. She wanted sleep as an end to thinking, as an end to reliving these horrors, but when such a time came that exhaustion forced her to sleep, she found her dreams to be even worse than her memories.

Sixty-Seven:
Thursday Morning

Crow awoke to the blaring of Raven's alarm clock. It was a noise that made her nauseous. She reached across Raven and turned off the sound, realizing as she looked at the clock that it must have been going off for the better part of an hour. "Oh, we're gonna be late," she moaned.

The air felt heavy, and as soon as Crow sat up, she winced as a sudden ache pressed on her temples. "Ugh, too fast," she said, wanting to lie back down. She shook Raven a little. "Raven? Hun, it's time to get up."

There was a snort, then a mumble: "Um seepy."

"What?"

"I'm sleepy." A yawn. Then: "What time is it?"

"It's late. We have to go to school now."

"Damn. Ugh. What the hell is the point of a suspension if they just take it away?" Raven got out of bed and stretched. She was wearing a white nightshirt and panties and Crow could see goose bumps on her long legs. She walked over to a window and pushed the blinds aside to look out. She rested a hand against the windowpane but pulled it away immediately. "Fuckin' cold."

Winter was in full swing in Omaha. The cold and snow often arrived as early as November, but it had been both colder and more snowy than recent years.

Crow walked over to the window, and looked out. She squinted, the sunlight off the fresh snow dazzling. "I need some aspirin," she yawned. Raven put an arm around her.

"That makes two of us," she said.

Sixty-Eight:
Dashboard Confessional

Emma felt as though she hadn't slept at all. She drove, bleary-eyed, through the new snow towards work, cursing every time the car fishtailed a little or otherwise went somewhat out-of-control. She had spent a good deal of the night lying in bed awake, trying not to think about things. She had tried reading several times but couldn't pay attention; she had turned the TV on but it was all infomercials; she had even tried doing a crossword puzzle but couldn't figure out most of the clues. "Genus of the true lilies? What am I, a scientist?"

Now, she was nervous. She knew what she wanted to do. She would tell Richardson the truth, tell him that she had been looking over data involving Arty and had found mention of another reactor, M, and was it also organic? And did he mind if she examined them? But she couldn't stop thinking about Carl and his grim fate.

What would she do anyway? What *If* Hanin had been entirely correct? What if the energy project and the biomorph project were sinister military plans that would do little else but invite oppression and bloodshed? Would she continue towards those goals? Would she go public with the knowledge? Would she sabotage everything?

"I'm a scientist, not a hero," she muttered, turning into the parking garage.

In the best situation, the goodwill of mankind would be served via her work. In the worst, she could help destroy mankind altogether.

But the truth of it was, as much as Emma feared such notions, her deepest worries (other than those regarding her own well-being) involved the fate of the subjects of NOD's (and therefore, her own) experimentation. It was wrong, all of it. She saw that now. A good paycheck and a blurry view of the "greater good" had shut her up for years, but now that the truth was spilling out like pus from a popped tumor, she realized the graduate student idealist in her had not entirely died. She truly did still want to help people.

She got out of the car, straightened her coat, and walked, slowly, towards her fate.

Sixty-Nine:
Visitation

Danny looked intently into Mina's brilliant blue eyes, thinking of the difference in them between *then* and *now*. Mina had changed.

Everything's about you today, he thought.

Is it? she asked, mentally pressing a puzzle piece into place. She could see that the puzzle had trees in it, and they were "real," like in the photographs from some of her books. *I am the Lorax. I speak for the trees.*

What?

Nothing.

They sat, minds quiet to each other for a time. Then, Mina asked, *What did you mean, everything's about me today?*

I saw the schedule. Everyone is supposed to keep playing like we have been. Except you. You're supposed to meet with Dr. Jacobson. He motioned for her to look at the space in front of him. He had spelled out "changes" with macaroni noodles.

Mina and Danny looked up suddenly, alerted by a powerful presence entering the room. They saw the guards at the door move to admit Keiko and Johnny.

Something's up, thought Danny. It was rare for them to make such an appearance.

They walked softly, slowly, precisely, across the room towards Danny and Mina's table. They were holding hands, and Johnny had a teddy bear pressed to his chest. They sat down, Keiko across from Mina and Johnny across from Danny. Mina saw them as never before, every line, wrinkle, and wispy hair brilliant and vibrant. She looked into their eyes, dulled by experiences but with an inner glimmer that could never be exorcised.

Another joins us today, came a thought, and it was impossible to tell which of the two had thought it.

Another like you, came another thought, as both children turned to face Mina.

Murderer? came Mina's panicked first thoughts.

No, dear, came a thought, as Keiko shook her head in an almost motherly way.

Older, like you, was the answer, and it came clearly from Johnny.

Be careful, suggested Keiko. *There could be interactions. Strong powers. We covered up once before, but this time, there will be consequences that no power on earth can hide.*

A prediction? Questioned Mina.

A fact.

This said, they got up and left, never having made a sound the entire time. When they had gone, Danny resumed playing, and said to Mina, *Something's going to happen, isn't it?*

Couldn't you hear, began Mina, but Danny shook his head. He spoke aloud, quite matter-of-factly.

"They weren't talking to me."

Seventy:
Briefing

"Sergeant Leonard Dillons." Joshua placed the paperwork on his desk and reached for a cigarette. "How's that leg of yours, soldier?"

"Great sir, thank you for asking."

Joshua lit his cigarette and took a puff. "Well, everything seems to be in order..."

He looked questioningly up and down the row and they responded, "Yes sir!"

"If you men will follow me...."

Joshua got up and prematurely extinguished his poorly timed cigarette. He looked at the five men in front of him, each dressed in green and brown fatigues, each carrying a duffel bag. He thought momentarily of the carnage that had taken place earlier in the week, then, dismissing that thought, he led them out of his office.

They walked quietly down the hallway and to a small out of the way elevator. This, they took down several floors, getting off into a small foyer with potted plants, several benches, end tables, and a reception counter. Besides the elevator the group had entered the room on and the door to the reception office, the room also had doors leading to two bathrooms and what appeared to be a large freight elevator.

Richardson walked over to the counter and spoke quietly, the soldiers in the room unable to hear him. After a few moments, he said, "Come on," and motioned for them to follow him over to the large elevator door. Using a keypad, he opened it, revealing that it was in fact a freight elevator. The six men got on, and with a pneumatic *whoosh*, it led them down three more floors, into a narrow but very high-ceilinged room. They got off the platform.

"Doors to your right lead to your quarters," said Joshua, motioning off to the side. "The armory's that way. We'll go there first." He turned to the left and started walking.

"What's in there, sir?" asked Dillons, pointing to two huge doors that occupied the entire wall directly across from the elevator."

"Top secret weapons stuff—don't worry about it," replied Joshua, thinking, *Why do so many of them ask questions? What's up with the army these days?* Dillons, however, just smiled behind his back.

He led them into a white hallway with several doors on each side. They went into one on the left. The room inside was stark white with several glass cabinets containing various firearms and ammunition. A white table in the center of the room was covered with neatly arranged handguns, assault rifles, name tags, and key cards. "Everyone, take a gun and a rifle, a name tag, and a key card."

They picked up their guns, checking the balance, the sights, and the ammo. Dillons picked up his card and looked at it.

SGT DILLONS, LEONARD (Security)
CLEARANCE LEVEL 1

He sighed. He knew it couldn't be otherwise, but he hated being at the bottom of the ladder.

"The rest of your stuff—ammunition, radios, and armor, as well as a packet for each of you explicitly detailing your duties and rights—is in the next room. A full briefing will be held there in exactly..." Joshua looked at his watch. "...twenty-seven minutes. Until then, I suggest you go over the information provided."

He led them into the next room, which looked like a much smaller version of a lecture hall complete with a projector and screen. The front most table had five seats and five sets of gear. A rack at the rear of the room, near the door, had five sets of body armor attached to it.

"The head of security will be here shortly, but I wanted to take this opportunity to speak with you five directly." He looked and sounded damn serious, and everyone gave him their full attention.

"Whatever they told you to make you take this job was not true. Your mission is not to guard against terrorists, spies, radical activists, the president's dog, or whatever BS They told you. This is not a prison though after what you may see you might wish it were that and nothing more." He leaned forward dramatically onto the table and looked each man into the eyes in turn before continuing. "You five are here to protect this institute from itself. The matters we deal in are dangerous and occasionally violent. Lethal force is inadvisable but unless you are told otherwise, it is authorized. Do I make myself clear?"

"YES SIR!!"

"Good," said Joshua, calmly standing straight and heading to the door. "Someone will be along shortly."

After he had left, one of the men turned to Dillons and began to speak. "So, do you think—"

"*Shh!*" interrupted Dillons. He pointed at the wall, then at his ear. The message was clear: *The walls have ears.*

"Sorry."

Within a short time, the briefing began. None of it was anything the men couldn't have learned via inside operatives. It was all mediocre stuff, just shift schedules, patrolling routes, security and safety guidelines, pay info, and leave schedules. After about forty-five minutes of this, the head of security led them into an adjacent room. It was also dazzlingly white, with glass gun cases and a glass and steel table in the center of the room. On the table were several bizarre guns. There appeared to be two types: One long, black, and roughly tubular, tapering to a wedge-shaped point. The other was like a shorter version of that one, with a thick cable running from the handle to a black backpack the size of a car battery.

The security head spoke. "For the next week you will be practicing with these, after which you will each pick one of the two types as your own PLF."

"PLF?" questioned one of the soldiers.

"Personal LASER Firearms. They come in two types. This longer one has its own power source and is good for three or four shots. There is a setting that allows all of its power to be used in a single shot, although this usually damages the weapon." He motioned for them to pick them up, to get a feel for them. Dillons thought that the weapon was horribly balanced—most of the weight was in the butt of the gun—probably the battery. Still, he thought it shouldn't be too hard to use, because he figured it shouldn't have a recoil.

He practiced holding it out as if to fire. *Pay dirt*, he thought.

"The other one," continued the man in charge, "has its power source in the connected backpack. It's good for twelve to fifteen shots but the backpack is quite cumbersome so I suggest you choose the rifle. This model is best only in emergencies. You fellas are lucky—right now you're the only squad with these. They arrived less than an hour ago."

"Can the power be discharged all at once?" asked one of the soldiers.

"It has two settings, but tests have shown that discharging ALL of the power has a tendency to…ignite the battery."

"Oh."

Dillons wasn't listening. He was looking down the sight of the rifle, thinking, *This is so cool.* "What's the lethality of this weapon?"

"Depends where you shoot. Accuracy is of prime importance. Your target won't have time to move after you squeeze that trigger. But fire at the wrong spot—it'll hurt like shit, like a goddamn fire inside, but the beam will cauterize the wound it makes, and depending on your target, he might not slow down at all."

Seventy-One:
Stupid Boy

Raven and Crow entered the classroom just moments before the bell rang. Both girls had dressed rather plainly, being late to awaken. Raven had wanted to braid her hair in long pigtails but there just wasn't time. She was wearing a shoulder-less green sweater over a black tank top and form-fitting blue jeans. Crow had thrown on some of Raven's clothes; a fuzzy orange sweater over a pair of loose khakis.

They quickly sat down next to each other in their seats in the rear of the room. Both realized as they did that they were on the receiving end of several awkward glances, a premonition that someone was about to do something that would be, at the very least, annoying.

It wasn't more than a few minutes before Raven was passed a drawing of three stick people in very vulgar positions. One had red hair and was obviously Crow; another had brown hair and slanted eyes and was obviously her. The third was a male, judging from the simplistic stick-and-circles dick it had. It seemed to be pushed into Crow's…stick-ass. Raven looked over in the direction the note had arrived from and groaned.

Tom fucking DelFranco.

"This is genius," she muttered to herself sarcastically.

Without caring or even knowing what the teacher had been saying, Raven shot her arm up into the air and interrupted her. "Ms. Hatcher, someone passed me this note and I'm not quite sure I understand it, could you explain it?"

Expecting the worst, the teacher walked over to Raven's desk and took the piece of paper from out of Raven's outstretched hands. A look of disgust crossed her face as she looked at the picture. Throwing her arms out in exasperation, she cried, "Honestly, can't you people grow up!?" She stormed back to her desk and tossed the picture into the garbage. Raven looked back and smirked at a very red-faced boy.

"So that's what was on the paper?" laughed Crow as she and Raven left for their second class. "Who sent it?"

"Him, as a matter of fact," answered Raven, pointing to the angry-looking boy who was fast approaching them.

"What do you think you were doing back there? I could've gotten in trouble!" Tom was livid, but the girls knew all too well he was capable of little more than posturing.

"And your point is?"

"You're a freak and you know it. Nobody likes it."

"Come here," said Crow, dragging him towards a group of senior boys she knew fairly well. Raven followed. "Hey, guys. Me and Raven here are in a relationship. We totally make out and stuff all the time. That bother you?"

"No," said one raising his eyebrow incredulously.

"That's...pretty hot," said another, as he laughed out loud.

The first turned to face Tom. "You giving them trouble?" He was a lot taller than Tom. To the point of instant intimidation.

"No," Tom said, looking down at his feet.

"Well, you better not. Crow and Raven are cool. You got a problem with them, you got a problem with me."

"Yeah, no problem." Tom ran off like a dog with its tail between its legs.

"Thanks, Chuck," Crow said.

"Yeah, you bet." He smiled and turned back to his friends.

Crow and Raven walked away. "Color me impressed!" said Raven.

"Art geeks. We got each other's backs."

"Why is everybody so stupid?" said Raven.

"I know. Nobody can even think up a good insult these days," said Crow, changing the nature of the insult. They giggled. "Although, that blow-up doll thing was kind of funny, you have to admit. At least from their side, I mean."

"America effing loves lesbians. What the hell is wrong with our school?"

"We're totally hot, too," said Raven, laughing.

"Yeah, what's not to like?" said Crow, laughing as well.

Making fun of themselves raised their spirits a bit.

By and by, they passed two students engaged in a fierce lip-lock in the middle of senior hall. Briefly, they stared at it wondering why that was considered okay in public if they usually weren't. Raven gave Crow a quick smooch on the cheek.

"I guess anything goes now, huh?"

Seventy-Two:
Absolute Terror

Mina sat across from Emma. She looked quite pretty, although very tired.

"Rough night?" asked Emma.

"I had nightmares. About…." She hesitated.

"Mina," said Emma sincerely, "I want you to know that we—that I—don't blame you for what happened." Although her original speculations had been that Mina had been biding her time, she was now thoroughly convinced that this entity called Matthew was behind the catastrophe and that Mina was just an unfortunate victim.

Mina put her head in her hands and tears escaped from her eyes. "I just keep seeing it, over and over…"

"I'm sorry," interrupted Emma, feeling bad for doing so, "but can I see your palms?"

Mina held her hands out.

"I thought so," said Emma. "Your ID tattoo is gone. I hadn't thought of that before, but it makes perfect sense."

Mina quickly hid her hands under the table.

"Don't be ashamed, Mina. The power you possess that allowed you to remove those markings is something to be proud of."

"It's not that," said Mina, shaking her head because she thought the truth was completely obvious.

"Mina," said Emma in her best attempt at a calm, motherly voice, "I know you have a lot on your mind. We can talk about it if you'd like; in fact, I want to. I want you to know that you don't have to feel bad about telling me anything, okay? I just want to do a few tests first."

"Tests?" asked Mina hesitantly.

Emma responded to her unspoken fears. "Don't worry; I just want to do some simple ones, nothing painful." Even so, Mina fidgeted nervously as Emma reached into her bag under the table. She sighed in relief when the doctor produced nothing more dangerous than a deck of large, white cards. She dealt them out into five equal piles as Mina patiently watched, a blank expression on her face. Picking the first one up, but not looking at it, she opened her mouth but was cut off.

"I can't do that," Mina said flatly. "I'd have to look at it just like you."

"Oh," said Emma. "How about if I look at it?" She turned the card so she could see it: wavy lines. "Well?"

"Star," said Mina. Emma turned the card around, showing her the actual picture. "I was going to guess waves first; they're my favorite."

"So you can't read minds," said Emma.

Mina's thoughts came flooding into Emma's head, accompanied by a dull ache. *No, but I can do this. And it doesn't hurt anymore.*

"Oh," Emma said sheepishly as she winced slightly. "Well, I guess we should just move onto the next test, all right?"

"You want to know what my 'powers' are, right?"

"Well... yeah."

"I'm pretty sure I've figured them all out. I can just show them to you, if you want."

"Um, okay, I guess." This wasn't really how Emma was used to doing these things. Usually, the subject just sat there and followed directions. But, usually, they were drugged up. Emma suddenly realized that working with Mina now was like talking to a normal person, whereas working with one of the other subjects was like...well, it wasn't like a normal person at all.

But all of them were, underneath the drugs and conditioning, weren't they?

This isn't right, thought Emma. *What have I been doing with my life?* She gathered the cards up into a single stack, consciously hiding her worry from her face.

"Please set the cards on the table," said Mina, and Emma obliged.

Mina rested her elbow on the table and laid her head in her hand. She looked at the stack of cards and slowly the top few rose up into the air and began to spin around each other in tight circles.

"That's a definite 'yes' for telekinesis," said Emma.

Mina's eyes followed the path of the cards as she sent them zooming away from the table. Emma felt rather nervous as the cards started moving quite quickly back towards Mina. Prior to them hitting her, however, a soft, yellowish glow surrounded the young girl. Several cards impacted it, bending as they ricocheted off; a few others merely bounced away, and the last two actually bounced off Mina herself, having passed through the shield as it faded.

"Aurakinetic shielding, definitely. It's closely related to telekinesis; both are the result of alterations in the density of your aura. Given that you can do both, it's likely that you can also levitate by forming a layer of solidified aura beneath your feet."

"I'm nervous about trying that. I think I can; I know I was floating when I...." She averted her vision as the sickening memory of her actions came back to her. Emma seemed to understand and quickly changed the subject.

"What I'm really interested in is your ability to quickly heal from injuries." Emma had an unpleasant flashback as well; it was the attempt at exploratory surgery that had left everyone involved feeling like a butcher. "Can you explain it at all?"

"Not really. I can show you."

"Are you hurt?"

Mina just closed her eyes and put her arm out, underside up, fist clenched. One of the cards rose up into the air and floated several feet away. A look of fierce concentration appeared on her face; as the card began rocketing towards her arm, Emma realized the expression wasn't born from the discipline needed to move the card, but rather the discipline needed to inflict injury upon oneself.

The card ripped across Mina's outstretched skin, not cutting too deep, but still drawing a line of blood across the pale girl's forearm. She winced at the stinging pain but held her arm rigid. Emma watched as the pulsation of the blood flow reversed and the cut closed up cleanly.

"Do you have to make it happen?"

"No," answered Mina, opening her eyes and withdrawing her arm. "It just happens by itself."

Emma wondered something. If Mina's body could constantly repair itself, and eliminate any and all toxins it absorbed, did that mean she was immortal? Or would her body still run down and die, perhaps faster than normal people because of the stress of healing constantly?

"There's one other thing I want to know about. Are you aware that your body is slightly different? That you…look slightly different."

"Yes. I'm…." she hesitated. She looked at her arms; her pale skin was flawless. There were no imperfections anywhere. No moles, no stretch marks, no birth marks. It was as though her entire body had been resurfaced. Her eyes were a deep, brilliant blue, though that was from the lack of the medications that deadened her.

Her muscle tone had improved. Even her breasts seemed fuller, more symmetrical.

Emma just nodded. "I have my theory. First, do you have any ideas?"

Was it Matthew? No…. Was it me? But not consciously….

"I think…it's my healing. It's shed my skin and replaced it. It's…improved my…."

"…physique," Emma guessed. "That's more or less what I think. It's complicated, but…."

How could she say this in a way that Mina would understand? Or should she even tell her at all?

"Surely, you notice, how the other children look sickly and never seem to grow, right?"

Mina nodded.

"You aren't like them. Your body was older when you became…*special*, I guess. It may just be that your powers are, well, *determined* to maintain and improve your health and form. Or, it may just be the way your healing factor works. I'm not sure. Or..."

"...or it could have been influenced by Matthew," Mina hazarded a guess.

"Maybe."

The whole concept of sexuality was something Mina was just beginning to pin down, but she wasn't completely sure she had it right. Out of the cloud of medication, however, her young mind was racing to catch up with her older body. She knew the mechanics, but the only practical experience had been a terrifying, violent assault on her mind and body.

Matthew was clearly frustrated and furious. She cringed, remembering how he had touched her. There was no way that was how such a thing was supposed to be rightly done. Perhaps his buried sexuality had manifested in her?

In the end, it seemed a moot point. Emma knew it was a question that would likely not be answered without a lot of research into Mina's abilities, and it would probably be one of the least important pieces of information she could glean from her.

This had been the most Mina could remember talking in quite some time. She barely knew what she was saying until the words fell out of her mouth, as concepts and notions clicked into place rapidly.

"When M-Matthew first touched me I could sense his frustration. It was all around him like a shell. It felt like he'd been reaching out for things all his life, and everyone had been holding them back."

Of course, thought Emma. *Hanin's notes indicated that the medication did not work on him, so he was always questioning things no one would tell him about. Like his past.*

Mina opened her mouth as if to say more, but then hung her head, almost shamefully.

"This is important, Mina. I know you don't want to talk about any of that, and I don't blame you, but I need to know everything I can to prevent it from happening again."

"When he r-r-" the word was forced, "raped me, I didn't understand it all then, but I think I do now. It wasn't about... sex, it was about control."

It always is, thought Emma. *Even when it is about sex.* That wasn't really fair; her failed relationships had no bearing here.

Emma knew without a doubt that there had been no physical presence in Mina's room when the incident had occurred, but she did not in any way doubt Mina's interpretation of events.

"Until Matthew did what he did, you couldn't do the things you can do, could you?"

Mina shook her head "no." Emma knew that there was a rare phenomenon wherein one person could unlock another's abilities. Keiko and Johnny had been that way with each other.

"When he was there it was like being hit with this force…everything hurt, but everything opened up…I can't really explain it." She looked at the bent cards, scattered on the floor. "It used to hurt to move things," she said absentmindedly.

"Can you tell me anything else about this force?" asked Emma.

"I don't know," said Mina. "It was like a surge of thoughts that came without words; it made my head warm and tingly. I could feel it passing through my body."

Nod energy?

Tears came to Mina's eyes. "I think I still feel him, Dr. Jacobson, all cold and clingy and hating me for getting away," she sobbed.

"What do you mean? Where!?" asked Emma, alarmed.

"He's there," answered Mina, pointing to the floor. "Down there."

Seventy-Three:
Mooch

Raven tossed back the small paper cup and sucked down its contents. Leaving the office, she walked beside Crow and the two of them started heading towards the cafeteria. "Honestly," she said, "I think I'm old enough to take my own damn medicine." Crow nodded her head in agreement, and the two of them went the rest of the way to the lunchroom in silence.

Once they had bought lunch (over-salted French fries, ranch dressing, and off-brand citrus soda pop,) they sat down at their usual table. It wasn't long before a smallish boy carrying an overloaded black backpack came to join them. All of his clothing was black: he had black tennis shoes, black jeans, and a black long-sleeved shirt with a white cross on. His fingernails were painted with black polish that had cracked and peeled in spots. "I am *so* Goth," he said as he stole a few French fries.

"Whatever," said Crow, giggling. "Weren't you trying to be 'glam' last week?"

"I don't like to talk about that," the boy said solemnly. "It didn't work."

"I remember when you were just a nerd," said Raven. Changing the subject, she asked, "So what's your name this week?"

"You may call me by my given name: Samael, dark lord of chaos." He stole another fry.

"I thought it was Samuel, evil cashier of the Maxi-Mart," corrected Raven.

"Whatever," he said, stuffing his mouth.

Some things, thought Crow, *never change. Unfortunately.*

"You are so weird," said Raven, shaking her head.

"That's why you love me."

"Yeah. Whatever. I just wish you'd buy your own lunch for a change."

"You're always saying this stuff goes right to your hips." Sam took a chug of her drink. "You guys want to do something after school?"

"Sure," answered Raven. "But we have to stop at Crow's house first and I promised my mom I'd pick up something at the store on the way home, so just meet us at my house around four, okay?"

"Okay," the boy agreed. "You want to get high?"

Crow and Raven looked nervously at each other. Crow spoke. "We're trying not to do that anymore."

"Bummer. Well, we can go see a movie or go to the mall or something."

"Sounds good," said Crow. "Do you have to work tonight?"

"I have the night off. The Den of Infinite Evil that is the Maxi-Mart will have to get by without me." He grabbed more of Raven's fries.

"Cool," she said, then, looking at her mostly-eaten lunch, she sighed, and pushed the Styrofoam tray over to the boy. "Just finish it."

"Thanks."

Seventy-Four:
Reaper

There was a knock at the side door. Mrs. Yamada opened it to see a Hispanic man in jeans and a green hooded sweatshirt smiling oddly at her. His hands were in the pouch in the front of the sweatshirt, and he appeared to be wringing them.

Her eyes narrowed suspiciously. "Can I help you?" she asked.

"I'm afraid not," the man said, shaking his head. "I'm afraid not."

Seventy-Five:
Shutdown

"I don't see why not. Anything you think can help you with your work is fine with me."

"Well, I was reading a paper on the biomechanics necessary for harvesting Nod energy, and it seemed as though this 'M' reactor was much more refined than Arty. So, I figured if I studied its chemical and cellular functions, I'd have a better idea as to what I should be shooting for."

"I had meant to show you 'M' after showing you Arty, but after your experience I thought it prudent to save it for another time. You have full clearance to examine it yourself; the guards by Arty can direct you to 'M.'"

I guess there was nothing to worry about here, thought Emma.

"Another thing, sir—"

"Joshua."

"—Joshua—I understand that 'M' is not very large? I was wondering if I might have it moved to a laboratory for analysis?"

"Under these circumstances, I can allow it, but keep in mind most staff members do not have clearance to view it. This will, of course, require deactivating it, so I will phone ahead."

"Offhand sir, do you know who does have clearance to view it?"

"At this time, only you and Jameson. I will have him accompany you."

Figures, thought Emma disgustedly.

"Is there anything else you need?"

"Nope."

"All right then. I'll have Jameson meet you at the elevator."

Emma left the office presently and Richardson notified Jameson to accompany her and report anything suspicious. He thought, though, that while Emma's inquisitiveness could prove to be a problem, at least now she seemed to be on the right track. After several minutes, there was a knock on his door and Jameson himself entered.

"I wondered if I might have a word with you before I left with Emma?"

"Of course. What did you need?"

"Any idea which DNA sample I'm supposed to use?"

"For what?" asked Richardson.

"For the Process," Jameson answered in a voice that clearly indicated that he thought the answer was obvious.

"How so?" said Richardson as he leaned forward, eyes narrowed.

Jameson held up some papers he was carrying and pointed at them. "Didn't you read these?" Richardson shook his head and Jameson rolled his eyes. "The initial steps of the Process involve the addition of psionically positive sample DNA via a neuron-affecting vector such as mutated HSV-1 into the brain itself. There's multiple vectors and multiple alterations, including chemical and radiation dosages, but that seems to be the start of it. A spinal probe is also involved, I think to carry the mutations down the entire central nervous system, but honestly, I'm not sure." He seemed flummoxed at this last point.

Richardson lit up a cigarette and leaned back in his chair, both intrigued by this information and annoyed by Jameson's lack of ability and belief that he, Lieutenant Colonel Joshua Richardson, AKA not a scientist, should have the answer.

"I had no idea it required an outside source. I always thought that the Process brought out innate abilities alone...." His voice trailed off. "Of course!" he cried, slamming his fist against his desk. "The test subjects aren't individual results of the same experiment; they're steps in it!" He took a long, satisfied drag.

"So it's a breeding program," said Jameson, suddenly understanding it as well. "The genetic mutations caused in one subject are used to create more mutations in the next."

"And that's why Hanin wanted a natural psychic for the next subject. The genetic pool was becoming too diluted. He needed a new source of raw DNA to thicken the mix."

"Forced evolution? I suppose then that the DNA should come from the last subject."

"Not necessarily, because we've often had multiple ones created at once. My guess is that Hanin may have had multiple 'evolutionary branches' going at the same time."

"I could use Mina's DNA. Her DNA has changed slightly, since the, er, event, and she's fully psi-active now."

"I think," said Richardson, "that that seems like a viable plan if nothing else should prove to be a better choice."

"One more thing, if I could?"

"Yes?"

"It would've been nice if I could've had access to these sooner," Jameson said, in an impolite and unprofessional tone, as he shook the papers he was holding. "The Process is really very complicated."

"Go see Emma now," Richardson scoffed, not about to be chastised by an inferior.

Some time later, Emma headed in silence down to the generators.

She glanced nervously at Spencer Jameson. He was as unpleasant to look at as he was to work with. His sharp cheekbones, sunken cheeks, and prominent widow's peak, as well as the slight hunch he walked with, gave her the impression of a vampire from the classic, black-and-white era of monster movies.

In short, his looks fit his personality as a weaselly fellow with a big mouth and not a lot of talent. There could only be one reason for why Richardson had appointed him to be Emma's second: He was watching her. Carl had been the most qualified; most of the staff had been more qualified than Jameson.

The thought of Carl brought a tear to Emma's eye, but Jameson seemed not to notice, too intent on whatever it was he was thinking about. Soon they reached the series of doors that would lead them into Project M's room. Entering the last one, Emma was surprised to find that it was nothing like Arty's room. It was a clean, white room, completely devoid of the organic nastiness that had identified Arty. People she had never seen before walked around with clipboards and white lab coats, going from monitor to monitor, sometimes sitting down and typing something, sometimes not.

A man with a nervous sort of look came over to Emma and shook her hand. He spoke in a hushed, hurried, absentminded sort of way. "Yes, well, Dr. Jacobson, of course you wouldn't be needing that bio-suit, didn't they tell you? M is this way, follow me, we've already begun to deactivate him, would you like to view him before we finish? Of course."

"Yes, I suppose so," said Emma, confused, as she followed the man to the rear of the room. There was a large white, rounded protuberance from the wall there, maybe eight feet tall. It had three sections that appeared as though they could open by sliding away from each other; one on either side that connected to large mechanisms, and one that seemed as thought it could open up into the ceiling.

"The portal room's right nearby, doctor, have you seen it yet?" The man seemed very proud.

"No, I haven't," said Emma.

"Well, it's 'absolutely restricted during use, so I'll just show you on the monitor." He led Emma and Jameson away from the three-part door toward a nearby monitor. He showed them a very high-definition view of the portal room, a sight that amazed Emma. It appeared to be a large room, but Emma didn't realize how large until she noticed a tiny door in one corner that appeared bug-sized compared to the view as a whole. A vast ring of soft yellow light sat, floating in the center of the room. Hazy rays arced away from it, becoming invisible a short distance away. Emma figured they must be the crossing ley lines, visible due to the high energy created by their proximity to one another.

In the center of the ring was what appeared to be a black sphere. Bolts of some form of energy constantly arced between it and the yellow torus. Directly above it was the tip of some wavering, tentacle-like structure.

"What's that?" asked Emma, pointing at the tentacle.

"Here, let me show you," said the man, zooming in on it. Up close, it still looked very much like a tentacle, save that it seemed to have some sort of maw on the end. Three large, tusk-like appendages stuck out from the end, a fleshy sheath covering them almost to their tips; it was like a three-sided pyramid with spikes sticking out of the base. As it gently swung from side to side, Emma could clearly see some sort of matter being sucked off of the black sphere, only to disappear into the maw.

"What is that?" asked Emma.

"That's Arty's tendril," said the man, eager to explain. "Energy is sucked into it from the portal, then converted into a usable power source in the distortion chamber above. The bulk of Arty sits in the room above that."

"The distortion chamber?" spoke Jameson, for the first time. "Doesn't that create intense vibrations?"

"Yes," said the man at the monitor. "The video correction is on now, let me show you...." He flipped a switch and the on-screen image became blurred as if the camera were being shaken very quickly. He flipped the switch again, and the image cleared up.

"What's that?" asked Emma, pointing to a round-tipped, slightly pointed structure that was also aimed at the black sphere, just above the yellow ring. It looked inorganic in nature.

"That houses Matthew's tendril," said the man.

"I'm sorry, what did you say?" asked Emma.

"I said it houses M's tendril," the man said nervously, and then muttered something to himself. Getting up, he started walking back towards the door they had been near earlier. He was speaking quickly now, with an awkward look on his face. "Shall we?" he said towards Emma and Jameson. Then, to someone else in the room, he said, "We're going to retrieve M now. Begun the shut-down sequence for Arty and prepare the lift elevator."

He led the two scientists over to the three-part door and opened it, revealing a long, white tunnel. "If you'd like," he said, "you can go on ahead now. I have to finish the prep work before I join you."

Emma and Jameson went ahead. Once the door had closed behind them and they had walked down the hall a ways, Emma spoke. "Did you know about them?"

"Not at all," answered Jameson. "They weren't part of the main staff, that's for sure."

After a bit more walking, the hallway gave a shudder. An automated voice came through speakers on the ceiling. "GENERATOR SHUTDOWN COMPLETE."

"I guess it's safe then," said Jameson, shrugging.

After a couple of turns and a one-floor descent, the two came to a door covered in warnings that was labeled "Project-M Generator Room. No Unauthorized Entry." They went in.

The room was no bigger than an average laboratory, although the ceiling was a bit higher. Standing in the center was a beige, cylindrical object that could only have been M.

It was between six and a half and seven feet tall, with slightly angled sides that terminated with a shallow curved cap that topped the object. It appeared to be scaly, as lines like cracks covered it in large, polygon-like shapes. The shapes seemed to be lined with fine hairs. Running around the entire thing in a spiral from top to bottom was a raised protrusion of flesh covered in a line of holes. Emma could see the protrusion expand and contract and reasoned that the holes might be for breathing. All in all, the structure was not nearly as disgusting as Arty, but was similarly disturbing in its bizarre alien organics.

Connected to M's base was all manner of tubes, wires, and mechanisms, which were in turn connected to a large device labeled, "Life Support." Emma had just walked over to examine it when the door opened and the man who had been speaking with her earlier walked in.

"Sorry," he said, "I never introduced myself. You can call me Jon." He shook Emma and Jameson's hands roughly. "I know who you two are. We know who all of you are."

"Really..." began Jameson.

"I'm sorry, that must have sounded funny. I mean, my staff is familiar with the names of all of the research scientists."

"Forgive me for asking, but just who is your staff?" asked Emma. "I wasn't familiar with any of them."

"We work here and at the substations," answered Jon. "We monitor and maintain the generators and the ley line network."

"Oh."

"Anyway," said Jon, moving over to M, "if you look at the ceiling above him you'll see posts that line up with the holes around the base. The posts descend and connect to the holes, and the whole structure lifts up into a dedicated elevator shaft that leads right up into M's normal laboratory. You two can ride up with it, if you like."

"No thanks," responded Emma, not wanting to be stuck in a closed-in space with this *thing* for any amount of time. Or with Jameson, for that matter.

"Well, his connection with the portal has already been severed. I just have to retract the tendril." Jon walked over to a monitor and began hastily typing on a keyboard. "Everything you need to know has been sent to the lab above. You know which one, right?"

"Yes," said Jameson.

"Good." There was a clunking noise accompanied by what sounded like slithering beneath the floor. "The tendril's been retracted. It's beneath the main structure. If you need to examine it, you'll have to raise M off the floor."

"Tendril…." Jameson muttered.

After Jameson and Emma had left, as they walked down the hallway, Jameson looked over at her and said, "That spaz called the generator 'Matthew.' That's the name of the boy Mina said raped her."

"Yes."

"What did he mean by that?"

"Beats me."

"You're not telling me something."

Emma couldn't resist. "I don't have to. My clearance is higher than yours. Anyway, let's get up to the lab. We've got work to do."

Seventy-Six:
Cut Off

The cold closed in as the steam escaped. Matthew could sense it…the other world was falling away and there was nothing he could do about it. She was there, he knew it, but too strong for him to take right now. He couldn't slip through before it was too late because he had nowhere to go. And the behemoth, the Gargantua to his Pantagruel, the 'Arty,' it just mumbled as it sucked space through its stupid mouth.

The sphere that cycled in and out of this meta-cosm was intact, but destination-less.

SOMEONE HAD REMOVED HIS FUCKING BODY!!

And all he could do was wait, wait for the glimmer of hope that it would be reconnected, and that he could escape, for the third time, and this time, do things right. For Anna hadn't worked, when he'd still been terrestrial, and Andrew hadn't worked through the portal, and Mina hadn't worked through the portal, for they had fought back, and if they had been less strong of mind, he could have succeeded. He knew a word that meant this, and it meant success, if ever he could attain it.

That word was "Angel."

Seventy-Seven:
After-School Plans

Raven walked up to the door to her home and moved the bag of groceries she was holding from one hand to the other so she could reach her keys. "I'll call Sam when we get inside," she said to Crow. She tried to unlock the door, but it already had been. "Oh," she said and pushed it open.

"Mom, I'm home," Raven said, putting the bag on the table. She opened the refrigerator and put a gallon of milk inside. As she continued to put away the items in the bag, she saw Crow take off her coat and walk into the hall in the direction of the living room. Momentarily, she completed her task and reached for the phone. She punched in Sam's phone number and held the receiver up to her ear, but heard nothing.

"What?" She hung the phone up, then listened for a dial tone, but there wasn't one. "Mom," she complained out loud, "did you skip the phone bill again?" She walked into the hallway and started heading toward her mother's room, but a noise in the opposite direction made her turn around. She walked into the living room, and—

"Don't move."

If the gun had been pointed at her, she probably would have risked it and ran, but the fact that it was pointed at Crow forced her to hold her ground. Crow was struggling in the man's grasp, but he seemed to have no trouble holding her. Whatever he'd done, he'd done it quickly and quietly, for the girl was both bound and gagged. He pushed her to the ground violently, (she went "mmph!") and he pressed his handgun hard up against her temple. Crow managed to kick him as he did so, but all he did was smack her hard on the head with his firearm, knocking her out.

The entire time, Raven was trying desperately to scream, but her lungs were as empty as a dead man's, and her legs had turned to jelly, forcing her to slide down into an awkward sitting position. It was like a bad dream where something was chasing her, and no matter how hard she tried to run, she just couldn't move. Abject terror was a feeling she had rarely, if ever, dealt with.

With Crow unconscious on the floor, the man was able to aim his gun at Raven without worry. "You can either come over here so I can tie you up, or I can shoot you," he said.

But, she did neither. She ran—not to the side door, and possible escape, but to her mother's room, and certain doom.

"Mommy! Mommy?"

She thrust the door open and fell down, panting and sobbing, her hands pressed against the wet carpet, the blood squeezing up between her fingers. She tried to grab the doorknob to pull herself up, but her hand slipped off. She clutched her heart, staining her clothes red, and gasped for the breath she felt would never come.

The man was behind her now, but he wasn't advancing. He was relishing the moment.

"Just one cut across the throat is all it takes. The bleeding doesn't stop until there's nothing left to come out." He reached over Raven and grabbed her dead mother's head by her hair with his stained, gloved hand. The blood stuck to her face where she had been lying in it, and her hair was matted against her cheek. Her lifeless eyes gazed uselessly into the distance.

The man dropped her back onto the floor (the noise was a combination of "splotch" and "thud") and said, "Your brother's on the other side of the bed, if you want to go look." But she wouldn't. She just kept staring at her mother's dead body, until there was a cold impact against the back of her head, and everything went black.

Dreams and nightmares scare the waking self into momentarily believing they're real, until the moment passes and clarity returns. Real-life horrors grip the heart and stop it, forcing it to wait…

And wait…

And wait…

For the moment of clarity that never comes.

Part Two
Joining Paths

Seventy-Eight:
Of Machines and Men

Emma stared intently at the monitor before her. "This is amazing," she said as much to herself as to Jameson. "You know, most power generators take energy from environmental sources and use it to move water in some form or another over a turbine, which is what really generates the electricity. But M and Arty are more like photovoltaic cells—they directly convert Nod energy into electricity, without any turbines—no middlemen, so to speak."

She didn't really care if she was saying things Jameson should hear or not. He doubtlessly knew at least as much as she did about the energy project, seeing as how he had clearance to view the reactors.

From behind her, she could hear the steady breathing of the mammoth organism, as well as the voice of Jameson. "Those X-rays should be ready by now if you want to bring 'em up."

"Just a minute..." she began. Then: "Wow." The information she had been looking through about Project M apparently included an exhaustive study of certain areas of the biomorph program that she had not seen elsewhere, either in the files she had access to or in Hanin's personal notes. Specifically, the information pertained to the methods necessary to convert a being into a structure capable of generating electricity from Nod energy.

"These predictions are amazing...if Hanin's vision could be realized... wow." She swiveled around, took off her glasses, and chewed on the end of the temple bar. "What were you saying?"

Jameson shook his head out of irritation and said, "I said the X-rays are probably done now."

"Oh." Emma spun back around in her chair and manipulated the onscreen data, bringing up several white-and-black images.

"It's amazing...such regular structure...not at all like Arty." The X-rays showed the cylindrical shape of M supported by a grid-like skeletal frame, with a thick column in the center that was likely at least in part, bone. As Emma examined the images, her eyes narrowed as she noticed a blotch of white near the structure's base on one side. "Hey Jameson, do we have another angle on this area?" she asked.

"I think so," he said, taking over mouse control. After a few seconds, he'd found it. "Here."

The image on the screen brought back the revulsion in Emma's thoughts by reminding her that the bizarre creature behind her had once been a human. At the bottom of the creature was the partial skeleton of a teenage child, the skull and spine fused with the main skeletal structure, the arms and legs appearing to have grown into the grid-work of the being. Empty, white eye sockets stared accusatorily at her. "I want to see it," she said.

"What, that? Emma, we can't just cut into it and have a look around. We could damage it."

"Why not?" she retorted, mumbling, "That's what we did to Mina." Jameson heard her.

"This isn't the same thing. Mina's abilities may be promising, but she's just a subject. This thing is like a finished project."

Emma narrowed her eyes. "How much do you know about what it is we're doing here?"

"I know," he answered, pausing, "that a form of energy exists that a psychic mind can harness, via certain bodily structures, and turn into a source of electricity. I know that Mina's powers of healing form the basis of those required to create the aforementioned bodily structures via bio-morphism. And —," he paused again, "I know you don't like me, but we're work partners, so you might as well get over it."

"Well…" began Emma. She was going to address Jameson's last point, but decided not to. No sense in being childish.

"Look at this readout of brain activity," she said instead, bringing up a graph of several wavy, horizontal lines. "All of this coordinates with autonomic brain functions and everything required to keep a body alive, but nothing more." She was absent-mindedly scrolling the graph backwards, into the past, coming across a point where the lines appeared scrambled, with a couple heading into the scramble and not coming out.

"I thought it wasn't supposed to have any higher brain functions," said Jameson, pointing at the extra lines on the graph.

"It's not…you know, the timing of this blurry spot would approximate when it was shut down and disconnected with the portal. I wonder how far this thing goes back…" She began scrolling the graph further and further back in time, until she reached the morning of Mina's possession. Immediately before and after the event, the graph showed a period of very high brain activity. During the event, it showed no such activity, just as it showed following the disconnection of M from the Nod portal.

"If I didn't know better," said Jameson, pointing at the screen, "I'd say that showed the brain functions of a normal—well, a normal psychic—brain."

"Mm-hm," Emma agreed, obviously deep in thought.

"Do you know something about this?" asked Jameson. Before Emma could answer, an announcement came over the P.A. calling Jameson to go to the service entrance on the first floor.

"I wonder what that's about," he said, leaving the room with an air of disappointment. His leaving gave Emma time to worry. How much did Jameson know? Did he have access to the report Hanin had mentioned, the one that theorized the link between Anna and Matthew? If he did, would he put together that with Mina's testimony, Jon the tech guy's slip of the tongue regarding M's name, and the data that had just been viewed? Honestly, connecting all of it seemed like a stretch for Jameson, Emma felt, but the uncertainty was worrisome. Actually, she wasn't sure why it would bother her if Jameson figured it out or not. Jameson was just a watchdog sent to see if she was working for or against Richardson and NOD itself, to see if she could handle the mountain of sometimes horrific information she had just received without cracking either morally or because of stress. As far as Richardson should be concerned, every step she was taking was forward, so what did it matter if Jameson figured out what M was?

As it was, M was a danger and Emma had to report her findings one way or another. She just needed more data first so she wouldn't have to credit the secret scribblings of Dr. Hanin. Those were best kept hidden.

As for proceeding with the work she was supposed to be doing, the sheer potential of M and Arty intrigued Emma so much that despite her reservations about its true purpose (military or otherwise), if there were a way to proceed without hurting anyone else, she would like to continue the studies.

After all, what scientist doesn't want to change the world?

The key was working with something that *couldn't* be hurt. Hanin had written of a being named Angel that had been created with no conscious mind. While he had been concerned that Matthew could use it for his own purposes, Emma believed that with M disconnected from Nod, such an occurrence was no longer a threat. Perhaps when she had learned more about M, she would pursue study of this Angel.

Emma had already begun going over some of Hanin's notes (the ones Richardson had given her.) It seemed truly that the groundwork for the Nod energy project was fully laid out—the only thing left was to actually *do* it while avoiding catastrophe.

Unfortunately, certain experiments in biomorphism seemed necessary to perform to gather data. Unfortunately, the only possible way to do those without involving the uncertainty of Angel was with Mina. Self-healing involved a changing of the body that was the cornerstone of biomorphism, which in turn was a cornerstone of being able to generate electricity from Nod energy. Unfortunately, the only subject that possessed even an inkling of such power was Mina (not that Emma was eager to subject any of the children—Mina included—to anymore harm.) But, she was in very deep.

Emma was all too aware that all of the tests into biomorphism with prepubescent subjects had resulted in unstable forms that deteriorated the subject or caused death. Only post-pubescent Matthew had obtained a stable from, which was right behind her…

"Fuck!" Emma yelled, practically having a heart attack as she turned around.

"Did I scare you? I'm sorry." Benny stared up at her with nearly-colorless eyes.

"Benny, you really shouldn't be here."

"That's Matthew, isn't it?" he asked, ignoring her.

"Yes," she said, not thinking. "Now, can I take you back somewhere?"

"Mark my words," he said, with a voice that seemed to come from somewhere other than his mouth, "this one will only be trouble. One of us sits unfinished, open to attack. Beware."

"Angel?" asked Emma, thinking of the stored kin to Matthew that Hanin had mentioned in his writing. But it shouldn't matter, with M deactivated….

"The message has been delivered," said Benny in his own voice. "Keiko and Johnny said we might have a new friend after today." Saying this, he descended through the floor, leaving Emma all alone, staring at the gentle breathing motions of the abomination that was Matthew.

Seventy-Nine:
Cover-Up?

Steve Phillips opened the door to his house, freshly-bought, used school books gripped under one arm, grocery bag full of supplies held by the other. Setting the bags down, he was about to take off his coat and pet his dog (a large white mutt named Candy,) when his mother, sitting on the couch holding his baby sister, told him with a sad tone in her voice to come watch the TV.

"Well," said the chubby officer on the left, "at this point the missing girls are our top priority, as they are our prime suspects for this brutal slaying."

The image of the cop and the reporter on the TV was replaced with two poorly taken school photos with the captions "Raven Yamada" and "Maria Fischer" beneath them. The voice-over, provided by the female reporter, said, "Again, viewers are urged to call the number at the bottom of the screen if they have any information about the whereabouts of the missing girls or know anything at all about the murder of local woman Molly Yamada and her son that occurred earlier this afternoon."

The image returned to that of the officer and the reporter.

"What can you say about the reports of an large, unmarked black work van seen in the vicinity of this neighborhood earlier today? Might it have something to do with this crime?"

The police officer calmly responded, "At this time we can neither confirm nor deny such reports. However, all of the evidence so far points toward the daughter and her friend as the culprits."

The reporter faced the camera and spoke. "Thank you, Officer Schuman. Now, to speak with Sam, a local boy who discovered the…"

Steve heard no more. He got up, went upstairs to his room, shut the door, and screamed.

Eighty:
Delivery

Carlos Gonzalez leered over his seat into the back of his van. "You know, you girls are probably on the news by now. Poor little girl, prime suspect in her own mother's slaying. Ran away with her BFF. Am I a genius, or what?"

Raven looked at the blood all over her hands, and thought of the knife that the man had covered in her fingerprints. She glared at the evil man with pure hatred in her eyes; staring until his face was scratched indelibly across her mind. She would not, could not, forget his face. If she made it out of this alive, she would hunt him to the ends of the Earth if that's what it took.

That was *if*; that was *then*. *Now* was a different story.

He had bound her, but not her mouth. She wanted to scream, but anger wasn't enough; fear was stronger. A life, her life, Crow's life, might be the punishment for any indiscretion, and by this point, her spirit had all but completely broke, and the man knew that, and she wasn't willing to risk anything more.

"Can you believe your mother actually asked me to do her a favor? Right before I cut her, she said 'Are you going to kill my baby girl?' and see, I don't like to lie. So I say, 'No, ma'am.' And she says, 'Please, please tell her to find her father!' Can you believe that?"

"Don't taunt the subject," came a voice from outside the van. Raven tried to get up to her knees so she could see out of the front door. She glanced at Crow lying beside her, still out cold. The Hispanic man got out of the van and began speaking in hushed tones to the man outside. Raven could only make out so much.

"…cer Jame…"

"…at's me. Do you ha…"

"…two."

"…two?"

"…gured, what the hell…"

Footsteps approached the rear of the vehicle and the sudden light pouring in as the doors were flung open made Raven squint her bloodshot eyes. When she became accustomed to the light, she could see that the man looking down at her had slicked-back hair and a pointy mustache. He looked like a rat in a lab coat. "Well," he said, "I guess I can use her for raw data. And as a guinea pig, huh? But you don't need to know about that, ha!" He stared down at Raven's tear-streaked face. "It won't be so bad," he said to her, "A whole new life awaits you!"

She glanced around frantically as she was pulled from her position and down a hallway. She looked around, sweating, as the walls slipped by in running daubs like a melting Van Gogh painting. She heard herself cry out as something hot came up her throat. Confusion set in, and she asked her mother, "Who is that, mommy? Is that blood on all those people?"

Raven lost it—stress, angst, hatred, heartbreak, misery, hallucination, and confusion—and blacked out.

Eighty-One:
The Process

Spencer Jameson watched as the last of the girl's pretty brown locks hit the floor. There was a click, and the whirring of the razor ceased. He looked from one bald head to another, dismayed at the bruises on both of them. "That motherfucker, there'd better not be any brain damage."

He was relieved, at least, that the primary subject, the Asian one, had been conscious earlier. The other one had remained unconscious since they had arrived.

He glanced over at the vomit-covered lab coat he had tossed into one corner. "Goddamn that girl was freaking out," he mumbled, referencing the seizure he had witnessed earlier. Turning his head side to side, he grunted in disbelief at his bizarre surroundings.

Most of the machines were sleek and modern, white plastic and stainless steel. As it had luckily turned out, there were several "seats" so he was able to tend to both subjects at once, rather than having to keep one subdued while the other was worked over.

The participant was clearly not intended to move during the procedure. There was a number of adjustable shackles, two for each limb, a belt for the waist, and a shackle for the neck that was intended to be fastened very tightly and used to support the neck and head at a very specific position.

It was not so much this contraption that had confused him so much, it was what he had seen on the way back to this room.

The leading hallway had had a legitimate brick arch doorway with the phrase "APPARATUS PSYONIQUE" in tarnished metal across the arch. The walls beyond were covered in a hellish combination of old computers, chemistry sets, next-generation electronics, and industrial revolution-era mechanisms. Pipes and valves led off in all directions behind it and to the sides, sections of them bent at funny angles and divided in odd manners. Wires and tubes spiraled around the structure and its components. Strange gurgling and beeping noises emanated from deep within.

The low light and strange surfaces gave an impression of filth and dinginess, but on closer inspection, everything was just as clean as anything else in a hospital laboratory. Spencer Jameson had the distinct feeling that he was being joked with; that all of this rubbish in the hallway was, merely nonsense, intended to give a steam-punk/electronic atmosphere to this area which was in a very real way the nexus of NOD. It was as though someone on the staff had had a large amount of time to fool around

Here he was, now, in the room at the end of the hall, in a lab like any other.

Several large artificial sequencers worked silently, slowly building through chemical reaction and organic process the DNA he was going to need to inject into the girls.

It would be infested into their brains and spines using the HSV-1 Herpes virus variant as a harmless vector. Speaking of that, there was a separate mechanism that was at this moment fabricating the delivery system, which seemed to exist of a cap of ultra-sharp, durable needles.

The whole thing made him quite queasy.

The problem...the only real problem was, the spinal injection. It had to be done manually. It was an absolute blessing how well this machine had been made, how brief the written instructions were and how useful the onscreen commands were. He'd honestly had a harder time making a dog tag at a touch-screen kiosk. However, these sort of things...he was under no false pretenses that his medical techniques were anything but sub-par. He'd gotten by on subterfuge, spying, tattling; he was good at determining who needed to know what, and how to go about getting that information. He could spot leadership, or at least ambition, from a mile a way, and it was his livelihood to make himself important to that situation.

Jameson stepped away from the girls and headed toward the mechanism's control panel, checking the status of the DNA preparation. He began the process that infested it into the transfer vector. He heard a noise behind him and looked back at the two girls, sheathed bald-headed on operating tables. One of them stirred slightly but neither awoke.

Leaving the console, he walked back to the table, producing a long hypodermic needle from his lab coat as he did so. He pulled the sheath off of the needle and tapped it a few times, squirting a bit of its contents out to remove air bubbles. He injected the primary subject first. Reaching into his pocket for a second needle, he repeated the process and had just finished injecting the other girl when she woke up.

"Aaahhhh!! Raven! Raven! Wake up! Help! Get help! Aaahhh!!"

Raven stirred, and groggily turned her head towards the noise that had awakened her. Why was Crow bald?

"Whazza ellskoing on?" she slurred.

Jameson took a fairly solid kick to his thigh, inches from his manhood, and cursed himself for not double-checking the shackles.

"Crow...kekkk the shet ooww...." Raven blacked out from the medicine.

Crow tried to take in her surroundings as tunnel vision began to set in, aware that only her feet were free. She flailed them towards the man, who looked increasingly blurry, though he had backed out of reach.

Everything was white and steel, but that too blurred...

Jason Chmielewski

She thought she was yelling, but it was barely a whisper.

"No! Raven! Wake up! Wake up!" Crow started sobbing.

Raven looked over at her, her head wobbling, a trail of drool reaching down to her chest, not even sure she was looking at Crow, seeing only a peach blur without the usual mane of fiery red hair.

"Love 'oo."

Hallucinating was a bitch. Sleep would take it all away.

It was at his point that something buried deep down inside Jameson made him hesitate, and he might have even contemplated stopping what he was doing had there really been a way out at this point. But he was a doomed man, a man marked by Old Scratch himself; he'd sold his soul long ago. There was no real resistance left in him.

Crow was still sobbing as Jameson lowered the framework above her head. "W-what are you going to do to us?" she choked out. Her breathing was beginning to feel labored and she was getting very drowsy.

The medicine was finally starting to take full effect, he noticed, because she was no longer fighting back as he fixed the shackles on her feet. "I'm going to make you a better you. You'd be better off if you'd just relax."

Jameson watched Crow's eyes slowly shut as he pulled the metal framework above the chair down further and reached inside of it, placing the interior cap firmly on her head. He walked over to the control console and pushed several buttons, then turned away as the framework automatically tightened around her head and unceremoniously and barbarically cut into her head and screwed itself onto her skull.

"Jesus...." he muttered, shaking his head. He may have been a shell of a man but he still had gag reflexes.

Jameson walked over to the primary subject, Raven. Save for their bruised faces and chrome domes, both girls were really quite attractive. It was a shame what he had to do to them. He was a creep in the bed but he didn't consider himself abusive.

He quickly dismissed such pointless thoughts and smiled, something that made him look worse than normal because of his sunken cheeks.

He returned to the main control console and saw that one batch of the vectored artificial DNA was ready. He might as well start with the secondary subject as a test run, as she was expendable anyway.

He picked up the spinal injector from the counter and sighed. Here, the otherwise good, concise instructions had been reduced to hasty scribbling in a steno pad.

He crossed his fingers.

A mere forty-five minutes later, Spencer Jameson stood in front of Joshua Richardson and gave his report.

"Of the two subjects, I regret to inform you that the secondary subject did not survive the Process."

"What was the cause of death?"

"Um, I'm not actually sure as of yet; any number of factors could have resulted in this outcome. Her body is being prepared for autopsy presently."

"Well, she was unexpected anyway, so no harm, I suppose. And the primary subject?"

"Is alive, sir, but as to the effectiveness of the treatment, it will be some time before the mutations set in and we can begin testing."

"I shall make the announcement to the staff regarding the presence of a new test subject in the morning," said Richardson, leaning back in his chair. "Until then, keep me advised."

"You bet," said Jameson, all-too happy to be leaving Joshua's office. He turned and quickly exited, his head held low, not out of guilt, but out of self-deprecation as he berated himself for screwing up.

Spencer Jameson knew what had killed the secondary subject. *He* had. The damn instructions were complicated, so complicated, scrawled onto a steno pad in a manner befitting an illiterate madman. He couldn't really be blamed, could he, could he, because after all, it wasn't like he really knew what he was doing.... He didn't know that the spinal probe had to be manually aligned and *just so*, and that if he didn't do that he ran the risk of completely severing the spinal cord....

He just didn't know.

Meanwhile, on a level so biologically small no one could have known, the living force that was Mina's DNA fused itself with the Asian, the Raven, the Black Bird that Brought Omen. It sank into her, judiciously choosing its work as would a sentient entity. Far beyond the brain it was intended for, it sank in, creeping down the young beauty's spine, insinuating itself into the core of her being, her uterus, her Fallopian tubes, her ovaries, her ovum. It knew its own path in existence, and like two negatives making a positive, it worked its way in, someday, someday, to make a grand statement out of the grotesque injustice of its presence. For sometimes, rarely, when important to the grand scheme of things, evil can bring about hope.

Eighty-Two:
Hot Damn

Leonard Dillons ("Sergeant" Leonard Dillons, as it were,) was mildly annoyed. Although target practice with the laser guns had been fun to begin with, the lack of sound and recoil stole any sense of tactile enjoyment quickly.

He wasn't used to this much inactivity and this little conversation. He had just finished patrolling the same white hallways for five hours. Walking back and forth, back and forth, he had lost count somewhere around sixty. His leg (the one that had been broken) was sore (maybe it was psychosomatic, who knows) and there was very little he could do about it.

He had to wait several days before he had leave of the Gates Building and could check in with HQ. Until then, he had to bide his time with boring, repetitive activities. He knew he was one of the new guards, but he had hoped he would at least get to guard the armory or be stationed on the floor where all the little psycho children stayed. But instead—

"Hey! Dillons!"

"Yes, Captain Davis?"

"Report to the guard house on 45. Guess there's a new patient that needs guarding."

"Yes sir!"

Well, at least now I might be able to do some good spying, Dillons thought as he got up.

Eighty-Three:
God Dammit

"Why the hell wasn't I notified?"

"Well, you were busy with M, and Jameson is certainly qualified, so I didn't want to disturb you."

"I'm sorry, Joshua, I just think that as staff head I should be present when the Process is applied to a test subject, especially since I do not as of yet have any practical experience with it."

"I'm sorry, Emma, I'll keep that in mind next time."

"Thank you. Now, may I see the new subject? And, do you have any information about her that I may need?"

"I'll have everything sent to your office. In the meantime, what I can tell you is that preliminary tests have shown that this subject, Raven, may have strong psychic inclinations. As such, she may be valuable to general studies, at the very least. Have you had any luck with M or Hanin's notes?"

Emma had had more luck than she cared to relate. "In a nutshell: In order for a psychic to draw energy from Nod, certain changes in body structure must occur. Apparently, the ability to change one's own body has its roots in the ability to heal one's own body, which is why I think Dr. Hanin believed Mina to be important to this project. Although, this puzzles me, because to the best of my knowledge, Mina did not manifest any healing powers during Dr. Hanin's time here."

"Anyway, it seems that outside means were necessary in order to alter M's and Arty's bodily structures so that they could draw energy from Nod. They had the innate ability, but needed an added stimulus, although truth be told I have not read far enough yet to know just how such a transformation was stimulated."

"Work with Mina should hopefully provide insight into how the aforementioned 'bodily changes' can come about in such a manner as to provide easier, better,"—she almost said *safer*—"more powerful reactions with Nod energy."

"That seems like it should about sum everything up," Richardson said. "What are your plans now?"

"I'm going to split my time between M and Mina. Mina's abilities seem to make her—more *aware* than the other subjects, and I believe that a personal touch is needed to keep her in line, so to speak. I've prepared some stimulus reaction tests for the rest of the staff to carry out with the other subjects. Fairly standard data gathering. Oh, and I'd like to see this new subject as soon as possible."

"You can see her right now if you'd like, but I should warn you that

Process records indicate it may be some time before she manifests any abilities. Her room is next to Mina's if you'd like to see her."

"Yes, I think I'd like to."

"Anything else, Emma?"

"No, sir."

"Please! Call me Joshua!"

"Sorry, Joshua." Emma didn't like referring to people she disliked by their first names. And, with each passing revelation, she found that she disliked Lieutenant Colonel Joshua Richardson more and more.

She left his office, heading for the women's bathroom. She avoided the mirror, feeling like her face must be covered in worry- and stress-lines after a week in hell like this one. A violent massacre, a dominated girl, a murder, and now this new subject, some girl taken from god-knows-where and subjected to god-knows-what. Was she an "acquisition?"

Joshua paged Jameson as he lit up a cigarette.

"Yes?"

"Don't let Emma know about the...failed subject. She doesn't need to worry about messy details like that."

"Understood."

Eighty-Four:
Damned

Mina was laying side ways on her bed, breathing heavily as she tried to straighten out herself and the world in general. Many, many concepts that she didn't even have names for were now assaulting her head.

She had always hated the tests the doctors performed on her. Now she had a second thought-that the doctors didn't have any *right* to do what they did.

They were *wrong*.

It was just like when the Once-Ler destroyed the Lorax's forest—he had no *right* to do it, but Mina couldn't express in words why. But she knew it was so.

She felt—the best word she could think of was *cramped*—in this room, in this floor, in this building. It made her twitchy and she frowned. She wanted to see "outside," but not just because she wanted to see what it looked like. There was another reason, but she couldn't name it. She knew if she tried hard enough, she could break through all the walls and people in the way until she was "outside," but somehow that was wrong. Or, maybe...it was just scary. Outside was all unknown. Here was—well, it was terrible, but it was known.

But if the doctors were wrong for what they did to her, was it still wrong for what she could do to them? Every time she thought of this, though, she remembered what she had done, and how terrible it made her feel even she knew it wasn't her fault.

She couldn't hurt people again, even if it was for her own good.

She rolled onto her face and spoke quietly, "What would you do?" as she thought of the emanations that always rose from deep below. Then she noticed something.

He—Matthew—was gone.

Eighty-Five:
Darkness

She sat in darkness, arms bound to her front, shaking her head slowly back and forth. A thick line of drool hung from her mouth, but she didn't realize it and wouldn't have cared if she had. She rocked forward and backward, muttering, "red hair, red hair," over and over again.

Something was missing.

She couldn't see it but the tile floor in front of her was cracking seemingly of its own accord.

"Pass out," she mumbled, feeling compelled to say that as a familiar pain came to her head. But she didn't pass out.

Cracks spider- webbed across the entire floor, even going under the door and out into the hall beyond. And the pain kept coming but the inner darkness never did. But the outer darkness was there, and wouldn't cease its empty existence.

"Red hair, red hair."

She tried to focus on a spot in the darkness—her eyes were playing tricks on her in the inky blackness and were making specks of light and color for her to see. Every where she looked, it was straight ahead, and even as she tried to focus it moved off to her side, because her head kept moving.

It was making her mad.

Tension built, and suddenly a soft, orange-yellow glow enveloped her, and for an instant she could see, and was happy. Then it vanished, and she forgot.

"Red hair, red hair."

She sat in darkness.

Eighty-Six:
Tabula Rasa

"Thank you—Dr. Jacobson," the man—"Sgt. Dillons"—said, as he handed Emma back her ID card and stepped aside.

She nodded to the guard and used her card to open the door in front of her. It opened into a small alcove with a second card-reader and door.

She paused a moment, wondering about the extreme level of security, when right next door, Mina's room didn't even have a door, just a curtain. But, given what had happened.... Then again, it might just be a precaution for newly "created" psychics. She was under no false pretenses though that any of these security measures really meant much in the face of such power these "children" had.

She slipped her card through the reader as the first door closed, and the second door opened into darkness. From the light of the smaller room she was in, Emma could make out a bed in the middle of the floor and a moving shape beyond the foot of it, seemingly rocking forwards and back. Was that the new subject?

"Hello?" Emma said as she fumbled for the light switch. Her hand ran into a hole where the switch should have been. She fumbled around for a second, and found a penlight in her lab coat. She briefly examined the hole and saw that cracks led up from the floor into the wall and seemed to have caused the section of the wall with the switch to actually fall out, as a chunk of plaster was visible on the ground below. Cut or torn wiring was visible in the hole. "What?" she mumbled, confused.

She heard her still, rocking, rocking.

Emma went back into the smaller room and looked for a panel on the wall. When she found it, she opened it, and flicked a switch labeled "Emergency Lighting Bypass." She walked back into the other room where fluorescent ceiling lights were starting to come on.

The bed was ahead of her, against the wall to her right. It seemed to be speckled with pieces of plaster, as did the floor in general. Cracks crisscrossed the floor and led up the walls and onto the ceiling. Evidently, they were the cause of the plaster on the ground, as the cracks seemed to have caused bits of the ceiling to fall off, as well as pieces of the walls. The chunk containing the light switch and the wiring was clearly the largest of the pieces.

Of course, it was not this damage that Emma was primarily concerned with. It was the girl who was bobbing back and forth at the foot of the bed. She was squinting, not yet accustomed to the lights being turned back on. She couldn't even cover her eyes, Emma noted, because of the straitjacket she was wearing. "And they just left you here like this?" Emma questioned, speaking out loud to herself. She walked over to the girl, bits of tile and ceiling crackling under her shoes.

The girl looked up at her. Her eyes and skin color gave away a lineage that was at least in part, Asian. She was probably even attractive, but the multiple stitched puncture wounds on her head, not to mention the huge bruise, made it hard to see her in a context other than "injured."

Something suddenly dawned on Emma. "You're a...teenager," she said, surprised.

"She's missing," the girl said with difficulty.

"Who's missing?"

"Red hair."

Red hair? Her mother or sister, maybe? Emma felt horrible not knowing where this innocent girl had been torn away from.

"You're pretty," the girl said.

"Thank you," said Emma, leaning forward and placing her hands on her knees. "Your name's Raven, right?"

"*She* was pretty," the girl said, and began sobbing. Without warning, the ground began shaking slightly, and cracks started spreading out from under her in all directions across the floor.

"So you *did* do that," said Emma as she backed away nervously.

Raven resumed rocking forward and backward, sobbing as she cried "red hair" over and over again. The lights flickered as ceiling bits fell down all around the room. Her rocking became quicker and quicker, and she was leaning farther and farther, and sobbing louder and louder, and....

Emma ran back over to her and quickly pulled a shot out of her pocket. She had a quick flashback of the incident with Mina, her hand, and the sedative, but she quickly put it out of her mind as she bent over and studied Raven with one hand. She used her mouth to remove the sheath, tapped the hypodermic lightly, squirted it, and then injected it into an exposed part of Raven's arm. Within moments her movements slowed and the room calmed down.

Emma tried to carry such a shot on her at all times. Most of the staff did. Situations like this demanded it. It was unfortunate that nearby supplies had run low during Mina's escapade...

"It'll be okay," Emma cooed, putting the sheath back on the shot and pocketing it. Seconds later, Raven was unconscious.

"I think it's safe to say you're telekinetic. But I thought it was supposed to take awhile for psychic phenomena to appear?" mused Emma. *I wonder if her mannerisms are a side effect of the Process?* She continued, in her head. *Will they disappear in time?*

Next door, Mina sat with her ear to the wall, trying desperately to hear something, anything. It wasn't just the shaking of the room that had alerted her; she could feel something, *someone*, of great power nearby. It felt the same way she did, and that scared her at the same time as it gave her a glimmer of undefined hope.

That night, Raven dreamt everything that had ever scared her as well as everything that ever could. She saw her and her mother, standing amidst a sea of red as a floating man struck down those around them. She saw her father, yelling, as a woman ran by. She saw a vast pillar of skulls and rotting, festering death rising out of the center of Omaha. Everything she'd ever imagined, she saw that night. And, when she awoke next morning, she remembered none of it. She was quickly losing all concepts of who she was and where she came from, and had no care to remember. Drugs were administered; they helped the transition of Raven Yamada into Raven X, empty vessel. Even the red hair she had seen so vividly during the night was quickly fading from memory. Dreams and emotions curled up and died; desires and derision fell away; identity and self-worth were hidden.

Control was achieved, much faster, much more completely, than anyone who didn't understand the drugs would have thought possible. Indeed, for many who did, the effectiveness of the medication was simply scary.

Maybe Mina had been drugged up for too long; even in her self-cleansing state now, she couldn't remember "before." Raven still had fleeting glimpses, but they too would soon die out completely and be no more.

She was almost—*almost*—a blank slate—tabula rasa.

Eighty-Seven:
Night

No one slept well that night. Mina slept a tentative sleep, her mind too busy to allow a defenseless state to take over. Raven slept an intensely troubled sleep, one of nightmares that were all too true, though she was comfortable, as Emma had removed her straitjacket and laid her in bed.

Emma slept wracked with worry and guilt over the stitched-up child who was waiting for her undivided attention, a young girl who cracked the floor through her own angst.

Richardson did not sleep. He often spent nights awake in insomnia-creating worry, fearful anxiety that he would wake the next day with no job. And then, if he was no longer deemed worth running NOD, why, with everything he knew....

Carlos also did not sleep—he spent the night with his wife, having the most invigorating sex he had since   well, since the last time he killed someone in cold blood.

Conversely, Marcus tossed and turned all night, not used to sleeping without his wife right next to him.

Dillons was kept up by his leg, which still hurt.

Even Jameson's sleep was troubled. He kept waking to the image of Crow, spasming, as something he'd done wrong, horribly wrong, had damaged her spinal cord beyond recovery, his goddamn twitchy hands turning the spinal probe into a spinal mutilator. In a fit of sheer panic, he cut her carotid artery, letting the life spill out more quickly from the convulsing girl than it would have otherwise.

Actually, only one person slept soundly that night—but it was a sleep from which she'd never awake—a cold, endless sleep of lost days and unfulfilled promises, the lies of future moments stolen away in one quick, stabbing gesture. Ironically, it was perhaps Crow who was the best off.

At least she would never feel pain again.

Eighty-Eight:
Friday Morning

Emma led Raven down the hallway, toward the playroom, where she would get the girl's medicine from the adjacent office.

The cocktail of drugs and sedation that Raven was on, being new to her, played havoc with her sense of balance, and she walked with difficulty, like a child who has just recently figured out how. Each step was wobbly and stunted, and even though Emma was holding one arm to steady her, Raven periodically held her other arm out to try and help her balance. She would also periodically scratch the stitches on her scalp and neck, but Emma kept telling her not to.

"They won't heal if you keep picking at them," Emma said, catching her scratching her head once again.

"S-sorry," she stuttered, reacting more to the tone than what was actually being said. The guards in the hallway tried their best to keep their eyes aimed ahead, but many couldn't help but stare at this damaged girl.

They went into the playroom, and Emma sat Raven down at a table and told her "not to scratch" while she went to get her medication.

Raven scratched. She realized this, and mumbled "sorry," to herself.

Mina walked over, with Danny tentatively following her.

"It was you, wasn't it?" asked Mina. "Next door?"

"Big boobs," said Raven, pointing at Mina's chest. She started laughing, but it quickly devolved into sobbing. She put her head down.

"Thank you," said Mina dryly. Was it sarcasm in her voice, or just annoyance? But when Raven started crying, Mina felt bad and sat down next to her. "What's wrong?"

The other children in the room were staring at Raven—not because of the way she looked (Anna's head was worse but they were too used to atrocities to stare at even her) but because she was *grown*. The air was abuzz with mental whispering.

Raven stopped crying, and slowly turned to look at Mina again. She was wearing a pink tee shirt and a pair of fitted white shorts. She had found both in the bottom of her drawers; she had never had reason or command to wear them before and in fact did not even know they were included in her mostly drab, utilitarian clothes. She had worn them specifically out of a growing urge to break up the drab boredom that blended each day into the next. None of the scientists she had passed in the halls had told her to change or even commented on the breach of normality, though she did get a few surprised looks. As she left her room to go get Danny, though, she caught a curious smile from Dr. Jacobson as she entered the next room. The children didn't seem to notice in the slightest, of course.

The clothes struck her as "cute"—nothing more—and that was why she had chosen them specifically. And though they were not actually revealing, they did nothing to hide her physique from Raven (or anyone else, for that matter.) And, at this point, Raven did take a moment to more closely examine Mina.

She was incredibly petite, no more than a couple inches above five feet, but with a perfect hourglass figure that was very voluptuous for her small frame; buxom, with a narrow waist and healthy hips and thighs, gentle, curvy calves, and slender arms with delicate hands. Her nearly-porcelain skin was flawless and almost seemed to glow from within. All of this, of course, in the sensual sense, was completely lost on the heavily drugged Raven.

She had a beautiful, round face with full cheeks and full lips and a short nose. Her long blond hair was parted on the left and she wore bangs swept to the right across her forehead. By far her most prominent facial features were her large, blue eyes, radiant as a deep, sun-lit lagoon, that seemed to carry an air of otherworldly sadness regardless of the expression she wore. Long, graceful lashes added to the sense of deep emotion she seemed to emanate unconsciously.

Raven *was* able to appreciate this; the recognition of faces was deeply seated in the mental workings of humans, and a part of her was able to recognize how stunning she was.

To an extent, at any rate.

"Y-you're c-cute," she stuttered.

"Thank you. You're cute, too," said Mina, who knew it was so, beneath the bruise and cuts. She had a pleasant shape to her face and good features, but Mina was saddened by the lack of any spark in her otherwise attractive brown eyes.

"T-thank you." Raven tried to remember who else was cute, but couldn't. She scratched at the back of her neck.

Mina sat, taking in all that this girl was. She could feel it, the same power she had felt last night, although it was much weaker now.

Another joins us today, another like you, they had said.

Be careful, Keiko had said. *There could be interactions. Strong powers. We covered up once before, but this time, there will be consequences that no power on earth can hide.*

There was a kind of meshing, a kind of syncopation between the two girls that Mina was dimly aware of.

Interactions?

Afraid to do so, but unwilling not to, Mina held her hand out towards Raven, and—

"Raven? We can go now. Oh, I see you've met Mina."

Mina hesitated as she looked up at Dr. Jacobson, standing above them with a small tray of medication in her hands. She balanced it with one arm so she could reach out and help Raven up. Mina withdrew her hand, cursing herself for being so slow, and watched the doctor and the girl walk away.

Emma took Raven to a laboratory where Jameson was waiting. As they walked, Emma kept glancing down at Raven, watching as her eyes slowly seemed to be closing from the depressants in the medication.

Docile.

They reached the lab and entered; Jameson seemed frantic.

"Umm, Emma, can you watch Raven a little longer? There's something I need to see Richardson about."

Emma wasn't going to take his words at face value. "If it pertains to our work here, you should speak with me first."

"Uh, that won't be necessary, thanks."

He was fidgeting. "There's something you're not telling me."

"And there's plenty you're not telling me. Look, someone has to stay with her, and we can't take her up there if both of us go."

And he walked out, leaving Emma behind.

Jameson was almost running when he reached Richardson's office.

Not as though a couple minutes will make much difference, he thought to himself.

He knocked and entered without waiting for a response.

"—good news, then?"

"Why, I—Jameson?"

He panted for a second, catching his breath as he looked from Richardson to the uniformed man in the room and back again.

"—sorry, sir."

"Is something the matter?"

"Possibly, yes."

Richardson looked over towards the other man. "Could you leave us alone for a couple minutes, Nick?"

"Certainly. I'll be in the hallway." The man in uniform left quietly and closed the door behind himself.

"Now, Spencer," said Richardson, "This had better be important."

"Well, I don't quite know the implications of it, yet, but," he hesitated. Richardson felt the moment might require it and lit up a cigarette.

"According to my readings, psychic phenomena do not usually manifest immediately after the Process is applied to a test subject."

"So I hear."

"However, Raven, the new subject, has already begun displaying alarmingly powerful telekinetic abilities."

"As I have gathered. Is that a problem?" Richardson puffed on his cigarette.

"She seems to be…not in control of her abilities." Jameson looked quite uneasy.

"How so?" questioned Richardson, leaning closer to Jameson.

"The early stages of the medication process that is intended to wipe her memories also blocks most conscious thought, as well as the creation of new long-term memories. In other words, the state of her mind is somewhat… random."

"So you're worried she might inadvertently cause harm with her powers?"

"In a word…yes."

Richardson leaned back. "Has anyone actually witnessed her exercising any abilities yet?"

"Yes. Dr. Jacobson checked in on her last night and witnessed it."

"And she was unhurt?"

"Yes."

"Short of having her complete this medicine cycle in a stasis tube, I don't see any other options."

Richardson paused, and after a moment, Jameson hazarded a suggestion.

"So you think I should place Raven in a sensory deprivation chamber?"

Richardson answered slowly, thoughtfully. "No…I wouldn't want to restrict development of her powers in any way. Carry on as you have been, but keep me informed."

"Yes, sir," Jameson said worriedly.

"Incidentally, Spencer, do you have any idea why the new subject reacted so fast?"

"The DNA used was sourced from Mina. It's only a guess, really, but since Mina has the ability to rapidly fix cellular damage to her body, perhaps the mutations were accelerated as well."

"Does Raven show any signs of any such healing ability?"

"Not as of yet," answered Jameson. "But again, theoretically it should be some time before all of her abilities manifest themselves. She is experiencing fairly normal reactions to all medications being given to her, though, so at this point I would guess that she does not yet have any healing properties. At least, not any on the scale of Mina's."

"You said, 'fairly normal?'"

Jameson looked down at the floor for a second, his right foot tracing nervous circles on the floor. "It's just that, I've never personally dealt with the onset of memory modification. There are tests that should be run, and in any case, only the subject truly knows how successful the treatment is. Or doesn't know, I guess I should say?" he looked confused.

"Let me see if I follow. You have a subject in which fast mutations are occurring, leading you to believe that possibly she carries the ability to heal."

"Yes, possibly."

"Yet, she experiences regular reactions to medication, leading you to believe that she doesn't heal."

"That's an oversimplification, but I suppose you could say that. In any case, time will answer all questions." He stood there for a second.

"Anything further?" said Richardson with more than a hint of annoyance.

"Oh. No. Thank you, sir." Jameson turned and left.

Richardson called for Kresge as the door was opened, and the man reentered.

"Sorry that took so long."

"What did he have to say?"

"It seems the new subject may not have the ability to heal."

"Then she's worthless, right?"

"Oh no," disagreed Richardson. "They're all useful in some way or another. And, if my understanding is correct, people with far less ability than the healer we have, have been very useful to the energy project, which, at face value, is still a worthwhile endeavor, if not the main goal."

"But you're disappointed."

"I'll wait for more information to decide. Jameson isn't the keenest doctor we have."

"Then why is he your snitch?"

"Because out of all the doctors, he's the greediest. He sold his soul long ago and hopes to keep reaping the rewards."

Some people will do anything for money, Kresge thought.

"Anyway," said Kresge, "are we in agreement about the transfer?"

"Of course," said Richardson calmly. I will notify the armory staff at once of the schedule, and the item shall be released to your staff as soon as you are ready."

"This was a lucky find, Joshua."

"It bothers me, of course. I was never properly notified of it. I had to read Dr. Utsugi's files to learn about it. But it seems everything was on track with her all along."

"It was brilliant, splitting the project so ingeniously. Letting Hanin think what he wanted, working to create the raw source without even knowing it.

Shame he got it shut down."

Richardson elaborated. "Utsugi knew Hanin was aware of more than he let on. How much more, we don't know. But it was genius of Utsugi, continuing the soldier project secretly without Hanin knowing he was still, at least, doing her mundane research the entire time."

"After the incidents, there was just so much bureaucratic red tape. For a self-controlled agency, we were muddled in, let's be frank, needless bullshit. Nobody, save maybe Dr. Utsugi herself, knew the whole of the project. Angel was shut down because only a couple people had access to all of the information. Luckily, of course, that—thing—is a moot point now, at least in regards to the work at hand."

Kresge had a look of smug success on his face as he continued. "The simple fact is that the disaster that occurred, Joshua, was a blessing," said Kresge. "It trimmed the fat. It may have been a setback in manpower, but at last, all the information is in one spot and as director, you are no longer handicapped by dealing with subordinates that know more than you. Now you know more than they do, as it should be." *And so do I,* he thought. "*We* have the secrets, not the people working beneath us."

"It was ridiculous," said Richardson, disgustedly. "How they expected me to coordinate two independently focused research groups without knowing all the details of what they were researching."

"Not to mention Yamada's team at Groom Lake. Their discoveries may have simplified everything we need out of this project."

Richardson looked irked. "I can't believe we were days away from setting up a practical test. If I hadn't read Utsugi's notes before the message from Groom Lake came through, I would have looked like I had my head up my ass about the whole thing."

"You did. We all did." Kresge chuckled. "Not anymore."

"Do you think the advisory board will be pleased with this display?"

"Yes. I hesitate to say it, but as long as everything goes right."

"Some measure of risk is unavoidable. I have faith, though. This should put *everything* back on track."

"This will be the first, full, live ammunition test of a conscious subject," Kresge said. "Yamada and his team had better be right about this."

"Domination is a rare talent, and a dangerous one," Richardson admitted. "If this—when this—goes well, we can end research into it, 'breed' against it."

"I wouldn't be so hasty. It's very interesting, and a unique ability in how it allows psychics to interact, from what I gather. Perhaps further down the line?"

"Perhaps. In the meantime, let's move forward with this test, and let the doctors get what they can out of their new pet projects."

"Agreed."

Eighty-Nine:
Piss Off

Doesn't it bother you? the boy said.

What?

Let's think about it mathematically. Let's call your boss "entity A" and you "entity B."

Okay.

Entity A wants entity B plus information C to equal product D. Follow?

Yeah.

*But all you're getting is maybe, **maybe**, one half of C. Kind of half-assed, don't you think?*

I guess so.

So, maybe they already have the other half of C, and you don't need to know about it.

Maybe.

Or, maybe Product D isn't what they're really after.

So what you're saying is…

…that your goals are not meant for your purpose. That the work you complete isn't going to be used on what you're working for.

So, what's the real goal?

Isn't it obvious? What's bothered you from the very beginning? Who backs your work?

Who?

Who?

Emma woke with a start. "The military," she said, but didn't know why. She felt confused as though she'd been dreaming, but didn't remember any. She had a dull ache in her head that made her wince.

"I can't believe I fell asleep," she said, dismayed at the small puddle of drool that was on the table she'd been leaning on. She glanced over at Raven, sleeping in a chair. It was one of the most bothersome things she had seen lately. On a scale of wrong to ten, it ranked at least a nine. This bruised, bald, cut-up adolescent from god-knows-where, rambling and slurring her words, dressed in a hospital gown and slippers, soon to be subjected to horrible tests in the name of *progress*.

"Well," said Emma, quietly, "if I accomplish what's wanted of me, people won't be treated like you anymore. Right?"

The room did not answer back. Emma wished she had been sure of her statement; maybe it would have appeased the guilt that was all-too normal to her now. But it was a poor justification, and she knew it. She felt strong for putting up with it at the same time as she felt weak for not doing anything about it, even though she knew there wasn't anything she could do.

Emma valued her life. She wasn't going to go against the system, not after it killed Carl and did *this* to a poor girl. She cursed herself, though. She used to feel strong and sure of things; now she knew she was devolving into a wishy-washy sort of person. Sleeping with the enemy, as it were, and not bold enough to leap from the boat.

What kind of person am I? She thought. She expected that seeing Richardson should fill her with venom and hatred for the man, and for NOD, and everything they stood for. But it didn't. Oh, she felt dislike, maybe extreme dislike, but did not despise the way she thought she should. Perhaps it was years of experimenting that had desensitized her. Maybe it was the medical profession in general. Maybe....

The human being is an odd creature, for only it can feel guilty about not feeling guilty enough.

"Knocky-knocky," said Jameson as he entered the room, talking as if he thought himself clever. "Have an accident?" he said, eyeing the drool on the table.

"Fell asleep," said Emma.

"Most unprofessional."

"Don't get me started."

"So how's Raven been?"

"Oh fine," said Emma, sarcastically. "She hasn't been breaking anything with her mind, if that's what you mean."

"Err...good. Well, I'm anxious to get her started on some tests, there is so much to go over, and I—"

Emma interrupted, anger in her voice. "Okay, since you're the expert in the Process, and—"

"I wouldn't say that—"

"—everything that it involves, guess what: you're in charge of Raven. She's your responsibility. I have too much to do, with Mina, and Matthew, or M, or whatever, and I don't know anyone else on this research team well enough to have them help me yet! Raven is yours. I expect a report at the end of the day and to be notified *whenever* you think I would want to be. Get her out of here."

"Yes ma'am," Jameson said sheepishly. He helped Raven get up and quickly took her out of the room.

"Jesus Christ," Emma said with grave irritation in her voice. *That was a hasty choice, but oh-fucking well. Maybe it will keep him off my back.*

Ninety:
Work

Emma scrolled through page after page of text on the computer screen in front of her. She yawned, and then looked over her shoulder at the chambered horror that was "M." She adjusted her glasses and squinted at the tiny letters on her monitor. She fidgeted a little, and then pushed her glasses up to the top of her head and rubbed her eyes. She fruitlessly blew a loose curl away from her face, only to have it return immediately.

For the last hour, she'd been sifting through file after file of data looking for some information on what she should be trying to accomplish with her research.

Mentally harnessed energy? Sitting—lurking, squatting, whatever—behind her was the proof that such a thing was possible. She was required to replicate it in a way that was…this was both humorous and bothersome to her… *commercially viable*. Right? That was what it came down to.

She even believed she had figured out *how* it produced power. Well, more or less. She glanced up at the ceiling above M…a series of concentric cylinders, each big enough to surround it, hung an inch or so out of the ceiling. They had turned out to be scanning devices…MRI…CAT…et cetera. And she had scanned M, and found out something spectacular.

The column in the center she had assumed to be bone, was in fact, a bone shell surrounding a densely packed neuron cluster. The electrical potential of it was astounding. She had found similar, though much smaller, clusters throughout the body of the thing, so, she had postulated, that that was how it generated power, in some way or another it "ate" Nod energy and converted it, through neurons, into electricity. The action potential would have to propagate to some sort of collection or disbursement organ to actually generate usable electricity, however. IF she was right.

They were just neural clusters though. Not brains. Not minds….

Mass production of a mindless, organic construct capable of tapping into an alternate reality filled with a limitless energy source. That was the goal.

She envisioned it as a beginning with a creature made with artificially sequenced DNA that would provide it with psychic abilities yet deny it a conscious mind. Then, she imagined, it would have to be exposed to various stimuli to produce a vessel with a capacity equal to (or exceeding) M.

The second aspect had been successfully completed at least once. M was a completed structure. Though Emma had absolutely no idea what it entailed, this process should be fully documented…somewhere. It was the first aspect that seemed farther out of reach.

Hanin's notes declared that "Angel" was created to be an unconscious, psychic organism. Emma would have to gain access to a lot of information, perhaps even the body of Angel itself, in order to even begin to grasp the concepts of just what would be necessary to recreate it.

Hanin's worry was that Matthew's malevolent soul was reaching through his old body and attacking psychics. Of particular worry was Angel. Hanin had written that Angel, possessing no conscious mind, would be easy prey. And Emma had of course seen evidence of higher brain functions in M's readouts.

So…she would leave that part for later. Right now, she would deal with lesser (relatively speaking) problem of stimulus-response regarding what was in effect shape change on a micro and macroscopic scale.

Actually, right now, she was going to go visit Mina.

Ninety-One:
Table

"What the hell am I supposed to be doing with you?"

Jameson looked over at the bald girl sitting in the chair near him. They were sitting in a pale gray room, ostensibly designed to evoke a lack of emotion or empathy. It had no specific function; it wasn't a lab, waiting room, or even a nursery. It was just a room, adjacent to several other similar rooms near a large block of labs. The paint was the same color as the labs; probably it was intended to be one but hadn't become necessary yet.

All that was in the room now was a small rectangular table and two chairs. Raven sat in one, a glassy look in her eyes. A trail of drool was hanging from the corner of her mouth.

"Euch, let me get that." Jameson looked around for some towels, or napkins, or anything he could use to wipe her spittle. Finding nothing, he graciously used his sleeve. "There."

He drummed his fingers on the table.

Tap-tap-tap-tap. Tap-tap-tap-tap. Tap-tap-tap-tap. He stopped. There was a rattling that had started while he was drumming his fingers. At first he thought the table was unsteady, but it was still moving after he had stopped.

He looked quizzically at Raven. She was motionless, fresh drool already hanging from her mouth. But the table was still rattling.

Spencer Jameson got up and backed away from the table. It was shaking visibly, and seemed to be under great stress. With one quick buckle, it snapped, sending splinters into the air. Jameson merely got hit by a few tiny flecks, but a large piece smacked Raven in the forehead. She slid; her chair flipped out from under her and she fell to the floor. She appeared unfazed.

"You are going to be trouble." He walked over to her and helped her up, and led her towards the door of the room.

"Come on, Raven. It's time for some tests." Jameson figured that at the very least, he could gather data with EKG's, brain pattern scans, and blood tests. At least that would be something to do until he figured out something better, right?

Ninety-Two:
Retirement Plans?

Carlos and Marcus sat across from each other at a card table, a deck of playing cards and two beers on it. Off to one side was an ashtray into which a cigar had recently been extinguished. The cards were scattered around a bit as though a game had been played and then stopped abruptly.

In fact, Carlos and Marcus were both restless. They were bored and out of contact with Leonard for possibly several more days. It was a situation neither man liked.

"Well, I'm going to be transferred to NOD at the next shift change," said Carlos. "It won't be the same without you."

"Yeah, but the takeover should happen soon enough, and then all three of us will be back together."

"The way it should be."

"Why aren't you gonna lead, Marcus?"

"They want me to lead an outside strike force in case you guys on the inside need help with the takeover."

Carlos had picked his hand back up half-heartedly, but threw it down now in disbelief and disgust. "An outside strike force? Really? We're just rotating in as guards, man. What the hell do we need that for?"

"I don't know, really. I think it's just a precaution, in case someone figures something out. I mean, as far as the 'real' army is concerned, we don't even exist. Someone gets wind of this, maybe they try and take us out."

"You don't really believe that, do you?"

"Ha! No." Marcus spoke smugly. "They couldn't take us out if they tried."

"What do you think it's all for, anyway?"

"Most of the missions we do for NOD amount to nothing more than industrial espionage. But some of the stuff we've seen…like those giant crystals that we always destroy…and those deformed babies. I dunno. It's supposed to be about psychics and weapons. But no one ever fully explained it to me, and I never really asked. Guess I was just too concerned with the paycheck to worry about the work."

"Not me," disagreed Carlos. "I love my work. The money is just a perk."

"Well, it seems that this takeover is supposed to get us lots of stuff: new weapons, a new, high-tech base of operations, new mission opportunities, all funded by Uncle Sam, still with no questions asked. It should be very good for business. Pretty simple reasons, really. No secret motives here, I don't think."

"Yeah. I suppose." Carlos looked worried. He had pulled out his knife and was picking at the table.

Marcus knew his friend's tone of voice and nervous antics well. "What's the matter?"

"Well, Carrie's always been a real trooper when it came to my work—always out of town, never able to tell her why, thinks I work for the government—but you know, she's pregnant now."

"And you're thinking it's time you settled down."

"Yeah. I mean, I know we're better soldiers than ninety percent of the people we fight, but you never know what's gonna happen in the field. I don't want her to wake up one day to a phone call that says, 'your husband's dead' and nothing else. I want to enjoy my life with her, especially because the baby's on the way."

"You've been great to this organization. Maybe they'll promote you—give you a desk job?" Marcus said hopefully.

"Yeah, guerrilla warfare requires a lot more paperwork than most people think."

They chuckled, and then each man sipped his beer.

"That's it then," said Carlos. "When this takeover is finished, I'm retiring from the soldier of fortune lifestyle. I'll be…a *secretary* of fortune! Sound good?"

"Heh-heh, sounds great!" They chugged their beers, and Marcus stood up and went to get some more from the nearby cooler.

Carlos sat, thinking his decision was sound but wondering what it would do to him. He loved the thrill of the hunt, the heat of the kill. No one else but his superiors knew the full extent of his predilection for carefully, thoroughly planned stealth violence. The missions they gave him quenched his thirst. So how would he be once those missions were gone?

He knew he would do anything for his wife, his family. But his desire to hunt the most dangerous animal was so strong…would he be strong enough to deny it? He sighed, shaking his head in doubt.

"Huh?" asked Marcus, sitting down with the fresh beers.

"Nothing," said Carlos.

Ninety-Three:
The Bad Guy

"Mina?"

"Come in."

Emma entered the room and saw Mina lying on her bed, looking at a book. She was scratching her right leg.

"You're going to hurt yourself if you keep that up," said Emma, not realizing it really didn't matter.

"I just need my legs shaved."

"On Saturday, I think you're...due..." The matter-of-factness of that statement, and the almost regular human vanity it displayed caught her off guard.

"Dr. Jacobson, what's a tree?"

Emma looked down at the book the girl was reading. It looked like a Dr. Seuss book. "Well, they don't look like that. Not really. Don't your other books tell you?"

"Yes and no," replied Mina, sitting up to face Emma. "They have pictures and descriptions, but I can't read all the words. And they don't describe everything, anyway." For a moment, Emma felt lost in Mina's expressive eyes, but she shook it off and mentally discounted it.

"Like what?"

"Like, are trees warm like people? Or are they cold? What do they feel like? And they sway in the wind." She pronounced it with a long "i." "What's wind?"

"That's wind," said Emma, emphasizing the pronunciation. "You know, when the air comes out of the duct? Wind's like that. Only...bigger."

"Faster?"

"Yes. No. Sometimes. I mean, there's more of it, it takes up more space, I...I don't know. It's funny, but I never thought about it before."

"Dogs."

"Hmm?" Emma had been trying to figure out how to explain wind to herself.

"Dogs. What are dogs like? I looked at some and thought, that's cute, but I don't know why. Some people are cute, but dogs don't look like them. Why are they both cute?"

Emma's thought was that whatever humanity the medication had been holding back inside Mina, though it had slowly been peeking through, had just cascaded out completely.

"You're cute."

"Why thank you, Mina. You're quite cute yourself."

Mina smiled a warm, genuinely happy smile of appreciation.

It made Emma Jacobson feel like the biggest schmuck in the world.

Mina was, by most standards, extremely attractive. Even if that hadn't been the case, she still would have been purposely dressed modestly and fitted with an IUD, at least until recently. The reasoning was technically practical, but sexist and deplorable in its assumptions. Emma had had a conversation about it not long ago with Carl, rest his soul.

"Look, Carl, Mina is post-pubescent. She is an intact female. This place is crawling with doctors and guards, and there is plenty of time when the test subjects are alone."

"She wouldn't have a relationship, though, the medication keeps emotions low and libido almost non-existent...Oh."

The justification? "Things" happened in institutions. Better prepared than not.

However Mina was no longer a mindless drone. She was as much a real person as she could be given her limited real-world knowledge, and Emma felt that she at least deserved to dress like a real person. To break up the monotony, maybe just a bit. Perhaps Emma was projecting her own ideas of helpfulness onto Mina, but even if that was the case, Mina *had* found the shorts and tee shirt buried under her usual assortment of shapeless tops, bathrobes, and sweat pants.

It had been Emma who had ordered the laundry staff to put them there, along with an assortment of similar choices.

It was becoming harder and harder to treat Mina like the subject of an experiment.

"Mina, I'd like you to accompany me to one of the laboratories," she said with a heavy heart.

Mina, who would have normally said "Okay," or "Yes," and jumped up immediately, simply sighed, closed her book, and shuffled to her feet.

As they walked to the laboratory Emma intended to use, they passed another doctor, a woman, and she and Emma stopped to converse for a moment.

"Cecily..."

"Dr. Jacobson."

"Emma is fine."

"All right then."

It had been a secret that Cecily Armstrong had been dating one of the guards killed in the recent incident. As it was a personal secret, among a group of people holding much bigger secrets, of course nearly everyone knew about it. Emma felt a lot of guilt in regards to the occurrence and wished she could in some way keep an eye on Cecily and make sure she was doing okay. It was an unusually motherly concern for her.

"What do you have planned for today?" asked Emma, trying to sound casual.

"I have the White Room booked for the next hour and a half. I'm working with Benny today." She whispered the next part. "Thank god medication affects him, unlike your charge," she motioned towards Mina before continuing. "Can you imagine how much trouble he could cause? His phasing ability makes him impossible to restrain. I think he's showing signs of teleportation, as well."

"Well," said Emma, intrigued, "do let me know how your research goes."

"Of course." Cecily turned to walk away.

"Cecily…"

"Yes?" She turned back.

"Nothing. Never mind." Emma was about to tell her that she would be there if she needed to talk to some one, but the truth was the two of them had never been close and Emma didn't want to sound condescending.

Once the two women had reached the lab, Emma motioned for Mina to sit down. She did, and Emma walked over to a cabinet and retrieved a small silver case. "Mina, I want to understand your healing ability. I believe it may be part of something greater."

The girl looked at her, not really appearing disinterested, but not fascinated either.

"There have been…people like you…who have been able to change their body's shape at will, or change parts of their bodies into other substances. You may have been right when you suggested that perhaps...Matthew...changed you, however." She could not say that name without a sense of dread tightening her gut. Mina, for her part, looked slightly embarrassed but also fearful at the mention of Matthew's name.

"I think though that you may have the ability to change yourself as you see fit, at least to a certain degree. You told me that when you get hurt, you don't *make* yourself heal; it happens by itself. What I want to know is if you have tried to stop it from happening."

"You mean," asked Mina, "that if I get cut, you want to know if I can make the cut stay open?"

"Precisely. If you can change your self, I think the first step to learning how would be to learn if you can control your healing."

"Are you going to hurt me?" Mina was scared, but not yet defiant.

Emma's awkward silence was all the answer Mina needed, but still, finally, she said, "I'd prefer not to."

What a useless sentence, Emma thought. The tests that she could run to try and understand Mina's powers could reveal fascinating, tantalizing knowledge, but they would amount to little more than torture: cutting and bruising her; exposing her to diseases, drugs, seeing how her body reacted to any number of physical and chemical attacks. Emma was not sure she could bring herself to do this, soon, if ever.

"I'm just saying, if you get hurt, concentrate and see if you can stop your healing for a moment. Do you think you can do this?"

"I don't know how, but I'll try...."

"Good! Let me know immediately, success or failure, if this happens. Now, if you could take off your top, I'd like to give you a physical and try and take some blood, and then I want to test your shielding powers. All right?"

"Okay," said Mina, slowly getting up and pulling off her shirt. She was wearing a bra—nothing fancy, but a regular bra, not the kind she was accustomed to. She pointed at it. "Should I—?" she began.

"No. Not yet, anyway."

Time to be poked and prodded, measured and ogled. She definitely did not like this anymore, but if there was a word for the wrong that was all around her, she did not know what it was.

Slave.

The word echoed in her mind, kind of like telepathy, but also like a memory. Like someone else had thought that thought once inside her head, and now she was remembering it, and only one person (that she knew of) had ever been in her head.

"Slave," she muttered, not truly knowing what it meant, but having a pretty good idea.

"I'm sorry, what?" asked Emma.

"Nothing," Mina said disdainfully as she set her shirt on a chair and walked over to the doctor.

Ninety-Four:
Contempt

He was having a particularly strong fit of self-loathing. He had explored this particular circle too many times, but here he was again. She could have been great for him, and he had started to make her perfect, and yet again he was rejected. This was the third time. The first two had been his fault; he had used the girl improperly and had shattered her; he had been too caught up in enjoying the boy and had been caught off-guard. This loss had not been his fault. Occupying her made his blood rush hot, metaphorically speaking. She awakened thoughts in his mind he never knew he could have, not having a body (or real-world knowledge) to go with them. He had fixed the mistakes they'd made in her, and in the end, she could have used him as much as he used her. It would have been beautiful, perfect.

But she had been stolen from him, before he could complete his "settling in."

It had occurred to him some time ago, having been around so much of both, that living and dying were essentially the same thing. You couldn't have one without the other. Every second a person was living, he or she was also inching towards death. That's what had made this girl so special when he had peered inside and seen what light flickered in her cells.

She could separate life from death. For her and her alone, life was different than death because she was not a slave to the latter. He would tell her this the next time he saw her…or was her.

Suddenly, he remembered something that he hadn't thought of in quite some time. He remembered another girl that he had met very many cycles ago, when his freedom had seemed assured for a moment. He realized that the chaos she would help bring would happen soon, and he hoped he would be there to see it.

Ninety-Five:
Electro-Cranial Aberrations

Raven stared at the man floating in the sky, and watched the torrent of red below him spin like a tornado, splashing the ground like so much spilled tomato soup.

She did not comprehend it at all. She looked up. Her mom was holding her hand so tightly it hurt.

"Mommy?"

She said something, but it was barely a whisper. She managed to say it again, slightly louder: "Run..."

People flew past them both like streams, away from the fruit punch twister. The muted silence was deafening for Molly Yamada as she tried to move her feet, tried to turn her head, tried to pull her daughter to safety. But then Death himself stepped down from his throne of blood and swiftly approached, and Molly could not gather the will to move her trembling legs from the spot; she knew if she moved at all she would fall and that would be the end of her.

"I know you," said Death. But he was a boy, just a boy. How could he be Death?

He looked quizzically at Molly, and eyed young Raven as well.

"No...not you. But he's all over you." As his eyes moved back down to glance at Raven, he added, "Dr. Yamada."

Happy to hear something she understood, Raven smiled at the mention and blurted out, "He's my Daddy!"

Death smiled, a sickly smile, and looked back at Molly. "But you...no...he is there. He's on you. In you. Well, he was. It's fading." He smiled a sick smile, his toxic green eyes filled with fire.

"I...I know what you are," Molly said, as though it could give her some semblance of power over him. But that was an empty hope; he was unquestionably in control.

Death replied matter-of-factly. "The body is Andy but the brain is Matt. Take your pick."

He looked down at Raven again and put his hand on her forehead. Molly pulled her back.

"Don't worry, Ex-Mrs.-her-daddy. You can thank the unlucky stars I had mercy on you today. But before you go, know this: there is something in your daughter, and when it comes out, no man, woman, or child on this planet will be able to stand in her way. It's a shame that machinations are already in place to make you forget all of this, because the lovely question you will never get to ask yourself is, did I let your child live because of what she is, or is she what she is because I let her live?"

"*I won't let you take her!*"

Raven awoke abruptly, panting and wheezing. For just the tiniest moment she was completely lucid and remembered everything, but then her head began emptying all over again.

"Dream," she said. "Red. Mommy."

"Ah," came a voice to her side. "You're awake."

Spencer Jameson walked over to the bed Raven had been lying on. "Our little tests really took a lot out of you, didn't they?"

Raven looked at him, scratched her head, and said, "Itchy head."

"Don't pick at your stitches," said Jameson, but it felt like a wasted effort.

"I have a book," he said, changing the subject. "And I have read a good portion of it, and it pertains to you." She was drooling. He sighed, knowing what he was doing was pointless, but he continued anyway. "The human aura is a particulate field construct tied to the body by a subconsciously exerted psychic force. It is comprised of recently discovered particles, including many that have not previously been theorized."

"Telekinesis is the process by which the human mind, consciously or unconsciously, shapes and molds this field in order to cause it to interact with physical objects and forces."

He leveled his face with hers and spoke softly, sinisterly. "It means you can place your aura around objects and lift them up, crack them in half, throw them, make them implode. You can short-circuit an electronic device, as long as you have an inkling of how it works. You can levitate, possibly even fly. If you have enough control, you can excite matter on a molecular level and cause fires or boil water, or slow matter down and freeze it. You may be able to align your aura, adding kinetic energy to your actions and knock out a heavyweight boxer in a single hit."

"The point is you are a girl no more. You are a tool, whether you or anyone else wishes it to be so. You are a breed of psychic potentially more dangerous than any other. I made you and once you have completed this…" He gestured, searching for a word as he watched her stare blankly ahead. "…integration cycle, you will understand and obey me. You may have part of Mina in you, but you will not act out like her. Understand?"

"Balls to the wall," she said randomly.

It wasn't really that Jameson had expected there to be a meaningful response; it was that he was scared and was trying to make himself feel better by talking in such a commanding sort of way. This girl, his to deal with thanks to Emma Jacobson, had already exhibited signs of dangerous telekinesis. Given the dangerous source of her added DNA, and the likelihood of her powers increasing in strength as they matured, he was rightly worried. He felt that by making his stand now, he would win a victory over the girl, but in truth the only victory he might have won was over his own fears. He wanted very much to convince himself he would be safe.

There was a whimpering, which brought Jameson out of his reverie of worry. Tears were dripping down Raven's face.

"We belong to the wretched," she said. The bed she was on began to shake.

It only took Jameson a few seconds to produce a tranquilizer shot. Raven had soon passed back out, and Jameson breathed a sigh of relief. It was because of the drugs, it must be, he thought. She was a powerful subject and the muddled state she was in was causing misfires of her nerves. That was all.

But he just knew…he didn't know how, but he knew…that as much telekinetic power Mina had expressed during her killing spree, Raven was unbelievably stronger.

It didn't matter. No one could stop the world from spinning, and no one could stop Spencer Jameson from making his name one people would remember. Someday. He was destined for greatness. Old Scratch would see to it; that was his contract with fate.

Ninety-Six:
Discovering the Waterfront

Dillons yawned. He was bored of his post, and his leg hurt. He was pretty sure it was just in his head, but it gave him something to dwell on. And, his previous thought that he could do some spying up here, "where the action was," had so far proven false.

He was feeling very disappointed.

He looked at the doorways near him; one had a curtain, another a double set of locked doors. In the dim, blue light that flooded the corridors at night, he strained to look each way down the corridor, looking for someone, anyone, anything, but he was all alone. He yawned.

In one of the rooms behind Dillons, Mina sat on her bed, in the dark, staring at her teddy bear by the soft glow of her nightlight.

It looked exactly like the bear she had wrecked before when she had felt cocky. The newness of regaining a true sense of self had quickly worn off once she had realized she was nothing more than an object, a thing to be poked and prodded while notes were scribbled on clipboards.

The bear bothered her. She put it face down on the bed where the camera in its eye couldn't see her.

She realized then that she knew what a camera was because she had read about them, but was never told. At what point had she realized what it meant to be watched? Apparently she could do nothing to avoid it, though, because she had already destroyed one peeping teddy, and here was another ready to take its place.

She walked over to her mirror, a full-length one that stood near the bathroom. If she had such thoughts, it would have struck her as odd that she had one at all, given that vanity was not an emotion held by her previous self. Of course, it had a wide-view camera embedded in it, but she didn't know that.

She looked at her self very carefully. It took time to adjust to the darkness further from her nightlight but she was able after a few moments to see her self fairly well.

She examined her face, turning it to the side and smiling. She liked what she saw. She liked her smile and her lips and her cheeks and her diamond blue eyes and the cascade of blond hair that reached almost to the middle of her back.

"I'm beautiful," she whispered. Not out of ego, but out of contentment about her own looks.

She looked at her body, covered by her nightgown. She had strong shoulders. She had cute little toes attached to dainty feet attached to legs with strong calf muscles. She had a firm rear end and a narrow waist, and a pair of breasts that were full and perky.

"I'm…" What was the word? "…sexy."

She smiled. It wasn't narcissism—it was empowerment. She felt… possessed, but not like with Matthew.

Like when she was in the shower the other day.

Like when she had realized, perhaps still subconsciously, that she was becoming her own person.

She reached both hands down without looking away from her reflection and pulled her nightgown up above her waist.

She had not put on any underwear this evening.

She stared intently at her groin. "Petals," she said, and thought of flowers.

Was it beautiful? It had mostly brought her pain. But the memory of that pain, and the incident that had caused it, while difficult and even anguishing to remember, did not carry with it the burden of guilt society so often unfairly placed on women in similar situations. She was free.

She held her nightgown against her stomach with her left hand, and delicately, soft like lily blossoms, she placed her right against the cleft of her vulva. She pushed in a bit, gently, unknowingly at first, exploring the contours, and felt a tingle. She bit her lip as she started to enjoy the motions of her hand, and then closed her eyes, and an image came to mind…

… She saw Matthew and he was getting on top of her, and….

And that was sex. And it had been harsh, and hurtful, and disgusting.

And yet she knew that that wasn't right, and she knew that what she was doing was somehow related to how it *could be right*. That the two situations were only mechanically similar; they were not emotionally similar.

She banished him from her mind and opened her eyes, watching herself in the mirror. She was breathing more deeply.

She took both hands, and pulled her nightgown over her head and threw it on the ground. She took a couple steps back, still looking intently at herself.

A soft touch, a hard touch—she was more often than not intrigued by the result.

At some point she found herself on her bed, finding herself racing quite quickly towards—whatever the actual outcome would be—she didn't know. She felt warm, and as though a pressure was building, and then, all at once, there was a release, an enrapturing series of releases, as wildfire spread through her nerves; her breaths, rapid and shallow. For a few dizzying moments, her mind was completely clear.

As her body calmed down and her breathing slowed, as she basked in the afterglow of a new experience, she raised her right hand, looking curiously at it. She lazily let it drop against the wall behind her head. There was a hot feeling, like a shock, not unpleasant, but startling, and she immediately pulled her hand away and stared at it again.

In the room next door, Raven removed her hand from the wall. The shock that had passed through her had made her almost lucid for a moment.

Her head hurt when she tried to form thoughts, but she remembered a feeling, from before, when she had seen the pretty girl and almost touched her hand. There was a connection, a brief connection of wills. But then the darkness swallowed Raven up again, and she forgot.

Mina lay in bed, thinking. The multitude of sensations had been overwhelming, but she swore it felt like she had shared the last moment with someone else. Not someone…bad…like Matthew, but someone…soothing. That girl? She wondered….

Raven was shaking a little when she got under her covers. A warm, happy feeling encompassed her, filling her with contentment. For the first time in a long time, either before or after the events that had so abruptly changed her life, she slept without worry.

Out in the hall, Leonard Dillons sighed, wishing for some action to liven things up a little.

Ninety-Seven:
Nothing Specific

Emma sat at home, sipping tea and reading a paper entitled "Aura Field Distension Dynamics." She had found it in the files she had access to. While it did not pertain directly to the work she needed to do with Mina, it was still quite interesting. It explained that some users of aurakinetic shielding were able to focus their shields around specific areas, including objects external to their own bodies. She wanted to try this with Mina. And, she felt it would be important to learn the limits of the girl's telekinetic abilities and levitation skills. She had worked a little with the girl today analyzing her shield abilities; they would continue that work tomorrow.

She sighed, looking at her watch. It *was* "tomorrow"; it was half past midnight and she wasn't even changed for bed. It wasn't that she couldn't have fallen asleep; it was almost that she was scared to. Outside her house, on the street out front, there was probably a car with spies in it, watching for a lack of discretion on her part. That wasn't what was really bugging her. A couple of days now after the event that had turned so many lives upside down, she was just starting to relax into a groove of sorts, but it was now that she was most afraid of what her mind might show her while she slept.

In a few hours she would be going back to work anyway. Usually, she got at least one weekend day off, but despite her frazzled nerves, now was no time to take time off.

It was during this last thought that she nodded off, and indeed, her sleep was fraught with concepts and imagery that would have startled and horrified a wakened mind. But in a couple hours she woke from discomfort, with no memories of dreams specific, only with an overall feeling of unfocused fear that made her shiver all the way to bed where, luckily for her, the Night Terrors bothered her no more that night.

Maybe they felt sorry for her, knowing her waking hours could be terrifying enough.

Ninety-Eight:
Saturday Morning

Emma sighed, seeing Spencer Jameson walking towards her from the opposite end of the hallway. He waved; she returned the gesture. They stopped within feet of each other, turning to face adjacent doorways. Emma's was curtained but had no actual door; Jameson's was an electronically locked blast door with an entry log in a slat in the wall and a guard with a gun nearby.

Jameson grabbed the log.

"Anything worth noting?" Emma asked.

Jameson flipped through the first two sheets, skimming them. "Nope. Night seems to have passed without cause for alarm." He turned to the door.

"Your ID, please, doctor," said the guard.

Jameson looked huffy as he handed over his identification to the guard. Emma smiled as she just walked right into the room in front of her.

"I'm sorry," she said a second later, her face flushed, as she turned away from the room. "I didn't think you'd be up yet, I was just going to leave your schedule."

Mina, startled, had dropped her towel. She was standing outside her bathroom door, completely naked. Her hair was soaked and her body was glistening.

"That's okay, I'd say knock first but I have no door, right?" *Not like I deserve that kind of thoughtfulness, right?*

Slave!

Mina touched her head, confused. She didn't understand the thoughts she'd just had.

Emma, still turned away, began speaking again, but Mina interrupted her. "Well, anyway, meet me at—,"

"I thought about what you said. About halting my healing. But there's nothing here to hurt myself on anyway. Except bruises, I guess. Those are easy to get."

"Well, I hope I made myself clear that I didn't want you hurting yourself on purpose."

"Of course!" Mina giggled.

Emma thought, *She's acting kind of spacey.* She added, *I hope she's all right,* but she quickly realized that there was no basis in the entire set of circumstances involving this girl to judge "all right" against.

Mina did feel a bit spacey, despite her inner anger a moment earlier. Although she couldn't have expressed the idea in words, she had been gifted with a new, (un-medicated) personality, and was now in the difficult process of integrating it into her former, bland, emotionless one.

Emma of course was completely aware of this, and it wasn't as though it was a completely unprecedented incident. Personality changes could come with brain injury, amnesia, amnesia recovery, the coming and going of a fugue state, any of a number of psychological conditions. But this was, of course, different, and there was no *specific* precedent to this, at least in her studies.

She expected Mina to be scatterbrained, at best. What Emma was worried about was the worst-case scenario, the one where Mina revolted against her captors and resumed killing. While at this point she fully believed the initial incident was not Mina's fault, and had the support of her boss in keeping Mina alive and conscious, she of course realized that Mina likely still had the power to cause great damage, if not the ability to specifically reenact the nature of the incident.

It was unnerving to hear her speak of, or at least hint at, hurting herself. It was made worse by the double standard that was, not wanting the children—subjects—to hurt themselves, while simultaneously exposing them to all manners of stressful, often painful experiments.

Emma could hear Mina rummaging through her clothes drawers. "Since you're already up and almost ready, why don't you just come with me when you're dressed?"

"Yes. That's fine."

Emma wondered if Mina felt guilt for what she—or at least her body—had done. The talk of hurting herself—did she demand penance of herself? Was it idle talk? Was it sarcasm? Was she even capable of that?

Just yesterday Mina had expressed extreme confusion at the transference of similar emotions between dissimilar subjects.

It was more and clear to Emma just how deeply the medications suppressed emotion and cognition. But of course, Mina was still a unique case, as her age and neurological makeup was different than the children's.

Was unique, Emma corrected herself. Though she didn't want to see Raven that way, she really was a second chance at a rare observation....Missed opportunities were not something scientists like her tended to be fond of.

There was a tap on Emma's shoulder that brought her out of thought, and she jumped a little. She turned around.

Mina was smiling up at her. She was wearing a long-sleeved, form-fitting black top with an ankle length, royal blue skirt.

"Could you...could you put my hair up? Like Dr. Verona...used to wear hers."

"Sure," said Emma, feeling guilty and oddly proud at the same time. Dr. Verona had died when Mina...Matthew...had destroyed the board room. "Turn around." She proceeded to put Mina's long, soft hair into a high ponytail.

Mina swayed her head back and forth, listening to the *swish* of her hair on her back. "Thank you, Dr. Jacobson."

"You're welcome, Mina," Emma said. She had a strange tightness in her gut.

Mina was practically skipping down the hall next to Emma. "So what am I going to be doing today?"

She sounded almost chipper.

"Well, first, we're going to stop at the playroom, I have to meet with some of the other doctors. Then, we're going to study your shielding some more."

"Okay."

By and by they arrived at the playroom, and Emma left Mina there while she stepped into an adjacent room.

This is very important.

Mina looked around. She could swear the thought had come from Anna, but that was ridiculous. She walked over to the girl and looked at what she was drawing.

"She's been working on that all morning," said Danny, who was suddenly standing next to Mina.

"You startled me," said Mina, gasping. She looked at Anna's picture; it looked like a schematic of a person; it was drawn with exacting attention to proportion. Mina, of course, just thought it was weird that Anna was drawing something other than her usual collection of lines and shapes.

"I wonder if he's a real person," said Mina.

"I don't think it's a real *he*," said Danny. Mina giggled, looking where he was now pointing. The picture seemed to be of a man, but he was clearly naked and clearly without genitals.

Just then, Jameson came into the room with Raven, and Mina's eyes immediately locked onto the girl. She was dressed in a white hospital gown covered in blue elephants and she had pink socks on. She was carrying a stuffed pony by the tail and was looking around without really appearing to focus on anything. But then she noticed Mina, and she held her hand out and tried to walk towards her, but just then Jameson started walking again and he took Raven by the hand through another door.

"Are you ready to go?"

Mina looked up. Emma was back in the room, holding a file folder. Mina nodded solemnly.

"All right, then, let's be on our way."

Ninety-Nine:
The Real Deal

Dr. Graley set the phone down and spoke to her son.

"I'm going to be out for much of tomorrow. Our agent has set up a munitions test in the desert and he insists I would want to see what Nod has to offer."

"Sounds interesting."

"Very much so. He wouldn't give me details over the phone, so I believe it is very interesting, indeed."

"Things have really died down here," said Marcus.

"Yes, I know. However, the time for action should be soon. I'm stepping up rotation of our soldiers into the Nod facility." She ran her fingers through her graying blond locks.

"Nervous?"

"Of course. Although I have the utmost confidence in you and your men, this represents a paradigm shift in this operation. Our unit will either live or die by this choice."

"Don't worry. We'll live; nothing can stand in our way."

One Hundred:
Leaving

"Thanks for stopping by, Emma."

"Yes, Joshua, well, you said it was important."

Richardson took a hit off his cigarette and adopted a pensive look. "Yes… you see, I'm leaving for the rest of the day. I'll be back on Monday. You have my cell number in case of an emergency?"

"Yes, of course."

"In the meantime, I trust everything is going well?"

"Yes. Mina seems…cooperative. We are working on her shielding capabilities today."

"Good. And Jameson?"

"Raven is still developing mentally. Dr. Jameson will notify me when it is necessary."

"Good. Well, it seems like everything is under control. Business as usual, while I'm gone."

"Yes, sir. Joshua."

Richardson dismissed Emma and started getting ready to go. As long as tomorrow went smoothly, he'd be guaranteed his position here at NOD. He was sure of it.

One Hundred One:
That's Levitation, Homes

"Mina, can I ask you a question," Emma asked into the microphone in front of her.

Mina answered from the inside of the reinforced glass booth, "Yes."

"How do you feel?" Emma had pen in hand as she was going to take notes.

"I feel fine."

"What I mean is, how do you...." Emma stopped herself. What she wanted to ask was how did Mina feel about these tests and her general treatment? There were unfortunately two crucial problems with directly asking that question. One was that Mina had no standard against which to measure her treatment. The other problem was that asking the question might imply that she shouldn't feel good about her treatment, which could skew the result. Regardless of what answer was appropriate, Emma did not want to color them.

"Are you happy?"

Mina seemed confused, and Emma immediately knew it was the wrong question to ask.

"I guess." Her answer was half-hearted at best. Again, she had nothing to compare with. Emma moved to scribble down something but stopped.

"If you don't mind me asking, what do you think about when you're alone?"

"Mostly I just read. I like *The Lorax*."

Emma was familiar with the story. It was about a greedy man that destroyed a forest and had to live with the repercussions as his acts hurt those around him. Mina's copy was dog-eared and well-worn.

It was about injustice. Might Mina have understood the theme without being able to name it exactly, and identified with it?

The word "liability" briefly entered Emma's head, but she didn't want to think that way. She took several notes.

"I was just wondering. Okay, are you ready?"

"Yes."

Mina faced to the side; Emma pressed a button. A tennis ball launched into the air, aimed above Mina's head. A yellow glow surrounded her; the ball passed over it, though. But by the time the second ball approached, Mina had refocused her shield into a parabolic shape that extended several feet above her head and seemed to fade away around her waist. The ball ricocheted off. The third ball passed through as the shield faded.

"Good," said Emma, turning off the tennis balls and scribbling onto her notepad. "You seem to be quite apt at reshaping your shield. Perhaps you can do it faster?"

"I'll try," said Mina. Mina stood still for a few seconds, and then formed another aural shield. Instead of initially appearing all around her, however, it was focused into a lens shape and appeared only in front of her. It was so well defined that the center of it was nearly opaque. Mina seemed to be straining, though, and she clenched her eyes shut. But the shield flickered and faded, and then all at once, it discharged, making an audible "pop" and blowing out several fluorescent lights in the process. Mina fell to her knees, panting, as a rain of sparks fell around her.

Emma leaned towards the microphone. "Perhaps we should call it quits for now? Are you tired?" Mina nodded. "All right, I'll open the door and you can come out."

"Wait…I want to try something first."

Emma watched an amber glow surround Mina's feet, much like her shield. It quickly faded, but as it did, Mina rose about a foot into the air, her toes dangling downward.

"Well, well, levitation! What made you change your mind?" Emma rapidly scribbled on her pad.

"I'm not afraid anymore," Mina said, matter-of-factly. She held up the hand she had placed against the wall last night while she had been exploring herself, smiling as she looked at it. "Not afraid at all," she muttered, and floated through the doorway as effortlessly and as gracefully as a butterfly.

One Hundred Two:
Free Radicals = Structural Damage

Emma sat in M's lab, looking over several piles of papers. The door opened, and Spencer Jameson entered.

"Ugh," he said, glancing at M.

"Can I help you?" asked Emma, not looking up from her papers.

"Uh, possibly. You know, this is like admitting defeat, but I could use your help. Do you have any ideas what I should be doing with Raven?"

Emma wasn't listening. "You know, I bet Mina's body does not suffer oxidation damage to her cells."

"Emma?"

She muttered to herself, then added, "Although I don't believe the Process would affect mtDNA, if I'm right then mitochondrial damage from free radicals might somehow be fixed by her own cellular processes."

Then: "I'm sorry, were you saying something?"

Jameson pulled a chair up next to Emma and sat down. "Do you have any ideas what I should be doing with Raven?"

"What have you done so far?"

"She's had a physical, blood work, sensor implants, just basic stuff like that. But do you know anything about working with someone who just completed the Process?"

"I was never privy to that sort of situation or the information involved in it. Just look stuff up."

"Raven isn't a typical case. She already manifests powers, but not cognitive control. I don't know what to do."

Emma turned to face him. She took her glasses off to wipe the lenses. "Let me ask you something—what did they tell you this job was when you took it?"

Jameson sighed. "They said I was going to catalog primate research specimens."

Emma put her glasses back on. "Okay, bad example. Let's say you worked in—regular—medical research. Don't you think now and then you'd come across a situation that had no precedent?"

"Well—yeah, but…"

"And what would you do in that case?"

Jameson looked sheepish. "I guess I would make an educated guess and create a procedure."

"Then that's what you should do here. It's my job to oversee your work and if you truly need help I will provide it. But right now I have a lot of data to go over so for now just do what seems best." He had asked a legitimate question, but Emma had never had much patience with the often-cocky Spencer Jameson.

She turned back to her papers, and Jameson just sat there looking at her for a moment, trying to think of a good way to ask again.

"I'm going to have to check her telomerase activity, examine cell division...." Emma mumbled presently.

"Emma?"

"Yes?"

"Uh...thanks." He got up, and left.

Emma rolled her chair over to a nearby table where she had set some x-rays taken earlier of M's tendril. She stared at the maw on the end as she turned the table's light on.

Slender, diffuse lines outlined what appeared to be three mouths, nested like wooden egg dolls, with vicious looking teeth. The structure was clearly jaw-like, although it was not connected at all to the head (or skull, at least) that she had discovered buried inside M.

Emma opened a folder and looked at a file she had found today in Hanin's —her—office. It was a set of four photocopies: three x-rays and one photograph. There were roughly scribbled notes and several rows of equations written in the margins. The first x-ray was a hand. The third appeared to be a mouth, but it was attached to an arm bone. The second x-ray was somewhere in between—it showed the arm bone, with the bones of the carpus rearranged and four of the fingers fused into two ring-like structures. The thumb was barely present. Emma wasn't sure what the equations meant, as well as some of the notes, but it was clear they were involved with biomorphism. Hopefully, they would explain what outside stimuli could force changes in the subject. That would be the key to duplicating the energy-creating structure of Arty and M.

Emma picked up the fourth paper and looked at it. There was only one line of writing on it: "Subject Terminated." Looking at the picture made her feel ill. It was a picture of a child, a test subject, with a small, misshapen head attached to the end of his left arm, the top of the skull connecting to his arm where his wrist should be. The eyes were wide open, glassy looking and highly dilated. A protrusion of bone came out where a normal head would have been attached to a neck.

Emma quietly turned the picture over, placed the papers back in the folder, and returned to work. Sometime later, she felt a tiny shaking sensation. Arty, she assumed for a second, but then she heard an alarm in the distance. Fearing the worst, she ran out of the room and looked around. She saw several scientists looking around questioningly, as well as three guards running towards an elevator. She moved to follow them, but one put a hand up and said, "Please, ma'am, this could be serious."

Emma wondered if he had been present during Mina's incident. She squinted in pain, the alarm suddenly blaring up in this section of hallway. "I'm in charge of the experiments here."

The guard motioned for her to follow, and together they rode the elevator up to floor 45—the floor that the children's dormitories were on.

The elevator door opened and immediately visible was the cause of the alarm and the shaking Emma had felt. It looked as though a chunk had been blown out of the wall. Raven was on the floor surrounded by rubble, bruised and cut in several spots. She was rocking back and forth quietly. A guard—a black man, "D" something, Emma couldn't remember—was pointing a weird-looking gun at her. He was sweating profusely, and seemed to be trembling. "Doctor?" he said.

Before Emma could even answer, the three guards she had rode up the elevator with had deployed themselves around the entrance way to the hall and had their guns pointed at Raven. Emma opened her mouth now to speak, but she realized then that the guard wasn't talking to her. She realized there was a person lying on the ground behind a particularly large chunk of rubble. He pulled himself up to his knees—it was Jameson—and answered the guard.

"No, no, you needn't fire. I'll take care of this." He pulled a black case out of his pocket and opened it. He took out a needle, and within seconds Raven had collapsed to the ground, unconscious. Jameson stood up.

"I want to thank you sir for your quick reactions," he said to the guard, feeling it necessary to say *something* to try and take the edge off the situation.

"Yes, thank you sir," said the guard.

The guards dispersed and Jameson motioned for Emma to come near. Together, they picked up Raven by her arms and carried her into her room. They laid her down on her bed, (she was quietly breathing, as if asleep) and then both doctors sat down on the bed. Jameson spoke.

"I was bringing her back to her room when she pointed at one of the guards and screamed. Then the wall she was next to exploded and knocked us both down. I think she took the brunt of the blast, but luckily, the biggest piece just fell to the ground and didn't hit her."

"You said she pointed at the guard? Like she was afraid of him, or recognized him?"

Jameson simply shrugged. "I don't know why?"

"Was it the guard outside?"

"No, someone he was talking to."

"I didn't see anyone else."

"Maybe he was the one that sounded the alarm."

Emma paused for a second, thinking. "I'll report this to Lieutenant Colonel Richardson."

"What should I do with Raven?"

"Well, tend to her wounds for now. And keep her drugged up. Sedate her as much as possible until she's acclimated to her medication." She got up, about to leave, then turned back and spoke. "And maybe do a damn CAT scan, she's had plenty of head trauma since she got here. Tables, walls—Jesus Christ, Jameson."

And with that, she left.

Some time later, once Jameson had also left the room, leaving Raven to sleep, a guard walked up by the door, and stood face-to-face with the room's guard.

"Leonard."

"Carlos, what are you doing here? You transfer already?"

"No. Look, it's harder to communicate here than we thought." He discretely handed Dillons an envelope. "That girl…was that my acquisition?"

"Think so."

"Guess she recognized me."

"The way I hear it, pretty soon she won't recognize her own mother."

"Good."

And he said good-bye, and left.

One Hundred Three:
Sunday Morning

Mina slowly woke up, yawning contentedly. She was holding her teddy bear. She gave it a light squeeze, thought better of it, and tossed it away. Looking around, she spied a note on her nightstand.

Mina-
Today I will be working with another subject. Please tend to your meals at the regular times. Practice your abilities if you wish but be careful.
                    -Dr. Jacobson

Mina was glad she could read (she wasn't sure that all of the children could,) but wished she had new books. She'd read all the ones she had countless times.

She sat up, readying herself to get up and get dressed, when she was stopped with an odd feeling, like sadness. She dismissed it and got up off of her bed.

As she got dressed she thought of very little. She had become accustomed to not feeling Matthew beneath her feet; she had gotten used to feeling differently than before the incident, even if she had new thoughts from time to time. It wasn't necessarily full complacency, at least as far as her feelings were concerned, but she wouldn't have resisted the doctors at this point without something out of the ordinary happening. It just wasn't something she had ever done and it wasn't something she now thought of as a course of action. She did, now and then, briefly entertain thoughts of breaking through the walls of the building to see what "outside" was, but she never seriously considered it.

She felt lazy today and she donned a light blue tank top and grabbed a pair of blue sweat pants. A thought occurred to her as she pulled them on. Today she would have plenty of free time. There was a good chance she could try to speak with Raven. Smiling, she put on a pair of pink bunny slippers, and left her room for the cafeteria.

As she walked down the hall, she noticed a guard was staring at her chest. The top she was wearing tended to hug her breasts rather tightly. She was used to having loose, or at least nondescript clothing; lately had been different, but all along she had been dimly aware that some of the men, doctors and guards alike, would stare at her chest and rear from time to time. A glance might not have bothered her, but there was something creepy about the way this man was looking at her.

She remembered suddenly the other night, when she had been lying on her bed, and she had fondled herself, and it had felt pleasurable, and it abruptly occurred to her then, after that line of thought, that the men staring at her chest might be doing so out of something related to sex.

She immediately thought of Matthew, and suddenly her perception of the guard changed from annoying to threatening. She put her hands over her chest and quickened her pace down the hall, feeling quite a bit less confident than she had when she'd gotten up.

One Hundred Four:
Proving Ground

"Welcome to our proving grounds, sir. One of the most barren places in this whole country."

Richardson looked around. Indeed, as far as the eye could see, he saw nothing but rocks, sand, and a handful of plants. And, of course, the army buildings and vehicles. It was cold, but there was no sign of precipitation.

The soldier led Richardson towards a group of people standing near an armored truck.

"You know the advisory board, of course?" spoke Nicholas Kresge.

"Ah, yes," said Richardson. "Wait, who's missing?"

A small, serious looking Asian woman spoke. "Dr. Zdorak and Admiral Jonas are busy with other matters."

"Ah. Of course." He motioned towards a woman standing next to Kresge. "And this is?"

"This is my assistant," said Kresge as the woman and Richardson shook hands.

He introduced them. "Lieutenant Colonel Richardson, this is Dr. Graley."

"How do you do," said Richardson, shaking the doctor's hand.

"Fine, fine, thank you." She smiled. "The pleasure's all mine, I'm sure."

One Hundred Five:
Letter

Dillons was sitting on his bunk, looking at the letter Carlos had given him.

Dear Leonard,
Hopefully it won't be much longer until I see you again, I miss you so
much. I spoke to the doctor. She said everything looks fine and we have nothing
to worry about. Your friend Mark called the other day, he said he had
everything ready for the party. Hope you'll be there. Hold tight, I'll see you
soon.

Love,
Carlene

It was easy enough to understand, and in fact didn't really say much. They probably just didn't want him to feel cut off and start worrying. It said several things distinctly: one, that Dr. Graley was completely confident that everything was going according to plan; two, that Marcus' group was ready for the strike if it became necessary; and three, that Carlos (Carlene!) would be transferred to NOD soon.

The thing about Carlos was that he always opted for the riskiest missions, sometimes even taking risks that weren't entirely necessary to get the job done. Even considering the danger inherent in his occupation, Carlos liked to live life on the edge even more so than his fellow operatives. On the edge of the edge. Dillons wondered if Carlos had been assigned to deliver this message to him, or if he had come of his own accord.

He shrugged, took some painkillers for his leg (psychobabble bullshit,) and proceeded to eat the letter.

One Hundred Six:
At Last

Mina had not seen Raven at breakfast, and she was now not in the playroom. It hadn't occurred to her that while she had the day off, Raven might not. She hoped that wasn't the case.

She sat still, trying to will her hand to feel the way it had the other day. Chemicals and reactions she had never experienced before had overwhelmed her body, but in the middle of it all, she was *sure* of that sensation.

It had been *her*. It had to be. And that had to mean something, right?

What are you doing?

Nothing, Danny.

Raven's not here.

How did you know I was thinking about her?

How do you think?

Keiko and Johnny. Do they know everything?

They know enough.

Do you know where she is?

She'll be here shortly.

What do you know, Danny?

I know nothing. I am the messenger. Would you like to play with the blocks?

Mina looked into his eyes. "No thanks," she said, and smiled. She glanced around the room. There, in the corner, a girl sat, watching bright flecks like embers dance around in front of her face. She spun them in intoxicating patterns, and Mina was caught up in it. She was unsure how much time had passed when the sound of a door opening stole her attention away.

Raven walked in, and Mina saw every detail perfectly. This was a girl stumbling forward, her head wobbling, her eyes darting back and forth in paranoia and fear. She wore white pajamas with light blue rabbits on them, and pink socks with yellow heels. Her hands clutched a plush green lizard. They were trembling, and her nails were bitten down to the point of painfulness. She had an expression on her face almost of pity. Mina could tell that yes, she had a pretty face, beautiful in fact, but it was hidden under cuts and bruises that looked worse than the last time Mina had seen her. Short brown hairs covered her head, but didn't hide the bruises and stitches there.

She looked over at Mina, and their eyes met. Raven dropped the lizard.

"Here, let me get that for you." Spencer Jameson reached down and grabbed the stuffed animal, handing it back to Raven. He walked over to a man standing nearby with a clipboard and handed him a piece of paper. "Keep her sedated," he said. "Notify me if anything…out of the ordinary happens." The man with the clipboard nodded, and Jameson left.

Mina stood up. She started walking towards Raven, who stood there, waiting. Mina had her hand held out. She could feel her heart beating.

Thump-thump. Thump-thump. Thump-thump.

There was a ringing in her ears, and then a voice in her head. But her heart was too loud; she couldn't make out what the voice was saying.

Thump-thump. Thump-thump. Thump-thump.

Her arm was straight out, her fingers inches from Raven.

Thump-thump. Thump-thump. Thump-thump.

She closed her fingers around the other girl's wrist.

There was no shock, no strange sensation, no feeling of closure. But she could feel the girl's warmth, and her pulse, and at that moment it matched hers beat for beat.

What is this?

"You want to sit down?"

Raven nodded. Mina led her to a table adjacent to a bench. She helped the girl into the seat and then sat next to her. Raven leaned against Mina's shoulder. Mina still held her hand.

Raven sighed. She smiled.

They sat there, side-by-side, and presently, Raven fell asleep. Mina looked at her warmly; she put an arm around her, and tried to make her more comfortable. And as Raven slept, Mina decided she felt pretty okay right now. And by and by, she nodded off as well. And both of their sleeps were untroubled.

One Hundred Seven:
Field Test

Richardson milled about in the dust, away from the pack of scientists and military who's-who's, kicking up small clouds as he paced. It was cold, but bearably so; apparently, today was "unusually warm" for northern Nevada at this time of year. He was smoking his last cigarette before the demonstration.

"So, this is a fully conscious subject? With no control unit?"

Kresge, who stood as still as a post regardless of Richardson's pacing, spoke. "Yamada claims his team has found a way to control a psychic through implants and conditioning. Implants that a healing-based biomorph can't reject."

"Even so, a conscious subject? That's still dangerous."

"They're all dangerous, Josh. I'd rather a manually controlled soldier than the alternative. You're the one who said domination was a dangerous ability."

"Of course it is. The whole, original idea was based around having a dominating unit control a squadron of soldiers. We never, well, *I* never knew how they were planning on controlling the control unit! Look at the Anna Incident. And Mina, the healer, said a 'Matthew' started her whole escapade."

"'Escapade'?" Kresge laughed. "You *do* have a sense of humor, don't you?"

Richardson inhaled and exhaled deeply, seeming to calm down, for the moment. "And what makes these implants so special that they actually stay inside the damn things?" he asked.

"He wouldn't say. Said it was 'still classified.' There's a reason Yamada himself isn't here. He doesn't want to risk—*coercion.*"

Richardson threw his arms up in exasperation, almost spitting out his cigarette. "So we're right back where we started! They know everything, we know nothing!" It was unlike him to lose his cool but the situation had him both irritated and anxious again over his own security.

"Don't worry," Kresge said. "We'll find out eventually. If nothing else, we'll take custody of the sample and dissect it ourselves. Besides, we have an ace in the hole."

"Oh yeah? What's that."

"That new subject, the teenager? That's Yamada's daughter. Now put that thing out, it's time." He turned to walk towards the waiting group, the nonchalance with which he had delivered that information metaphorically stabbing Richardson in the gut.

Richardson noticed from his position in the pack the unwavering direction of the sight of the people around him. It unnerved him a little, that all of them were staring straight forwards except for him. It seemed inhuman, somehow, like he was the only person with real thoughts on his mind other than what lay directly ahead. And he did have thoughts, and many of them involved worry. The worst of them was that the experiment they were about to attempt would go horribly wrong, and he would lose—among other things—his life.

Presently though, they arrived at a small building overlooking a shallow valley that, on closer inspection, looked to be in fact a crater. It had been partially obscured, built up to provide obstacles for training, but given the area's notorious history it was likely a bomb crater.

They stopped close enough to the edge to be able to see the whole of its insides. Down at the bottom were a tank and several concrete objects near which stood several soldiers. The man standing next to Kresge addressed the group. "This building is a blast shelter. If you'd all step inside, please."

Richardson noticed that none of the group budged an inch. "We'll all be fine here, soldier," said Kresge.

"As you wish, sir."

The door to the building opened, and a cute, mousy woman with long, wavy brown hair, glasses, and a lab coat—stepped out, carrying a metal briefcase. Behind her walked—floated—a being in a long, black cloak with a hood. None of his body was visible.

The woman greeted Kresge with an attempt at a handshake and spoke excitedly. "Hi, I'm Amy—"

He cut her off quickly. "You're our T-4, correct?"

The woman, Amy, felt deflated as she lowered her hand. "Yes, sir." She set her briefcase on a nearby metal folding stand and opened it up.

"Would you introduce our friend...Amy?" asked Kresge.

"Yes, yes, of course." As Amy fumbled with the contents of her case, she shot nary a glance at the robed figure that stood so menacingly behind her. "This is Tom. I will be telling you a little about him as the demonstration goes on. Tom, please take off your robe."

"Tom" did so in a very dramatic way, and even the most stalwart of the advisory board members gasped. Richardson couldn't help but gasp himself, but neither Kresge nor Dr. Graley made a noise.

Tom stood near or slightly past the six-foot mark. It was clear that he was naked, but he had no visible genitals. His head was bald, and his hands, feet, and head were all fairly normal looking, though quite pale, almost blue. The rest of his body was a dark black, covered by glowing red lines that crisscrossed and connected forming irregular polygons. The visual effect was not unlike cooling lava that had cracked, revealing the boiling and viscous liquid beneath. He appeared quite strong, though lithe. He said nothing, and made no movements other than blinking his yellow eyes occasionally.

"You will notice," she said, "that there are many controls within the briefcase I have." She motioned towards it, and indeed, there were several switches and screens within the case. "Should anything happen, that large red switch will activate a toxin held within Tom that will render him temporarily incapacitated." She giggled nervously after saying this. "As we, um, have not fully tested any of this yet, it is a necessity, I'm afraid."

Richardson felt his stomach turn.

Amy turned toward Kresge. "Shall we begin, sir?"

He nodded. One of the soldiers nearby said something into a walkie-talkie, and Richardson looked into the crater and saw that the men in it were scrambling into various positions.

"All right Tom," said Amy, "Hide yourself."

The air around Tom became excited. At the spots where his blackness terminated against the pale skin of his head, hands, and feet, his red lines spread outward like growing roots or veins. Behind them trailed the blackness, and once his entire body was red and black, the space surrounding him wavered and he vanished.

"Okay, um, you see, Tom's aura is bending and redirecting light to hide him visibly. The effect is not perfect; if either Tom or the objects behind him move quickly, the refraction effect sort of has to play 'catch-up' and the image will be somewhat distorted. Also, the cloak is not all-inclusive as far as all wavelengths are considered, but it is still quite effective."

Richardson looked at the spot where Tom was supposed to be. He did a double take when he thought he saw two grayish spots hanging in mid-air several feet above the ground.

"You may notice that you can see something where Tom's eyes should be. In order for him to see, he must weaken the cloak to let light into his eyes. Though this is not a huge giveaway, I assume your people are working on a second-sight correction for this problem? Anyway, let's begin, shall we?"

She turned around. "Okay, Tom, just like we discussed, incapacitate?" There was a wavering in the view ahead of Amy indicating that Tom was moving. When it had passed, she walked over to her case and began watching the readouts. "Some of Tom's powers include personal shielding, morphable bone blades, and telekinetic force blasts. We should see examples of all of these shortly."

Tom listened to the whistling of the wind as he flew towards his target. He smiled. He felt alive.

This was his purpose.

All of the ants scrambled around, not knowing which way to shoot. He taunted them, dropping his cloak and forcing sixteen-inch bone spurs out of his underarms at the same time. He barrel-rolled to the right, missing several rounds of gunfire. He heard them impact against the cliff wall far behind himself. Flying forward, he saw a hand-held laser being aimed at himself, and he calmly erected a pale, sea green shield in front of himself just before the man fired. The laser made a "pfft" noise against it as its power dissipated.

He re-cloaked.

On the ground below, the soldiers in the tank were looking for the faint infrared signal that would mark Tom's airborne form. The turret was swung to face his previous location, and when the sighting had been made, the aim was readjusted and the order to fire was given. The shell had barely left the cannon when a telekinetic attack blew it up. The resulting explosion crippled the turret and was concussive enough to force the tank backwards several feet.

With ground-troops scrambling around trying to get to safety and to get a fix on Tom, the defenseless tank was a sitting duck. Tom dove for it. He held his right arm out, blade extended, and focused his aura into a kinetic edge that sharpened and strengthened his blade. He swept along the side of the tank, digging into it to a depth of half a foot, all along its side. Rising into the air and reversing his facing as he climbed behind the tank, he fired a series of telekinetic projectiles into the gash along the vehicle's armor. It exploded from the inside out, blowing off the turret completely and bursting the armor plating open like it was the shell of a detonated grenade.

"Ooh, dear," said Amy. "Mr. Kresge, sir?" she asked, turning around.
"Please, continue, dear."
Meanwhile, Dr. Graley furiously took notes.

Tom hovered, watching the soldiers scramble around several sections of wall. A few were firing indiscriminately into the air. It was clear they had no idea where he was. He dove at one, his right arm held out. His blade sliced the man in two quite cleanly. His gun continued to fire as his top half began sliding to the ground even before the bottom half had time to topple. Tom watched this, smiling, as he flew past, rolling onto his back and looking down the length of his body to the man trying to flee the scene of his fresh kill. He unleashed a torrent of telekinetic pulses that hammered the man against a nearby wall and cut wet red holes throughout his body.

God, thought Richardson, *this isn't a test, it's a massacre*. But still, Kresge did not give the order to cease. And Richardson saw (and was surprised by how much it bothered him) the trembling hand of Amy, the scientist, poised above the controls in her briefcase, desperately awaiting the order to stop. The soldiers nearby stood steadfast and true, even as their colleagues were splattered against the crater's floor below.

For a brief instant, despite all he had seen already, Joshua Richardson questioned his own sanity.

The gunfire was dying down. There were a few desperate *rat-tat-tats*, but none were made with any attempt at aiming. Morale was broken but no one ran because no one knew which way was safe, and likely as not, no direction really was safe. Finally, a soldier rose, unable to resign himself to death without a fighting chance.

Tom flew towards him at full force. He erected his shield at the last possible moment, and crushed the young American against a wall section with such force that the wall cracked and fell over, the man's burst insides sliding down the stone and mortar with sickening slowness.

There were only two left. One had fainted, and was beheaded without resistance. The other one had begun running, but Tom impaled him from behind with both blades, pulling him up into the air. With one quick, calculated motion, he pushed one blade up towards the soldier's shoulder, the other, down towards the opposite hip, raining the man onto the rock below.

"Are they all dead?" Kresge asked Amy.

She looked over her displays. "Yes," she said, hesitantly.

"Push the switch."

She did, and a faint cloud of dust appeared in the crater below. When the dust cleared, a figure of red, black, and pale, pale white, was visible, unconscious on the rough ground.

Nicholas Kresge turned towards the advisory board. "If you can find a soldier more ruthless or efficient than him, I will eat my hat," he said, and walked away.

As he passed Richardson, he quietly said, "Don't worry, Joshua, that was exactly the demonstration I was promised."

As nonchalantly as possible, Richardson walked over to the opposite side of the shelter and proceeded to empty the contents of his stomach.

One Hundred Eight:
Head Trip

Sometimes my mind plays tricks on me, and I see things that aren't really happening right then. Sometimes I black out. Well, I used to, anyway.

A woman, a man, naked. Another woman, cries. A teddy bear falls. A scream. Bloodshed. A man confronts the child. He is familiar? A fight. Girl yells at girl. A new girl. A fight. Reconciliation. Death surrounds her. Damnation.

Mina awoke with a start, images and thoughts fading from her mind like an echo fades into quiet. She looked down and smiled. Raven was sleeping still, her head lying against Mina. Something about that just felt right; her heart seemed warm.

The remnants of her dreams all but gone, Mina closed her eyes for a moment. She thought of this girl, Raven, and wondered why she didn't talk. Mina felt confident though that she would, in time. She decided it was her duty to help the girl get used to life here, as Danny and the other children had helped her.

"Mina?"

Mina opened her eyes, briefly startled. A doctor was standing in front of her. She didn't know her name.

"I'm sorry to bother you, but Raven needs to eat now. I'm going to take her to the cafeteria."

"I can take her," offered Mina.

"Thank you, but I have to see someone there. You are, of course, welcome to come along."

So Mina woke Raven up. The doctor wiped a bit of drool from the girl's face, and helped her up. Holding her stuffed lizard, Raven shuffled along next to the doctor with Mina right behind.

At the cafeteria, Mina sat down with Raven. She saw the doctor hand the server a bottle of pills. Probably something that was supposed to go in Raven's food. Soon, Raven was eating—applesauce, some kind of liquid meat food, and potatoes. She used her spoon sloppily, her hand trembling the whole time. Her entire fist was clasped extremely tightly around the handle

Mina looked across the table at the battered girl. She felt completely compelled to stay with her. She could have sworn that there had been some— force—that beckoned her to do so. But, maybe it was just because Raven was the only other one like her among all of her peers. The only other one who did not look like a ghostly child. Maybe it was the newness of the girl, the knowledge that she would need help to get by. Maybe…maybe it was just her face, undoubtedly good-looking, but presently, battered and bruised.

Maybe it was more than that. Something undefined.

Raven sniffled. "Dead," she said.

"Who's dead?" asked Mina, suddenly concerned.

"I dunno."

"Do you want to…are you able to…do you need to talk?"

Mina grabbed her forehead, a sudden ache appearing in response to a series of images and concepts that glanced across her mind much too quickly to be individually acknowledged.

Please, not that fast, Mina thought to Raven. Raven looked shocked upon receiving this message. She dropped her spoon. The *clank* was very loud in the mostly empty room. She began to cry.

"I'm sorry," said Mina, moving to grab the spoon.

A server came over quickly. "Is everything all right?" he asked.

"Yes," said Mina, "I, um, think she isn't used to..tele…tele…mind-talking, yet. I startled her." The word failed her. Why?

This seemed to satisfy the server, and he walked away. When he was some distance away, Mina turned back to Raven, who was holding a new spoon the server had brought over, although she wasn't eating with it.

"Were you trying to tell me something?"

"Tell?" said Raven. "Telephone, *rrring*!" She giggled and her head drooped, her eyes almost shutting.

"You're drugged, aren't you? But differently than the rest?" asked Mina rhetorically.

"It won't stop ringing!" exclaimed a confused Raven, right before she passed out, visibly pained. It didn't seem as though she was actually answering Mina, just that she was saying whatever came to mind.

There was a presence behind Mina. She turned around.

"Hi," said Benny. "I came through the ceiling. Well, it's a floor, now." He shrugged.

They keep her drugged? Mina said to him. *Well, more than usual?*

She broke some stuff. They're scared. Danny would know more. They talk to him.

I want to talk to them.

Go ask them.

Mina didn't want to leave Raven, but if she could talk with Keiko and Johnny, maybe they could tell her more about Raven. They always seemed to know more than they should.

Mina was halfway down the hall near the playroom, looking for Keiko and Johnny, when she collapsed to the floor under tremendous mental strain. It felt like her eyes were open, but it seemed like dreaming. She felt drills in her skull.

There were too many images, tactile impressions, odors and sounds for her to deal with. A voice was audible in her head, barely able to cut through the din.

It was a voice both male and female. It was Keiko and Johnny.

The drugs affect her slowly, building to a point where the crescendo signals quasi-permanence. She nears that point where dosage changes and memories mellow. You made a connection before that and as long as she is scattered she won't know whose head to dream in.

Mina rocked around on the ground, holding her head tightly. Guards stood around her; doctors had been sent for, but her eyes and ears were shut to the outside.

She reaches out to you because you reached out to her. Soon, everything will normalize and she will be level, but incomplete.

"I don't understand!" Mina yelled. "I don't know all your words, or all your meanings!"

The medicine she takes, that we all take, changes you. Soon, those effects will root fully and she will be capable of regular conscious thought, but as a lesser person than you. Like all of us. You are immune.

"Lesser?" Mina was sweating profusely, the barrage of subconscious thoughts nearing her to delirium.

You are capable of thought and actions we are not, because of the drugs.

Drugs.

Drugs.

drugsdrugsdrugsdrugsdrugsdrugsdrugsdrugsdrugsdrugsdrugsdrugsdrugsdrugs drugsdrugsdrugsdrugsdrugsdrugsdrugsdrugsdrugsdrugsdrugsdrugsdrugsdrugs drugsdrugsdrugsdrugsdrugsdrugsdrugsdrugsdrugsdrugsdrugsdrugsdrugsdrugs

It was every voice in the building, and it was in her head. But the strength of the revelation cleared her and set her free.

Everyone was unable of incitement because of the medication that she herself was immune to.

She had never touched herself before the incident.

She had never questioned her place, or the right of the doctors to do what they did.

There had been talk of "before" this place, but never any concern about it. But when Matthew had controlled her, she had searched for files about her past. It didn't feel like her concern as much as his; she had sort of become him, wrestling with concepts even now, afterward, she had trouble understanding. But, it had still been her past they looked up.

Mina promised herself, whatever happened to Raven now, she would help her know herself someday, no matter what. That's what the dream was, right? Raven's memories, or attempts at memories?

"Pupil dilation is normal."

She'll tear the world apart one day. If you help her free herself, it will happen.

It's the right thing to do.

"Blood pressure is normalizing. Mina?"

The voice in her head became strictly female. It was Keiko, and if Mina had had the faculties to discern this fact, she would have marveled at how baby-like and unfinished Keiko's voice was.

I have seen another way. You can be her handle. We make no promises; nothing is definite. You cannot save everyone, but you may be able to save her, at least.

"Mina?"

Save her from who?

From herself. Keep her human. Well, as human as you are, at least.

There was a fit of giggling in Mina's head.

Is this a game to you?

"Mina?"

Mina realized she was staring up at someone blurry. She focused. It was Dr. Jacobson. She was surrounded by a halo? No—lights. Like an operating room.

"It's not a game," she muttered. Mina tried to sit up, and discovered she was restrained. She grunted.

"Mina?" said Dr. Jacobson. "Should I release you?"

"I'm okay," she said groggily.

Dr. Jacobson, assisted by a woman doctor Mina did not know by name, unclasped the leather straps on Mina's arms and legs. "What happened, Mina?" Dr. Jacobson asked.

"I was with Raven, and I left to see…um, and my head hurt really badly." It was definitely not the whole truth, but Mina was unsure if she wanted to say the whole truth, even after she'd sifted through it. What exactly did happen?

Mina glanced over at the other doctor, and Emma understood and asked her to leave. When it was just the two of them, Mina spoke again.

"Whatever's happening to Raven isn't done yet."

"What do you mean?" asked Emma, a skeptical look on her face. Mina didn't want to tell her everything that had transpired for fear of what the doctor would think. However, the fact that she was restrained within the previous five minutes was not lost on her. After what had happened, there was no way she could afford to look…

What was the word?

Crazy?

Was it a no-win situation?

"Raven spoke to me. Tele…pathically. With images and words."

Emma looked both intrigued and worried. "What did you see? What did she say?"

"I couldn't tell, everything happened all at once. I think it's because… she's on medication, right doctor?"

Emma saw what Mina meant, and conceded this point to her. "Raven is on a different medication than the other children. It is very likely that for the remainder of the time she is taking this medication, she will be confused. Is that what you meant by it isn't done yet?"

"Yes. That was my guess," Mina lied. She hadn't guessed; Keiko and Johnny had told her, in their traditional roundabout way. "Her thoughts seemed very confused."

Emma spoke. "You seem okay now, but I want you to let me know if anything like this happens again, okay?"

"Okay."

"Promise?"

"Promise."

"Anyway, Raven asked for you. She was napping in the cafeteria, but I was notified that she had woken with a start and appeared very troubled."

"Does she know my name?"

"I don't know. She just asked for 'the girl.' I assumed that was you." Mina looked hopefully up at Emma, who audibly gasped at just how unearthly blue Mina's eyes were.

No, they weren't unearthly blue; they were earthly blue. Emma felt she could see the entire world reflected in those eyes, and it was all she could do to pull her gaze away. For the briefest moment, she felt utterly intoxicated. It didn't seem to be something she could get used to.

"You may leave."

Emma watched Mina leave, and she had a sudden crazy thought. Not of anything specific, it was more like a premonition or a feeling, that Mina meant something very significant, and not just for her work.

"Ah ha!" cried Emma, having a eureka moment, pushing away the feeling she had just had and conjuring a new idea involving the possibility of duality between Mina and Raven, just like…

Keiko and Johnny, thought Mina as she walked down the hallway towards their room. *Maybe…*

She had wanted very much to go back and see Raven, but she felt this was important, too. She had reached their room but before she had even announced her presence they had told her to *Come in.*

There was a pink, bubble-shaped couch in front of a flickering TV. They sat on the floor, watching the soft glow in dim light.

They spoke together.

You want us to explain what Raven means.

Yes.

Johnny looked up at Mina and spoke quite frankly. "We don't know."

"What do you mean?"

He continued talking, although now it was Keiko's voice that issued from his mouth.

"We see some things clearly, and other things we see indistinctly, and sometimes there are different paths."

"What do you see clearly about Raven?" asked Mina.

"That she will tear the world apart."

"Indistinctly?"

"Whether that is good or bad."

"Any different paths?"

"Whether or not you save her."

"Can you be more specific, please?" Mina was on her knees. Everything about this girl seemed so important to her suddenly. Maybe it was the idea that she could provide Raven's salvation that appealed to her, because in a way it would be like making up for the salvation she could not find for herself for killing those people. Even if it hadn't been her fault.

They spoke into her head now, as they intently watched the television.

Jump into the fire or pull her from it. Succeed, or fail.

"That's not much of a choice!"

We never said you had a choice, only that there were different paths.

"That doesn't make any sense."

Continue as you are going and you will reach a point. There, you will either succeed, or fail. It is unclear.

Mina put her head in her hands and started crying. "I don't understand anything," she sobbed. "Nothing, nothing at all."

Johnny walked over and put a hand on her shoulder. It was small, and chubby: a toddler's hand. He smiled warmly, and said to her, "You will. When you are free. Then you will understand everything."

"Everything that matters, anyway," said Keiko.

"And stop beating yourself up inside," said Johnny. "Matthew killed those people, not you."

Keiko, too, smiled warmly. "You'll have it easier than we do. You won't have to live in each other's heads—only in each other's hearts."

Mina walked huffily down the hall. She didn't know why she was so bothered with what Keiko and Johnny had told her.

And then it hit her: she didn't know why she was so bothered by *anything*. She never had been before.

It was more than a crisis of character—it was a crisis of *everything*.

Who the hell was she?

Was there a good reason for her to believe Keiko and Johnny?

Or Danny?

Or Dr. Jacobson?

She looked at her hand. Was that all that was truly real? And was it really?

But, the last things the children had each said—they gave her comfort.

She began running, and she didn't stop until she found Raven, in her room, next to Mina's own room.

"My name's Mina," she panted, out of breath. She held her hand out.

Raven looked confused. "Raven?" she asked as much of herself as of Mina. She reached her hand out, and Mina grasped it firmly in her own. And there was that spark—whether it was in her hand or her heart, Mina could not tell. But it was there. A kindred spirit was with her, trapped in the prison of her own mind.

Raven was new, and unformed. "I don't remember," she sobbed, and Mina held the taller girl closely. "I know there's important things, but I don't remember what they are."

"One day," Mina whispered, "one day we'll leave this place and find all of our memories."

Raven nodded. The fog tried to creep back in, robbing her of the need to remember. Slowly, it succeeded, but Mina meant what she said. One day.

One Hundred Nine:
And So

The next two-and-a-half weeks brought a few changes, though not to everyone.

Although Mina spent a good deal of time with Raven, talking to her, reading to her, and playing with her and with Danny and the others in the playroom, there were only a handful of occasions where Raven seemed at able to speak intelligently with Mina. Only rarely did she say something that seemed anything other than nonsense. There were no more instances of Raven filling Mina's head with thoughts and images, at least.

Despite the rareness of direct communication, Mina treasured her time with Raven and couldn't help but feel a leap in her heart whenever she went to spend time with her. Raven clearly reciprocated some affection; she had begun eschewing her stuffed lizard in exchange for having a free hand with which to hold Mina's. Even when she was unable to speak in meaningful ways, she would smile, and every now and then, Mina could swear she saw some sort of glimmer deep in her blank stare.

Raven's physical and chemical state left her constantly fatigued, so fairly often she would nod off while Mina read to her on her bed. Mina would lovingly place an arm around her, and would let her sleep, feeling content to bring her comfort.

Mina easily accepted this routine, and the atrocities that had been committed by her body, while never far from mind, bothered her less and less. Though not under the effects of any medication or therapy of any sort, she accepted her surroundings nearly as much as she always had, for they were familiar to her and seemed, at least right now, to pose no threat.

The reasons that Raven and Mina had so much free time were two fold. One reason was that although Spencer Jameson supervised Raven, she had not yet completed the cycle of memory-altering drugs, and was still considered unready for experimentation. The other reason for the open schedule was that Emma, having done some research spurred on by the notes she had recently discovered, was well on her way to formulating various testable theories regarding biomorphic stimulus response. Unable to do all of the math herself, she had several mathematicians and bio- and particle physicists working with her.

Keiko and Johnny remained quiet. When they had nothing to say, they said nothing.

Dr. Graley was very impressed with the demonstration she had witnessed with her co-conspirator, General Nicholas Kresge, and was eager to commence with the operation; however, the full guard staff rotation of NOD was still incomplete. Kresge was happier than he had been for quite some time.

Lieutenant Colonel Joshua Richardson was also quite upbeat, time having cleared his mind of the poison of the atrocity he'd seen, and certain that the demonstration that the advisory board had recently witnessed would insure his position for quite some time, once he realized how positively they had felt towards it. Little did he know his superior was involved in a plot that worked best with him out of the way.

And, far away yet right next door, a being lived, biding its time, waiting for its chance to work out a plot of its own.

One Hundred Ten:
Breakthrough!

Emma looked at the scaly tentacle on the monitor in front of her and shivered. "Reminds me of my last boyfriend," she quipped.

That thought, instead of taking the creepy edge off of M's alien body structure, only served to remind her that she had not had a boyfriend for several months. Almost a year, as a matter of fact. She was an attractive, successful woman. So, what was the matter?

"I'm too damn successful," she muttered, trying to remember the last time she had had more than two days off in a row, and couldn't. Hell, she rarely had two days off in a row.

Sighing, she flicked a switch and a faint hum filled the room. A series of lights lit up on the device next to M. It had been built hastily by her and her staff to test out some theories they had worked out. Based on the equations written on the x-rays she had discovered (which she had been assured were related to relatively simple particle physics) a device consisting of several radiation emitters had been slapped together. Theoretically, it would produce a biomorphic reaction, but precisely what reaction that would be was unknown.

M was sheathed in a high-tech, lead-based fabric that was highly resistant to radiation. A collection of instruments and sensors surrounded his tendril, exposed within the lead sheath. Among them, of course, was the camera that fed the image she was currently looking at to her monitor.

She glanced over at the male scientist who was assisting her. Jameson had turned down the request to help with this project, citing important work with Raven as a priority. So, Emma had to rely on the next highest-ranked doctor. Of course, it had been her who had set his security level, after all.

"Are you ready?" the doctor asked, standing next to a large control kiosk that was connected to the instruments around the tendril via a lead-lined tube that passed through the sheath. Emma replied yes, and the man began entering data and pressing buttons on the machine. "Okay," he said, after a bit.

Emma pressed a switch on her control panel that had a sticker label above it that read in bold black-on-yellow, "PRESS TO START." Immediately, the image on the monitor showed signs of interference.

"Raising radiation to point-one-two percent maximum output," said the male scientist. The image yellowed a bit; Emma noticed that the hairs lined up on the tendril and began to wave in unison with each other.

"Point-one-five," said Emma.

"Point-one-five," said her assistant.

The hairs beat faster.

"Point-two-oh," said Emma.

"Point-two-oh," said the scientist.

The hairs beat faster; the image was slightly fuzzy and greenish.

"Point-two-five," said Emma, excited.

"Point-two-five," was the reply.

The lines that delineated M's surface into polygonal shapes began to glow red. On the green-tinted monitor, they looked to be a bright brown.

"Point-two-eight," said Emma. Her assistant, staring at the image in his own monitor, silently adjusted. The hairs seemed to burn away and the glow pulsed dimmer, than brighter.

"Point-three-oh," said Emma. The results were instantaneous; the bare skin sections on the monitor became black and the red lines became very bright. The monitor's image was becoming increasingly fuzzier, though.

Emma quickly jotted down a note on a nearby sheet. *Visual confirmation of channel-1 radiation effect lambda-upsilon occurred between .28 and .30 % of maximum output.*

"Start channel two radiation at twelve percent maximum output," said Emma enthusiastically.

Immediately with the compliance of this command, the surface of the tendril pulsed and writhed in sections, bumps forming, running along a length of the skin, and then disappearing.

"I believe the desired effect has been achieved, has it not, doctor?" said the male scientist, quite happy with the result.

"Yes, but I'd like to continue the experiment. Raise channel two to twenty-five percent."

"Doctor?"

"It's all right."

"As you say."

The skin of the tendril writhed spastically, but when the radiation reached the level that Emma had specified, the monitor's image became totally garbled. Every couple seconds, an image would appear that was just barely discernible but it would be gone so fast that it was hard to tell what any one specific image contained.

It seemed that the whole tendril was now writhing, as it was in a wholly different position in each clearer image. Then it seemed to stay in one place, but the surface changed. A rapid succession of images interspersed throughout the static gave impressions of limbs, heads, unknown organic structures forming and un-forming out of the tendril. A toothy grin, an eye, a finger, among the many unknown, fleeting images. It was impossible to tell how frequent the changes were, except that with each usable image, the structure was different.

Emma stood up.

"Doctor?"

Emma looked at her assistant. "Shut off channel two."

He was just about to do so, when a sudden explosion of energy knocked him out of his chair and knocked Emma flat on her ass.

"Shit," said Emma, getting up. Much of M's lead sheath had been blown open, due to an explosion apparently located around the instrument cluster of the tail. The whole area was smoking, and faint flickers of fire were visible through the smoke. Several red lights flickered on the ceiling and an alarm began blaring.

"Abort fire suppression!" Emma yelled, reaching for a fire extinguisher. "Authorization Jacobson, Emma!"

"FIRE SYSTEM ABORTED," said a computerized voice as Emma pushed away the torn edge of the lead sheath and used the extinguisher on the smoldering mechanisms.

"What's the status of the instruments?" she asked loudly.

Her assistant pulled himself into his chair. "Um, all experimental instruments offline. I read radiation levels as no threat."

"What was that explosion!?"

"Ah, my readings indicate it was possibly psionic in origin, although the stray radiation makes making a decision difficult. Either we pushed it too far, or the instruments themselves."

"Wow," said Emma, more interested in what she was seeing than in what she had heard.

As the smoke cleared, Emma could see that the inside of the lead containment sheath was spattered with blood. M's tendril, now its usual color save for charred and blistered areas, had a large chunk missing, and blood was gushing out. But the blood was slowing because the missing area was shrinking, as were the marks of fire damage.

M was healing itself as rapidly as Mina was able to

"Back to square one?"

"No," answered Emma. "We're on the right track. It's all connected, no doubt about it. Healing and biomorphics." She bit her tongue before saying any more; no one she had worked with knew where she was going with this, and she wanted to keep it that way, at least for now.

Something came over her then and there, something that helped her push away many of the doubts she had had. She had just tasted discovery, and it filled her with an urge to do more.

Back to the moment, she wanted to inspect the wound. Pulling a pair of latex gloves out of her lab coat, she put them on and reached out to grab the tendril and turn it so she could get a better look.

"Jesus Christ!" she yelled, pulling her hands back.

"What?"

Emma stared at the inside of the wound.

There were eyes staring up at her. After a moment, they seemed to flee into the shaft of the tendril, as though they were independent organisms unconnected to the larger one. It was exceedingly disturbing, and continued to drive home the point that while the M generator may have once been human, it was now something completely different, something completely alien.

The other scientist, now standing next to Emma and looking into the hole that had all but closed up, said, "I'm going to be sick." Emma agreed, but said nothing to that extent.

The damaged area of the tentacle was now marked with nothing more serious than a gash. Emma pulled off the gloves. "Get me a full read out of all the sensors' information," she said, a very bothered look on her face.

"Yes, ma'am."

One Hundred Eleven:
Coming Out of It

Raven scratched furiously with both hands. "All my stitches itch," she said sorrowfully.

Mina carefully pulled the girl's hands away from her head. "All your stitches have been taken out," she reminded her futilely.

Mina looked Raven's head over. Her hair, now visibly brown, had grown long enough in the last couple of weeks to hide any bruises or scars she may have had left on her head. Her face was healed completely and it was obvious now that she was absolutely beautiful. There were moments when Mina wanted to touch a finger to her lips, to feel their softness, but she resisted.

But those eyes—they were dead.

They were brown, and peculiar in a way Mina was not very familiar with, which made them even more alluring. There was the one lady—Utsugi—and some of the children, maybe, who had similarities, but Raven's were much prettier.

But there was no sparkle there. Well, that wasn't entirely true. Now and then Mina swore she could see something. But, by and large, they were the eyes of someone who had never seen anything worth remembering.

Or had seen but couldn't remember?

There was a difference, though. Raven would look at Mina deliberately, sometimes, and it was the same gaze she had when she looked at the wall.

But she didn't smile at the wall. Only at Mina.

"My prescription's low," said Raven.

"What are you talking about?" asked Mina, wishing she could make heads or tales of the girl's jabbering.

"The nervous system's down, I know."

She sounded like she was repeating something rather than trying to convey some message. But it was hard to tell; most of her speech was in monotone except when she sounded deeply sad.

"It's so cold, Mina," Raven said, surprising Mina greatly, as she rarely used names, even in moments of full coherence. She had had a crayon in her right hand, which she dropped before hugging Mina tightly. She responded by hugging Raven back.

"What's the matter, Raven?"

Raven just whimpered.

"It's all right, I don't expect you to say anything."

"My head hurts. I wish it would stop."

"Do you hear that?" Jameson said to nobody in particular, watching Raven through the playroom's two-way window. "The final stage is almost complete!"

He was excited because Raven was showing signs that the last round of medications needed to alter her memory state had almost completed their necessary cycle. It was the matter-of-fact, meaningful things she was saying with increasing regularity: she was starting to make sense when she spoke.

"Air is orangey," Raven said.

Well, starting to make sense, at least.

Within the last week, Raven had shown signs that she was coming out of the drug-induced stupor she had been in. She still said bizarre and apparently meaningless things on a regular basis, but she had been steadily improving. Soon, she would be ready for the mood-altering drugs all of the subjects took to keep them in line.

Almost all of them.

Jameson had nothing but contempt for Mina. Regardless of whether or not the "possession" story was true—the one the entire faculty seemed to be aware of, regardless of individual clearance level—he didn't trust her. He wasn't exactly scared of her, but she was unmedicated, uncontrolled—an unknown.

Lately, Emma had been busy with the M generator, and her research, and Mina was basically free to do as she wished, which, most of the time, was to spend time with Raven, Jameson's charge. Raven, being not through her drug cycle yet, was also not restricted by scheduling, as she was not ready for regular research yet. This gave the two of them plenty of time together, and it irked Jameson.

On one hand, it confused the hell out of him. Mina—seemingly pleasant, naive, free-minded; and Raven—sedated and practically a vegetable—had somehow formed some kind of friendship. They were essentially inseparable, even holding hands when they walked together. It just didn't make sense.

The other problem was that this relationship was likely to continue, and even grow, once Raven was fully cycled. Even though—hopefully—she would be just as simple-minded and easy to deal with as the children were, she would be far more of a person than she was now. And Jameson had a feeling that this relationship was going to interfere with his work with Raven, because of Mina's potential to be willful, a trait unprecedented among the test subjects.

And, he needed to do great things with Raven, ground-breaking and important tests and experiments—he had to convert Raven's raw power into something fine-tuned, controllable, impressive, and most of all, most likely, usable and reproducible.

It wasn't just his thirst for greatness, it was the fact that getting paid to be a snitch only worked so long as one had someone to snitch on, and given the professionalism Emma had shown very recently regarding her work, Jameson might not have much to snitch on for long.

Raven had really only become his charge due to Emma's whims, but it *could* be a step to greatness—only the two of them had personal charges, and only they were post-pubescent test subjects.

Post-pubescence. He looked at them. They were sharing a bench seat, Raven's legs up with her feet on the seat and her knees to her chest, leaning against Mina with her eyes closed. Mina was casually sitting, with an arm around Raven, gently stroking her hair.

Jameson felt a sudden rush of self-loathing and annoyance at the thoughts that ran through his head. But, there was no denying that they were a pair of very attractive girls. Raven, once her bruises had healed and her hair had started to grow back, had proven to be a stunner, even with her dull, lifeless eyes. Though she was generally dressed in shapeless pajamas or sweats, he had performed her physical and she was slender but nicely proportioned, with gentle curves.

Mina was unnaturally beautiful, though there was a childish quality to her face, probably because of its roundness and plump cheeks. She had—for whatever reason—been allowed to wear more "civilian" clothes as of late, and though today she was wearing sweat pants and a hoodie, he'd seen enough to become acutely aware of how curvaceous her diminutive frame really was.

With disgust, he shook his head, trying to dismiss such thoughts.

He needed to get out more, away from this damned building, and hit the dive bars and skin joints.

One Hundred Twelve:
9362469232:2

Steve Phillips lay on his bed, thinking, *This is going to be the worst Christmas ever.*

Snow was falling outside.

It had been falling since the end of November. Omaha summers were hot and humid; winters could be on the milder side of cold during the days, but there was usually plenty of snowfall. This year, temperatures had stayed fairly low and there wasn't much time for melting.

A stack of books sat in a corner next to a large binder and other college-related paraphernalia.

Other, none-college paraphernalia sat on the TV tray next to his bed.

His room was a mess of scratched-up CD's and clothes.

Raven used to give him crap, ask him why he didn't just get an MP3 player. He said he liked the sound on the CD's better.

There were nearly always scratched; nearly always had been.

Raven.

There was a stack of boxes in the corner, filled with Raven's clothes, music, her favorite books, whatever him and that little freak Sam were able to get in one trip, that night he'd gotten drunk and high and decided he would be damned before he'd leave her shit to get sold off at some auction or destroyed.

She was out there. Somewhere. She had to be.

The refrain of the song he was listening to came on for the second time. It was an old CD; this was the only track that didn't skip.

It was the only track that perfectly described how he felt at this exact minute.

He pulled the CD out of the player and threw it at the wall edgewise, where it shattered into several pieces and tumbled onto the floor.

"Fags," he said in disgust, and rolled over.

One Hundred Thirteen:
Congratulations

Emma Jacobson had made a very important decision.

She was done playing games with Richardson.

She needed full disclosure.

She entered his office.

He was sitting at his desk, reading something off of his laptop and finishing up a cigarette.

"Very good work," he said.

"Thank you," said Emma. "Now, what I'd like to talk to you about is—,"

He cut her off. "I've already raised your security clearance, Emma. Please, have a seat." He motioned to a chair in front of his desk as he put out the smoldering butt of his cigarette. After she had taken a seat, he closed the laptop and folded his hands.

"Emma, you are no doubt wondering why you had to arrive at conclusions and methods that have already been determined by your predecessors. Frankly, I wasn't sure if I could trust you at first and I did not allow all of the information you would require in your work to be provided immediately. There were certain other things contained in the same security clearance. Specifically, there were many—atrocious—results of Dr. Utsugi's biomorphism project. In their own ways, they were far more atrocious than Arty or M. I was afraid…"

"It would be too much for me to handle," Emma finished for him. She was feeling brave and for some reason, exhilarated and oddly secure. She offered information. "Listen…I found things that Dr. Hanin had written. I know that it was a military project. He also mentioned a prototype psychic called Angel."

"Yes, well," Richardson cleared his throat, trying to hide his surprise. "There is much that I am still learning myself. I was not privy to everything before. I want to assure you, however, that regardless of what you may have read, the weapons division of biomorphics research no longer exists." He bent closer to her, trying to speak in a warm, caring voice. "All of the work we do now is dedicated to two things: good, old fashioned scientific research, and the energy project. All of the work done here, Emma, while it may seem brutal at times, will one day make the entire world a better place."

Richardson was still big on the posturing, talking about how grand NOD's work was, and Emma still did not trust him very much. But she trusted him enough, after his glowing accolades towards her, to believe that her life was not in danger.

Richardson sat up straight. "I was pleasantly surprised that you worked out those stimulus-response reactions for M by yourself. It took your predecessors much longer to arrive at that point."

"Thank you, sir, but of course, I had some things to point me in the right direction, and my staff did most of the work with the equations—,"

"Of course, of course, Emma. Credit where credit is due. But this is your project, and you did the experiment based on theories you had worked out. Never forget that subordinates are…subordinates. They help, but you are the one that is truly responsible."

Emma couldn't help but smile. A part of her felt a little giddy, even though it was obvious he was talking her up on purpose. "Hopefully the information I can access now will allow me to start experimenting on Mina." She felt her stomach drop as soon as she realized what she said.

"Sir…" she began.

"Yes?"

She was going to ask Richardson's opinion about what she had read regarding Hanin's belief that somehow Matthew's…soul, or whatever…was able to reach through the M generator to possess other psychics. She fully believed at this point that this was what happened to Mina. And, there were the anomalous readouts of M's brain activity. She had been checking them everyday, and since he—it—had been detached from the Nod portal, those waveforms had not reappeared. Still, that was not conclusive proof that it was harmless now. Then, there was the existence of Angel, and the fear Hanin had regarding its potential powers…in the hands of Matthew.

Richardson knew of and believed that Anna had been possessed by Matthew, and was not ruling that out as the cause behind Mina's insurrection. But he was mostly unconcerned, believing the benefits to far outweigh the risks.

"Never mind," she said. "I have work to get to."

"Of course," agreed Richardson. "Oh, by the way…how is Raven progressing?"

"Dr. Jameson has reported that she has nearly completed her initial medication cycle."

"I know you'll be busy with Mina, Emma, but try to find time to work with both girls, all right?"

"Yes, of course."

"I will email you the information regarding your security clearance."

"Thank you…Joshua." Emma left his office, closing the door behind her. Against better judgment, she felt almost thrilled to have access to new information about her work, regardless of whether Lieutenant Colonel Richardson was being absolutely truthful or not. She had a feeling he wasn't; but discovery could be such a rush and Emma was eager to get started.

Angel, though, was a big question. Emma partially wished she had pushed for more information. If he held the key to a psychic with no conscious brain function, he might very well be the only way to render a humane outcome to the energy project.

Eventually, she would have to cross that bridge.

One Hundred Fourteen:
Dream Time

Raven crawled around on her bed, alternating between moving on all fours and rocking forward and backwards with her arms wrapped around bent legs. Voices kept trying to say things in her head but they faded in and they faded out and she didn't know what they were talking about.

It was building to an avalanche, a crescendo, a cascade failure of her brain to work as a normal person's. There would come a sudden change, and then her chemistry would accept the maintenance drugs that would keep her in a perpetual state of foggy acceptance, denying her access to feelings and memories until eventually, even her unconscious mind would forget her past and it would be forever lost to her.

She cocked her head to the side and looked at the wall by the door. There was a patch that was whiter than the rest of the wall, where it had been fixed and plastered and repainted after she had broken it.

She concentrated without knowing why, and she had a distinct awareness of every molecule in a very specific area. And she spoke to them without words, and they did her bidding.

Her bidding was not nearly as focused and precise as her ability to cause it was.

The plaster merely crumbled onto the floor, exposing the wiring and framework beneath it.

This tiny act, coupled with the maelstrom in her head, was enough to make Raven pass out.

She dreamt of a seizure, and a kind face lined in red light that asked her if she was okay, and arms that held her and made her feel all right. But then the dream dropped away, and all that accompanied her until she awoke was a tangled mess of black and green nothingness.

Mina's sleep was very troubled. She dreamt of horrible things, of a cabin in the winter woods, a relic of older times, snow drifts almost as tall as she was pressed up against the sides like an icy comforter wrapped around a freezing child.

She saw the girl inside, young and cold and naked and all alone.

But then the girl was outside, and she could hear the wind howl, much louder than the heating ducts ever got. And Mina felt certain that she herself would pass out, but she was already asleep, and could not.

There were two men. They died.

Did the girl kill them? Or...?

To provide for the girl, they must die.
It all went red.
And she was warm, for a little while.
There was a great gnashing of teeth.
Stringy, red, disgusting.
Gnashing of teeth.
Voraciously filling herself so death would not come.
But death never came.
Gnashing.
She gulped; swallowed, and threw up.
Of Teeth.
She bit again, and this stayed down.
And when it was gone, she waited.
But death never came, gnashing its teeth.

Mina woke up with a scream, her body slick with sweat. She reached to wipe away the blood that was on her mouth, but it wasn't there anymore.

Was it ever?

Years ago, her head seemed to answer, but the details faded leaving her with faint glimpses of her dreams and horrible fear. She took some solace in that Matthew was not below, but even the fear of him had faded and this was little comfort.

Was she the little girl in her dream? She couldn't remember her face, or her hair, or any fine details.

They left her to die, she thought. *That girl was left there on purpose.* She couldn't have said why she was sure of this, for it was only a dream. Right?

The behemoth slept in the basement, the faint buzzing of its TVs accompanied by the out of sync beatings of its hearts and the breeze of its respiration. Part of it was as just awake as part of it was asleep, and both parts shared the same thought: *We hope our end draws near.*

He stayed in the emptiness, fretting, in a place that was like having eyes shut so tight you saw things, and couldn't tell the difference between light and dark. He watched great circles spin and spheres turn and hyperspheres rotate inward and outward simultaneously.

Not even the most nebulous of links existed anymore between his ether-self and his matter-self. If the body was dead, he was truly forsaken.

The elders asked him to pass along the dreaming roads and watch creation smite Armageddon and watch apocalypse beget The Beginning. To follow the circles was to understand everything.

He watched pure energy be born and die at the same time. The child was its mother's mother, and mother and child were one and the same.

The others said words to him, nod and dreamtime and astral and ether and quiddity and altjeringa and sea of stars and any other word or phrase they held dear from literature or life that described this brave new world to them.

But they all bored him.

There were no sins of the flesh, no touch as he cherished it, or at least believed he did.

No lives to hold in his hands.

No truths to learn.

They spoke of pleasure and bonding that he could try and delight in if that was all he wanted in life.

But he did not want to fuck vortices.

They spoke of the city of dreams and truth, of Gloria Incandessa, the Light Behind the Shroud, the Secret Under the Veil, that he could explore, if his ways were changed and his transgressions pardoned. There, soul could be made flesh, and space be made matter, and he could find the realism he craved, perhaps.

He would have none of that.

The Outlands were his home, the Badlands of roving beings and threats that were the literal manifestations of the chaos that slept all around.

A world without entropy and rot had to have some outlet for its negative forces, and so the wraiths and jabberwockies crept to kill and eat the unwary.

He would kill too, but in the real world…or he'd die trying.

One Hundred Fifteen:
Professionalism

Introduction to Psychic Phenomena Theory in Regards
to Artificial Psychic Organisms 88.dfg15-62
(For complete transcript please refer to PNR 1q46)

Psychic phenomena (also referred to as psionic
phenomena) is properly referred to as ENA (extra-
neural activity.) ENA is any and all manifestations
of brain activity not directly included among
regularly expected functions of the human mind, such
as: autonomic activity, thoughts and chemical-
emotional activity, normal bodily control and
function, standard sensory perception, etc.

Most psychic abilities seem to be carried on
recessive genes and are thus dormant among most of
their carriers. In some cases, conditions similar to
epilepsy and various mental illnesses seem to result
from carrying such recessive genes. It is hoped that
through the stimulatory effects of what is known as
"The Process," such recessive genes can be triggered
and supplemented through added abilities, via the
activation of implanted genetic structure.

Unfortunately, an exhaustive study of human DNA is
outside of the budgetary limits of this facility.
Additionally, it is of the writers' opinion that the
Human Genome Project is not up to the task this
facility would require and is therefore not valid as
a final resource.

It is thus the policy of this facility that the
creation of an artificially sequenced psychic
organism is understandably difficult. It is by
unfortunate necessity that result-oriented base pair
sequencing is based on theoretical results and
suspect data. In layman's terms, genetics is an
extremely complex area of study and mistakes will

```
happen with predictable regularity.

    However, let us remember that experimental work is
the core of all science. It is often easier to
disprove than to prove; yet both take knowledge
farther.
```

Emma had been browsing new files since she had arrived at work this morning, but this was the first one that contained data regarding the artificial creation of psychics. The facts surrounding the trio of prototypical perfect psychics Matthew, Andrew, and Angel intrigued her greatly, although it was hard to say if this was due more to the potential threat of Matthew, or to the fact that all the information regarding them that she had come across so far was highly interesting, yet tantalizingly brief.

In regards to her work, cloning wasn't an area she was concerned with. If she reached a stage where the creation of a being seemed like the next logical step, than she would worry about that then. All that she truly needed to worry about now was getting familiarized with the energy project data that was contained in the files she now had access to.

She had some ideas for experiments, such as a larger scale version of the one that had produced a biomorphic reaction in M's tendril. She thought it better to do some reading first, however, not only to avoid repeating steps her predecessors had already taken, but also to try and avoid problems like the small explosion that had occurred in her last experiment. She was a little giddy, however, finally feeling like she had some actual meat to sink her professional teeth into.

Emma had a saying she liked, although in truth she thought it more than she ever said it aloud. It was that all science was ninety-nine percent information gathering and only one percent actual experimenting. She wasn't sure if she'd read it somewhere or made it up herself, but it had never seemed truer than during the last month. True, it was to be expected that one would have a lot of reading to do after being promoted as far above her old station as she had been, but with the way Richardson had dicked her around and hid information from her, she'd wasted a lot of time. She was fairly certain that when she had thought of something specific to do, more often than not she was just repeating an experiment that she hadn't been allowed to read about yet.

It was rather frustrating.

Emma thought of Richardson. She had actively found him attractive not all that long ago, and those feelings had changed to revulsion and fear fairly easily. She would never forget Carl's death, nor would her stomach ever stop turning at the thought of the experiments NOD did on children and some of the disastrous results.

But, Emma was a scientist. And the problem with science is that it involves so many slow processes. Biology, astronomy, and geology all involve changes that take thousands, even millions of lifetimes to complete. Even quicker work in the sciences is often unfinished by the time of its progenitor's death. In a result-oriented society that breeds the kind of people that want things and wants them now, the slow truth of science is a hard fact to swallow.

How exciting it was, then, for Emma, who faced the truth of work without any grand accomplishments so far, and yet now saw a light at the end of that tunnel. She truly felt as though she was on the verge of something; Hanin and Utsugi had been on the verge of something when they had died, and now it was up to her to finish it. She had a gut feeling that nothing was being held back; Joshua—Richardson—had spread everything wide open, she just had to connect the dots.

She could make humanity a better thing. So many scientists wished to do just that, and so many of them wound up doing nothing of the sort, or worse yet, wound up building guns and bombs. Emma had the rare chance to actually have that wish granted.

It was not uncommon for a man or woman of thought to occasionally push aside some morals and convictions, and even the law itself, when faced with such exciting new discoveries. In medical school Emma had learned about men who had dug up corpses to perform dissections when such treatment of a human body was tantamount to sacrilege. But had they not risked imprisonment (and holy hell itself) the study of medicine could very well still be in dark ages.

Emma thought of work she had to do. Mina was her key, the person whose manipulations of flesh could lead the world into a paradise of free energy and the loss of the problems that arose from its current short supply. Emma was under no delusions that the work would be easy or quick. She was under no delusions that fights of morality and legality would not break out if her work succeeded, but she believed in the greater good of it. Indeed, for all her thoughts on the matter she was under no delusions of grandeur, but the idea of paving the way into such a brave new world of knowledge and hope was so intoxicating to Emma that the idea of experimenting on Mina did in fact bother her less and less with every passing minute.

Emma had a scar on her right hand that had been given to her by Mina. She thought of it, then of the bar code that should have been tattooed on Mina's palm but no longer was. Unlike Mina, she could not make her ills go away with nary so much as a thought, but that was okay. Her scar was a memento of the hard work and losses that would guide her to something truly important, something that one day, would change the world.

And it all began with a little girl and an organic machine named M.

One Hundred Sixteen:
Falls into Place

Rarely did Lieutenant Colonel Joshua Richardson, head of the NOD facility of the Gates Institute of Omaha, dirty his hands by coming so close to the work his people toiled on. But every now and then he would stand at the sidelines, or sit in on an experiment, and today he felt like having a look around.

He stood behind the mirror of the children's playroom and watched the sickly, eerily pale children go about their business. They would play simple games, all that the drugs would let them grasp, he supposed. Here and there he would catch a glimpse of some child's power. In this most cases, it was usually telekinesis, as someone pulled something over that was out of reach, or gave something to someone halfway across the room. There was the occasional levitation of a subject. Today he saw a little girl, all skin and bones and practically bald, drawing with three crayons simultaneously, without touching any of them. He smirked.

But his thoughts were broken up when a girl completely unlike the rest entered the room.

This had to be Mina. He had heard the hushed rumors, the rude comments. She was certainly as attractive as he had been led to believe, and she walked with a delicate grace that was unconsciously sensual.

He didn't give a rat's ass about any of that. He was a man; she was a child. He had no problem with real women.

He caught a glance of her face, however, and it gave him pause. A second later, and it was as though she knew he was there, as she seemed to be looking right into his eyes.

God help him, his heart skipped a beat at the sight of those eyes.

After what felt like an eternity, she looked away, and Richardson suddenly realized he'd been holding his breath.

He shook his head, partly out of disbelief, partly to try and clear his faculties, and started to leave, heading back to his office. He intended to put in a call to Nicholas Kresge when he got there, so he was rightly surprised when he entered his office and found Kresge there, eyeing a painting of a World War 2 destroyer on the wall.

"That one's new," said Richardson.

"You always liked boats. Why you're an army man like me is beyond my understanding."

"Never really had the sea legs. I just like the machinery. To what do I owe this surprise visit?" Richardson sat down at his desk and lit a cigarette.

"Those things are going to kill you," said Kresge, sitting down as well.

"I don't doubt it," Richardson answered, taking a drag.

"I got your notification about Dr. Jacobson's security clearance increase."

"Yes," said Richardson, "I'm quite certain now that she can be trusted. Maybe not forever, but for a while. For long enough."

"What makes you so sure?"

Richardson flicked some ashes into his ashtray. "She wants to make a mark on the world. I don't know if its ego or altruism, but she wants it. Remember Buck Johnson?"

"He shouldn't have survived that sortie. But he did."

"And you remember that look in his eyes? Gratitude. To a higher power, I suppose, but I saw the same look in Emma's eyes when she realized all that could lie ahead."

"What she thinks lies ahead."

"Whatever." Richardson took a long hit off his cigarette. "I'm certain she won't give us any hassle for awhile. No matter what she has to do, she'll keep doing it now as long as she feels her noble goal is in reach."

"You're absolutely sure?"

"The only thing that's ever held her back is her wish not to hurt others. But when you work in experimental medicine, you're going to hurt others. I think she gets that now."

"Fine, Joshua, but whatever happens, it's on your hands."

"Fine by me."

Kresge looked concerned. "Anyway, do we really need her anymore? We have Setsuna's toy."

"Truthfully, Nick, when I was placed in charge of this facility following the Andrew Incident, there were certain things I was not notified of. I should have had access to all the files, but I didn't. I guess since the weapons project was officially shut down, the advisory board decided I didn't need to know everything."

"Nor did I," said Kresge with a chuckle. "But she continued her work, correct?"

"Some research, yes. But as far as I can tell, she created no more prototypes." Richardson glanced at his cigarette; the last inch had burned out. He twisted it against the ashtray. "From what I have read though, Dr. Utsugi left a trail of errors a mile long just trying to create the one soldier we saw. We need Emma to create the 'raw source.' We need a psychic that possesses certain powers that we can, effectively clone ad infinitum."

"A psychic like this Mina," added Kresge, understanding fully.

"Exactly. Mina possesses the two main skills we need for the raw source— biomorphic healing that hopefully will pave the way toward shape change and the bodily structures the soldier will need, and telekinesis. Although I gather she is rather weak in that area; she can levitate but is unable to fly. Which is why our new subject, Raven, may prove to be very useful. Jameson believes she will possess exceptional telekinetic abilities. And then we—"

"Cross multiply and divide," interjected Kresge, chuckling again.

"More or less."

"And the other children?"

"Research is always important. You never know when something will prove useful. Plus, I don't like to put all my eggs in one basket."

"Damn close, though."

"Point taken," admitted Richardson, given that he currently only had one scientist working on anything truly important. "Anyway, let Emma think she's going to bring free energy to the world. All the work she's doing to that end is the same work necessary to create our raw source: the biomorphism, the energy production, so says the research. Once she's got it down to numbers and equations, I figure even a fool like Jameson could apply Dr. Utsugi's methods to create the soldiers."

"What about the 'mindlessness' of the energy project? We don't exactly need that anymore."

"It wouldn't hurt to know how, though. The energy project could prove a lucrative, secondary goal. Speaking of that, though, what about our 'super-soldier'? Your Dr. Graley oversaw the transfer back here, correct?"

"About that," Kresge began, placing his hands in his pockets, something he only did when upset. "We have him. He's on ice."

"And?"

"And they took out the implants. He was only out of our sight for a few minutes."

"Dammit," Richardson exclaimed. "What about playing our hand?"

"Relax. All in due time." Kresge did not want to cause a stir between NOD branches until every single soldier in his was under his direct command: the Black Army.

"We could use those implants to keep Mina under control, Nick. She's unmedicated. She *can't* be medicated."

"Any trouble with her recently?"

"A minor incident in a hallway the other day, but that was linked to a telepathic intrusion from another subject. There were no casualties and it's under control."

"So she's fine." Kresge took his hands out of his pockets and straightened his uniform top. "What of Matthew's supposed possession of Mina?"

"I can't discount it, but it doesn't sit right with me. Regardless, an atrocity was committed, but I have no more proof that he was behind it than I do of Mina doing it purposefully."

"But how would she know his name?"

"The children talk, Nick. They know more than they let on, I fear."

"But they don't care. The medicine keeps them that way."

"Yes. Except for her." Richardson was going to bring up the implants again, but thought better of pressing the issue.

Nicholas Kresge turned to leave. As he walked out, he spoke.

"Just keep an eye on her, Josh. Let me know if anything goes south."

One Hundred Seventeen:
Biokinesis

"Mina, I have some questions I want to ask you. They may make you uncomfortable, but it is very important to me for you to answer as best and as truthfully as you can."

Mina nodded absent-mindedly, but the necessary bluntness of Dr. Jacobson's question (there was no pussy-footing around a subject like this) grabbed her attention.

"Mina, when you attacked Dr. Benton, his cause of death appeared to be cardiac arrest. Something stopped his heart. Did you cause that?"

"I...I think so."

"Is that something you can still do?"

Mina raised her hand, looking at the spot on her palm where her bar code used to be. She remembered vividly the feeling of energy pulsing from that area, warming her hand but at the same time feeling like it was sucking the life from her...when in reality it was sucking someone else's life out, so to speak.

She had a brief daydream...she stood up and held her hand out...the energy arced out and tapped into Emma's nervous system. She was dead within seconds.

Mina shook her head, trying to make the image disappear. "I don't know," she answered.

"Also," said Emma, looking at some papers, "there was a soldier that was believed to have been set on fire by you. Do you know how you might have done that?"

"How do you mean?" asked Mina, a little scared and quite anxious.

"I mean did you literally set fire to him, with actual flames, or did he just 'burst into flames?'"

"The second one, I guess."

"I see." Emma put the papers down and adjusted her glasses. "And you're not sure if you can still do that?"

"No. I wouldn't want to try."

"I don't blame you, obviously. The thing is, Mina, is that abilities such as that go beyond the realm of standard telekinesis. The abilities of telekinesis that you have generally include the ability to move objects and affect their structure, but this does not apply to most living organisms. Do you understand what I'm saying?"

She thought back to when she had demonstrated her healing ability by making a card fly across her skin, cutting it. "That, telekinesis couldn't just make a person get hurt, without hitting them with something?"

"More or less. This is a little violent, but the easiest way I can think of to explain it, is that with telekinesis, you could throw someone against a wall, but you couldn't simply will his bones to break. If you were pyrokinetic, you could set fire to the area around a person, but you couldn't just make him start burning without external flames. Got it?"

"Uh-huh."

"Okay," said Emma, and she sighed at having to be so crude, "but what you did was express signs of biokinetics, which *is* the ability to directly affect other people's physical body, for better or for worse. And what I am wondering is whether or not you possess that ability, or if it was simply a side-effect of your…condition."

So, Mina thought, *she wants to know if I did it, or if Matthew did it.* That was what it came down to, although Mina knew that Emma wasn't speaking in terms of blame. She couldn't have explained why, but now that she thought about it, it seemed like that power was something neither she nor Matthew could have used on their own (whatever Matthew actually was;) it was more like something they could do when they were together. Like a combination of their respective abilities.

She tried to will a spark, a flame, of some sort of life force into existence, but there was nothing. She tried to remember the first time she had used telekinesis, to determine if she knew her powers innately or had to figure out how to use them. But she couldn't remember the first time.

"I don't think I can do it. I'm pretty sure."

"Okay, thanks. But if you think of anything else, let me know?"

Mina nodded.

Emma thought about Mina and how naive the girl really was, for someone who had seen and done the things she had. She had no real world knowledge, although that wasn't her fault, but she seemed to have some sort of innocence about her that went beyond that fact.

Perhaps because she had only recently started really living?

"Mina, I'd like you to come with me. There are some tests I'd like to run."

One Hundred Eighteen:
Full Collapse

Raven sat at the table in the playroom, her stuffed lizard next to her. Mina hadn't been around today and she felt the need to bring it with her.

She was drawing with crayons, something that seemed familiar but that she couldn't remember the name of. It had a tall, narrow brown part with a big circular green area on top of it. Presently, she was drawing lots of red circles on the green part. "Prophase, metaphase, anaphase, telophase. Adenine, thymine, guanine, cytosine." She tried to ponder what she had said, but all she could think of was, "The Lix is made of sperm and shit."

She smiled, and went back to drawing.

The bottom of the room fell out. Colored spots of light were spattered on her eyes as she fell.

She suddenly realized that she was on the floor. The only thing that had fallen was her.

"What happened?" she sighed, in a song-song voice.

Her head began pounding and she put her hands over her eyes. Her head felt like it was getting bigger as the inside got tighter. She fell onto her side and curled her legs up. The pain was intense. There were sirens and chirping birds and barking dogs and yelling and laughing and screaming and giggling and talking and horns and bells and guitars and every noise she had ever heard or could ever hear. A thousand scattered images raced by her eyelids leaving motion blurs a mile long. She tried to cry out for help, a thought stabbing outward to someone who cared....

Some distance away, Mina stumbled, a sudden ache in her head.

And Raven's head continued to spin. She was unsure how long this episode continued.

"I think the neural cascade has occurred."

Dendrite, dendrite, axon.

There was a light in her eyes.

"This is Dr. Jameson," a voice said.

She tried to connect words. *Doctor? Nurse?* she thought. The children kept laughing. Then...

It stopped.

She sat up with a start, panting, her head feeling like it was going to split. She was slick with sweat.

There was a man looking at her, an ordinary, seemingly nondescript man. She too felt nondescript.

"Do you know your name?"

Name? She had a name?

"No," she said.

"Your name is Raven," the man said.

That seemed a little silly for a name. Beth or Emily, maybe, but Raven? Wasn't that a bird?

There was a painful twinge in the front of her head. "Yes, that sounds right."

"My name is Dr. Jameson. I'm going to be your…" He searched for the right word. "…caretaker," he finally decided.

"Good for me, huh," Raven said noncommittally, but not sarcastically. "My head hurts."

A woman dressed like the doctor brought her some pills and some water, and she took them.

"Aspirin?"

"Valium."

"Oh."

What was aspirin? It was…oh yeah, for headaches, it was… ah… oh… Blackness.

She dreamed long and hard, about two girls, one blond, one a redhead. They frolicked while holding hands through a field of lilies that never ended. But the sun burned the redhead into a used-up match, and the blond fell ill and grew a deathly green. But still they frolicked, laughing and dancing the whole way to nowhere, to a nonsense song that looped endlessly.

When she awoke again, her mouth tasted salty and overly wet and she turned over. There was a bucket conveniently placed next to the bed she was now in, and she threw up a little. Then she realized there was an IV attached to her arm and she followed it up to a sac of some greenish liquid suspended from a thin metal stand.

Her eyes felt puffy, and everything was slightly blurry. She tried to focus on the IV line but saw a smudge moving beyond it. She focused on that, and it resolved into a man entering the room.

"You've been unconscious for over an hour, Raven," the man said to her. "How do you feel?"

Am I Raven? Yes…yes I am. He's talking to me.

"I don't know. Tired?" Her head hurt as soon as she spoke. It was like her own voice was making her ears ring.

"Does your head bother you?"

His voice, too.

"It hurts."

"That will go away in time." He had a pad of paper with him, and a pen.

"Raven, do you know where you are?"

"No."

"Does that bother you?"

She pondered this thought. "Not really," she answered, truthfully.

The man scribbled quickly on his pad.

"Do you know your name?"

"Raven?" she asked. Someone had told her that. It seemed right. A girl had....

"Yes. Do you know your full name?"

"No."

"Would you lie to me?"

Raven shrugged.

The man scribbled some more notes. In a previous life, Raven might have found his appearance alone off-putting; a narrow man with a narrow face and greasy-looking hair, with a nervous air about him. But now she felt entirely apathetic to him. To everything.

"My name is Dr. Jameson. I introduced myself earlier, but I doubt you remember. You passed out shortly thereafter."

Remember? The word seemed almost absurd. It seemed to Raven that it should have a broad, important meaning behind it, but instead it seemed very trivial.

"I saw you," she said, nodding. "Caretaker, you said."

"Yes. I will be your caretaker."

"Is this a hospital?" she asked.

"Yes. Of sorts. Many important discoveries are made here, and you will be a part of that."

She narrowed her eyes. "I broke walls?" She had vague impressions of cracked plaster.

"Yes, but don't worry about that. You have great powers, and with your help I will study them."

"Okay." Seemed reasonable enough.

Something kept popping into her head. A girl...with red hair? Yes, but... no, blond hair.

A girl with blond hair.

"There's a girl with blond hair?" asked Raven.

"Yes. A friend of yours, I suppose. Her caretaker, Dr. Jacobson, has asked that the two of you be studied together so you will be spending time with her."

"Good." Raven glanced to her side, and there was a stuffed lizard on the stand next to the hospital bed. She snatched it and held it in her arms. *Mina,* she thought. The lizard? No, the girl. Of course. She had a memory of a sweet, caring smile and long, blond hair, swaying as the girl turned around. It was coming back to her.

"Now Raven, I am going to bring a wheelchair in here and you are going to sit in it. I am going to show you the various rooms you have access to, and explain the rules, all right?"

"Good. It smells like vomit in here." There was an image pressing on her subconscious of a dried vomit stain on a carpeted floor, but the memory couldn't break through. She had a déjà vu moment, though the feeling quickly passed.

It was at this moment that another man entered the room, a balding brown-haired man with a light blue shirt, a white lab coat, and a clipboard. "Sir?" he asked.

"Yes?" responded Jameson.

"Do you have the subject's schedule for the pharmacist and hygienist?"

Jameson walked over and spoke in a voice that was subdued, though not a whisper. He handed a slip of paper to the other doctor. "She needs this one to re-grow her hair, and…"

"We can do that?" asked the balding man excitedly.

Jameson unwittingly glanced up at the man's hairline. "Sorry, it only makes existing hair grow faster. It can't…replace hair." The man's face fell a little; then he eyed Jameson questioningly. "I want my charge to feel… comfortable…with herself."

"Anyway," he continued, "that slip also notes the medication she needs to stabilize her memory state. As for the hygienist, I want Raven to have assisted bathing ever second day, and a haircut every two weeks. I want her shaved twice a week. The hygienist should attend to her skin health and eyebrows, you know, whatever female stuff…whatever." He was definitely out of his element. "Ah…if she thinks I'm wrong about anything…just tell her to make sure everything's right, okay?"

"Um…sure." He briefly looked over the paper from Jameson.

"Anyway, I don't think she should be made to attend to all of her own hygiene until after her memory state is permanently altered and she is used to life at this institute. All right?"

"Yes sir," said the other doctor. He scribbled a few lines of notes, and then left the room.

Jameson turned back around. "And where were we? Ah yes, I was going to take you for a tour. Doctor?"

The balding man reappeared in the doorway after a moment. "Yes?" he asked.

"Could you have a wheelchair brought in here? I'm going to show Raven the facility but I don't want her to wear herself out walking."

"Certainly."

Jameson looked at her, sitting in the bed, staring quite contentedly at nothing in particular. She was attractive; she had good features. *Okay*, he admitted to himself, *maybe growing her hair back quickly is more for me than her, but with all the damn hours I devote to this place I deserve something nice to look at, right?*

Jameson had shown Raven her room and the cafeteria, both of which had seemed familiar. She had met the woman who would be taking care of what Dr. Jameson had called her "personal needs." Now, he was taking her into what he called "the playroom." It was mostly empty, a plain white room with several sets of tables and chairs and benches, a couple toy boxes at one end, and a wall made mostly of mirrors. There were several bookshelves with a small number of well-worn books on them, as well as some drawing supplies.

There were several children in there, playing with various simple toys. Any ordinary teenager would have been creeped out at the way they looked, their mixtures of childish features, wrinkles, and ivory skin off-putting, at least. But Raven, in her permanently drugged state, paid them no heed.

"This is the playroom," explained Jameson. "When you are not eating, sleeping, or in my or another doctor's care, you may spend your time here or in your room."

Such was the briefness of all of Jameson's room descriptions. He turned the wheelchair around, ready to leave and take Raven back to her room, when the door opened and Mina walked in.

She was rubbing her left forearm and looked like she had been crying. She was looking slightly downward but her head rose when she saw Raven. She sniffled.

Raven's heart fluttered upon seeing Mina. This was the girl she had asked about. Recollections as recent as the day before were hazy, but she could not forget her. She absent-mindedly dropped her stuffed animal and rose to her feet. The first step was a stumble, but the next few were strong, with purpose.

She stood a couple feet from Mina, who smiled, the pink under her eyes fading.

"I know you," said Raven. "We sit together." She stepped forward and threw her arms tightly around her. "Mina," she said matter-of-factly, as though she were giving her that name.

Mina happily returned the embrace, but looked questioningly at Jameson over Raven's shoulder.

"She feels much better than she has been," he explained. "I think you'll find it much more rewarding to spend time with her now." Whereas he had been confused by their friendship, Emma was intrigued, and she wanted him to encourage them to spend time together.

Raven breathed in deeply. "Your hair smells nice," she said happily.

"Thanks. I used a citrus shampoo."

Jameson rolled his eyes at this banal exchange. He decided now was as good a time as any to leave them together, and leaving early for the day suddenly seemed like a good idea. He had a nice wad of cash to blow and had been lonely for almost two weeks now. He just had to check in with Emma, and…

"Mina, would you take Raven back to her room for me? Something's come up."

"Sure." Mina was happy to take Raven away from Jameson. There was something about him she didn't like. Well, more so than she disliked the other doctors, at least.

They started to walk away. *No need for the wheelchair, I guess,* he thought.

As they walked, they casually grasped each other's hand, reaching out simultaneously, as though it was second nature.

"You looked sad," said Raven after the girls had walked a ways down the hallway in silence. It was an observation, really; she wasn't looking for an explanation.

"Some of the things you have to do here are…" Mina tried to think of the right word. "…unpleasant." *Not that you'll care,* she thought, sadly. *Just like everyone else.*

Conversing with Raven, as with an actual person, brought a level of joy to Mina's heart that she hadn't expected. But it was tempered by sorrow as she assumed Raven would be as docile as the other children.

But they weren't *really* empty, where they? Danny, Benny, Keiko, Johnny, at least…they had *something* going on in there. Maybe not Anna or the rest, but they did. So maybe, just maybe….

"Do you have great powers?"

"What do you mean?" asked Mina.

"Dr. Jameson said I have a power. Do you have one too?"

Mina shrugged. "I heal really fast if I get hurt. I can float, and move things without touching them."

"Oh." She waited a moment, and then added, "What can I do?"

"I don't know. Break stuff, I know that. I couldn't always do those things, though, not before…." She stopped. There was no sense in bringing up Matthew now.

"Before what?"

Mina didn't want to answer. She waited a few moments, and then sent a thought to Raven.

Can you hear me in your head?

Raven looked startled as she glanced around. "Did you say that?"

Yes, sort of. I think we can all do this. It's like thinking, but you have to concentrate on the person you want to hear you, like you intend to talk to them. It's hard to—

Like this? interrupted Raven. The ability had come quite quickly to her once she knew of its existence.

Exactly! answered Mina. *Now, please talk to me now like this, while we're out here, and not out loud, okay?*

Okay, I guess.

What do you remember?

Remember? Raven wasn't sure what she meant.

What's the oldest thing you remember?

I woke up in the hospital bed, and Dr. Jameson said he was my caretaker.

Anything earlier than that?

There wasn't much, but Raven smiled. *Just you, really. You read to me. You walked with me. You held my hand. Not much else. Sorry.*

Mina couldn't help but smile at this. Suddenly, the idea that Raven might have forgotten her seemed like it would have made her miserable.

You don't remember before you got here?

This concept was very difficult for Raven to grasp. Since waking, it had not occurred to her that she would have had to have come *here* from somewhere else. She just accepted the fact that she was in this "hospital," and didn't question it. The fuzzy memories she had all took place here as well.

And the longer she stayed here and the more medicine they pumped into her, the closer she would come to never remembering "before."

I'm going to save you, Mina thought to herself. *Somehow.*

By this time they had reached their rooms. Mina motioned for Raven to follow her. "You can come in for a bit if you'd like. I can tell you about this place or something."

Should we talk like this? Raven asked telepathically.

When we don't want anyone to hear what we say, yes, answered Mina, smiling at Raven's cleverness.

Mina entered her room, pushing aside the curtain so that Raven could enter easily. She motioned for Raven to hop up onto her bed, which was the only surface to sit on other than the floor. She rubbed her forearm again and pushed back the tears that almost crept out again. "Give me a minute; I have to change my clothes."

There was a sadness in Dr. Jacobson's eyes that Mina had not seen before. They were sitting across from each other at a table; Emma looked at the top Mina was wearing. It was a fairly tight black tee shirt with a pink and white heart on the front that was distended by her curves.

"I had the staff put regular clothes in your drawers. Choices I thought were cute. It breaks protocol, but I thought you deserved a greater sense of humanity. Something...a little something...to make the days different."

Mina sat still, unsure what to say. She supposed she was thankful. Anything to break the monotony was nice.

Emma took her glasses off with her left hand and reached for a nearby tissue with her right. She wiped the corners of her eyes.

"I thought, seeing you as a person would make it easier to treat you as more than an experiment."

Mina sighed. She was becoming increasingly intelligent, increasingly better at insight into conversations and statements.

"Mina, to do my job, I'm going to have...hurt you again."

Please don't hurt me, Mina thought.

Please don't hurt me, Emma thought.

It had started simply enough, with small cuts, tests to see if Mina could control her healing ability.

It had ended with screaming that still rang in Emma's ears. Despite Emma's attempts at anesthesia, Mina could feel almost the entire slice as a six-inch length of her forearm was removed as a tissue sample. It grew back, of course, but the pain lingered.

Mina lacked the will for revenge, and she didn't have the heart for anger. She had seen what those things did. When Dr. Jacobson released her for the day, she merely left, sobbing, hoping to find Raven, and with her, some measure of solace.

Now that Mina had found Raven, she was faced with confusion and mixed emotions. Though she had clearly forged an emotional bond with the girl that continued even now, she was completely different. She should be happy, knowing that she could have actual conversations with her, maybe even learn about her—but it had been so simple before. Raven was someone to look after and care for. Now she was...

...what was she?

Mina stood in front of her dresser with her back to Raven. She pulled her shirt off with both hands, being careful not to let her long hair get caught up in it. She threw the top into a laundry basket nearby and reached behind herself to unhook her bra, a new kind she had been given to wear that was not like the more modest, utilitarian ones she had previously worn.

Her skin is so pretty! Raven thought. She was entranced by Mina's pale, even-toned skin, especially the curve at the small of her back, where her waist was narrowest. She sighed involuntarily, but Mina didn't hear her. The thoughts went no further than idle observation.

Mina opened her dresser and pulled out an ankle length, yellow nightgown. She threw it on in one motion and pulled her hair out of the neck hole, spreading it outwards with her hands. She bent down, placing her hands up the bottom of her gown, and pulled her pants off. Those she also threw into the hamper before turning to face Raven.

Raven had never seen anything quite like Mina. Truthfully, never was not a very long time for her anymore, but that was how she felt. She had a brief moment of memory of something connected to the motions Mina had gone through; something other than changing clothes. It was nothing specific, though; it was akin to the feeling of having a word on the tip of her tongue.

She looked at Mina and there was a spark, small and insignificant, but it faded even faster than it had arrived.

And then she remembered something similar, a hand on a wall, and a shock through her body. But it was gone.

Mina smiled, the happiest she had looked all day. This was going to be good, she decided. It was going to be better this way. There was a lightness in her step, in her heart, as she walked over to the bed and sat down next to Raven. It didn't matter how she was, just that she was better than before.

"I want to talk to you so much. I can't wait to. I'm just so tired. The…tests today were…exhausting." If her body had worked any other way, she would have been wracked with pain, and likely crippled.

"What kind of tests?" asked Raven. *Grades?* she thought for a fleeting moment.

"Mostly…." Today had been different. The tests had always been unpleasant in one way or another, even painful, but Mina had never endured one like this before. "The doctors—scientists—work with you to see what kind of powers you have. What you can do with them."

Like this! Raven thought to her, apparently proud of herself.

"Yes," said Mina, a morose expression on her face. "I don't know why they test us."

"If that's what they do, why wouldn't they?"

Complacency. *It's still better this way,* Mina thought, partially as an attempt to convince herself. It was best not to push too much. For as much as Mina *had* grown in insightfulness and mental complexity, she was no where near the state of a "normal" person, and Raven, for all her new-found conversational skills, was even further away.

It was best to take it slow, to provide friendship and support, and see how this girl, awakened from one dream into another, would be. Until the time was right.

"I'm tired, too," said Raven, yawning. Her brain chemistry was still reeling and it had been a difficult day for her as well.

"Can I sleep here with you?"

"Of course," Mina said with a warm grin. It wouldn't be the first time. Not everything had changed with Raven.

Raven curled up next to Mina, and Mina put an arm around her. "Are you cold?"

"No. Not with you."

Raven closed her eyes and was the first to nod off. Mina watched her for a time, the slow rise and fall of her chest as she gently breathed, her sad, mostly empty eyes shut to the world. Mina couldn't help but feel something for her, an odd collection of friendship, devotion, the will to protect, and the will to serve.

She wished, as her eyelids became heavy and her long lashes fluttered as she started to pass out, that there was a word for this feeling, something that had started small like a jitter in her stomach or a skip in her heart, and had been growing, growing, growing....

Emma, eager to think of something good after the atrocity of her earlier actions, actually opened her mouth to offer information to Spencer Jameson.

"By the way, I took tissue and blood samples from Mina today." That wasn't the good part, of course.

"And what did you find out?"

Would he even understand? She thought, crassly. And then: *Well, despite him being a fuck-up, he does have a doctorate too.*

"Her telomeres are completely normal."

"So her cells obey the hayflick limit."

"Yes, but her tissue has a substantially high quantity of stem cells."

"That could account for her rapid healing."

Good, he's keeping up, though Emma.

"She may be, for all intents and purposes, immortal. Her system seems to contain an abundance of anti-oxidants that prevent mtDNA degradation."

"But the trade-off for aging is cancer. The longer a being lives, the greater the chance of cancerous tissue forming from bad chromosome duplication."

"It's a possibility. She may end up dying just like anyone else, possibly even sooner."

Jameson thought about everything Emma had said so far. "So, her healing, while certainly amazing, may be entirely biological in origin, and not psychic at all."

Here was where the interesting part collided with the guilt Emma was trying to hold back. "Ah, I tested for that. I ran some scans on her arm as she...healed it...and there was definitely increased psychoactivity. It ended as soon as the healing was completed."

"So, her healing is still controlled by her psionic abilities."

"There's more." This was the worst part, but the most fascinating, the absolute proof of that hypothesis. "I took a...sizable tissue sample. Once I stabilized it, I injured it."

"And?"

"No healing at all. No effect without her psychic presence. Completely non-psi-active."

"Well," Jameson joked, "I guess we don't have to worry about growing two Minas if we cut her in half."

Emma gave him the evil eye. That was just...awful. After a moment, she decided to keep going, anyway. "It also seems that she has no control over her healing. It seems to be entirely autonomic. Or, she hasn't figured out how to slow or stop it, but I doubt that. She's taken to everything else I've asked of her very quickly."

The elephant in the room was that if this WAS absolutely true, if she had no voluntary control, then any test designed to prove otherwise was merely an exercise in torture. Still...she had to know. There was still data she needed to gather, either way, before she could perform any of the biomorphism tests.

She sat in silence.

After a time, Jameson looked up at a monitor.

"Well, it seems they're bonding after all."

The monitor showed a view of Mina's room; both her and Raven were lying on her bed, passed out.

"It's just a hunch of mine, I know it's silly. But Keiko and Johnny are a prime example of linked-pair powers. These two...maybe it's the similarity in age, or rather the difference in appearance from the others, that pairs them. But it could very well occur."

Especially because part of Mina exists in Raven, thought Jameson.

"Even if it doesn't happen, this is an unprecedented level of friendship among the children"—that wasn't the right word, of course—"and I find it fascinating. Anyway, I'm tired. I'm going to go soon; you should, too."

"Yeah. I guess I should go now." He thought of the fat, sweaty wad of bills he had. He had some quality time to get to; he nodded, and left the room.

Emma sat there for some time, contemplating the equation that was Mina X Raven, if it really was one at all. This was really a side project for her, something she wanted to do to sate her own curiosity. The generator was her given goal, but the way Keiko and Johnny seemed to share abilities and thoughts instantly interested her quite a bit. So it was no surprise how intrigued she was when Mina seemed to feel the shock of Raven's mind being altered, the way Raven followed Mina around like a sick puppy even when she couldn't understand a damn thing the girl said…was it an after-effect of her interaction with "Matthew?" Did it have to do with some trait the girls shared?

Still, as much as Emma believed that Mina was not responsible for the deaths her body had caused, and as much as a part of her disliked NOD's (and her recent own) treatment of human beings, she hoped this was not an indication that Raven was affected differently than the children by the medication. With as much telekinetic power as she could possibly possess, the thought of it being entirely within her own control to do with as she pleased frightened Emma. In other words, she hoped she would be controllable. Mina, at least, had been docile since the disaster.

Having resigned herself to business as usual, Emma got up out of her chair and went home.

The children spoke that night, across rooms and hallways and floors, of the coming end that had been prophesied. They spoke without passion, with a matter-of-factness that belied the topic of their discourse: freedom.

For it was not something they lusted after; it was not something they felt denied of. For they were incapable of non-complacency.

It was simply the next logical step in their evolution.

And already the wheels turned. But they knew great hardship lay ahead, for it was foretold by two of their own.

One Hundred Nineteen:
Morning View

Mina awoke lazily the next morning, aware of a warmth next to her that wasn't always there. She was briefly confused at the presence next to her before she had opened her eyes, but then she saw Raven curled up next to her, lightly pressing against her, sound asleep.

"Hey. Hey, wake up," Mina said, jostling Raven lightly. Soon the girl stirred, opened her eyes, and yawned.

"Hi." She smiled too.

"It's morning. We have to see what they want us to do today. I have to take a shower."

"There's someone who's supposed to give me a bath. Dr. Jameson said he didn't want me to worry about that myself yet." She sat up and got out of bed, and asked, "Which way should I go?"

"Your room is the next one. I'll walk you."

"Oh, that's right."

Mina took Raven to her room (funny that hers had security doors and a guard had to let her in,) and went back to her own room to shower.

She smiled the whole time, thinking about nothing in particular.

Presently, Mina entered the playroom, having showered and eaten.

Danny, Anna, Benny, and others Mina were less familiar with were in the room. There were a few telepathic "hellos" but for the most part they paid her no heed.

She sat next to Danny. *Do you know where Dr. Jacobson is?* She asked.

She was in here a while ago. Keiko and Johnny spoke to me. Dr. Jacobson thinks you and Raven could be like them. They don't agree.

What do you mean like them?

That you and her could think together and use your powers together.

Well, what do Keiko and Johnny think? Keiko had said something before about living in each other's hearts, not minds.

They think that it will not be that way, but that you two do share a connection. They said that the doctors put some of you in her head.

Did that explain certain…moments? Was that the reason?

"You're the messenger," Mina said aloud, repeating what Danny had said to her before. Then, silently: *Do you care?*

I care no more than I am allowed to.

I want to understand them. What are they?

Someone entered the room. "Mina?"

Mina turned around. It was Emma. "Please come with me."
Danny sent one last thought to Mina.
I don't know.

One Hundred Twenty:
Mind Over Matter

"I'm sorry," Emma said as she tightened the restraints around Mina's ankles. "I can't imagine how unpleasant this is for you. If you can appreciate it, know at least that you are helping to make the world a better place for everyone in it."

Mina had no concept of how big the world was. Ergo, the idea of "helping the world" was completely lost on her.

Emma left the small room through a glass door. The wall it was connected to was also glass; it divided the lab so that they were in two parts. She looked at the device that Mina was attached to. Why anyone would create such a thing was beyond her; it seemed cruel and oddly specific; she had even discovered it by accident. But now it kept her from doing the deed herself.

Little did she know that Dr. Utsugi had built the device years ago, for the exact same tests, with the exact same reasoning. It had worked perfectly; it had helped her distance herself from her guilt until she literally did not feel it anymore, and now Emma was on that path herself.

Emma sat at a small console and began pressing buttons. "Okay, once again Mina, you will feel a slight scraping at first and then a light cut will be made." She had never wanted to do this. A week ago she wouldn't have. But now? Now she did it. And justified it to herself by trying to make herself believe she had justified it to Mina. "Again, try to withhold your healing ability."

It was a light scratch at first, just like Emma had said. It wasn't enough to make Mina cry but it was uncomfortable. Then the pressure increased, drawing a narrow red line across her ankles. The slight angle of the table she was on made the blood drip down her skin into her rolled-down socks.

The cuts were deeper than Emma would admit to herself. It was agony, but Mina bit her lip, desperate not to cry out. She tried to hold her powers back, wanting this test or whatever it was to be a success so it could be over, but still her skin closed back up right behind the paths of the tiny surgical steel blades. For her part, Emma wanted Mina to succeed so she could stop testing her. All the girl had to do was to be able to control her power, and then they could move on.

It hurt so much. Fresh skin would grow only to be sliced apart again and again. The nerves had little time to recover before they screamed new signals of pain.

An odd thought passed through Raven's head.
When the skin is sad, it cries bloody tears. When the tears dry up, the skin

can be happy again.

"What was it you wanted, again?"

Jameson looked over at her and gave a sickly smile, the attempt of someone who had not on many occasions smiled without an ulterior motive. Raven naively smiled back.

"I can't do it," Mina cried out. She could stand it no more.

"Please, just a little longer."

"I can't!" Tears were running down her face as the blood from her ankles was forming a puddle on the floor.

"You don't know what my other choice is," Emma muttered to herself.

Raven watched the block float above her open hand.

"Try another at the same time," Jameson suggested.

She did; it was easy. She made them rotate around each other.

"Try another."

She did. Again, easy. Jameson kept suggesting she try more. She kept trying, and succeeding. She had twelve circling with ease and had run out of blocks. They rotated around a common point; as they did she spun the group perpendicularly to their rotation so that they slowly marked out a spherical space.

"Can you move each one separately?"

This took Raven several tries before she could move even four objects in different directions. When she was moving all twelve in the same direction, it was like driftwood being swept away by a current. She manipulated the current, not the individual objects. Each additional object made the whole ordeal only infinitesimally more difficult. Moving them separately was markedly more difficult; if she concentrated too much on one, the others would fall to the ground. But, with Jameson's coaching, she succeeded in moving five.

"We'll work more on that later. How are you feeling?"

"Fine," she said without emotion.

Mina was in the corner of the room. The table she had been strapped to was lying on the floor, the mechanisms and restraints ripped and broken.

Like a terrorized dog, Mina was trying to get as far as possible from the object of her misery. She randomly invoked aurakinetic shielding. The scene reminded Emma all too vividly of when she had found Mina after Carl had tried operating on her.

"Mina?"

Mina did not acknowledge her.

"Mina, I'm sorry, you have no idea how sorry I am."

Then why did you do it?

"Mina, please, it's the least painful way. I know you can do this. You have all the signs."

What, I bleed? Is that a sign? That you can cut me forever and I never stop bleeding?

"Mina, please, you can take the rest of the day off, just come out of the corner."

Mina's head jerked up. She ran out of the room, pushing Emma back from her with telekinesis, making her stumble and almost fall. She did not want the good doctor to lay another hand on her today. She ran right for her room, and curled up like a fetus in the womb of her bed. Emma monitored her until she reached her room, then sat down and sighed. She would have to get the White Room ready. She had no choice. But it probably would've had to happen eventually, she reasoned. It was a necessary step.

One Hundred Twenty-One:
Business is Business

Nicholas Kresge sat in his car in the rural back roads near Omaha, watching gentle December snow fall onto the whitewashed earth around him.

He felt old today. He ran his hand over his head. He had a full head of hair, but it was gray and thinning. Windy days would play havoc with him if he didn't wear a hat.

He was powerfully built, from a life of service and daily routines, but the aches were real and more and more common. He wasn't going to last forever, and his plan could easily take years to reach fruition. He prayed he would live long enough to see the nation he dreamed of.

"We're behind schedule, Amanda. Why the delay?"

Dr. Graley spoke without turning to face him; she was also watching the snowfall. "I've run into some problems appropriating resources. No more than a couple weeks until that's sorted out. However, apparently some of the guards are filing grievances about being removed from duty ahead of their scheduled rotation. Except for the occasional massacre, NOD's an easy job and some of them want to stay."

"You should have told me sooner," Kresge said gruffly. "I'll take care of that."

They sat for a minute in silence.

"What do you hope to gain from this takeover?"

"Hmm?" she looked at him, puzzled. "Resources. Combat advantages. Financial gains. You know all this."

"But you're still all just patriotic Americans, huh?"

"We're a branch of the military, Nicholas. I would hope that my boys were patriotic citizens."

"The Black Army, NOD—it's all gray. A very, very deep shade of gray." He stopped; he didn't need to lecture her. She was all too aware of the limbo that both of their organizations existed in.

"And you? Are you a 'patriotic American'?"

"This country," he said, motioning outwards with his hands, "was great, once upon a time. Now, it's crumbling under its own infrastructure and indifferent citizens. It's not the nation it should be anymore. It's not number one."

They had touched on this subject many times, (after all, the takeover had been initiated by the two of them,) but the notion of Kresge's motives being patriotism first and foremost still struck Dr. Graley as incredulous.

"You're not honestly going to sit there and tell me a takeover like this is less about money and more about a sense of national pride? Nicholas, what we're doing, were NOD a publicly recognized facility, would be treasonous."

"Money? I've got plenty of money. I'm a professional soldier, Amanda. I make a good salary and I don't have the time to spend it. All of my children are through college and married and my grandchildren have trust funds. I don't need more money."

She harrumphed.

"Let me tell you a thing about America," he continued. "The first mistake we made was letting the Soviets beat us into space. But we beat them to the moon. At least fifteen countries are carrying out the same types of experiments we are, but we are the only nation with the resources to *stop* the other ones. And, thanks to our secret operations, our 'Black Army,' we've never had an international incident."

"So how will a new regime at NOD help our country?"

"We've been pussyfooting around the research for too long. We've made strides, but weakly and slowly. We'll have our soldiers, our psychic warriors, but we *will* have unlimited energy as well. America," he stressed, "will have unlimited energy. That alone will put us ahead of the rest, where we should be. No more of our economy being under the thumb of OPEC, for one thing."

"And you will see to this?"

"I will. I don't take no for an answer, and I don't like being told to wait. I know more than the advisory committee and I'm less squeamish than Richardson. I run a tidy, efficient ship. And unlike him, I know whose strings to pull, and how."

"And we fit into your plan how?" Her eyes narrowed as she said this.

"You and your people have been more than helpful. Stay on the right side —my side—and you will be rewarded beyond your wildest dreams. The U.S. government will still have access to NOD's advances. But so will you. NOD is practically autonomous. It has the right to do as it sees fit in studying new sciences. With no one to answer to, our mission couldn't be simpler. No one will ever realize a transition has occurred. As long as the military receives advances, we will receive funding."

"Speaking of advances..." Dr. Graley baited.

"How are the laser rifles?" asked Kresge.

"They're lovely. We've made some modifications and are now testing them for field use. But I was speaking of the biological advances."

"Once everything is in place I will show you our generators. The soldier project is underway. I don't like the way Richardson tiptoed around it after the disaster, but he assures me everything is under control. I will make some changes after I control the facility, of course. He puts too much 'faith' in people's ability to choose between morals and money."

"Theoretically we are already in control," said Dr. Graley. "The guard is almost completely Black Army members."

"The only formality is the removal of Richardson," said Kresge.

"Didn't you say before that you had served with him?"

"Yes. I do regret what I have to do, even though we've had our differences. But business and duty come first."

One Hundred Twenty-Two:
Our Girls

Jameson spoke out after a terse silence. "I have had great progress with Raven already."

"Oh?" said Emma, absent-mindedly. "That's good."

"What's on your mind?" sighed Jameson as the two of them sat at the meeting room table, discussing their charges.

"I know it's not what I am supposed to be working on, but I'm very curious as to what kind of connection there could be between our girls. I've done some reading. There are two kinds: an apathetic connection, wherein the participants are aware of the other's existence, but nothing else, usually. No emotions, thoughts, abilities, et cetera are shared except occasionally, in times of severe mental stress. This has shown up among test subjects very rarely. The other kind is a sympathetic connection, which is even more rare. It is the kind that Johnny and Keiko have, where telepathy seems able to cross any distance, where the subjects have constant empathy for each other and can tap into one another's abilities."

"So what do you think Raven and Mina have?"

"Well, I'm almost sure there is a connection of sorts, but at this point it could be either."

"And why the fascination?" Jameson asked.

"I've seen an awful lot here," Emma explained, "and a lot of awful things. But the idea of two people being that close, it…there's a kind of hope I get from that."

"Oh," said Jameson noncommittally.

"So you said things were progressing well with Raven?"

"Yes, she's already able to move five objects independently. If she proves to be as strong a telekin as I think, she may be able to fly. What about Mina?"

"I'm not having any luck. I need to pin down the limits of her powers. I need her to temporarily halt her healing, but how am I supposed to explain to her how to do something that I don't understand?"

"So you've hurt her."

"What?" Emma did not immediately follow that transition.

"Well, in order to examine her healing ability she would have to be injured."

"Oh. That." Emma looked ashamed.

Jameson briefly put his arm around her, and in a congratulatory way said, "Welcome to the wonderful world of experimental science."

Emma felt sick.

"Anyway," she said, "I'm going to begin modifications to the White Room tomorrow, I want to run some radiation sequences on Mina and see how she reacts."

One Hundred Twenty-Three:
Inspection and Introspection

Raven sat on the bed. Mina had shared her clothes with her; she wore a sky blue tee shirt; a yellow chick adorned the front, and khaki shorts with no belt; her slender, almond legs looked freshly shaved.

She looked very nice; clean and groomed; her hair was already several inches long.

"Can you read?" Mina asked.

Raven thought for a moment. "Yes," she said, finally.

Mina passed her a book. It was well-worn.

"The Lo-rax. What's a Lorax?"

"It's made up. It's the orange guy on the cover."

"What's it about?" asked Raven.

"It's about this guy that cuts down all of the Lorax's trees, then feels sorry about it, and asks a kid to plant a new one."

Raven knew exactly what a tree was, but could not remember ever having seen one. This did not bother her.

"You can read it if you want."

"Okay."

They sat in silence for a while. Then Mina spoke again.

"Do you have a mother?"

Mina knew what a mother was. A mother was a woman that gave birth to a person. She had wondered recently if she herself had one.

"I don't think so." Raven looked confused. "Do you?"

"I don't know."

Mina suddenly felt a great deal of compassion towards Raven. Keiko and Johnny had told her that Raven's memory would "mellow." If that meant she would forget everything she had known from "before," absolutely everything, than that wasn't right. It wasn't how a person should be treated.

She glanced at her ankles. Of course, they had healed completely and no longer hurt, but she could still remember the pain of the cutting. That wasn't right either.

Mina wanted to go, to leave the place she was trapped in. But she was scared. She had no concept of what outside was. She might as well have lived her life in a float chamber, for all the real-world experience she had.

And here was a girl who, for all Mina knew, could have had all the knowledge about the world there was to have, and yet she had access to none of it.

I want to leave, Mina thought. But she didn't know how.

Emma glanced at an image on the computer screen in front of her; she had no desire to really study the ghastly thing. Since Richardson had raised her clearance, she could now directly access most files regarding biomorph experiments, including those involved with the creation of human weapons, not just energy generators.

It seemed that a biomorphic growth, such as the "bone-blades" she kept running across, generally resulted not from the repositioning and reconfiguring of existing tissue, but in the creation and growth of entirely new cells. It was this fact that further bolstered her belief that Mina's abilities could be linked to biomorphism, given that her regenerative abilities activated on the cellular level and were very efficient.

The raw matter for these cell growths, the information stated, came usually from the participant's own fat and energy stores, but sometimes it was pulled from his or her own aura, or even the air and earth surrounding the subject. In a successful test, once the subject was told to eliminate the biomorphic structure, one of three things occurred. In the case of such structures as the "bone blades," the object was often retracted into the subject's body, where it lay dormant but still fully formed. Otherwise, the cells comprising the structure were systematically killed via apoptosis, at which point the leftover matter either was reabsorbed, or in a third scenario, fell away like dead skin or a lizard's tail.

Emma briefly wondered if the latter two methods might also prove to be a boon for cancer research.

As for unsuccessful tests, Emma had already read of the horrible things that could occur, but these new files contained even more atrocities. She read of one instance where a biomorphic growth could not be controlled, and had spread like cancer through the participant's body, killing the subject in a matter of days. It had been at this point that Emma wondered if cancer and tumors were merely improperly activated biomorphic reactions, given the file she had read earlier stating that psychic abilities seemed to be carried on recessive genes and when they activated among the general populace, they often functioned as diseases. It was certainly something to think about.

There was another subject that had successfully created an extra pair of working, though underdeveloped arms. However when she had attempted to undo the change, instead of just the extra arms being destroyed, her immune system had attacked her entire body, literally corroding it from the outside in.

The list went on and on. A staggering number of people, children, really, had been through this institute before her arrival, and possibly during her time here, as well. However, Emma had a good deal of faith in Mina. Her ability to heal seemed unparalleled among the subjects she had read about so far; there seemed to be little doubt that her body would be able to fix any damage caused to it by itself or other sources. As for actual biomorphism, well....

Mina lay next to Raven, and they looked into each other's eyes. Mina could swear a slight glimmer was there. Their hands were between them, lightly clasped together.

What do you like? Mina asked.

Food? hazarded Raven. She did not know what Mina meant.

I like to read. I have read all the books I have many times.

A hobby, Raven understood. *I don't have one.*

Hobby? Mina had never contemplated that before. She knew the literal meaning of the word but understood vaguely that it denoted a division between free time and work time, and being a literal prisoner "free time" had never truly been separate from work time.

Something you do because you like it.

Mina smiled.

Raven's mind replaced words of its own accord, playing clever games that she was oblivious to. *Someone you do because you like her,* she thought to herself. A mere month ago she would have found that parallel logic humorous and clever, but now she dismissed it as a busy person might any errant thought.

What do you want? Mina asked.

That was a very hard question to answer. She didn't really "want" anything.

I like spending time with you. I guess I want that. What do you want?

There was a tightness in Mina's throat; it felt like her heart had leapt up there and was crowding out her windpipe.

I want...to touch your lips. It was true; she had for quite some time, though she wasn't sure why.

Okay, Raven responded plainly.

Mina breathed deeply and unclasped a hand. She moved very slowly, very tentatively, as though she was afraid Raven might change her mind at any moment. Presently, her hand reached Raven's face, and she gently brushed her middle and forefinger across Raven's lips.

They were as soft as a gentle breeze.

That's not how people touch lips, Raven told her. She put her hands up to Mina's shoulders and lightly pushed her onto her back, simultaneously getting above her. She had her knees to Mina's sides, and slipped her hands onto the bed so she wasn't leaning on her.

She looked at Mina's face, and smiled. Mina looked up at Raven, her short hair resting against the sides of her beautiful face. She was completely at a loss for words.

Raven sighed deeply, a happy sigh, leaned her head down, and kissed Mina. It was the briefest of kisses, barely more than a brush of lip against lip, but Mina's cheeks turned as pink as cherry blossoms.

Raven leaned back up and looked down at Mina, smiling at the innocent girl's blushing face. There were no thoughts in her mind, no mental processes encouraging or discouraging this. It was her heart that was calling the shots.

There was definitely life in her eyes.

She leaned back down, and kissed Mina properly, passionately.

One Hundred Twenty-Four:
Strength

    M sat in the center of the lab, unattended to except by its own life-support system. Emma had been spending very little time on it recently, but it did not care. It had not the mind it needed to care.

    Every day Emma checked NOD's energy needs. The facility was running at a surplus so she felt no need to reconnect M to the power grid knowing that sooner or later she would need to study it further. Also, there was always the nagging thought that reconnecting M to Nod would recall that bizarre brain pattern she and Jameson had discovered, and the idea that that might cause a reenactment of the Mina incident. But this was one of many things that bothered Emma less and less with each passing day, as distance through time and personal successes bred complacency.

    Today Emma was sitting with Jameson in a small control booth that was part of a much larger, but mostly empty room. In the center of the room sat Raven, levitating a crate the size of a small car about three feet off the floor.

    "How heavy is it?" asked Emma.

    "Uh, I forget, but it's filled with sandbags."

    Emma looked impressed. She leaned closer to Jameson. "Her hair's growing quickly," she said. "Do you know how long it is?"

    "Over six inches," said Jameson, proudly, despite it having little to do with him.

    Raven rotated the box and moved it slowly up and down. "Check this out," said Jameson. He flicked on a microphone and spoke into it.

    "Raven? Can you show Dr. Jacobson that thing we talked about? With your fist?"

    Raven looked up at the booth, behind her, and nodded. Emma leaned forward, interested.

    Raven held out her right hand, open, palm up. She concentrated on the flow of energy around her hand until she could almost make it out at the edges of her visual acuity. She felt her aura spark to life as she controlled that flow, forming lines of force that traveled the length of her forearm and wrapped around her hand, forming spikes of kinetic energy that pointed in the direction of the fist she was making.

    She pulled her arm back and punched at the box with all the force she could muster, both physical and telekinetic.

    There was a great cracking and puffing noise as wood splintered and sawdust and sand billowed out. A great hole about a foot in diameter encircled the area where the blow had landed, and sand poured out amidst the cloud of debris. At precisely the opposite end of the crate, a loud crack was heard, and flecks of wood scattered into the air as sand began pouring out of that side also.

"You can set the box down," said Jameson into the microphone. Raven did so, coughing and rubbing sand out of her eyes.

"I'm quite impressed," said Emma. "The shockwave traveled the entire length of the box. Have you determined its force yet?"

"Not yet. We're still fine-tuning it."

"Just out of curiosity, has she flown yet?"

"Not yet. I've just had her working with independent control of objects, except for the telekinetic enhancement to that punch. Although, everything I've given her to lift, she has been able to. I'm running out of heavy things."

"Have you worked on shielding?"

"She was able to develop one earlier, but we haven't worked on it really. I'm planning on doing that with her today."

"Well, so far, so good," said Emma, getting up. "I have to be off. I need to check up on the modifications to the White Room."

"All right then," said Jameson.

As Emma walked out of the room, she briefly entertained the notion that maybe she had judged Jameson too harshly, that maybe he was a decent scientist, if not a decent man. But she quickly dismissed the thought.

Hours later, Raven entered Mina's room. Mina, who had been given the day off by Dr. Jacobson, was sitting in bed, half under the covers, reading a book entitled *Our Lovely World*. Raven looked exhausted; she walked slowly and with less than usual coordination. Still, though, she had that far away, unconcerned look in her eyes. Mina motioned for her to sit next to her, and she did, climbing on the bed with slow deliberation.

"Here," said Mina, reaching for something on her nightstand and handing it to Raven, "you left your lizard in here."

"Thanks," said Raven, smiling as she took the small plush animal. It was nice to have, and she vaguely remembered a time when she wouldn't allow it out of her sight, but that time felt longer and longer ago.

"Do you want to see what a real lizard looks like?" asked Mina.

"Sure."

Mina turned to the index of *Our Lovely World* and found a page with pictures of lizards. She showed it to Raven: skinks and Gila monsters and Komodo dragons and frilled lizards that ran on water.

"I've seen this before," said Raven, pointing at the frilled lizard, her tightly held stuffed animal brushing against the page.

"Where?" asked Mina.

Raven shrugged. "Not sure," she said.

"You seem tired," Mina said.

"I'm exhausted," Raven elaborated. "I worked on telekinesis and shielding all day with Dr. Jameson."

"What color is your shield?" asked Mina, wondering if it would be like hers.

"Yellow-orange. Yours?"

"Yellow." Mina smiled.

They sat for a while, looking at the pictures in silence. Then, Raven spoke again.

"Mina, there was a boy, he asked what it was like outside."

Mina looked surprised. "What did you tell him?"

"I didn't know what he meant. Outside what?"

"I think we're in a building." Mina flipped through the book until she found a picture of a landscape with trees and rocks and grass and mountains in the distance. "I think this is what outside looks like."

Trees.

"There's buildings too," said Raven, her eyes narrowing. "All over."

"Do you know any in particular?"

"No."

Mina sighed, wishing she knew what such a landscape would look like.

"Mina?"

"Yes?"

"Something's missing."

"What do you mean?"

"Something in my head is missing. I know it. I feel like I've forgotten something important." The phrase she was looking for was *like I used to be something more.*

Mina put her arm around Raven. "Do you promise not to say anything to anyone if I tell you something?"

"Sure," said Raven.

"When you arrived here, you looked like someone had hurt you. I think someone brought you here, without you wanting to come here."

"That doesn't seem right."

"It isn't."

"I want to leave, Raven."

"Leave? To where?"

"Whatever's outside."

Raven thought about this for a moment. "I'd like that. I want to see trees again."

Again? She could clearly envision a tree in her mind. Therefore, she must have seen one before. Right?

"I've never seen a tree," Mina said, facing the book but staring blankly. "I'm almost positive." It could be the drugs, though. She couldn't even remember her first day here. And there *had* to be a *first* day.

Mina concentrated on the camera in Raven's lizard's eye. She tried to gain awareness of its functions, but could not make out the slightest whir of it changing focus. She wanted to crush it, but they would just replace it.

The evening was quite relaxing for them; Raven was not called back for any more testing and Mina of course had the day to herself so they spent the rest of their time together. They went to the cafeteria to eat, and then they spent some time in the playroom. Mina introduced most of the other children to Raven, the "new" Raven. Some of them demonstrated their abilities; Raven found them quite impressive and on several occasions Mina laughed good-naturedly at Raven's astonishment at a world Mina was used to. As usual, Keiko and Johnny were off by themselves, and Mina made no attempt to find them or even mention them to Raven, as their powers were off-putting as were their mannerisms and speech patterns, and Mina thought it best not to worry Raven yet with such riddles as they would doubtlessly provide. More than that, Mina did not want them telling her more that Raven was some sort of destiny for her.

Mina was fully aware that this Raven she had known was the latest in three iterations of the girl. The first was unknown to her; it was Raven from Before. Then was Raven the muddled; the girl Mina had met first, one who was practically impossible to speak to but somehow still likeable and possessed of a good heart. Then was Raven as she was now, an adjusting girl, bereft of memory, sweet but naive...about most things.

She had trouble eating pudding neatly, and that Mina found oddly cute. It made both girls giggle. When Raven smiled, Mina could practically feel her heart. It was warm, and caring, and troubled, but attractive.

Mina knew that the Raven she was beginning to know was not the "real" Raven, but she liked her and did not want to be told again by Keiko and Johnny that she would destroy the world. Which to Mina was ironic for she could not truly care less about "the world," having no recollections of ever having experienced anything in it other than the hallways of her shallow existence inside NOD. She thought of her earlier anger towards them and wondered if it might have been irrelevant.

So Mina purposely avoided the two children, which was not hard as they rarely left their room. And she spent the rest of the evening reading to Raven, reading several children's books that had always been over her head, until now, and she found herself laughing at jokes she had never even recognized *were* jokes. To Mina's delight, Raven understood most of them too, so maybe there was hope for her yet.

Mina had a hope that she would not voice, that she still didn't really understand, that, before they found sleep that evening, she and Raven would touch again, the way they had the previous day, that she would feel her again on her lips and against her tongue.

She was not disappointed.

One Hundred Twenty-Five:
Dissension?

Mina awoke the next morning, alone. She found a note on her dresser from Dr. Jacobson telling her that she had another day off—she had probably sent Raven to her own room when she dropped off the note. Mina was quite happy about this because recently Emma's tests had been rather brutal. The note also mentioned that Raven had the day off as well so if the two of them liked they could spend it together.

Truthfully, both Jameson and Emma had plenty of experiments they could run with Raven. Mina was somewhat on standby due to the fact that the White Room was still being updated for several tests Emma wished to run. The only reason they were both given the day off was because Emma wished to observe them together for a full day to see how they interacted and if there was any sign of their powers intermingling.

They started the day off simply enough. After Mina took a shower and dressed, she went to Raven's room and saw that she was awake. She dressed and they went to breakfast together. Danny and another boy named Francis were telekinetically playing catch with a piece of applesauce, releasing control right before it hit the other person so that he had to jump in right away and push it back before he got hit. Benny surprised everyone by putting his hand up to block the applesauce. Francis was taken off guard because Benny let the food phase through his hand and it hit Francis in the forehead. They all laughed loudly. It was the liveliest Mina had seen any of them in quite some time.

Mina and Raven sat with them and ate. Raven had problems holding her spoon and almost dropped applesauce on her pants. She caught most of it in midair with her powers, which put a smile on her face and Mina's.

This led Danny to question how strong Raven thought she might be. She tried to lift the table next to them, and realized after she heard a crack that they were bolted down. She stopped trying and grinned sheepishly, but one of the cafeteria monitors heard the noise and came over. She left after reminding them not to use their powers unless "accompanied by a doctor in a laboratory setting."

So they resumed eating. Mina watched Raven's hand tremble as she held her spoon. It struck her as odd as she realized that Raven only seemed to have these problems now while eating, and only after she had eaten a bit.

Mina's vision followed the spoon down to the almost-empty bowl beneath it. She lost track of the conversation at the table (mostly, it was about recent tests and powers; what else did such children have to talk about?) as a thought began to surface in her head.

Medication was usually given at meal time. Something Raven was being given had the side-effect of temporarily disturbing her fine motor skills. Mina didn't know the words to so eloquently explain her idea, but she guessed at the concept well enough.

She looked around at the children around her. None of them were having any trouble eating. She could not remember having any trouble eating. Except— no, there it was, dimly, a time, when she did.

She had a hunch, but it was hard to be sure.

Raven.

Yes?

You told me once they give you medicine for your hair. Is it a pill or something?

The lady that takes care of me rubs it into my scalp once a day. She said it's 'topical.'

Thanks.

Mina smiled. That was out of the way; she didn't have to worry about that variable, and the reaction the doctors might have if her hair stopped growing.

It was something else, some other method—Raven was being given a drug that the other subjects were not. She had a feeling, a very strong feeling, that whatever it was, it was the key to freeing Raven's mind.

Raven was sitting to Mina's right, and her left hand was resting on the bench next to her. Mina grasped it gently, and Raven glanced at her, smiled, and then continued to eat.

After breakfast, the two girls looked for something to do. In truth, there was little to do with time off other than play with blocks and toys, draw, and read. Mina had, in a simpler time, played with the children, and sometimes even alone, but even then she had recognized that it was not fulfilling for her in the way it was for the younger ones—or rather, the ones that *looked* younger, despite their wrinkles and pallid skin. Drawing was an option, but she was not very talented in that area and it didn't really hold her attention.

So the two girls went back to Mina's yellow room and looked for a book. There was nothing Mina had not read yet, but they picked one out with animal pictures and Mina asked Raven if she'd like to read. To their surprise, she took quickly to it, reading smoothly and with proper inflection. She even read easily words Mina understood from context clues, but was unsure how to pronounce.

"You sound like you've been reading for quite some time," Mina said after awhile.

"It just seems natural," Raven said.

Mina watched the girl read, and as time went by she noticed less and less the words Raven said and noticed more and more Raven herself. She had an effortless beauty that made Mina smile, and she read so tirelessly and easily that Mina was left feeling amazed.

"You went to school, didn't you?" Mina asked.

"School?" Raven looked puzzled. School was a place you sat, and other people sat, and a teacher told you things and tested you on what you had learned. The thought put a frown on her face and filled her with a disdain she did not know the origin of.

"Maybe. I don't know."

Mina felt a hole in her heart, a sudden drop in her gut. She desperately wanted to learn everything there was to know about this girl. But she couldn't. She couldn't learn anything.

Raven, she said to the other girl telepathically. Raven answered the same way without hesitating.

Yes?

The medicine you're given—I think some of it, at least, is different than what the others are given. I think some of it makes you not remember before you were here.

That doesn't seem nice. Her thoughts were cheery, in an "I don't like it but don't really care" sort of way.

I think, if we look at what you're taking and what Benny or Danny is taking, we can figure out what's different, and maybe you can stop taking the one that's changing you.

It was another hunch, but Keiko and Johnny had told her that Raven's memory would continue to change. The only logical vector was medication.

Raven was unexpectedly sharp-witted regarding this idea. *Is that why you asked me what my hair medicine was? Because, if it was a pill I stopped taking, they'd realize it.*

Raven's intuitiveness pleasantly surprised Mina. Maybe, it wasn't too late. Maybe, this could work.

Raven smiled back, and spoke next, guessing Mina's next thought. *Don't worry, I won't tell anyone about this. You can trust me.*

I believe it's you I can trust. I just don't know about the drugs.

Raven grasped Mina's hand, and placed it against her heart. Mina could feel the steady thumping as Raven developed an odd moment of clarity, a moment of thinking outside the literal, a moment of philosophy.

As long as you can trust that my heart will keep beating, you can trust me. This is what friends are.

Dead brown eyes stared into lagoon blue eyes, and for a second, those dead eyes flickered alive once again.

When we leave, thought Mina to Raven, *it would be nice if you remembered about the Outside so we'd be prepared. I have no idea what to expect.*

What do you mean?

Well, here we get food from the same person every day. Is there someone Outside who gives us food? What about showers and clothes? Where do we go for those?

A word appeared in Raven's head. *What's money?*

Money?

It seems important. I thought of it when you asked about food and clothes.

I have no idea. Then: *No, I've heard of it before. One doctor asked another, "Did you win any money at the track." And the other said, "No, I lost all my...."* She stumbled over the next thing. *"Ca" something. Starts with a "k." Or "c."*

Cash. It's the same thing. As money.

I remember that because I wondered what "the track" is. We have a track here, for running around.

I don't know, thought Raven.

Raven lifted several books off of the bed with her telekinesis. Effortlessly, she floated them side-by-side and opened to pictures.

Book one: a green vista, a plain with few trees, a heard of hoofed herbivores (wildebeest, bison?) in the near background.

Book two: a rainforest. Tree trunks everywhere, covered in moss and other greenery. The focus: a monkey holding onto the side of the central tree.

Book three: a skyline. Clearly drawn. Buildings built out of unevenly angled walls with useless doors and windows dominated the scene. At the front of the picture was a boy; at the end of the street (angled so that it appeared far away) was a strange creature.

Book four: a dinosaur. Deinonychus antirrhopus. Fearsome-looking, it had a long, sharply curved claw on each foot and a dangerous maw.

"I know none of this," Raven said.

"But that doesn't bother you."

"Not really, no."

Emma listened closely.

"I don't like the sound of that," Jameson said.

"What?" Emma asked.

"It sounds like dissent."

"Do you blame them?" Which really meant "I blame myself."

"Mina, no; Raven, yes. She should not be bothered by such things."

"She just said she wasn't."

"But still, she shouldn't be thinking of them at all. It's all Mina's fault for putting such thoughts in her head."

"So what," asked Emma exasperatedly, "do you want to keep them separated or something?"

"Actually, I would. But unfortunately, that isn't my choice to make." He glared at her.

"Mina is dangerous. Raven isn't. She's drugged, remember?"

"Raven is acting anomalously. She has been all along. There are things she's said, and things she's done. Surely you remember a couple?"

"Overall, I feel she has conformed to the guidelines of the relaxants and memory modifiers. Especially since they have not been tested on anyone in her age range, except Mina, who is herself anomalous."

Jameson pointed at a nearby wall. "Raven could punch a hole through that wall."

"So could Mina."

"Raven could punch a hole straight through this building."

"Do you want me to be jealous of your charge or something?"

Richardson, who had been sitting quietly behind the pair of doctors, took this moment to speak up. "This bickering is quite unbecoming of you two. At any rate, doctor,"—he was facing Emma—"I don't see any cause to believe that the girls could form any sort of mental union that would increase their powers. Continue with these experiments if you must, but remember your primary goal."

"Of course. I, uh, the White Room is almost ready for the next series of experiments."

"Good. Spencer?"

"Yes?"

"Keep me posted on Raven's abilities. I want to know the full extent of her powers as soon as possible."

One Hundred Twenty-Six:
Experimentation

It still smelled like her.

It had been quite an ordeal, getting her belongings; and now it was an ordeal of the soul having to see them every day, as each day passing made the hope that she would return grow fainter and fainter.

Steve Phillips had been looking over an art history book; he had signed up for school at Omaha Community College, for the winter term. The school ran four terms a year, one a season, and he had made the cutoff for the one beginning in January.

But the book might as well have been blank, for it held his interest to the same degree. He had, after a time, finally given in, and walked over to her belongings and taken out the first thing he found.

It was a tee shirt, a blank, white, tee shirt.

There was a moment in time, a night that seemed to last forever, where he had been able to express his love for her. Just once.

She, clearly, had not been returning that love; it was a moment wherein, he assumed, she just decided to try something for the sake of trying. For she could never love him, she could never truly love any man, right? It was for that reason, though, that that night pained him rather than filling him with joy.

The stars had been beautiful that night.

He had grown past some of the pain he once had at trying to be a friend to someone he was in love with. He was happy when she was happy, sad when she was sad, but still, the ache of unrequited love can never be completely lost while it still exists.

And they had lain there under the stars for a time, then, without word or glance, they got up. He walked her home, hugged her goodbye, and left.

They had never brought it up. Not once. The very next day, they were hanging out, completely normal as usual. But of course she remembered; and it was not a thing he could ever forget.

God, how he loved her. But right now, more than anything, he just wanted his friend back.

One Hundred Twenty-Seven:
Touchdown

Marcus flicked the paper football, aiming for the uprights created by Carlos' fingers.

He missed.

"I am so fucking bored," he said.

"Hey," said Carlos, "at least you get to play with the laser rifles in the field tests. I'm on the rotation into NOD so I don't have *anything* to do. At *all*."

"Yeah the lasers," replied Marcus, setting up another shot, "they're the most unfulfilling weapons I've ever used. Absolutely no kick. Point and click, you're done. Barely effective, too, I've been told. Kill shot, or you cauterize the wound and are left with a really pissed-off foe with a painful hole egging them on."

Flick. Miss.

"You've been in there, right?"

"In where?"

"NOD?"

"Oh yeah, when I went to see Dillons."

"What's it like in there?"

Flick. Miss.

Carlos lit a cigar and took a gentle puff. "I didn't see much, but it's a huge building. The floor I was on, I just saw labs and dormitories. Dillons is, well, was at any rate, when I was there, guarding the girl I acquired during my last mission."

"How did you get in there?"

"That part was easy. Got a guard uniform from the doctor and walked right in the front door. Crappy security for such a hush-hush place; a scientist held a security elevator open for me, and I took it straight up to the floors where all the crazy shit happens. Didn't have to bull shit anyone or break into anything at all."

Marcus grinned. "Sounds like cake."

"It is," said Carlos, hitting his cigar again. "It's gonna be easy as hell."

Flick. Score.

"Touchdown!" exclaimed Marcus.

"About damn time."

One Hundred Twenty-Eight:
Albtraum

Mina tossed and turned. The dreams had come again; dreams of blood and flesh and a child. And death.

The wind howled so fiercely; the cabin creaked, everything dark blue and black, the angles odd, the whole scene like a demented cartoon. She walked, her naked feet frozen to the core, the skin blue, but never blackening. The crunch of snow accompanied each step, her short legs sinking in almost to the knee. Several times she fell; the bite of the air alone was unbearable but each belly flop into a snowdrift sent her into hyperventilation; she should have been dead from hypothermia alone.

The blood was frozen to her hands, her face. She pounded on the cabin, *let me in, let me in, mein Gott im Himmel!*

She woke with a start, sweating, and held her hands up to her face,,,in the dark, they could have been red, she couldn't be sure, but as her eyes adjusted, she became aware that in fact, they were fine, completely clean, and normal.

"Are you okay?" came a groggy but concerned voice from behind her. The hand, above the covers on Mina's waist, fluttered slightly as Raven adjusted herself. Mina immediately felt relieved, just knowing she was there—they hadn't slept apart in several days, since before Raven had had her change. In the past, Raven had occasionally passed out while she was sitting with Mina, and she had let her sleep, but now they made the conscious decision to share a bed at night. It felt comforting.

Mina placed her hand on top of Raven's and grasped it. "Yes. Thanks."

"Good," said Raven, satisfied, as she began to nod back off.

Mina sighed with relief, her heart still beating fast, and tried to get comfortable. Words and phrases leapt through her head, odd sounding words that she felt vaguely familiar with, but couldn't understand. They were harsh-sounding, blunt. She tried to push them out. Eventually, sleep would come again, but would it be troubled still? At least, she wouldn't have to be alone.

One Hundred Twenty-Nine:
Busy Day

The next day brought anticipation.

Emma Jacobson rode the elevator down to the White Room, where she would meet Mina. A mix of apprehension, excitement, fear, and guilt clouded her mind. Great things might be discovered, but at the hands of human pain. Offhandedly, she realized that Christmas had come and gone, without a single card to remind her. It was little matter; if she had been at all religious when she was younger, she certainly wasn't anymore.

Spencer Jameson was less excited then Emma, but he also had no trepidation. Today, he would experiment with Raven's levitation in a large, open lab space—maybe even see if she could fly.

Carlos Gonzalez was packing up his gear, excited for a change of pace. Dr. Graley and General Kresge had both pulled some strings, and his unit, the last replacement unit, was moving into NOD today.

Nicholas Kresge stood in Joshua Richardson's office, feeling his plan coming to fruition finally, since he had talked to Amanda Graley earlier about the last guard rotation.

"I glanced at the roster for today, Joshua. I see Dr. Jacobson is using the White Room."

Lieutenant Colonel Richardson took a slow hit from his cigarette, inhaling deeply and exhaling gently. He tapped the ashes off the end against his ashtray. "I'm expecting a full report on Mina afterwards."

"And the other girl?"

"Spencer says her telekinesis is unbelievably strong. I doubt she could be used directly, but her DNA is on file and ready to be analyzed."

"Very good. On another subject, do you remember Dr. Graley, my assistant?"

"Yeah, from the soldier test. Sure."

"Well, she's going to be working at another branch of NOD, and I need to have both generators up and running soon. She's going to be coming by in the next couple of days to see them."

"Emma's been studying M, but she has her hands full with Mina right now, I'll let her know it needs to be reactivated temporarily. In any case, if she's going to be using the White Room, we'll need the extra power." He took another hit. "I should have it online by tomorrow, if not today."

"Sounds great. Keep me posted."

"Will do."

Kresge left the office as Richardson finished his cigarette and put it out.

Today would be a good day.

Elsewhere, elsewhen, elsehow, there was another whose anticipation had nearly run out. Matthew had almost reached his breaking point. He had grown virtually suicidal.

He would harass the yellow bringers of pain, swaying in and out of their range on self-referencing arcs, seeing how close he could get to utter annihilation before he turned back. He had even considered trying to penetrate the Shroud, to see how close he could get to the center of the Light, how much damage he could cause, before they stopped him.

But that was foolhardy. His brain, (or whatever the ethereal counterpart was) was hardwired to think linearly, and as much as he understood now the method of thinking in round-about circles and spheres, he was still used to falling back on old-fashioned straight line deduction, resentment, and frustration.

Wait a little longer, he told himself *Just a little longer.*

After so many failed attempts, he did see himself now as the punisher of them, they who had locked him up, who had forced him into this predicament.

They would all perish; but, in time—he would look for opportunities first.

One Hundred Thirty:
White Room Return

Emma sat in the control room of the White Room, awaiting Mina's arrival. In the next room over were the bulky, modified equipment that had just been completed for her last night. She (with help) had worked out extensions to Hanin's equations, had found other information in his files, and had deduced experimental procedures that she was now ready to test.

Over the last week she had come to a hypothesis regarding biomorphism. Arty—as well as the test subjects who had not survived—were a result of self-controlled attempts at biomorphism, which had almost universally been failures. But M's regular structure was the result of carefully applied external stimuli. So she had reasoned that a being did not possess the knowledge to correctly reshape its own body.

For a human had no inherent knowledge of its own body's structure—the reactions, the cellular biology, the placement and functions of nerves, etc. So how could a being like that be expected to create and maintain, then later undo, a stable structural change to its own body?

Hopefully, whether truly biomorphic or not, Mina would have verifiable reactions to today's tests. Emma was fairly certain that no change would be dangerous or permanent; Mina's healing was impressively quick and strong.

By and by, Mina stepped into the White Room, this time, naked and unchained. Freedom of movement (growth, maybe) was a must. Emma leaned forward and clicked on the mic.

"How are you today Mina?"

"Fine, Dr. Jacobson," she lied. She was filled with dread and anticipation.

"That's good. Well, if you will, please make your way to the rings at the center of the room."

Mina slowly began walking, unenthusiastically hunched over. It seemed abnormally dim in the room today. She hadn't been in the White Room for quite some time, but the walls seemed less bright than usual, and seemed to pulse quite sluggishly.

Emma had a twinge of guilt watching Mina getting ready for the test. What could another life have given her? Art? Music? Science? She was too short and too voluptuous to be a model—well, a fashion model, at least—but given talents could she have been an actress? She was smart; could she have been a writer, perhaps, or a teacher? But here she was, a tool of the state.

Mina had her arms crossed, though not out of any attempt to conceal herself. Here she was, wide open and ready for abuse, in front of the eyes of one. One who had seemed humane for a while, but who had quickly turned around.

"I'm going to begin the tests now."

"Yes, doctor."

Couldn't she, if she had wanted to, smash through the ceiling? Found the ground floor and broken out? Why was she so complacent? Mina berated herself.

It was for Raven, she realized. That was why she waited. She was afraid she wasn't ready, that she was too weak. But the longer they stayed, the weaker she'd be.

Emma began the power-up sequences on the radiation emitters. The first test was simply one of basic reaction to stimuli. After less than a minute borderline levels were reached, and Emma began flooding the center of the White Room with exotic particles.

The reaction began gently, a slow burn creeping its way up Mina's spine to her brain. A faint glow from within her skin was apparent. Emma considered this to be a success, so far, and moved onto step two.

The radiation output was heightened and changed, and the glow increased, appearing to cover Mina's body with faintly reddish outlines of polygons. Mina began to feel somewhat wobbly and lightheaded. Emma proceeded to step three.

The lines shone with intense light, oh, and they hurt, now, and Mina was afraid she would burst into flames, but she didn't. The skin inside the polygons began to tremble and pulsate of its own accord, as though she had air pockets under them that alternately inflated and deflated.

"Now, maximum baseline stimulus output," Emma said to herself as she increased the output once again.

Mina fell to the ground, convulsing, her body turned to black between the glow. The pulsating of her skin was intense, threatening to rip her flesh off...

...and it did. Mina was wrong, she wasn't going to burst into flames.

She was just going to burst.

It was like a thousand tiny explosions all over her body, as each section of skin popped open, spraying the air and ground with a mist of blood. Her nerves flared up, excruciatingly painful, and then died. Either she was protected by shock, or her nerves themselves had been broken as well.

"Abort! Abort!" Emma yelled; it took her a half-beat to remember that she was alone, and she quickly shut the system down herself.

Her left arm pinned beneath her by her fall, Mina groggily looked at her right arm; despite the blurriness of her vision, she could tell that she was starting to heal. Her body had reclaimed some of its spewed blood but she had lost quite a bit.

Emma's heart beat quickly. It was a moment before she was sure that yes, indeed, Mina was going to be all right. She sat back in her chair, and exhaled deeply as Mina clumsily stood up.

Is that what you were hoping for? Mina thought to herself.

Emma leaned into the mic. "All right Mina, take a moment to rest, and then we'll start the next test." There was a tightness in her chest, a tangled feeling in her guts, but she did the best to dismiss them, or at least, to ignore.

One Hundred Thirty-One:
Reunion

Dillons led Carlos into the restroom, one of the few places in NOD not under constant surveillance. They exchanged a hug, a big, testosterone induced back-slapping manly hug. The bigger black man put his hand on the shoulder of the smaller, lithe Hispanic.

"Here to stay, huh?"

"Yeah you got it. Dr. Graley pulled some strings. The troop rotation is complete. But what's with this private first class bullshit?"

"Aw, you know it don't mean nothin'. I'm just a sergeant here."

"So what's it like? I got debriefing in thirty."

"Boring, but at least now we got each other, ha! Nah, for as much crazy shit as they have going on here, nothing seems to happen. I've been guarding that chick—the one you acquired—and there's been a little funny business, like tremors and stuff, but not enough to keep the day interesting. It's been quiet actually for awhile—she isn't even in her room most of the time anymore."

"That's okay, once we have this facility secure, you and me are gonna rejoin Marcus on the outside."

"I can't wait. How's Marcus doing? How's your wife?"

At this point, the door to the bathroom opened abruptly and a freckled, red-haired man in a lab coat came in. Seeing the soldiers standing opposite each other with the bigger one's hand on the other's shoulder, he held his hands up at shoulder height in front of him. He said "Don't ask, don't tell," and backed out.

"Nice," said Carlos sarcastically. Dillons removed his arm and grinned. "Anyway, Marcus is fine, but he's bored too, we haven't had any missions since this stuff all started. And Carrie's good, due next month."

"You excited?"

"Hell yeah."

"But you said, boring here? You know how I am, I need to see action. That's why I took this job."

"Just try and ride it out for awhile. That's all we can do."

"Yep."

"Yep."

One Hundred Thirty-Two:
About to Break

Mina was sitting in the corner of her room, her knees to her chest and her hands on her shins. She was rocking forwards and backwards; her breathing was haggard, and her eyes looked unfocused, when Raven came in to see her that afternoon.

A look of intense concern shown on Raven's face. "What's wrong?"

Pulled out of her stupor by a comforting voice, Mina looked over at Raven and ran to her, throwing her arms around her and crying against her cheek.

"It was awful, absolutely awful," she sobbed. "For hours…the tests…the pain. Oh we have to leave, we have to be free, this isn't right!"

Raven led Mina over to the bed and helped her up onto it, and sat there, holding her as she cried. After a time, Mina calmed a bit, and Raven spoke.

"I missed you at breakfast and lunch."

"Dr. Jacobson didn't want me to eat. She didn't want me to throw up anything."

Raven backed away a bit from Mina and reached a hand into her pocket, smiling as she did so. She held her hand out to Mina and opened it just enough so that she could see inside.

There were several pills laying on her palm.

These are the ones no one else takes. I held them in my mouth— telekinetically—and took the rest. When the nurse left, I hid them in my pocket.

It was always possible that the other pills were just as bad, but Mina was sure this was, at least, beneficial.

Watch, Raven thought to her. She looked at the pills intently, and they were suddenly gone, reduced into a cloud of atomized dust.

Everything's going to be okay, Mina responded, a giant grin on her face. Overcome with the happy prospect that really, truly, everything *was* going to be all right, with her own pain momentarily forgotten, she surprised both of them by taking the initiative and pushing Raven against the covers and joyfully kissing her.

She still didn't understand the feelings that led to this or the feelings that came from it, but by God, did it ever feel right.

One Hundred Thirty-Three:
Paradox

Emma looked at the report she had typed up for Richardson. Disjointed sections caught her eye one by one down the page.

```
Mina herself is unsuitable for biomorphic usage
due to her healing ability quickly erasing any
changes made in her structure.
```

Oh, what a horror the last test had been. The shape, the inhumanity of it, thank god, thank Jesus fucking Christ Mina was able to save herself from it.

```
However, as a test subject, she has provided
valuable data and should continue to do so.
```

Provided she continued to *live* through the tests.

```
It is of my opinion that Mina is not currently
capable of generating biokinetic abilities as she
apparently did during the attack on Dr. Benton and
the guards.
```

She couldn't prove it, but it seemed true.

```
In regards to Mina's testimony, and Dr. Hanin's
report regarding the Anna incident, I can find no
other alternative to explain her aberrant behavior
other than psychic possession by the former test
subject known as Matthew. Unfortunately I cannot
determine by what vector this came about. I believe
it to be some sort of function of the M Generator,
however, and recommend it be kept offline until a
more thorough series of tests can be run.
```

Too much? Too little?

She decided she wouldn't submit the paper until she had time to think about it and rewrite it. She leaned back in her chair, drumming her fingers on her desk. And then slowly, from out of nowhere, a thought crept into her head.

Recently, when Richardson had raised her security clearance, she had received a list of files and rooms she now had access too. Among other places, Dr. Utsugi's office was listed. The clearance level on both Hanin's and Utsugi's offices had not been changed after the Mina incident, and the thought had never occurred to her before, but if Utsugi worked beneath Hanin, why was her office held under tighter security?

Emma's current security level was higher than Hanin's had been… meaning Hanin did not have private access to Utsugi's office, even though Utsugi was his subordinate.

Meaning Utsugi's clearance level was higher than Hanin's.

Meaning…it was time for some snooping.

One Hundred Thirty-Four:
Calm

Mina sat with Raven, the taller girl's arm around her. Mina had, at her insistence, told her the day's events, and Raven had seemed able to grasp the implications of it. Raven had had an easy day; some telekinesis tests, and some successful levitation tests. Raven told Mina that Dr. Jameson wanted to test her levitation further, to see if she could fly. Mina smiled at this idea.

Their closeness calmed Mina; she truly felt like more of a person just because of Raven's presence. Raven, at least in the hellhole of NOD, was more of a person with Mina then she could have been without.

One Hundred Thirty-Five:
Dr. Utsugi's Files

Emma sat at Utsugi's desk, rifling through sheet after sheet of carefully hand-printed notes. It was here; it was all here. Basic descriptions, psychic theories, the energy project, the soldier project, the truth.

On psychic basics, the aura, and mental intrusion:

The aura is the foundation for much of psychic science. It seems to be a field of potential energy that surrounds a living being; psionically manipulated, it can be solidified, projected out as particles, used to lift and move objects; indeed every year we discover more functions of the aura than we could have imagined existed.

But the most intriguing aspect of it to myself is one of its most basic features, one that affects all beings, not just psychics.

The aura appears to be a shield that keeps minds separate. And as such, it protects the mind and body, as an extension of the mind, from psychic intrusion. Intrusion must be carefully defined to understand this fact, however.

As a first example, telepathy is not intrusive; so far, every being tested whether psychic or not, has the ability to sense telepathic thoughts directed at him or her. Thus telepathy itself is a psychic ability, but the ability to perceive it is a sense, no different than vision or hearing. So we see that telepathy is not intrusive.

Now with telekinesis, careful explanation must be given. A kinetic edge (also referred to as an inertial increase) can be applied to a physical object, which is used to hurt a human. In this case, the telekinesis itself is not intruding on the target; rather, it is adding to the energy of the physical attack, and thus is not intrusive. A "telekinetic" blast is also not intrusive; the solidified portion of the aura that can be projected at a target is no longer part of the aura, it is in fact a rapidly evaporating solid projectile in this sense no different from a bullet. The telekinesis merely forms and propels the object. The end result is that telekinesis cannot be used directly to penetrate the human body or cause other harm; though, a human as a whole may be a target.

The catchall phrase of "intrusion" is used for rare psychic abilities that allow bypasses of the aura. These would include abilities such as mind reading and mental control (domination.) Also however is the notion of biokinesis; that a person capable of both telekinesis and domination could bypass a human's aura protection and directly cause telekinesis upon the body. As a weapon, this would be dangerous, though extraordinary.

On her relationship with Hanin, and his work:

It pains me sometimes to think of the lies I must constantly inflict about Mahir. We have grown quite close as colleagues, and it shames me that he thinks his work on the energy project is for the greatness of mankind. Surely, the work coming out of it is valuable in its own right, but he is truly defining the science of biomorphism to further my experiments in the soldier project.

On the nature of the soldier project:

The fallibility of this project is that at some point, it requires a very strong psychic to obey a regular human. I agree whole-heartedly that the soldiers themselves should have no conscience mind; once the raw source known as "Angel" has matured we shall see if it is possible for a being such as that to possess psychic power; however to test that we need a subject that possess mental domination but is still controllable. Matthew tests poorly and seems weak; Andrew shows promise but without a Matthew, he is useless.

The Angel itself possesses genetic coding for both telekinesis and biomorphism; however causing biomorphism to work in the manner we intend is still beyond us. Every day that Hanin and I work on our parallel projects we get one step closer, however.

In regards to the Anna incident:

It seems then in fact that Matthew was capable of domination; however, it seems his brain was burned out controlling Anna. I cannot say with any certainty what caused this, as it is the first and only verifiable case of psychic possession I have witnessed. However, I must say also that Anna's brain does not work quite like any other we have studied. Photokinesis is still a mystery; how can the mind manipulate that which moves at light speed?

Following the Andrew Incident:

It seems that now the Angel will be lost to us. It was never completed, and now, seeming that a force of possession still exists despite Matthew's death, a being as potentially powerful as the Angel would be, must be, kept out of his grasp. For in its genetic coding lies Mahir's energy algorithms, leading me to believe it may be able to feed limitlessly off of Nod energy, super-powering it. However, I will continue working on biomorphism to try and clearly define the stimulus approach. It is of my opinion that no being, unless fully aware of the infinitesimals of how his body worked, could safely and correctly perform biomorphism. So, I feel that external stimuli must be applied in specific manners to compensate. Mahir has worked out much of the beginnings in creating the M Generator; I shall go a step further.

On the virtual completion of the biomorph project:

At last, for all intents and purposes, the mathematical side of biomorphism has been completed. The fruits of my labor, my secret subject Tom, has become a perfect warrior. Though he is of conscious mind, Yamada tells me that he and his team have created implants that cannot be rejected by a biomorphic body. With proper stimulation through these implants, we will no longer need a "control unit" and that solves the very dangerous problem of trying to control a being capable of domination.

I shall prepare and submit a report tomorrow; for now, I will house him in the secondary cryonics lab behind the breaker room, along with my other "fruits"... the steps along the way that led to Tom.

There hasn't been a case of possession in years. Hopefully, after presenting Tom, I can reactivate the Angel project and perform the same experiments on him that created Tom in his current from. It may still be useful to create a soldier that does not possess higher brain functions.

The first, and least important thing that confused Emma was that, if for all intents and purposes biomorphism had been a fully understood area of study by Dr. Utsugi, why was she still working to that end? Unless, of course, her superiors had not found out about it.

Emma looked at the date on the paper she had just read. It was dated exactly one day before the Mina incident.

Utsugi had never submitted a report. She hadn't lived long enough.

And this... secondary cryonics lab? Tom, and the subjects that had led to his creation?

Emma strengthened her resolve, and got up. She felt, no, she knew, that she was one final step from the truth about NOD. She had to go to the cryonics lab.

She left immediately for the main breaker room.

One Hundred Thirty-Six:
The Truth, Part One

Emma had never been to the breaker room; had never known a secret lab was connected to it. Now, amidst the jumble of mechanisms and wires she saw plainly a large door with an access terminal on the side. Hoping against hope, she slid her ID card, and sure enough, she had the clearance to enter.

It was a cold room, as cryonics would suggest. Her breath blew out in foggy clouds; she shivered, wishing she'd worn pants today and not a skirt.

The color scheme of the room made her feel even colder than she already was; it was a mix of white, frost blue, and gunmetal. It was a sizable room, with a control bay on one side and the frost-covered cryonic tubes on the other.

Unlike their depictions in popular fiction, the tubes would of course be opaque and fully sealed, so she went to the control bay to peruse their contents.

The results were shocking; inhuman atrocities, each worse than the next. The grotesqueries of their altered anatomies, peeled and curled flesh, piercing bones, exposed muscle and tendon, spars, spurs, claws, extra sensory organs, altered sensory organs, unknown forms… it horrified her and nauseated her simultaneously. These were worse than the failures she'd seen. They had died; these, presumably, were still alive in their tortured states.

And then, after nearly thirty of these monsters, Emma found Tom, and a temporary calm came over her. He was, in some way…beautiful.

He was built like an athlete; a runner. Strong, yet lithe. Classically handsome face, though hairless, and pale, like his hands and feet. No body hair, not even any genitals, but his sculpted form was black, blacker than any African Emma had ever seen, and crisscrossed by red lines, the same she'd seen on Mina in the White Room.

Her temporary peace was shattered when she noticed recently dated information among its statistics:

```
Removal Authorization:
    [Joint Authorization]
    Kresge, Nicholas (General)
    Richardson, Joshua (Lieutenant Colonel)
Replacement Authorization:
    [Joint Authorization]
    Kresge, Nicholas (General)
    Yamada, Daichi (Doctor)
```

What had they done? There had to be a record. She ran to the elevator to find out.

One Hundred Thirty-Seven:
Culmination (Almost)

It was a moment, a moment of definition. Sense was coming out of chaos, worlds needed to be built on the ashes of the fallen. Raven had taken the first step towards unlocking herself, her mind, her body, her heart. Renewing, regrowing, rebuilding.

The closeness they felt, the gentle touch, the consoling, the words without speaking, had built to a head with this day, this day where Raven, in her increasingly-less clouded state, had been able to comfort Mina after her second worst day ever, with good news, a kiss, an embrace, and a tear.

Raven had saved Mina.

Mina closed her eyes and leaned toward Raven, and kissed her.

"I'm supposed to save you," she whispered softly, the emphasis on *you*.

Raven pressed into the kiss and ran a hand gently through Mina's soft, sweet-smelling hair. She placed the other hand against her cheek.

Mina opened her eyes.

Raven's were alight, a fire burning fiercely in them. She pulled her head back and smiled at Mina. Mina gasped.

Was this? No, but it was close. There was a freedom there that was on the very edge of bursting free; a few steps still needing to be taken before Raven was fully whole. Mina knew this on a guttural level, and at the same time, she all at once understood the terrible unity of desire and restraint. Her skin was flushed, her heart a-flutter.

Returning Raven's smile, Mina began to move behind her, to hold her, and to lay down with her, to sleep, to wait. A hand brushed against Raven's waist and she could sense her taught abdomen through her shirt. She gulped. A fire raging in her now as well, Mina spooned Raven and comforted herself in the scent of her hair as they dozed off, slowly calming down.

They slept soundly. For once, Mina's sleep would not be troubled.

One Hundred Thirty-Eight:
The Truth, Part Two

Emma was in the security files room, searching, Tom, Tom, Tom.
Nothing, nothing, nothing.

She had been reading for hours, looking at horrors for hours. It was well
into the early morning and she was determined to put the final piece into place
in the puzzle she'd finally almost solved.

At her clearance level, there were 1336 computer files she did not have
access to.

Then: a thought. Maybe, the old protocols were still in place.

Richardson had mentioned in their first meeting after the Mina Incident
that Hanin and Utsugi had given her unusually high clearance; she had said that
they trusted her to get files for them on occasion. And it hit her. Why oh why, oh
why fucking why, hadn't she thought of this in the first place?

```
Logged in as: Jacobson, Emma (Doctor)
```

Click.

```
Proxy Login:
```

She typed.

```
SetsunaUtsugi
```

Click.

```
Password:
```

```
TobeyMaguire69
*************
```

```
Proxy Login confirmed. Clearance Level Equivalent.
```

She searched, "Tom" and over a hundred files showed up. She clicked on
the most recent. It was a video file. She gasped at what she saw.

There was Richardson, and that man Kresge, and a host of others. And
there was Tom. And then; a massacre. Gently, gracefully, he dispatched every
man down in the crater with ruthless efficiency.

This was her fault. She had not made it; but she was remaking it. The blood of those men was on her hands.

And the mix of emotions, greed and morals, came to a head, and she felt a wave of guilt and responsibility come over her like none she'd ever felt.

One Hundred Thirty-Nine:
The Truth, Part Three

Raven woke with a start. She had slept well for several hours, and while she did, her brain undid the work of the medication. Whether it was from missing a single day's stabilizing drugs, the factor of her age, or something related to Mina and the nucleotides they shared, she would never know.

But, she remembered everything.

"Oh, god," she said aloud as her life before NOD, only tenuously lost to her, came flooding back.

She began shaking, it was too much, the flood of emotions, memories, experience ravaging her mind.

She inhaled a deep, hollow breath, and caught herself before she screamed. She held her hand up to her mouth.

She looked next to her. Mina was still sleeping, the gentle rise and fall of her chest with each breath counting out a steady, calm rhythm.

Mina was comfort.

Mina was beautiful.

Mina was thoughtful.

Mina was freedom.

Mina was love.

Raven put her arms around the girl, and leaned over and kissed her on the forehead. She rubbed away a tear at her mother's memory. And...her. She was dead, as well. She had not seen the final blow, but she knew it to be true.

"Raven?" Mina awoke easily, dreaming only lightly.

She sat up in Raven's arms, turning her upper body to face her, and put her arms around Raven. They held each other tenderly for a moment, and then Raven spoke.

"You did it. You saved me. And now it's time for me to save you."

"What do you mean?"

"We're going to leave. I remember everything."

"You do!?"

"My name is Raven Yamada. I'm eighteen years old. A man killed my mother and my brother, kidnapped me and my girlfriend, and brought us to this place. They experimented on both of us, and she died." She had a steely resolve in her voice as she spoke. *I can fill in the details later*, she thought.

"That's horrible!!" Of course Mina knew the words kidnap and murder; water cooler talk encompassed everything imaginable and the scientists and guards at NOD were no different.

"We have to get out of here. We can use our powers."

Mina was scared, but ready. The outside…she was going to see the outside. And Raven was going to take her there. She looked into Raven's eyes, no longer dead brown, but glowing with the glory of life, as they had from time to time, only now, it would be forever. And Raven looked into hers, so blue they could have been made of the sky itself, and they kissed.

"All right, let's go."

"Don't you want to know what they did to her before you go?" The unexpected voice made both girls jump. Looking towards the sound, they saw Benny, pulling himself up through the floor with his elbows.

"I can take you to her. It won't take more than a couple minutes." He was now standing up. "Go ahead and change, I won't peak." He turned his back and covered his eyes. It wouldn't have affected him in the slightest, but he understood manners and modesty.

Is it all right? Raven asked Mina.

Of course, I understand. She really didn't, other than the fact that Raven needed closure of some sort.

They dressed with easy clothes: tee shirts, drawstring pajama pants (duckies and turtles) and rubber slippers.

"Are you ready?"

"Yes," Raven said.

They sent you, didn't they? Mina asked Benny.

Yes. They said it was time.

"Hold my hands." Benny turned around and held out his hands. Both girls grasped one, and then the three of them fell through the floor like it was made out of air.

One Hundred Forty:
Back Downstairs

Emma dashed into her office, not really knowing if—not really caring if—there would be repercussions for her snooping in Utsugi's office, the secondary cryonics lab, or the security flies room. She hadn't thought that far ahead; she hadn't thought more than a couple seconds ahead since she had left the file room.

What to do, what to do. Flee? Stay? Accept responsibility, and hope for the best? Maybe the loss of job and life. Maybe grim determination to go ahead despite the costs. Maybe....

A note on her desk. Quickly now, quickly...*Emma...scientist coming to see generators...had Jameson reactivate M...Richardson.*

That was not good. Definitely not good. Dr. Utsugi had thought it was safe, the day before Matthew came through and killed her.

A crackle over the intercom.

"Emma?" It was Richardson. Oh shit. "Better get to the cryonics lab." Emma apparently wasn't the only one who had stayed late into the night.

What? Oh, the main lab, probably. Hopefully. Unless....

"Mina, Raven, and Benny are there. I'm sending a couple squads also. Try and get there quickly."

"Yes, sir."

Crackle.

What the hell!?

One Hundred Forty-One:
Where to Now?

Raven stared at the drawer. She knew what cryonics was. She'd seen and read enough science fiction. This was a cryonics lab.

This drawer wasn't a cryonic vessel meant for the storage of life.

It was a mortuary drawer.

Tears welled up in her eyes as she looked at the label on it:

```
Fischer, Maria. 17.
Cause of Death: Neck Trauma.
```

Raven wanted to hit something, so hard, to keep the tears back and make her hurt, and feel pissed off instead of sad. She had just come back to the world, through the spark of love, just to feel empty, lost, and alone.

She reached for the handle. Mina stood a few feet back, tense and worried, and Benny stood back further still, calm and neutral.

It was locked. With a snapping sound, she fixed that problem with her mind. She pulled it open, quickly, a thin white sheet all that was between her and her former love. The frozen air that came out of the drawer chilled Raven to the bone. The sheet itself was numbing to the touch.

But Raven didn't notice this—she was already feeling cold and numb.

She grabbed the sheet at one end, and hesitated, not knowing which was worse, to pull quickly or pull slowly.

She chose quickly.

She dropped the sheet as soon as it had been removed and it wafted down with a flourish, cold and dry. She put both hands over her mouth and gasped.

There she was. Crow. Rock hard frozen, blue and dead. Her body—naked —no longer the joy of lust. Her heart no longer the beating of love. Her mind no longer a whirlpool of thoughts and ideas.

Her head had been shaved, and purplish bruises from that *fucking asshole with the gun* speckled it. A nasty wound had been roughly stitched up towards the rear of her neck.

But the eyes were the worst part of it. Open, blank, staring straight up, never to see again.

Mina stared at the scene ahead of her, new, painful emotions coursing through her body. She had seen death, she had caused death, and knew it hurt others but she had never seen their pain before. This was entirely new territory for her (as most life experiences would be.) But this one was shocking in its raw unpleasantness.

Raven took a step back. She wanted to cry, to fall down, to push away the grimness of reality, but that sadness, that emptiness was being replaced with a new emotion: rage. Her hands fell to her side and formed fists.

"These assholes aren't gonna keep her body," she said, glancing around for anything flammable. There were chemicals, tubes, pipes, air canisters…she didn't know what any of it was. Then a thought. She picked up Crow with her mind and held her hand (freezing, frozen, rigid) as she floated next to her. She stepped past a gasping Mina and grabbed Benny's hand seconds before she walked into the wall between the morgue and the main cryonics bay. He complied with her unspoken wishes and they passed through the wall.

Standing beyond the control panel, they were still some fifty feet away from the rows of cryo-tubes. Raven, almost fumbling her mental grip on Crow's body, steeled her resolve and let out a telekinetic pulse so intense it visibly distorted her view momentarily. The effect was massive; every tube imploded and the mess of coolants from the mechanisms behind them billowed out in a heavy, deadly white cloud that quickly hid the view of shattered machinery and pulverized, disinterred frozen body parts. Ironically, something flammable *had* been ignited off of a bared wire, and the fire suppression system came on in the area around the tubes, the water passing through the cloud and clattering as hail as it hit the ground.

It had taken Mina several seconds to leave the morgue area and come around through the door to the side of the bay; she saw the results of the explosive noise she had heard, and watched silently as Raven levitated Crow's body into the roiling mist. By now, it had begun to spread thinly along the floor; Raven casually levitated above it, still fully aware of its biting touch; Benny floated out of it harmlessly, out of phase with the physical world.

The thinning vapor was still strong enough to instantly freeze nearly anything it touched; Crow's body, now lying on the ground, was quickly covered in water, which, with the gasses, froze it to a coldness naturally found nowhere on earth. Again, Raven focused her power, and concentrated solely on Crow; she was there one second, the next, she had been absolutely shattered into pieces no larger than grains of sand.

Almost as good as cremation.

The rage was intense. She could feel her body tingle, begin to burn, an animalistic simplification of the human mind trying to take over. And then, she looked at Mina—and her body began to cool and her breathing slowed. Mina looked at her with a mix of care, concern, and fear.

Poor girl, she thought, *I've scared her.*

She ran over to Mina and threw her arms around her; they were still cold from the bay.

"Never leave me, please. I can't bear it again."

A moment's hesitation, then Mina returned the embrace.

"Never."

Carlos ran down the hallway, a half-beat behind Dillons, who despite still complaining about his leg (it should have been fine by now; clearly, he was victim of a mental issue) was keeping well ahead of the two squads they had with them.

"I thought you said nothing ever happens here, huh?"

"Nothing usually does!"

Because of her superior familiarity with the building's layout, Emma had beaten them to the cryonics lab. Only Benny was there. Briefly, Emma stared in disgust at the mangled machinery and slowly thawing remains. Then:

"Where did they go, Benny? I need to know."

You want to see them, don't you?

"Yes, very much." The absolute strain of everything, learning the truth of the truth, the state of this room, the wrongdoings, the cover-ups, the lies, the pain…Emma almost broke down then and there. She thought of the scar on her hand, and knew she deserved much worse; she should shoulder the weight for her alternating naivete and indifference.

Then take my hand.

She held her hand out, and….

Presently, the soldiers burst into the cryonics lab, and it was…

Empty.

Except, unbeknownst to anyone (or just one) there was a flicker of life in the room, a ragged, half-frozen form flapping around, wedged in behind a crumpled storage tube that had served as its icy prison until just now. Desperately clinging to life and trying to heal the damage it had taken from this abrupt re-animation, it found its footing, and crawled like a slug out of its cubby hole. When it sensed the beings had left, it began feeding itself on the slowly thawing pieces of the dead.

One Hundred Forty-Two:
Leaving

"It's best if we leave from up high," said Raven. "Less chance of hitting anything. I can do this, you know; I'm sure of it."

"I have faith in you," Mina said, smiling.

They stepped out of the elevator Benny had pushed them into (or more specifically, through the door of.) They ran down a hallway until it split into a T-section near some offices. Raven could feel it; mere feet away, on the other side of this wall, was freedom. She began to focus her strength, and....

There was a grunt as something fell to the floor. Emma had never phased before, and the funny thing about it was one couldn't breathe because there was literally *nothing to* breathe. The act of un-phasing created a nice her-and-Benny-shaped vacuum (mustn't co-exist with existing matter, she imagined) and it was a second before she felt fresh air moving into her lungs. Benny made his exit silently, descending into the morass that was the Gates Building.

"Dr. Jacobson," said Mina, puzzled, taking a tentative step towards her.

"Don't go near her," said Raven, venom in her voice. "She's a monster just like the rest of them."

"Please," said Emma, looking up, tears streaming down her face, tears she had started crying while passing through purgatory, no breath in her guilty lungs. Raven's heart softened slightly and she paused. It was at this moment that Emma realized that somehow, Raven was as complete a person as Mina, as herself.

"Please, listen, I've, I've seen it, seen it all, where this goes. I thought... thought I..." A moment of clarity struck her. She pointed at her ears, her eyes, then the walls and ceilings around them. Raven and Mina both nodded, Raven, from common sense, and Mina, from the remembrance of her stuffed animal and room.

Mina walked up to Emma and calmly erected a shield around the two of them. Raven concentrated, and let out a telekinetic blast that was strong enough to crack the walls and blow out any surveillance equipment or other electronics in the area.

"I've seen...what's down the road from here...what I've been working on." She sniffled, a viscous noise of phlegm and tears. "Everything I've done to you..."

She looked at Mina. God, Mina, who deserved more than this. "I know you can't forgive me. Don't forgive me. But it's so much worse. Much, much worse than what you've been through."

Raven walked over and knelt down in front of her. Emma was suddenly very, very afraid, and Raven could tell.

"I'm not going to hurt you." She was very hardened from her memories and recent ordeals, but the soft warm presence of Mina kept her calm. She saw the lost kindness in the doctor's frail brown eyes. "What do you want?"

"I want you both to get as far from here as possible."

"That's what we want, too," said Mina.

Far off in the distance, down the hallway, was the echoing sound of shouting and booted footsteps.

Emma took a billfold and a pen out of her pocket. She scrawled a number on the top bill. "This is a safe line. They don't know about it. Call me if you have no other options." She tossed the money to Mina, who caught it. "Use it. Use it all. Get away from here. Start over, far, far away."

"How can we trust you?" asked Raven.

The sound of footsteps was closer.

"Because if they think I helped your escape, they'll kill me. You have to make it look good. You know what to do."

Raven spoke to Mina, a sob in her voice.

"Please sweetie, look away."

Mina did, a tear on her cheek. She heard the sound of fist on face and of unconscious woman hitting the ground. The last thought Emma had before she blacked out was *Fuck, Raven's implants!*

The guards arrived just in time to see Raven blow a hole in the wall, the glory of dawn cascading into the dim hallway. Specs of snow blew in, melting into insignificant wet spots as they hit the floor. Raven grabbed Mina, kissed her on the forehead, and the two were gone into the sky. Two women, who had met under extraordinary circumstances, who barely truly knew each other, yet were bound by a love that was itself extraordinary.

The guards saw the woman on the ground, unconscious, but breathing. The rasp of a walkie-talkie. A click.

"Lieutenant colonel?"

"Let them go. The Asian's tagged; we'll find them soon enough."

The black man, the one whose head wouldn't let him use his leg correctly except when he was too riled up to think about it, knelt to look at the woman's name tag.

"Dr. Jacobson is here. She's been knocked out."

"Bring her to me."

In the darkness, in the depths of the bowels of the building, amidst sparking wires, a used-up fire, and the melting of the (tasted) dead, a being, half formed, half-frozen still, lurched forward. Its undeveloped eyes opened, and the smattering of blurs and spots it saw were heaven, for the being piggybacking on its brain had seen his recently regained circle form a line, pointing to this very being, and he had followed that path whole-heartedly.

Matthew had a new home.

Part Three
One Path For Two

One Hundred Forty-Three:
Freedom

The thrill of flying for the first time was lost on Raven. When the distance between her and hell had increased and her emotions had settled, the adrenaline wore off, and she realized something they never tell you in superhero movies: flying was freezing. True, the air was rife with winter chill and she and Mina weren't exactly dressed for it, but even so she imagined the slightly thinner air and the screaming wind against her would be chilly regardless of the season.

By the time they set down in a wooded area, right next to a shopping mall some distance from the center of Omaha, both girls were positively numb.

Raven, startled that everything that had transpired had apparently taken place within a few miles of her own home, had picked this area because she was almost certain not to run into anyone who would recognize her here. It was a decent distance from her neighborhood and was not a particularly popular area; the people there had fallen onto hard times since the "wonderful" businesses of the Gates building had done so much to help the city's reconstruction and civil pride since the "terrorist" attacks so long ago.

A thousand thoughts ran through Raven's recently whole mind, but she focused on two. She had to. For now, anyway.

Mina, first. Then, me.

"We have to get some supplies."

Mina nodded. Raven had carefully set Mina down when they reached ground level and stepped down a couple feet away; now Mina moved back to embrace her again.

"I have faith in you. I always will."

They quickly walked out of the woods and into the mall, garnering many an odd glance because of their weather-inappropriate clothing. Mina (bless her heart) understood discretion being the better part of valor, and despite being surrounded by a cornucopia of new sights and sounds, calmly followed Raven's lead.

The pair walked into a clothing store, quickly picked out winter coats and a few changes of clothes, which they paid for with Emma's cash. They grabbed backpacks and a couple of blankets from nearby shops as well, as Raven realized night might not provide a place for them to stay. They left as quickly as they came, off to ask questions, answer questions, and figure out what to do next.

"...for the second time, prompting the mayor to call for a special

inspection of the Gates Building. Some onlookers claim to have seen a figure emerge from the hole, one saying that 'it just flew away like a superhero' but no footage of this was obtained. More on this story as it develops."

Samantha Phillips stood up. She listened carefully; her daughter was still asleep; her son, at school, getting his classes finalized. Quietly, she muted the TV and opened the front door and stepped out onto the porch.

She rubbed her arms; it was chilly, but thankfully, windless. Flurries danced around her, pulled down by gravity but trying not to relinquish their freedom just yet. The sun had not been up for very long, though it had warmed a bit since the night's chill.

The snow had been present for what already felt like eternity. It always came early to Omaha, and stayed well past its welcome. Even the holidays this year, having just passed within the week, seemed not to benefit any seasonal cheer from the great white blanket. Still, spring was coming, albeit quite a distance off.

Spring *was* coming, though, and with it, change

One Hundred Forty-Four:
Imprinting

There would be questions.

Oh yes, there would be questions. But at this moment, all US Army Lieutenant Colonel Joshua Richardson could say, as he stood and perused the violent destruction of the cryonics bay which eventually led to the escape of two of his charges, his two best charges, was, "Oh shit."

Skitter. A noise in the darkness.

A moment of hesitation, a moment of anticipation, a moment of fear.

Skitter. Step step step.

"Who's there?"

This one will be my thrall.

One Hundred Forty-Five:
Doubt

Doubt flooded Raven's mind. Thrust back into a world she had apparently only left weeks ago, absolutely nothing of her was as it had been then. The numbing cold and warm soul beside her kept her from breaking down just yet over her losses, but the fire inside her now begged her to question her sanity. She tightened her grip slightly on Mina's hand, feeling the gentle heat of her body despite the gloves they both wore. She looked at the shorter girl, who met her eyes and gave her a well-intentioned smile. She returned it, out of love, but there was still a sadness behind it.

They trudged on.

Raven wasn't out there enough to believe that anything that had happened recently was just in her head. Despite her pre-existing mental condition, she in no way believed that she had descended into a world of her own creation, though the thought had crossed her mind.

As they walked in the silence of winter, the rustling of their clothes and haggard breaths the only noise outside of the lick of carnivorous winds, Raven continually went over the mental actions of her new abilities. She had read of such things, in fiction, mostly, and had always wondered if such a thing were possible. The idea of having such powers, however, and even having them permanently, as more than a fleeting exercise of wills, escaped from all rational understanding she had of the world.

She glanced again at Mina, beside her, who now also appeared deep in thought, and was confused by her as well. Though she did not deny the connection they had, and in fact understood it as love, she knew so little about the young woman. She did not feel guilt at Crow's memory, however; Crow was never one to hold a grudge or to hold others back. She would want Raven to be happy, and perhaps Mina was the key to that. Raven couldn't say that she was ready to move on, as she had literally just been faced with what happened to Crow, but she felt no desire to push Mina away.

On the thoughts of her murdered mother and brother, Raven felt the fire of revenge in herself. She had never thought of herself as a vengeful or anger-prone individual, but thinking of the way she had tried to set up Crow, maybe she was. Certainly, however, murder of a loved one was an unforgivable crime, so any anger she felt was completely justified. Whether it was her hardened, settling mind, or the cold, she was unable to shed a tear for her losses.

Raven had full recollection of her time at the institute and had more or less pieced together what had happened. Although she had not the knowledge to know the full picture, the scientists had apparently felt no need to keep quiet around her. It was clearly a military facility, designed for human experimentation in areas of (apparently) psychic phenomena. She had met several doctors and had been fairly ambivalent about them, except for that rat-faced fucker, Jameson, the man directly responsible for Crow's death.

The difficulties of her former life had been completely swept away to be replaced with complete unknowns of a new life, and for all her losses, a part of her was glad at the thought of being able to start fresh. With no clear concept of what to do next, there was one thing that Raven absolutely did not, and would never, doubt.

She halted her walk.

"Mina."

"Yes?"

They faced each other.

"I love you." There was very little she had ever said with such conviction in her entire life.

There was a word for it. Mina's face lit up in a way it had never done before, as she understood completely what Raven meant.

"I love you, too."

As they embraced, for a time, they were blissfully unaware of both the cold and the stares of passersby who thought it queer that two young women should stand oblivious in the middle of a growing snowstorm and kiss.

One Hundred Forty-Six:
Brief Interrogation

Emma sat across from Richardson is his office, holding a cold compress against her left cheek. The dark beginnings of a bruise had set in and she hoped nothing would prove to be broken.

She also hoped her hasty actions would be covered well enough to prevent greater injuries. It seemed though, that as she watched Richardson hastily thumb through a small stack of papers, that she caught the occasional glint of terror in his eyes as well.

Presently, he spoke. "Emma, I need to know, to your best recollection, what happened."

What to say, really? she thought.

"I had finished with Mina for the afternoon and had sent her to her room. I was typing up a report for you, when I remembered I had access to Dr. Utsugi's office, and went there to see if she had left any useful information in her personal files." No sense in lying about this part, she decided. "I found some information about the cryonics lab, which apparently contained some prior test subjects I might be able to learn some things from. I put the report on hold, went to the lab, and then went to a file room for more research." She wondered if her snooping for information about "Tom" would be found out and held against her, or accepted as something she *should* be looking into.

"I got your call to go to the cryonics lab and went back there. Raven and Mina had already left, but I managed to head them off on the upper floors."

"How did you get there before the guards?" asked Richardson, his eyes narrowing shrewdly.

Fuck. Definitely not protocol. She had to choose her lies carefully; the building's surveillance was *very* thorough. "Benny—the test subject that can phase—took me there. Straight through the building."

Richardson seemed to be giving a questioning stare, and Emma felt obliged to embellish.

"Under the circumstances, it seemed worth the risk. Both girls were clearly acting far outside expected parameters."

"And when you got to them?"

How much was recorded? Emma wondered. "I'm not completely sure, the phasing left me winded and confused—I asked Raven to stop, she seemed to be taking the lead over Mina, and she used a telekinetic burst. But...it didn't hurt me. She avoided hurting me with it, I think."

"But then she punched you?"

"Yes. But," she explained, feeling compelled to point out her attacker's self control, "according to Jameson, she can amplify her physical prowess to cause grievous damages. She only hit me hard enough to knock me out. And then the next thing I remember was the guards waking me up and bringing me here."

"Mercy. Interesting. Lucky for you, and possibly, lucky for us all." Richardson seemed satisfied, and lit up a cigarette. "It's been a trying month or two, Emma. Very trying. There's going to be fallout."

To Emma's partial relief, Richardson seemed genuinely worried, as though he was in jeopardy. "Go home. Rest. I'll call you when we need you."

"Are you sure?"

"No experiments for the time being. This is going to be a nightmare to deal with. Rest, research if you want to. See a doctor. That bruise looks awful."

"Thank you, sir." He did not correct her to "Joshua."

"That will be all, doctor," he finished. She stood up and left the room, closing the door behind her.

Lieutenant Colonel Richardson leaned back and sighed. He pulled a black-labeled bottle and a low-ball glass out of his desk and poured himself a stereotypical glass of scotch. He downed it and pressed a button on his intercom.

"Sir?"

"Double the security on doctor Jacobson. I want to know when she takes a goddamn shit."

"Yes, sir."

He kicked his desk, sighed, and lit up another smoke as soon as the first was done.

One Hundred Forty-Seven:
Discovery

The snow, cold, and wind brought dark thoughts into Mina's head. She had of course read of seasons, but had no conscious memory of any. This feeling, however, was the same as in her worst dreams of violence and guilt.

She looked over at Raven. She was content to give her heart to her, despite knowing next to nothing about her. But that was the quandary of Mina's existence; she knew next to nothing about anyone, or even herself.

The sights, sounds, smells, around her were fascinating, being akin to a person of full faculties experiencing everything for the first time. She didn't miss a flurry, or a winter bird, a squirrel, a brick, or a sidewalk crack; the aroma of fast food and restaurant fare alike permeated her senses; the sound of alley cats and the thumping of a car decked out with sub-woofers was all new and intriguing to her. Every little detail was an experience, cataloged and filed by her brain as it tried to take in a world that was unknown but not entirely alien in concept.

The cold was a persistent annoyance but nothing she feared (save for the dark thoughts it brought up.) She could not be hurt by it, but Raven was another story. The snow was falling faster and faster, the day-time sun all but hidden by the gray clouds covering the sky in greater and greater quantity.

She looked again at Raven—a stern look on her face, but one of a beauty Mina was only recently really beginning to take joy in.

They walked by a park abutting a semi-wooded area protected by the city, and connected to a larger forested area blocked on one side by a highway. In the clearing, Mina saw a white-tailed fawn, somehow born well out of season, and locked eyes momentarily. There was an eerie innocence in those sad brown eyes. She knew what the animal was, from her books, and that it was very young, very new to the world.

We're not unalike, you and I, she thought. *Individuals thrown into a world outside of our understanding.*

After a time, it seemed their fairly straight-line travel was born of an urge to keep moving, rather than any idea of where to go. The wind-swept snowstorm had become oppressive and dangerous, and unsure what else to do to keep them moving forward, Raven began speaking as a distraction from the weather.

She took the time to explain basic concepts and objects to Mina—restaurants, libraries, police, how to cross the street, cars, airplanes—each came up as it seemed to need to, and then unfolded into a litany of related topics, seemingly without end.

"Am I talking to much?" asked Raven. "Is this too much too fast?"

"No, it's fine," said Mina, smiling. "If I forget anything, I'll ask. It's important to know these things."

"It's so weird. I've never had to explain things like this—well, I guess I have, from time to time, but just little things here and there, like to kids and stuff. I'm not around them very often anyway. And, well, you look about my age. But you've never seen any of these things. It just seems like it would be overwhelming."

"I've read about some of them," Mina reminded Raven, "and I've heard people talk about a lot of them. But..." She narrowed her eyes, trying to think how best to put things into words. "Okay, I know what a building is. But I didn't know what someone's house looked like compared to that food place, for example. Well, I sort of did." She thought of *The Lorax* and other illustrated books, "but it's much clearer now."

Raven sighed from relief. "At least, it makes it easier that you understand that you don't understand, I guess. Something like that." She laughed. Mina laughed also, and there was a bit of a skip in their next few steps, as difficult as the mounting snow made that.

After a time, Mina put a difficult question forth.

"Raven, what are we?"

Was she looking for a label for their relationship? Their label as psychics? Their place among humans? None of these were exactly easy answers.

"Woo. That's a big question." She turned to face Mina. "Is it okay if I can't answer that right now? I promise I will as soon as I can."

Mina nodded. Raven changed the subject. She couldn't see the sun or any clocks at the moment but she doubted it was any much later than midday. "We need to find something to eat and somewhere to stay the night. Even if this storm lets up soon we can't walk forever."

And I don't know exactly where we're walking too, anyway, she thought to herself.

One Hundred Forty-Eight:
Wht_rabbit.obj

No doubt he's shitting bricks right now, Emma thought of Richardson. No matter what exactly had led up to the spectacle that was the girls' escape, Lieutenant Colonel Richardson would more than likely be held accountable.

Not that others wouldn't, as well....

NOD did not seem to be an organization that took kindly to failure or dissent.

The snow was making driving difficult as Emma drove home. She didn't bother to turn the radio on; all talk shows and music would have seemed pointless and shallow.

She tried to piece together what had happened, and she was missing key elements. Mina had not been the aggressor, so she ruled out Matthew as a driving force. If anyone was in charge, it had seemed to be Raven, but despite Emma's worry that M's reactivation may have loosed the psychopath's will upon them once more, she was certain Raven was not carrying his psyche. She had acted with intelligence, but with restraint, whereas Matthew had never once showed mercy or care outside of the whims of his twisted personality.

Perhaps Raven was like Mina? But no, she had seemed under the control of the medication and had showed signs of great psychic ability, with healing never appearing as one of them.

Had Mina somehow reached out and swept the shadows from Raven's mind? Little, at this point, was outside the realm of theory. Maybe, however, Jameson was right and she had just been ignoring or uncaring of the truth; that Raven was not under the full control of the drugs at any point.

Maybe they were just two friends who wanted (and deserved) a better life, and had made a break for it.

The number Emma had given to Raven and Mina was for a pay-as-you-go phone she had purchased right after Carl's death, in case she needed an unregistered (meaning, untapped) number with which to call someone, should things get hairy. In all honesty, however, she had no guarantees it was any safer than her house line or primary cell. Her house, her car, hell, her purse could be bugged, for all she knew, and she knew was under direct surveillance from time to time.

The rational thinker in her made pointed out how rashly she had acted. Overwhelming guilt at beginning to tolerate a project of torture and bio-weaponry had caused her to make some weighty decisions; she did not regret what happened, but partly, at least, regretted her hand in it, if only for her own safety.

So she had helped "save" two girls. What of it? What of the dozens of other test subjects? Was it fair to free those two and not the others? Would they even be able to live in the outside world? Would they even be free? Unlikely. As soon as the world got wind of their abilities, another organization would jump in and scoop them up for their own agendas, if NOD didn't take them back first. It was entirely possible that she had risked her very existence for an ultimately meaningless act of insubordination.

The small voice of humanitarianism in her tried to tell her any good act is meaningful, but she still doubted the lasting effects of her actions. Powers like those the girls had would be difficult to hide. And, though Raven had less implants than the rest of the children, (some biorhythm sensors, mainly; the bulk would have been fitted after she had gone through complete mental stabilization and the nature of her powers had been completely ascertained,) the existence of her GPS sensor was nagging Emma.

That was the real kicker. It meant quite likely that whenever someone at NOD decided it was time to take her back, they would know exactly where she was.

The rabbit hole was deep, indeed, and though Emma had no real desire to climb all the way down, she feared she was already trapped well within it. In all honesty, she had no idea what to do next.

One Hundred Forty-Nine:
Advantageous Occurrence

"I'm on my way as soon as I get off the phone. I have to be honest, this doesn't look good for you."

On the other end of the line, General Nicholas Kresge was faced with a rare moment indeed: the cat had gained quite a hold on Lieutenant Colonel Joshua Richardson's tongue.

"Let me rephrase that," Kresge spoke after a moment of silence. "I have no intention of any punishment, so to speak, and I doubt the committee will either. You've been an asset to the military and to this program. I think though, that in light of the recent events, you will likely be removed from your position."

Richardson attempted to stifle a sigh of relief, but Kresge heard it anyway.

"In any case, what happens next is up to the advisory board. I'll let you know when I'm almost there." A beat. "Goodbye." *Click.*

Kresge put his cell phone away and leaned on the sink, staring into the mirror in the private bathroom he had made this sensitive call from.

He was a fairly old man. Nearly sixty, he was a grandfather, though not one of those "young grandparents" he despised. His children had gotten properly married at a reasonable age, and produced children in their mid-to-late twenties.

Most of them.

He was very fit for his age (which he honestly told himself wasn't really that old, nowadays,) but time and work had put cracks in his body and lines on his face.

He had no desire to see Richardson capitally punished for what happened at the Gates Building over the past couple months. They had served in the past together, and Kresge had been instrumental in getting Richardson his current (dubious) position at NOD. Though neither would have called the other friend, they respected each other. Perhaps part of that was a certain ease of morals in getting things done.

And, of getting things done...he could promise Richardson all the safety he wanted, but in truth, the advisory board was unpredictable. They were results-oriented, and despite some promising advances, and "Tom," the super-soldier's demonstration, they had been waiting a long time for results and had not yet truly received any.

Still, Kresge couldn't deny that this situation was fortuitous. Richardson's removal would likely come about without any need for further meddling, and Kresge would be in prime position to suggest himself as a replacement. Despite the drawbacks of the deaths and the escapes, he himself couldn't be in a better spot.

It was time to get going, however, and he washed his hands, more out of some subconscious, deep-seated need, rather than as a result of any usage of the bathroom he was in. As he did so, he muttered.

"Nothing sacred, nothing harmed."

One Hundred Fifty:
Secret Identities?

Raven closed the flimsy door behind her and set two bags down on the small, round table that was next to the wall. She rubbed her hands together and blew hot air into her palms.

"The storm's letting up but it's still cold as hell." She took off her coat and threw it on the chair in the corner. This place was a dump, but the walls were free of water damage and stains, and she hadn't seen a single cockroach or other pest.

That was a good sign.

She walked over to the bed in the middle of the single room and smiled at Mina, who was sitting in the middle of it. Her hair was wrapped in a towel, and she was wearing navy sweat pants and an over-sized gray top that had slid off of one shoulder. She grabbed the bottom of it and pulled forward, showing how poorly it fit her.

"We got too big of a size on this one," she said, smiling up at Raven.

Raven took in Mina's beautiful gaze and glanced at her exposed shoulder. "I don't mind," she responded.

"I'm going to take a shower and change. There's some snacks in the bags. Don't eat anything that says 'microwave instructions' I'll have to show you what to do with those."

"Okay. Thanks."

Raven walked into the bathroom with a change of clothes and set them down before undressing to shower. She was glad they had found this motel; it was fairly cheap and fairly clean. The truth was that while Dr. Jacobson's money had been a godsend in getting them this far, they were already almost broke.

Tomorrow they would have to find a way to survive and tonight they needed to form a plan. For starters, they would go see Steve tomorrow. Raven had no idea if he could offer any real, long-term help, but he could probably offer them a place to stay, at least for awhile.

Hopefully, after she explained what had happened, he would forgive her for disappearing. But to explain, she would have to show him....

She almost laughed at her train of thought. She was no superhero; there was no such thing. She didn't have to hide her powers from her friends. She would show him what she could do, he would believe her, he would forgive her.

But psychic powers weren't supposed to be real either, and showing him could put him in danger.

Then again, just being around him could put him in danger. But I don't really have a choice.

And, after everything that had happened to her, she no longer believed anything, anyplace, was really safe at all.

Across town, Emma was lying in bed, exhausted physically and mentally drained. She would be asleep by mid-afternoon, but it didn't really matter to her. It had been weeks since she had enjoyed a regular sleep schedule.

One Hundred Fifty-One:
Drinking to "Access"

"Are you drunk?"

The truth was, Lieutenant Colonel Joshua Richardson had had several drinks today. But the real problem was the other thing pounding on his skull.

"I've had a couple drinks, Nick. I think you would, too, under the circumstances?" He sighed. "I'm tired. That's all."

"You can get your rest soon enough." Richardson looked up at this, not sure what he meant.

General Nicholas Kresge looked around Richardson's office, as he stood, several feet from his desk, where the Lieutenant Colonel was sitting. He couldn't put his finger on it, but something was wrong. Something *felt* wrong. He looked over at the desk. The ashtray was full, and there were three half-smoked cigarettes sitting on it, burnt down to unused ashes.

"I mean you can go home and get some fucking sleep," Kresge elaborated, aware of Richardson's confusion, and suddenly, very annoyed at the mess NOD was in, despite it being good for him, in theory. "Soon."

Richardson lowered his head and shoulders in a sign of relief. He rubbed his forehead.

"God, it reeks of cigarettes in here."

Richardson winced as a quick pang of pain shot through his head from temple to temple. "Are you going to stand here and berate me, or are you going to tell me what you found out?"

"Fair enough. I made some calls on the way over. The advisory board is split on what to do, regarding the entire situation. I've been told not to expect any sort of resolution just yet." It had aggravated him to no end to hear this from them, but he still had his hand to play, was still confident Richardson would be deposed in the end.

"Which means? For me?" No point in beating around the bush.

"It means," said Kresge, putting both hands on Richardson's desk and leaning so close he could smell the stink of tar and alcohol on his breath, "after this conversation, you go home, you get some damn sleep, you get up in the morning, and you come to work. Each day. Until you hear otherwise."

He stood up.

"What about a capture team? We have Raven's GPS activated."

"The advisory board...doesn't want to cause an uproar. We're in the news again, Josh. Another hole blown out of the side of this building. If we send a team for them now, If this Raven is as strong as she's supposed to be, it could be the Andrew Incident all over again. They think, right now, she's going to lay low and avoid attention. We'll send a team once she's had some freedom, starts getting confident that she's safe. But they want us to be ready for a deluding just in case."

"All right then. What about our bargaining chip? What if we DON'T get her back? Then we don't have anything worth offering Yamada."

That's very interesting. I want that information.

"At the moment, not a big deal," Kresge said, smiling unexpectedly. "None of what's happened is being shared with the other branches, outside of what they can see on the news. Committee's orders. As long as that girl doesn't go public, Yamada thinks we still have his daughter."

"Good."

"Oh, and I'll still be bringing Dr. Graley to see the generators. Make sure at least those are working tomorrow, all right?"

"Sure. Should be fine. Purring like kittens." A presence was exploring his thoughts, and he was having trouble focusing. "Anything else, 'sir'?"

"No. Get some sleep, Josh." Richardson saluted him; Kresge "harrumphed" and left.

Richardson pulled his liquor and his glass back out of his desk and poured himself another drink. "It's all your fault," he said, to himself, to whomever. A sudden ache in his head made him wince. "Don't do that," he asked, his eyes shut as he downed his drink in one swallow. He kicked his desk, causing the bottle to wobble. He steadied it.

He lit a cigarette and took a long drag, and poured another drink. What was he doing? Forcing a hangover? Attempting a suicide? There was only enough drink in the office for the first, and he really didn't relish either idea much anyway.

He was not a man to drink to extremes. Amsterdam had taught him tolerance, experience had taught him temperance, and money had taught him elegance. Liquor was a treat for the senses and a welcome break for the mind, that was all. He had had many downs in his life but had not in a very long time attempted to solve them with booze. If he had a vice, it was smoking. He would readily admit that.

But he felt so defenseless, so naked. It was completely abnormal to him and horrifying in the way it made him feel weak. To be powerless to control his destiny was not a feeling he could tolerate; it was as though the retching at such a thought began in his very soul.

It wasn't the uncertainty of his post or even his life, it was this *thing*, bouncing around in his head, pulling his strings, scanning for knowledge.

He had decided not to tell Kresge about the damage to the cryonics lab.

No, he hadn't decided that.

He had, however, given the order for the staff to begin repairs and make sure it was in working condition.

No, he hadn't done that either.

His cigarette half gone, his drink gone, he poured yet another, his hands shaking. Maybe, addling his mind would make it more difficult; in all likelihood, it would make it easier.

He finished the cigarette and the last drink. He set the glass down roughly and got up. As he went to a side room to go lay down for awhile, he looked back towards the scotch, slurred "stay there," and left.

His desk creaked a little.

Sleep would be of little comfort for him. The booze muddling his mind was the least of his concerns.

The colors and shapes were nearly as vivid as the pain that accompanied the unwinding of his ego and the assertion of a dominance over his final choices and actions. Though it wasn't as powerful as it could be, Matthew was satisfied, believing the future would bring him a better vessel than this puny "Angel" with which to work his actions. Satisfied with the level of control he would have over Richardson, he formerly introduced himself, to which, Richardson admitted, he was not surprised.

One Hundred Fifty-Two:
Girlfriends

"Some of this is really good!"

Raven laughed aloud at this observation. "That's only because you've been eating that laboratory food forever!" She turned over an empty microwavable burrito package and looked at the nutritional information. "Ugh, none of this stuff is good for us, anyway. I'm gonna have to teach you how to eat well, hun."

"Tomorrow, we're going to see my friend Steve. If we're lucky, his mom might make us a home-cooked meal."

Mina cocked her head a little to the side and placed a hand on Raven's soft cheek. She knew this would hurt her. But she needed to know about her. "Tell me...about Steve. Please. About your family. The things you talked about before we left. About...the girl in the basement. I need to know about you."

Raven bit her lip. She could already feel her heart wrenching. She nodded. She managed a sad smile. "You deserve to know."

She talked at great length about her mother, and her brother. How none of them got along very well but that her mother was a good person who deserved better than the lots he got in life; how she hadn't seen her father in years and considered him the reason their family life seemed to fall apart.

She told Mina the truth about herself, that she wasn't the most responsible or thoughtful person; that she had always enjoyed reading, though, and had always tried to be a good friend to Steve, who wasn't her only friend, but he was her best friend and the only real constant one. She explained how he loved her and she didn't feel the same back, and how that was hard on him.

She talked about school, and prejudice, and day-to-day life, and real life, and the women she'd loved, or at least thought she did.

From time to time she broke into tears, but she persevered, knowing it was right to get all of this off of her chest. Mina sat, ever attentive, stroking her back, trying to comfort her.

She told Mina about her hallucinations, and her blackouts, and the events leading up to her kidnapping; how everything had felt better, how she had realized her mother deserved better from her; how Crow was steadfast and willing to work through all of Raven's own issues with her; how asking for help really was okay. And then...

...and then how, just then, it had fallen apart, all hope had been ripped apart, at the moment she thought everything was going to be all right, she found her mother and brother dead, murdered, and a man threatening her and Crow, and then she had been taken to the institute...

"...and the girl in the basement, that was Crow, my girlfriend," she sobbed.

"I thought so," said Mina, remembering the brief explanations Raven had given her before they had escaped. She threw her arms around Raven completely and held her as she grieved. She glanced at the curtained windows; it looked dark outside. It had been an incredibly taxing day, physically, mentally, and emotionally, and they had been awake since before dawn. Sleep would come soon, but not yet.

When Raven's sobs had lessened to a whimper, when the flow of tears had all but stopped, Mina backed away slightly and looked at her, her deep blues eyes connecting with Raven's brown eyes. She wiped away her tears with soft fingertips.

"Is that what we are? Girlfriends?"

Was that all she meant when she asked that? The simplest question? But how complex is the answer? Does she really understand what that means?

Raven smiled despite her still-wet eyes and nodded rapidly.

Mina desperately wanted to tell Raven about Matthew, about what he did, and what she did, to expose the load on her heart and mind, but now was not the time.

"I feel safe with you, here," Mina said, returning Raven's smile. She was ready to give of herself to another person, and believed that person now ready to receive her. Though she wasn't exactly sure of the manner, she had no doubt that Raven's heart and hands would guide her. She gently pushed the girl down to the bed, and kissed her, Raven gratefully accepting her comforting touches.

One Hundred Fifty-Three:
Midnight Interlude

That night, Mina and Raven slept soundly, Raven cuddled in Mina's warm embrace. Emma had awoken not long after midnight, worried about what the next day would bring her at work. She wasn't even sure what day of the week it was anymore, but she would go in, without fail. Anything else would raise suspicion.

Richardson was awake, but for a wholly different reason. He was stone sober; or at least felt that way. Matthew's presence in his mind was both maddening and centering.

"I can't destroy it yet. Kresge needs to see it first. Then I can do what you ask."

Your sense of self-preservation is annoying, but like it or not, I need you right now. Fine. We wait. As soon as he's come and gone, destroy it. I will not be sent back to that purgatory, that limbo.

Richardson smiled drolly, knowing that Matthew had given him the very information he could use against him, but would not allow him the will to do anything with it. "Fine. As you will it, 'master,'" he said sarcastically.

One Hundred Fifty-Four:
Busy Morning

The morning sun peeked in on Raven and Mina, gently waking Mina first, Raven second. She rolled over and smiled at Mina and pulled her tightly to her. "I love you," she said simply.

"I love you too."

They got up and readied for their day. Raven was glad it was fairly early; she'd rather spend more of the day with Steve, if possible, than looking for him.

She was not looking forward to introducing Mina to the public bus, but if she could find a good route, that was the best chance at getting across town rapidly. The weather report on the TV seemed promising; fairly cold, but mild weather and no storm like yesterday.

The morning brought Jameson a confusing encounter. He was called to Richardson's office almost as soon as he arrived at work, and when he got there, there was no answer. He turned around just in time to see Richardson coming down the hall towards him, wearing sweatpants and a tee.

"Sorry, Spence, I was here all night. I was just showering at the gym. Thought I'd be quicker. C'mon inside."

Once inside, Richardson sat at his desk and motioned for Jameson to sit down. The chair was facing the desk and looked very comfortable, and it did not take any time at all for Jameson to realize he had never seen this chair in here before. Letting his underlings sit in comfort while he talked to them was not something Richardson frequently did.

"Sir?" he began.

"Please, Spence, call me Joshua! How long have we known each other?"

"Um..."

Richardson didn't give him a chance to attempt an answer. "All right, so today, you're leading some of the staff on repairing the cryo-bay in the subbasements."

"Yes, I got your email yesterday."

"Okay, well, here's the thing. If you find any...remains...including any cryonic storage chambers whose contents are listed as "deceased" since yesterday...I want you to set those aside in secondary storage, okay? Keep 'em nice and chilled, and let me know later how much you have. Not frozen—cold. Like, refrigerated."

"Okay?"

"Trust me. Super important." Richardson smiled. It was a fake, simpering smile, meant for pacification, maybe even idle threats, rather than to convey happiness of any sort.

"Yes. Sure. Absolutely." Jameson was nervous and could feel the sweat forming on his brow. "Um, sir?"

"Joshua!"

"Um, Joshua—the girls—are we going after them?" Raven was his charge, after all. This could be construed as his fault.

Richardson waved a hand nonchalantly. "Don't even worry about that. It's already being taken care of."

"Okay then. Anything else?"

"Nope. Have at it!"

Jameson got up and left, glad to be out of such an uncomfortable position.

"Do you really think he's going to respond to me acting like that?"

I know what you think of him. And you're right, he's outlived his usefulness. You can keep making him feel important and then put him in a position of no real power, or you can kill him. I figured you'd prefer the first option; less mess to clean up.

"Look, I did exactly as you wanted," Richardson yelled angrily. "You better be right, my ass is on the line here."

Like I care, Matthew thought. But he kept that to himself.

Richardson kicked his desk. The thing inside hissed at him. He wondered, briefly, if he could reach in quickly enough and strangle the thing before it could react, but he knew it would know that was coming. *Fuck,* he realized, *it probably already knows I just thought about that, too.*

Jameson had quickly reached a lower level and was rushing down a hallway to a secondary elevator. He passed two armed guards on patrol and muttered, "These guys here, they have the easy job. I'm the one with my life in danger."

"You hear that guy?" Dillons asked Carlos. "*We* have it easy? What a dick."

"I know that guy. He's the one I met when I had my 'drop-off' here. Something Jameson. Rat-faced fucker. I don't like him; he's shady."

"Ha! That means a lot, coming from you, right buddy?"

Carlos gave him a dirty look for that jab, but then he smiled. It was true, and kind of a compliment, actually.

"So, anyway," Carlos began, changing the subject, "yesterday: what the fuck? If that's the kind of crap that's going on here, I'm not sure I want any."

"Well, good news is, my leg's fixed."

"It's *been* fixed."

"I know; I just finally wrapped my head around that when I realized I ran all that way yesterday without any problems."

"Anyway, like I said: If that's the kind of shit that goes down here, I want out. I don't want to get my stuffing blown out by some kid with...with...whatever the hell that shit is. I got a kid on the way."

"Telekinesis. I thought you were gonna put in for a desk job?"

"My paperwork skills aren't exactly high-grade, *hombre*."

"Hey! But you're bilingual, right? That's something," Dillons said hopefully.

"No man," Carlos said, shaking his head. "I know like ten words in Spanish and most of them are curse words."

"Hey, you're gonna have to teach me those sometime."

"Yeah, sure," Carlos answered, grinning at the thought.

Emma made her way towards Richardson's office. He hadn't called her in but she'd made her decision last night to come in regardless. She knocked, and he beckoned her to enter.

"Emma! I didn't call you in today. You're supposed to be resting!" He looked at the bruise on her face and winced. It had become a dark bluish-purple.

"I'm sorry," she responded, avoiding using either *sir* or *Joshua*, "I felt, under the circumstances, I would be remiss not to come in."

"Well, I don't really have much work for you. I mean—there's the obvious, your charge is gone—and Jameson is heading the cleanup and restoration of the cryo lab."

"I could help with that."

"Oh no no no no," he said very quickly, waving his hand dismissively. "Totally beneath you. Nope. Won't have you do that." *Jameson won't question why we're saving the remains, but she will.*

Emma narrowed her eyes; he was speaking oddly. Time to push a bit.

"Sir, the M generator—I have my concerns."

"I got your report. I'll be dealing with it, personally."

"I—," she stopped herself. *I never submitted that report.*

"Just do rounds. Check in on the kids, see how they're doing. It's been a traumatic period for all of us. Take it easy."

"Yes, sir." He dismissed her, and she left.

She rushed away from his office, put off just enough by his behavior to begin considering bizarre explanations.

It wasn't that he'd been overly friendly—he'd used that tactic in the past. It was that his speaking seemed hyped up, very unnatural for him. Clearly, he'd accessed her files, too, and had read her report—or was bluffing, although that seemed an unlikely strategy to take.

She slowly became sure that Matthew was once again in the building, and maybe that had something to do with Richardson's odd behavior. She needed to access the M-lab to check the generator's readouts (they were classified and thus not available from any of the local servers,) but if her hunch was true, that would immediately alert him to her snooping, and put her in danger.

But, what if he used another test subject as a time bomb? Emma was now more glad than ever that Raven and Mina had escaped.

One Hundred Fifty-Five:
Reunion

The bus ride, as Raven had suspected, was not very pleasant. The Omaha Metro system was not well maintained and had not been for as long as she could remember. Perhaps it was due to the seemingly endless supply of rambling, filthy-looking people that seemed to get on and off in equal numbers at every stop. Their crazy eyes were matched only by their crazy stories, which she did her best to tune out on the rare occasion that she had no choice but to take a bus; today, however, she hazarded a listen here and there and was confused to hear how similar all of their ravings were.

At one point, the bus had become overcrowded to the point where Raven would have to have had Mina ride on her lap, except that she had already instructed her to do so and had her arms protectively around her. Better safe than sorry, she had thought. She felt Mina was safer being that much closer. Not that she didn't have...defenses...at her disposal, but she'd rather hold her close, if that was enough to prevent any issues.

Their stop was quite close to Steve's house and only a couple other people disembarked.

"It smelled...bad...in there," Mina said, her nose scrunched up.

"That's what a dirty toilet smells like," Raven said, chuckling.

"People pee in there?"

"Sometimes. Uh, but they're not supposed to! We still use toilets in the real world."

"Thanks, I've figured that one out." Both girls laughed.

The walk to Steve's house only took a few minutes and they walked up to the porch.

"I'm really nervous," said Raven. "It's been...awhile...and it's been weird...and we have a long history."

"I know. It's okay. You've told me. Take your time."

Not everything, Raven thought to herself.

Finally she mustered the courage to knock. Steve's mother, Samantha, answered.

"Hi, I—Raven?" She pushed the screen open and hugged Raven in a tight embrace. "There's so much—oh my god, come in, both of you."

"I'd love to, but..." she began.

"Oh, you're not Crow?" It had just dawned on Samantha that the girl with Raven wasn't, in fact, Crow. In her shock to see Raven, the truth hadn't immediately registered.

"No," said Raven. "This is Mina. Crow's—gone." She could feel tears trying to force their way out, but she forced them back down. She was tired of crying, and surely there would be more tears when she talked to Steve, but she didn't have the time for that now. She knew emotions could be a sign of strength, not weakness, that one was human, but she was weary of it.

"There's a lot, I guess, I have to tell you. But, I really need to see Steve. Is he here?"

"Okay," said Mrs. Phillips, feeling a bit deflated, but understanding. "He's not here. He started school. He's at the community college. Right now."

"That's, actually, great! Good for him." Raven smiled, genuinely happy that he had gone through with it. But, she would have to disrupt that, for today at least. It was selfish of her, maybe, but he would want to know she was fine.

Wouldn't he?

"Do you happen to know his schedule? And—do you think we could leave our backpacks here?"

Steve was bored out of his mind. Lecture classes were, clearly, the worst, and freshmen geography was a snore-fest. Despite doing less-than-fair in most of his high school courses, he'd already found this one to be remedial enough that he slept through at least half of each lesson so far and had aced the first test.

Today, though, he couldn't sleep, and his right leg kept twitching. He felt like something was going to happen.

He had taken a seat near the upper back, hoping that meant the teacher wouldn't call on him for anything. As it had turned out, though, with a class this size, he hadn't bothered to learn anyone's names, and only pointed at people who raised their hand.

Steve never raised his hand.

The seat did however give him a good view of the entire classroom, almost like a fish's-eye view. He could see all three walls and part of the slanted ceiling and both doors easily.

At the door—was that? There was a girl with her hands at the side of her face, her nose pressed up against the window, looking in.

He squinted. It couldn't be, but—it had to be!

He shoved his books into his backpack and practically jumped down to the lower row, running to the stairs and the door.

"Mr.—," began the teacher, and stopped when he realized he didn't know the student's name, and honestly, didn't really care if he left.

Steve was at the door in seconds.

It was her. Other than her hair only reaching down to her shoulders, it was the same beautiful sight he had burned into memory.

He threw the door open and picked her up in a long overdue hug. When he sat her down, she could see tears of joy streaming down his face.

"Don't look at me, I'm blubbering like a pussy," he said.

"Dude," Raven said, dead-pan, "I have been crying so *damn much*...don't worry about it. It just means you're alive."

"Thanks," Steve said, wiping his face. "I'm just glad *you're* alive."

Mina looked quizzically at Raven.

"Pussy?"

Mina and Steve were introduced to each other and it wasn't long before they were driving to Steve's house in his worn-out four door clunker of an automobile. Raven hadn't said anything specifically about who Mina was to her, but the fact that they held hands all the way to the parking lot, and that Raven sat in the back with her rather than taking shotgun told him all he needed to know.

"So, I promise I'll tell you everything that happened. But I need to ask you if we can stay at your house for at least a few days until we figure something out."

"That's not a problem with me, Raven," Steve answered, "but you're going to have to talk to my Mom about everything too. The last we heard, you and Crow were wanted for the murder of your family."

"I—seriously? That's what they said happened? You don't believe that, do you?"

"Of course not. My Mom doesn't either. But she's going to need an explanation before letting a fugitive stay at our house."

Raven knew a little of her and Steve's past, from what he had been willing to tell her. Her ex-husband—Steve's dad—was a real piece of work: alcoholic, abusive, and a small-time career criminal who used their home from time to time like a flophouse for friends and colleagues that were on the lam or otherwise engaged in illicit activities with him. When the law finally caught up with him on murder charges, she moved and filed for divorce while he was in prison, though Raven and almost everyone else referred to her as "Mrs."

"No, I understand. After everything your mom's been through."

"Look, she loves you like a part of the family. I know she'll let you stay. But, yeah, she's gonna want to hear the whole story first."

It wasn't long before the four of them, Raven, Mina, Steve, and Mrs. Phillips, were seated around their dining room table, crammed into the corner of a small and overcrowded kitchen. Gracie, Steve's step-sister, was fast asleep in the next room.

Raven smiled at Mrs. Phillips. She had always liked her. She was kind, perhaps too kind; that may have been what had gotten her into trouble with her husband in the past. But she had always treated Raven (and whoever she happened to bring with her) as family.

She was tall, like her son, a short coif of sandy-brown hair styled around a face that was pretty but had seen its share of troubles. Her eyes were gray; two other traits (hair and eye color) that she also shared with Steve.

"Are you sure you want to do this?" Raven asked Mina, concerned. "You don't need to."

"No. I should. It's okay."

They had telepathically formed a plan of action as far as explaining everything to the Phillips.

It did not involve easing them in.

"We're going to show you...something. You won't believe anything I say unless you see this first."

Raven held her hand out, palm open, towards the silverware drawer. Strictly speaking, she could use her powers without any of the pointing and gesturing so commonly seen in movies and comics on the subject, but it did seem to help with concentrating and aiming.

One of the drawers slid open. Steve gasped and Mrs. Phillips held her hands up to her mouth in shock.

A steak knife flew out, handle first, towards Raven. She caught it, and handed it to Mina.

A determined look on her face, Mina pushed her left sleeve up and laid her arm on the table, palm up. She made a fist.

"No—," Mrs. Phillips began tentatively.

Mina winced as she drew a two inch gash across her forearm without touching the knife. In seconds it was gone. She laid the knife to rest.

"Holy shit," said Steve.

"You're like...superheroes!" Mrs. Phillips exclaimed.

Smiling despite herself, Raven claimed, nonchalantly, "That's only a fraction of what we can do."

"So, to begin...."

Raven did most of the talking. She explained how Crow and her had gone to her house one day to find her mother and brother murdered, and the man responsible kidnapped both of them. She told them how a doctor named Jameson had subjected both of them to a tortuous process that had shoved needles into their skulls. After that she was partially vegetative for what seemed like an eternity, but she met Mina, and something about her had helped keep her sense of self centered. Eventually she had developed strong telekinetic powers (Mina was telekinetic as well, and could heal injuries to herself in a moment.)

She skipped over their budding relationship—it could be inferred given their obvious current status as girlfriends—but explained that one day, everything just seemed to fall into place and she remembered everything. She found Crow, who was dead, and atomized her remains as a sort of cremation. Then, she and Mina had flown out of a hole she had made in the building they were in, which turned out to be none other than Omaha's own illustrious Gates Building.

"You flew," Steve said, incredulously.

"Yeah. I can fly."

"You really are like a superhero."

Raven shook her head. "I don't plan on it."

"So, this shit is real? Government conspiracies, human experimentation, psychic fucking powers!"

"Steve!" Mrs. Phillips chastised her son with a simple utterance of his name. "Shit" was apparently okay, but "fuck" was a step too far, in her presence.

"Sorry."

"I don't really know if it's government or private," Raven began.

"I saw people in uniforms. I recognize them now from things I've learned. They were...military uniforms." Mina smiled at Raven, glad for the girl's help in acclimating her to the outside world.

"So, government. They're going to be coming after you." Steve looked upset as he said this and worry lines crossed his mother's brow.

"Which is why, either way, we need to lie low for a couple days and then figure out what actually to do." Raven's eyes seemed to plead with Mrs. Phillips'.

"Did you come straight here?" she asked.

"No, we landed a few miles away yesterday and came here by bus. I don't think anyone knows where we are."

"No, but they are going to expect you to go home, probably. You can stay, girls, I can't turn you away, Raven, but you need to figure something else out quickly. I don't want my family in danger."

"Of course. Thank you, I understand." It was difficult for Raven to make eye contact with her, knowing the weight and history behind that statement.

Wanting to cut the tension, Steve spoke up. "So, it couldn't have just been you two, right? What else was going on there?"

Mina chimed in and told them about the other test subjects, what they were like, their powers. She told them about Keiko and Johnny but didn't tell anyone about their predictions.

"Wow," Steve said, when she was done, "that's like, exactly out of this movie I saw once. Makes you wonder who really knows what."

"There's something else I need to do," Raven said, sighing as she put her elbow on the table and leaned her head against her hand.

"I need to see Crow's dad."

"I'll take you," Steve offered. "I've been in touch, a little. He's probably home. He's been on work leave ever since she died—disappeared."

Raven felt like she had a rock in her stomach. She stood up, and looked at Mina. "C'mon hun, I need your support."

"Of course."

Raven looked at Mrs. Phillips, directly in the eyes, this time. "Thank you. Thanks for everything."

Raven had been in Crow's father's house for a good twenty minutes while Steve and Mina sat in his car, the radio playing a rock station at low volume and the air between them silent and awkward.

"So...." Steve finally said.

"Yes?"

"Um...." He wanted to ask about her, felt he probably should, but didn't really know what he would say. Instead, he asked about Raven. "Is she okay?"

"I think so. She's cried a lot, but she's smiled a lot."

"I'd cry a lot too, if half the people I knew were murdered and I was kidnapped." He immediately regretted how bluntly he'd said that, but she didn't seem to mind.

"Of course." She said it softly, matter-of-factly.

"So you...you've never been outside of that facility?"

"Not that I remember."

He exhaled. "Wooooo...that's intense. Crazy."

"It seemed fine. Until I realized it wasn't."

Steve was about to ask for some extrapolation, when he heard the rear door open and shut. He turned around. Raven was there, her eyelids puffy.

"I am so fucking sick of crying," she said.

"How did it go?" Steve asked, concerned.

"As well as it could have, I guess. I did the same thing as with you, told him he wouldn't believe me unless I showed him something first, so I levitated his coffee table. After that, he was all ears. I skipped most of it—just the basics of what happened to me and how Crow got dragged up into it."

Mina reached out and tenderly grasped her hand, stroking her fingers in a reassuring way. Raven managed a smile.

"He was happy, I guess, to at least know what happened. He told me to call him if I ever need anything. I probably won't. I don't want to be a reminder of his daughter's death. I'm really not sure what he's going to do now. If he's just going to let it go, or try and dig into this. I told him they were dangerous."

"Oh," she said, her tone of voice changed. "He wasn't as naive as I thought. He knew we were going out the whole time."

"Hmm. Funny. Sometimes they surprise you." Steve breathed deeply and exhaled. "So, what next?"

"Can we just go somewhere for awhile," Raven asked, "somewhere calm to just, I don't know, sit for a bit?"

"Sure thing."

One Hundred Fifty-Six:
Sever the Tie

"Joshua."

"Nick. Dr. Graley."

A round of hand-shaking ensued.

"Right this way," Richardson said, holding his hand out. "We're going to see R.T. first. M has been deactivated and is in its dedicated laboratory, so you'll be able to examine it up close."

Richardson had asked Kresge in private earlier if Dr. Graley should be allowed to see the actual anatomy of Arty. It was more out of the annoyance of preparing for the encounter, and the pressure Matthew was putting him under, rather than any concern for her well-being.

Amanda Graley was baffled by the need for an environmental suit. She had not been given any information regarding the nature of R.T. or its local environment. As they got closer to their goal, the suit's readout alerted her to changes in humidity, temperature, and oxygen levels—uncomfortable changes, but not life-threatening.

Eventually they reached a door covered in labels written in many, many languages; judging by the one written in English, they were warnings. As Richardson opened the door, Dr. Graley heard what sounded like the agitated whispers of dozens of people. She immediately felt the beginnings of a migraine.

There was a sudden pain in her neck, and the migraine immediately began to dissipate. The readout on her suit indicated it had provided intravenous pain relief; suddenly she understood why the need for the suit; it was much more advanced than she had assumed, probably equipped to deal with a multitude of needs. She found the idea intriguing and felt she would need to discuss the applications later with Kresge.

As Kresge and Dr. Graley entered the room, Richardson turned the lights on without so much as a warning.

The buzzing wall of TVs weren't even noticed by Dr. Graley, only the overwhelmingly *organic* nature of the room. She knew that the generators were psychic organisms, but she hadn't expected *this*.

It was all slimy coils, and fat, and what looked like giant, unfolded lung matter hanging like drapes. She followed the drapes to the ceiling, and...

...it was like some great green slimy organism had exploded against the ceiling, and it was covered in more eyes than she could count, human-looking eyes, and guessing from the distance between the floor and the ceiling, some were almost the size of beach balls.

The agitated mumbling reached a fever pitch.

Richardson cried out and stumbled backwards, and there was an audible "hiss" as his suit performed some function to counter.

We know he's got you, he heard, in his head, a myriad of voices speaking slightly out of sync, pounding at his brain.

"Josh. Josh!" Kresge moved to help Richardson as Dr. Graley stared gape-jawed at the ceiling.

But the ceiling was not looking back. All eyes were on Richardson.

"I'm fine," said Richardson, regaining his balance. "It's just a little...agitated today."

"And this...this generates electricity?"

"Yeah," Richardson said with some difficulty. "Come with me, I'll show you the portal room."

They left quickly, led by Richardson, who had not expected the assault Arty had made on him as a result of Matthew's presence.

After viewing the portal room, with no further issues, Richardson took Kresge and Dr. Graley up to the M laboratory. Kresge had ordered M deactivated at this point so that Dr. Graley could see it up close; this put a smile on Richardson's face as it would place the thing right where he—rather, where Matthew—wanted it.

Dr. Graley was visibly excited at the sight of the still disturbing, but much less grotesque object, that performed the same function as Arty.

Kresge took the lead on this one, not wanting to give Richardson another chance to make a scene, regardless of the reason.

"This is the Prototype II Generator. It's much smaller than R.T., the Prototype I, obviously, and while its output is much lower, it has a much higher efficiency in regards to its volume. It also has the benefit of being an orderly structure created from one organism, whereas the other is an ungodly mess created from dozens of organisms."

"People," Dr. Graley said, under her breath, in a neutral tone. She stepped close to the object, and tentatively placed a hand on it. She could feel it gently breathing. "Can it be duplicated?"

Kresge glanced at Richardson for a moment. "We're working on that—yes. It'll just take some time to iron out the process."

Dr. Graley spoke. "I'm suitably impressed. Nick? You'll see that I get the information I need?"

"Of course."

"Walk me out?"

He nodded.

Outside, Amanda Graley got into the driver's seat of her car and Nicholas

Kresge got into the passenger's seat.

"I wasn't quite expecting something on that scale," she said to Kresge.

"I thought you would be impressed. The soldier project still remains my primary goal, but the energy project, as a side effect, could be very important, just as I told you."

"I underestimated it. My apologies."

"Duly noted," he said.

"As for the removal of Richardson? You weren't very specific on the phone."

"It's only a matter of time, I'm sure. Two recent, high-profile incidents under his watch? I can't imagine the committee keeping him on after that."

"But they are. Right now," she pointed out.

Kresge himself wasn't completely sure of their motives, but answered as best he could to placate her. "It's a delicate situation. Internal affairs have to normalize before any more shake-ups happen. Remember, we just recently lost our entire senior staff."

"If you say so, Nick. I have some other questions, but they'll have to wait. I have places to be."

"As do I. I'll be in touch soon, Amanda."

"Good-bye."

Kresge nodded and left her car, walking over to his own.

He tried to believe what he said. Nothing else would make sense to be true.

Joshua Richardson stood in one of the doorways in the M laboratory, watching the underlying, grid-like structure of the M Generator become exposed as skin, fat, and other soft tissue burned with an intense hellfire. Acrid, noxious smoke billowed off of it, pulled up through the ventilation system to be purified and expelled.

There was a LOT of soft tissue.

When finally, he was certain that it was dead, that all that was really left was charring and splintering bones, he activated the intercom.

"I need a fire team to my location. There's been an accident, and the suppression system isn't working."

There was an immediate answer. "Location noted. Get to safety; we're on our way."

"Acknowledged."

He left the doorway and nonchalantly took the path to the hallway.

That's good. It can't possibly heal from that. It's dead.

"Good."

Matthew was ecstatic; he was now bound to this plane, with no connection to Nod. He could now proceed with his actual plan....

One Hundred Fifty-Seven:
Deer/Dear

Raven sat down on the bench next to Steve, shivering slightly. "C'mere," she said to the girl in front of her.

Mina leaned forward so her face was right in front of Raven's. Her cheeks were rosy from the cold. Raven brushed away a lock of hair that the wind had been gently playing with. "Listen, sweetie, I have to talk to Steve for a bit, okay?" Mina nodded.

They were in a small park that abutted a nature reserve and the area was surrounded on two sides by light woods with trails leading into them. The park itself wasn't more than a few benches and some playground equipment, but the trees were numerous and probably, inhabited.

Raven motioned around them. "All of this shit—stuff—is new to you, right?" Mina smiled and spoke.

"Yes."

Raven couldn't help but smile back. She couldn't imagine what it was like seeing a tree, or a chipmunk, or even snow, for the first time. "Look around. Just don't go too far, okay?" Mina nodded again, and turned. When she was several yards away, something dawned on Raven.

"Oh! Don't eat any yellow snow!"

She leaned back against the bench and exhaled a mist of breath. She breathed in deeply.

"She could have stuck around," Steve said. "I don't have anything to say she can't hear. At least, I don't think so."

"Nah, it's okay. I just don't want her to be bored. Words aren't exactly her thing yet." She thought about what she had said. *No, not exactly.* "I should say, she has no problem talking, we talk constantly, but she doesn't have enough life experiences yet. She needs to—just be around stuff. She'll get there." Something dawned on her.

"Shit. Did it sound like I was talking down to her?"

"If it did, I don't think she noticed."

"It's not like she's a child or anything—not by far—but—," she trailed off.

"She said in the car that she's never been outside that institute," Steve said.

"Exactly."

Steve let that sink in for a moment, and then spoke. "Okay, so—she's your girlfriend?"

"Yes. We're together." Raven wasn't sure how to explain it to Steve, as she couldn't explain it to herself. She looked over at Mina. She was wearing a pale green winter peacoat. A pleated skirt peeked out from underneath, and beneath that, she wore white stockings and winter boots that matched her coat. A black beret sat on top of her head. The wind gently swished her long blonde locks around. Raven had picked out the outfit for her; she thought it was cute. Nothing she would ever wear, but it suited Mina.

"I love her, Steve. With all my heart. I can't explain it. I barely know her. I don't think there is much of her to even know. It's like she's...it's like she's *new*. But there's a connection." She turned to face him and he was surprised to see that her eyes were wet. "She *saved* me, Steve. I was nothing. Whatever those bastards did to me, whatever gave me these—," It was cliched, what with the sorts of things she read and watched, and she didn't want to say it but there wasn't really any other terms that fit so well, "—these powers, they had me drugged too, I could barely form a coherent thought."

"I remember it, too. All of it. It's not like when they say someone's a vegetable and they want to communicate but can't—my mind was literally empty."

"And she saved me. I can't explain how, but it was like she reached into my heart and mind and fixed everything they did. And then we left."

"I love her. Intensely. And she loves me. She's said it, but she doesn't have to. I can *feel* it." She laughed. "This is gonna sound lame, but—it's like we're *soulmates*."

"Okay. Fair enough," responded Steve. "I'm sorry to bring it up, but, what about Crow?"

Raven was half expecting that name would drive her to tears, but instead, she felt rage welling up inside her. "The bastards that killed her, and my mom, and my brother, if I ever see them again, I'll...." She was speaking through clenched teeth.

"Woah woah woah woah, let's back up a step. Sorry." Steve had his hands up in apology. "I just meant...." He paused. Maybe this wasn't anything better to say. Maybe it was worse. "Are you...are you okay with someone else?"

The look on Raven's face was clear indication that he probably shouldn't have said that. *Stupid, stupid!* He looked down, bashfully. "I'm sorry."

"No, it's okay." Raven sighed. She looked toward the sky. "I get what you mean. Do I miss her? Yes. Am I over her? That's hard to say. I'm in love, Steve. I don't think you can love two people at once, not really. And I love Mina."

"Crow got stolen from me. We didn't break up. We didn't drift apart. She was murdered." Now, the tears came. Not long, not intense; her tears had been cried, mostly, but they were there, all the same. "She'll always be important to me."

Steve rubbed her shoulder. "Sorry."

"It's okay."

They sat there, silently, for a bit. They watched over at the edge of the woods, where Mina was holding her hand out towards a whitetail doe, who was tentatively sniffing it. The sight did not surprise Raven at all. Of course the deer wouldn't be frightened.

"Ok, let's lighten things up," Steve said. "She's really cute." He dragged out "really." "I'm willing to bet, under that coat, she's pretty hot, too, hmm?" He winked at Raven.

She smiled coyly. "Oh my god, dude. The body she's got. It's *ridiculous*. Just all curves."

Steve smiled back at her, but there was something behind that smile, something lingeringly painful, involuntary. Raven picked up on it immediately, and lowered her head, unable to look him in the eye.

"Steve...I'm sorry."

"For what?"

"For hurting you." *So much for lightening things up.*

It took him a second to realize what she meant, but realization hit him like a ton of teenage angst.

Steve had transferred into Raven's middle school when his mother had divorced his abusive father and they had moved into low-cost housing in Omaha. He was a year above her. They met during lunch when he was being picked on and she had stood up for him. He was short and chubby (a few months only from his big growth spurt) and had a terrible complexion that only in the present had really begun to clear up.

It had embarrassed him, but this tiny girl was so cute, and so loud-mouthed, he fell for her almost immediately. They became fast friends, having similar tastes in music and literature, and similar, frankly common, teenage issues.

Time went on, far more quickly than it seemed to them in their youth, and on the very day Steve was going to tell Raven that he liked her, she dropped a bombshell that had shattered his world.

She had come out to him. She told him that she was gay. That he was her best friend and the only one she could tell. That she had known for almost a year and had been hiding it.

And...he did the only thing he could do. He buried his feelings and told her it was okay, that it didn't change anything to him. That he would be her friend no matter what.

It was what she needed to hear.

Late in the next year, when she was in eighth grade and he had moved on to the ninth grade, she began dating a lovely young girl named Natalie who was already out at their school, and in the process, Raven came out as well.

Summer vacation was a whirlwind. It was mainly the three of them, Steve being the best friend he could, all the while his heart ached. And then, in late autumn, when the high heat and humidity of summer had started to wane, when all three were attending the high school, Natalie dumped Raven.

Of course it was an absolute tragedy for Raven; every breakup was, but this was her first, and the perverse nature of high school meant that she still had to see her ex-girlfriend every day, and in a cruel twist of fate, she had to work with her on a group project in British literature. It had incidentally ruined what until then had been the only class she actually looked forward to.

Of course, too, this was the girl that had taken her virginity. Several lays later it would seem like a meaningless moment, but *now*, it was huge.

And, on the weekend, Steve had taken Raven to one of the hills near farm country to look at the stars, shoot the shit, get drunk, and forget.

His motives were entirely pure.

They lay next to each other on a blanket. A half-empty pizza box was thrown off to the side, an enticing snack to any animals that may have passed by. The Milky Way shown above like a dusty river of fireflies, and it might, under other circumstances, have been romantic, but their young bodies and the half-finished fifth of peach vodka meant only the buzzed awkwardness of youth.

That, and their completely incompatible sexualities.

And yet....

A shooting star. They both made wishes.

A week later, Raven met Michelle, who would be her girlfriend until the Second Great Break-Up, then resume going out with her after the Third. (The Fourth would be followed by her meeting Crow.)

For Steve, it was much quicker, but only a shadow of what he actually wanted. One second he was watching the sky, the next, Raven's face was above him, smirking. She was holding herself up with outstretched arms....

And then they weren't outstretched anymore. And then her hands were at his cheeks and her tongue was in his mouth.

And then....

He wasn't stupid enough to think it was more than what it was, but he wasn't smart enough to say no. In the same night, he had his physical desires fulfilled but became no closer to having his emotional ones fulfilled, and in fact, this night would pain him for a long time to come.

"So that night, when we..." It wasn't an easy thing for him to articulate, and he finished abruptly. "...you knew. That...I like you. Liked you." He blurted out the last part quickly.

"Steve, I know you have feelings for me. Or had, at least until recently; I've been gone. I had no idea then. I was naive and had just gotten out of my first relationship. I wouldn't have realized it then unless you told me to my face." Raven took a moment, choosing her next words carefully. "I'm sorry. It must have hurt all along. Mostly, though, I'm sorry I took advantage of you. I don't know if it gave you false hope, or not, but I'm sorry."

"I mean...yeah, it was great. But it hurt. I knew it didn't mean we were gonna get together or anything, but still though. Anyway, I kind of always felt bad for taking advantage of *you*."

"As I recall, I made the first move, bonehead!"

"True. But why?"

"I don't know. I was hurt. You were sweet. I was curious. You were...safe, I guess."

"Wow," he said, taken slightly aback. "Don't know how I should feel about that."

"I'm sorry. You know I don't mean that as an insult!" Raven sighed.

"I know. Ha." He started laughing.

"What is it?"

"Honestly, that takes a huge load off my mind. I feel a bit...freer."

"Okay, but why did you put up with it? I know just how much it hurts not to have someone you want."

"Because you were worth it, as a friend," he answered simply. She smiled brightly.

They sat there for a time, watching Mina learn. She was staying outside of the woods, but was examining the trees. She took her gloves off and touched one, her delicate fingers soft against the rough bark of a bur oak.

"What's funny is, this wasn't at all what I wanted to talk about," Raven admitted. "But I'm glad we did."

"Yeah," Steve agreed quietly. That sense of freedom and elation he had just gained was eroding against the thought of what was to come. Raven immediately put some of his worries into words.

"What I need to figure out is how to survive and live a life when I'm an escaped experimental test subject of a completely illegal government project. God, that sounds so stupid when I say it out loud. In any case, they're not going to let me—us—go. Not with what we can know, what we can do."

"Can you show me again?" Steve asked. "It's just so weird."

"Look," said Raven, pointing towards the snow at their feet. She willed it, and small chunks began to rise and clump themselves into a tightly-packed snow ball. It floated up into the air and in front of Steve's face.

"You wouldn't!" he said.

She smirked. "Fine," she said, defeated. The snowball zoomed off seemingly of its own power and collided with a tree. Mina heard it and looked over at them, smiling.

"That's so crazy," Steve said.

"You haven't seen the half of it."

"What's flying like, by the way?"

"Um, well...exhilarating. Terrifying. Cold as hell."

He imagined her flying through the air like a superhero, the wind whipping past her. "Yeah, I guess it would be. I never thought of that."

"So," he continued, "do we know if you're all right? What if this—whatever they did to you—makes you sick?"

"I'm not sure. In some ways, I think I'm better."

"What do you mean?"

"I haven't had a single hallucination or anything since this all happened."

"Well, I guess there's a silver lining then? Jeez, what a way to get there, though."

A thought suddenly occurred to Raven. *Son of a bitch!* "Even if I was still sick, I don't think I could trust a doctor anyway. I think that's why they came after me. I had a really bad episode and Crow told my mother, and she took me to the doctor. She told me a man came to her offering to treat me at a facility for five years. They came for me not long after."

She leaned forward and hung her head. "They killed my family. I don't think they even wanted Crow. If she hadn't been there, she'd be...." She trailed off. *Goddamit, Raven, stop blubbering!* A shadow appeared on the ground in front of her. She looked up.

Mina had walked over and was looking down at her, smiling. Her beautiful eyes, like twin blue lagoons, held so much new-found joy that Raven couldn't help but feel better.

Mina leaned forward and embraced her. She kissed Raven on the cheek, and then pressed her own cheek against Raven's, the flesh cool from the wintry air.

"You saved me again, huh?" chuckled Raven.

"I will always be here," Mina said, softly.

Raven stood up, and Mina straightened up and stepped forward as she did so. Raven returned her embrace and kissed her briefly, on the lips.

"That deer really like you, huh, sweetie?"

Mina nodded. "You can be my dear," she said, not aware of the difference in spelling.

"You know, my mom always called me that."

"Oh," said Mina, looking worried. "I'm sorry if that makes you sad. I won't call you that."

"No," said Raven, smiling radiantly as she grasped both of Mina's hands. "I think it's a wonderful idea." Mina smiled back.

Raven breathed in deeply. "C'mon, let's go back to Steve's. It's cold. We can figure out what to do next later."

One Hundred Fifty-Eight:
Lunchtime

A call came in to Richardson's office. "Um, sir, uh, Joshua—we have all of the dead remains ready."

"Great job, Spence!" came the reply. "How about the repairs?"

"They're coming along. We can probably be done by tomorrow."

Richardson waited for input from Matthew, but there was none.

"That's fine. Burn the midnight oil."

Great, thought Jameson. *An all-nighter.*

"So...what do you want me to do with them? The remains?"

Transport them to the White Room. We're going there.

"Transport them to the White Room. I'm going to have them analyzed and destroyed."

"Okay...hey, the guys are getting a little antsy, there's rumors there was a fire upstairs?"

Richardson thought hard before he answered. Better to keep Jameson in the loop; keep him thinking he was important. So far, it had worked.

"You can tell them there was, but this next part stays between you, me, and Emma, until I say otherwise? Got it?"

"Of course," answered Jameson, mystified.

"There was a malfunction returning the M Generator to its active position. Its gone. Completely destroyed in the conflagration."

"Oh wow...." Jameson actually did feel a twinge of importance at knowing this fact. "That's awful. Of course. I won't speak a word of it. I'll get on that transport right away."

"Thanks, Spence."

Richardson looked now at the large cabinet door in his desk. "Now, how do we get you there without being seen?"

It won't be long before that's not an issue.

The cabinet door burst open, and *it* jumped out.

It could have stood at about two feet tall, but it was hunched over. Its body was little more in form than a curved cylinder, with a small, triangular, leathery tail. Its arms and legs were thin and weak looking; small hands with short fingers; short toes and high ankles. It walked like an animal, on its toes and forefeet, its knees close to its body.

It had a head that was barely differentiated from its body, like a round stump with underdeveloped ears and nose, with large, protuberant eyes and a small mouth filled with razor-sharp, triangular teeth. Its coloration was bluish-gray, changing into vibrant purple at its extremities. From its neck protruded sickly pink, feathery gills that laid on its back like undeveloped wings.

The Angel. Barely more than a fetus, with Matthew acting as its brain jockey.

Throw me in a bag or something. Getting out will be more interesting.

Richardson glanced over at his gym bag. That would do nicely. It would probably smell a bit, but that wasn't his problem.

He did feel a little strange walking down the hallways, but other than the odd guard patrol here and there, he didn't see anyone. Any working staff would either be with the test subjects or down in the cryo bay.

When he got to the white room, there was a couple of large coolers sitting on wheeled carts. Jameson was next to them.

"Sir, Joshua, I," he began, pausing for a moment as he looked confusedly at Richardson's gym bag, "I figured you could use me for the analysis?" *Surely, he wasn't going to try and do it by himself?* Jameson suddenly found the fact that Richardson was here personally to be very weird.

"Oh, no need, I have some junior staff on the way. No, I need you in the cryonics lab. Much more important. This is just tag-and-bag kind of work."

"Oh. Okay, then. Well, I'll be off."

"Good man."

When Jameson left, Richardson locked off the room completely. He set his bag down and unzipped it. The creature immediately leapt out and telekinetically threw open one of the coolers. He jumped in, and in moments, Richardson could hear the sickening crunch of bones and the sickening squishes and tearing of flesh.

Matthew had explained to him this need. The Angel was incomplete *and* not fully grown. Consuming psi-active tissue had already enabled it to grow when he first took control of it; more should help it reach full size and a greater level of power.

After several minutes, it jumped out of the first cooler and into the second, having opened it without so much as a touch. It moved quickly; Richardson knew it was the Angel, of course, but he didn't get a clear look at it. It was much larger than it had been earlier, however, that much was evident.

When it was finally done eating, it climbed out of the second cooler, and Richardson recoiled in horror when he finally saw what *it* had become.

The Angel had grown to around four and a half feet in height, upright, with a torso much more like a human's, with muscle definition but no nipples, navel, or genitalia. It still stood on its toes, but its thighs had grown longer in relation to the overall length of its legs so the knees were visibly farther from its body in relation to its earlier proportions. Otherwise, its arms and legs had remained much the same, but with more human-like hands and stronger musculature. The purple color turned to red at the fingertips, with blood-red, sharp claws at least an inch long at the end of each digit.

It now had a neck, and its gills had either automatized or been absorbed. On top of that neck sat a head, almost human, but far enough off that it was unsettling to look at. It was taller and longer than a human's head, almost without a chin, and the mouth had retained the sharp fangs that the Angel had had in its near-fetal state. The nose was flattened against the face, and the eyes were narrow, with brilliant green irises and pupils that were slightly vertical in orientation.

It spoke aloud, now, in a voice that was at the same time raspy and ethereal. "Look, Joshua, at this pathetic thing. How is *this* supposed to be my 'brother?'"

Richardson was confused; he didn't know what Matthew meant, but he didn't say anything in response.

It turned around suddenly, looking at the floor. A tail, about two feet long and tapered like a lizard's, swayed aggressively. "Shut up!" it yelled.

Turning back to Richardson, it pointed at its head. "This thing's brain is still a mushy mess. I think I can rectify that; first, I want to see Arty." He looked back at the floor, and smiled, a creepy, toothy grin.

"How I am going to get you there?" Richardson asked. "Every hallway is under surveillance, at the very least, and we'd have to pass guards and other personnel." Perhaps Matthew didn't care about secrecy?

"Is the boy, 'Benjamin' still here?"

"Yes, Benny is among our subjects." Richardson looked concerned.

"Good. Call him. He'll take us."

Richardson opened his mouth to protest but Matthew cut him off. "The 'kids' already know I'm here. Anything in the building with any semblance of psychic power knows I'm here. It doesn't matter."

One Hundred Fifty-Nine:
Temporary Home

Rather than going directly back to Steve's, Raven had suggested they stop at a used book store. She and Mina had picked up a couple of novels, an illustrated science book, and a couple picture books. Mina was very happy with the idea, and Raven wanted to encourage her to keep reading, since it was the closest thing to a hobby the girl had. Emma's money was all but gone, but Raven didn't mind. She didn't know what they were going to do in the long run, but she knew the money wasn't going to last very long anyway.

Steve took them up to his room, where his mother had placed the girls' backpacks when they had arrived that morning.

"So, um, you two can stay in my room while you're here. I'll sleep on the couch in the living room."

"I feel bad kicking you out of your bed, Steve," Raven said.

"It's ah, okay," he responded, fidgeting. "You two, you've got a road ahead of you, I can't imagine—you deserve your privacy and some time together while —I dunno, while you have a roof over your head, at least." It suddenly dawned on Steve and Raven what *running* actually meant. There was silence for a moment as they both thought about the implications.

Mina was concerned at the look of worry on Raven's face. "What's wrong?"

"This isn't going to be easy. I don't have a plan, I don't know where we're going to go, but we have to get away from here. We can't let *them* catch us."

Mina knew who "them" was, of course, but she wasn't too worried. "It's a big world out here, right? We'll be fine." She smiled, and it cheered Raven up a little, but she knew that Mina really didn't understand the needs of living—money, food, shelter—and how hard that was going to be for two young girls on the run to obtain. Steve, meanwhile, was concerned about this, but also the realization that his best friend, whom he had thought lost forever, was about to leave his life again. He was eager to change the topic.

"Oh, by the way, I got a bunch of your stuff." He pointed to some boxes in the corner.

"Really!?" Raven walked over and looked through the boxes. It was a somewhat random assortment of the few CDs she owned, her MP3 player, books, various knickknacks, and clothes—underwear included. "Wow, thanks!" She turned to Mina. "You're only a couple inches shorter than me. My clothes should fit you." She held up one of her bras. "Although, we're gonna have to get some cash to get you a couple more bras; no way in hell mine are going to fit you."

Mina and Steve both blushed.

"Oh, this was on your porch too. I think it had just came." Steve grabbed a box off of his floor and handed it to Raven. "The postmark is Japanese, I think."

"Oh," she said, softly, realization washing over her. She opened the package and pulled out a plastic-wrapped uniform.

"What is it?" Steve asked.

"It's an authentic *seifuku*—Japanese schoolgirl uniform. Crow, um, wanted to role-play."

"Oh."

"Well, I'm keeping it. I paid for it. Maybe I'll get some use out of it anyway." She grinned slyly at Mina, who completely missed the connotation.

Steve, feeling slightly uncomfortable, changed the subject. "My mom has to leave for work in a couple hours, I'm going to go help her with Gracie."

"Where's Trent?" Mina asked, referring to Mrs. Phillip's boyfriend and Gracie's father.

"His dad's sick and he's staying with him right now. It's been tough on my mom; I'm at school four days a week, and she's up in the morning with Gracie and then has her night shifts at work. I have to take care of Gracie until her bedtime. Uh, anyway, why don't you guys settle in and come downstairs? There should be dinner soon."

"All right," said Raven, thinking about the fact that "settling in" didn't really mean much; all they had were backpacks with blankets and clothes in them.

After Steve left, Mina sat down on his bed and Raven realized she had a very anxious look on her face.

"What's wrong?" She sat down on the opposite side of the bed.

"I have to tell you about something," Mina answered, looking downward.

Raven moved closer and grabbed her hand. "It's okay. You can tell me anything."

Mina looked up. "This was just a bit before you showed up. I was—," she struggled with the words, not just in choosing the right ones, but also in just talking about it. "—possessed. There was a boy, named Matthew—I don't think he was really there. I'm not sure how to explain it."

Raven looked concerned more than she did confused, but she felt both.

"He took over my body. It was...I'm not sure it really happened, it might have just been in my mind, but he raped me and got...inside my head." Raven's hold on her hand tightened. "I don't know how else to explain it."

"He...raped you?"

"It was, I think..." She struggled. She'd heard the phrase before, in unrelated talk. "A psychic projection. It seemed real, but it was his way of taking over my mind."

"I didn't really have much ability until then. Telepathy was painful, my telekinesis was weak, and I couldn't heal—at least, I don't think I could." She remembered the tests she had been subjected to in the White Room, the ones that often resulted in an intense heat that didn't hurt her. It was very confusing to look back on, now.

She was looking down again, and Raven saw a tear land on her lap. Mina hadn't allowed herself to truly think about what had happened until now, hadn't really explored the emotions of it.

"With him, I had more powers, I could affect people directly. And then, he—he made me kill them. I destroyed an entire room of doctors. I ripped a guard in half, took one's head off, set one on fire. There were others, too."

Raven felt like she had just been punched in the gut. Even at face value, it was a lot to take in. Mina looked up at her, and her beautiful blue eyes were full of tears.

"He's mad I got away. I could tell. He wants me back."

"I don't remember him," Raven said.

"He isn't always there. He comes and goes, somehow. But I'm afraid he'll find me again. I did such awful things...."

Raven was trying to wrap her head around this sudden confession and was doing her best to keep up. "It's okay. I'm sure the memories are awful. But no guilt, okay? If he made you do those things, it's not your fault."

"Somehow, he gave me my powers. He took away the lines on my hand."

Raven could remember now seeing bar codes tattooed on the children's palms, but she had never received one and had never seen one on Mina.

"Just...try to let the guilt go, please?"

"I'll try."

Raven pulled Mina towards her and embraced her. She didn't really understand all of this, but she knew what had to be done.

"We have to get as far from that place as possible."

One Hundred Sixty:
Cannot Stop the Battery

Richardson sat with Benny in the waiting room. Matthew—the Angel, Angel—he didn't really know anymore—had gone on ahead to see Arty alone.

"He's in your head," Benny said. "We can tell."

"We?" asked Richardson, though he suspected the answer.

"Well, Keiko and Johnny figured it out first. But we all felt it when he arrived. Danny's glad Mina got away before he came back."

"Just what..." Richardson began, unsure how to continue. He wanted to ask nothing less than exactly how the test subjects thought, how they interacted, what they thought of their existence and what, if anything, they knew about Matthew and what was going to happen. It was an enormous question, though, and he didn't know how to express it. Most of these children—whatever age they actually were aside—had been here since before he got his position at NOD, and that was a decade ago.

"What do Keiko and Johnny know?" he asked, settling on a single question, for now.

Benny smiled impishly. "We're all going to meet our destinies soon."

"Is that the best you can tell me?"

"That's all I know! They never tell anyone *everything.* Sometimes stuff changes."

Richardson leaned forward and put his head in his hands. Luckily, at least, Matthew's touch on his mind was weak at the moment; he was clearly preoccupied. Briefly, he considered running, but guessed that that was ultimately futile.

"What about him? Why are you helping him?"

"They said just to do what he says. That that will keep him from hurting us, probably, and it seems to be the right path, in the end."

Look at me, decorated soldier, trying to get advice on how to deal with a mind-controlling monster from an ancient child and his two fortune-telling buddies. Nothing about that sentence makes the least bit of sense.

He didn't have much time to himself as in mere moments, Matthew walked back into the room, looking refreshed and proud of himself.

"They know their place, now. I shouldn't really tell you this, Joshua, but you can't work against me, can you? You see, Arty's power is my power. I can skim a little off of the top. This weak brain is holding me back from drawing off more. It's time I fixed that."

"Where to next, then?" sighed Richardson.

"The file room where I took that girl's body. I need to know my history.

Then, we take action."

One Hundred Sixty-One:
Truce

Emma Jacobson drummed her fingers nervously against the table. She had taken a seat in the back of the coffee shop, where she could see the door and windows.

She felt that her paranoia was entirely justified.

Finally, after what seemed like forever, Jameson came in and sat down opposite her. He unwrapped a scarf and set it next to him, and opened up his coat.

"Jameson, what the hell, having us both leaving for coffee before the work day's up? This looks suspicious, you have to realize that."

"Good. You're scared, too. I guess we're on the same page, then." His normally perfectly slicked-back hair was unkempt, and he had bags under his eyes. Emma did as well, but had done her best to conceal them.

A waitress came over and Jameson told her he was fine. She walked away with a cross look on her face. Emma sipped her drink, a chai tea, and told him, "They really don't like it when you don't order anything."

"Whatever. Anyway, the reason I had you come here. You're the only one I can really talk to about this." *I hope,* he added in his mind. "Something's wrong with Richardson. He's acting very oddly."

"Of course he is. After the last two incidents? He's probably going to lose his job." She was going to take this slow, to see what Jameson knew or at least what he thought he knew.

"The M Generator was destroyed. It burned up completely. The fire suppression never came on."

"I didn't know that."

"He told me you were the only other person I was allowed to mention it to."

He's keeping all of his eggs in one basket, she thought.

"I think Richardson did it. Because...I think Matthew told him too."

"All right, Jameson, fair enough, we are on the same page. I think Matthew's—spirit, soul, whatever—is back in the building. And I think he might be affecting Richardson."

"That's not all. Look, I know you all think I'm useless and stupid." Jameson was being remarkably candid, Emma thought. "But I pay attention to things. Did you know that the entire guard contingent has been replaced in the last couple months?"

"So?"

"So, they usually only do a few quarterly. And their service records are available at our clearance level. All of the new ones are classified." He was sweating a bit. "Something big is going on."

Emma feigned calmness and sipped her tea, but she was starting to worry more than she already had. She might as well be open with him at this point. What was there to lose?

"That General Kresge has been around a lot more lately than usual. And—I have to make sure you're really on my side, here, Jameson?"

Perhaps honesty was the best policy here. "Emma, I was supposed to snoop on you. That's why Richardson put me as your second and not Carl. But—we're well past that now. You've done what they wanted, and I trust you more than I trust him."

"Fine." She sighed. That was good enough. "There's a creature—a creation —of Utsugi's called 'Tom.' Kresge and Richardson recently had it activated. There was a test run...it massacred an entire squad of soldiers. With ease. I saw the video."

"Meaning?"

Dumbass. "This has been a military project all along. We're building a soldier, Jameson. The *perfect* soldier."

Jameson thought back to a mere week ago, when he had thought his time to shine was right around the corner. When he, Spencer Jameson, a fairly mediocre student who had somehow landed a cushy job at an ultra-high security research facility, was in the process of training and studying possibly the most powerful telekinetic subject that NOD had ever seen. He had thought the act of delivering this prize of new research would be enough.

But he—as he had suspected, all along—he was just a pawn, a cog in a machine, deprived of his own true purpose in the bigger picture. It *was* just research. A side project, clearly not instrumental to anything important.

His ego deflated finally, once and for all, and he put his elbow on the table and rested his chin on his hand.

"I really am just a fuck-up."

Emma couldn't help but smile. "Maybe it's just the circumstances, Spencer, but this is the first real conversation we've ever had. This is the most honest I think you've ever been with me."

"So, what do we do?"

"Nothing, I guess. Watch and wait. Richardson told me to get some rest. I think...I'm going to do just that."

"He wants me working. I've been in charge of fixing the cryonics storage bay."

"Good luck with that." She finished her tea. "If you see him, tell him I went home sick. Fatigue. I'll email him later."

"Yeah, good luck with that, too," Jameson replied. "I'm going back before they miss me." He buttoned up his coat and threw his scarf around his neck. With a nod to Emma, he got up, and left.

She stared down at her tea, thinking. Getting out of Dodge might just be the smartest thing to do.

One Hundred Sixty-Two:
Plans

It struck Richardson suddenly how odd it looked, this barely humanoid creature with its lizard-like tail, leaning over a table and reading. There was a dull ache in his head.

What did it mean, exactly, about skimming power from Arty?

He could tell it was getting mad; the ache in his head was worsening, and he could feel exactly where it was coming from.

"In all my years, I never once cried. This is the closest I've come," came the raspy, bizarrely high-pitched dual voice. A clawed fist slammed onto the table in rage. The other hand picked up the sheets of paper and scattered them.

He turned to face Richardson. There was a fire in his green eyes.

"Matthew is dead. He never really existed. No 'the' either; I am Angel. Do you know," he began, pointing behind himself, "what those papers say?"

Richardson opened his mouth, afraid to answer, but "Angel" didn't give him a chance to.

"I'm not real. I was made by your people. From scratch, grown in a tube. All my life I've been frustrated, a prisoner, here and elsewhere, wanting to know who my parents were, what my childhood was like. *I never even had those things.*" He looked down in disgust at the body he was inhabiting. "No wonder this "brother" of mine is inhuman. It's just as fake as I am, isn't it?"

"Your project was suspended before I started here. I don't—"

Angel cut him off. "'Project?' My, 'project!?' I should have known, knowing the others. But they kept telling me I was special, and I believed it. I should have figured it out when I finally met my other 'brother,' Andrew."

"You—you did that too!" Richardson exclaimed, suddenly understanding.

"Your 'Andrew Incident?' Yes. But he was a shell of a being. Drugged into submission. I think I was left mostly untreated because your scientists thought I was useless. Useless!" He laughed. "I was exactly what they wanted—the 'control unit'! But I didn't let them know. I was afraid of that power once I discovered it."

"But, Anna—" Richardson began again.

"Anna was different. She had no defenses against me. I figured I could go where I wanted with her and find out the truth—this truth. But she surprised me. She burned me out of her mind. And then you took my body and made a *battery* out of it. But I was still connected. I still wanted to know. When the time was right, I came back for my brother. He was as good as dead. So I took him outside."

"Why did you kill people?"

Angel rolled his eyes. "With Anna, they were in my way. With Andrew—it just felt right." He walked closer to Richardson, who tried to back away but ran into a wall. Mere inches from his face, Angel continued. "Your people made me, and Andrew, for killing. Maybe we just had the instinct?"

He backed away, and yelled incredulously. "Even Arty used to be real people! Even that...that...monstrosity! But not me."

"I'm going to control them, Joshua. Those physically diseased vermin in the frozen basement. I'm going to do exactly what you built me for, and I'm going to spread them into your sick, twisted world."

Richardson was reasonably terrified.

"Arty's power is nearly limitless. I just need a better brain to use it all." His eyes brightened, and he walked back over to the files. After a few moments he found what he wanted. He flipped through the pages quickly, and began laughing maniacally. "This is too perfect."

He turned back to Richardson. "I want Mina. I can make a better body with her...in her. We're...compatible."

"You know her powers," Richardson said defiantly. "She can't be subdued. She'll resist any drugs we use and escape again."

"I'm in your head; I know most of what you know, Joshua. Call in your threat. Get the implants. We can subdue her with those."

One Hundred Sixty-Three:
Overview

The night passed peacefully for Raven and Mina. They read some of their books, watched a movie with Steve, and eventually the two of them retired to his room for the evening. His bed was old and not exactly the most comfortable, but it was better than nothing.

In the morning, Steve left for school, and Raven told Mina that they were going to help clean the house as thanks for letting them stay. With Steve at school and Trent gone, with Mrs. Phillips occupied with her daughter much of the day and at work at night, not much was getting done. Mina happily agreed; Raven was not fond of chores but it was the right thing to do, and she could teach Mina some domestic skills in the process.

Elsewhere, Emma Jacobson sat on her bed, knees under her chin, and stared at the packed bags she had placed at the foot, unsure what her next move really would be.

Angel had Benny with him and was using him to explore the Gates Building. He could feel the siphoned power from Arty coursing through his body, and it was a simple thought to scramble surveillance and lock and unlock doors wherever he went. He wanted a seat, a throne room, even, and though he liked the White Room, it was so...low. There was a space on forty-four he liked, though it was filled with the egg-shaped chambers he remembered being terrified of.

Nicholas Kresge was at a diner getting breakfast when his cell phone went off. It was Amanda; he ignored it. He was tired of her insistence that he push the advisory board to action; he was influential, but he was but one man.

He had learned patience over his many years in the military; she, apparently, had not. It was understandable; she was an army physician of high rank who had assumed command during a risky military operation in which her commanding officer had been killed. The resulting success of the action was attributed to her quick thinking, and she had been later hand-picked by the Black Army leaders to lead a contingent of black ops soldiers. She was used to quick missions with immediate results, and the fact that her own son was under her command made her all the more impatient, as his welfare was also in question.

A small meeting led by Leonard Dillons put his people on edge; the Black Army had not only taken control of the entire guard structure in the Gates Building, but they ran the surveillance room as well, and one of the men had noticed the cameras shutting on and off and the doors unlocking and locking in a way that suggested someone was moving through the building, taking great pains to be unseen and unreachable as he or she did so. Knowing what they did about the nature of NOD, there was not much they could do without calling attention to themselves; it was perfectly possible that this was nothing out of the ordinary, perhaps the movement of a top-secret object (or person,) and it should be left alone.

Still, Dillons' gut feeling was that it was something else, and he told his people to be on high alert. Carlos simply leaned against a wall the whole time, showing no emotion, playing solitary catch with his knife.

Marcus Graley knocked on the door of his mother's office. "Come in," she said.

"Sir, with all due respect, I'm bored."

She sighed. "At ease, son. Take a seat."

He sat down. "Mother, we haven't had a mission in weeks and I don't like being cut off from the guys in the Gates Building." Primarily, he meant Leonard and Carlos. "When do we make our move?"

She looked at her cell phone sitting on her desk. Nick was a busy man but she couldn't shake the feeling he was ignoring her. She put her head in her hands, resting her elbows on her desk. "Honestly, I'm not sure. There's been another incident and yet, Richardson is still in charge. Until General Kresge takes over, we have to bide our time."

"As for the lack of missions, I've made requests but there's nothing available right now. Everything seems to be in a lull."

Marcus was a career soldier and didn't like inactivity. He didn't want to be acting as a "guard," either, but at least it would be a change in venue. "I guess I'll take the boys out for paintball or laser tag. Call it a 'training exercise.'"

Spencer Jameson was doing rounds, as he was not expecting Emma in today after their conversation. He had not seen Benny anywhere but had confirmed that he had received breakfast and his medication, so it was alright, if puzzling. It really didn't matter to him, though. He could feel the world around him unraveling; things had been set into motion that he only knew a little of, but there was a dark energy in the air, an almost tangible sense of quiet dread. Perhaps he would take some time with Keiko and Johnny; he had never given their "powers" much respect, but what harm could it do?

Some time later, when the east coast was heading to work, Joshua Richardson made a phone call to the Nevada branch of NOD, where he calmly explained to a furious (and worried) Dr. Daichi Yamada that their newest test subject just happened to be his daughter, and that he was curious why his records had clearly been tampered with and showed no family. The terms for her to be provided with "proper care" was that Yamada was to come to the Omaha branch with his healer-proof implant technology, and use it to subdue a test subject for an experiment. He agreed.

Some time after that, an anxiety-ridden Dr. Yamada chartered a NOD private jet to Nebraska for the following day, and set about preparing his instruments and tech for the trip. When his director rightly questioned what he was planning on doing, he told the truth: that the director of NOD-Omaha was ransoming his daughter in exchange for shared research. She, a rather understanding woman, saw the panic in his eyes and told him to do what he "felt was right, within the confines of NOD's classification," and that she would be personally calling Richardson later to chew him out and tell him he would get his "goddamned tech."

The rest of the day passed wonderfully for the Phillips household. Mrs. Phillips was ecstatic at the amount of help Raven and Mina were, and Mina spent the day learning mundane tasks and being genuinely happy about them. Raven had found an old apron and the girlishness in her found Mina adorable in it, especially later when they were alone and it was the only thing she was wearing.

When Steve got home from school he tried to do his homework, but Raven kept bugging him to take them to a movie, and after an hour and a half of barely any progress he gave in and they went. It was Mina's first. When they returned to Steve's house, dinner was ready: a pot roast that had spent all day in the oven and was incredibly tender. Mrs. Phillips was a talented cook. Not long afterwards, she left for work, and Steve, Raven, and Mina took care of Gracie until she fell asleep. Raven couldn't help but smile at Steve's skill with his sister; he would make a good father to someone, someday.

Around midday Emma found herself at a motel on the edge of town; she barely remembered the ride there. It was if she'd been on autopilot since the morning. She found herself paying for a week's stay.

The room was fairly clean and had a full-sized, ancient fridge, a two-burner mini-stove, and a microwave. She was pleasantly surprised. She stocked the fridge with some basics and surveyed the room; it would do. She had a place to run to, temporarily, if need be. She was fairly certain she had not been followed; there was no car outside her house this morning, either. It was puzzling, but she was happy about it. What she didn't know was that, following the events of the previous day, Richardson had called off the active surveillance on her. She frankly wasn't his biggest concern anymore and he wanted as many guards at the facility as possible for when the shit inevitably hit the fan.

Jameson did go to see Keiko and Johnny, and the experience left him feeling more shaken then he was previously. He had pleaded for some information, something useful. All they could tell him was that he had no place in the things that were to come; that pathways had begun shifting due to certain choices, but no current outcome seemed favorable to him.

For a moment, he thought about just putting a bullet in his head, but he decided he wouldn't go out that way. When push came to shove, he'd do what he always did; put Spencer first and wriggle his way out.

Angel spent most of the day telekinetically "adjusting" floor forty-four, creating a living space for himself. His hubris bade him build a throne out of repurposed pieces of the SDF Chambers and other objects in the large space. He began setting up room for a court in front of his new throne. His id and ego fought as his plan unfolded; once he learned from Richardson that Yamada would be arriving as soon as tomorrow, and that repairs had been completed in the cryo-lab and most of the stored experiments were still biologically viable, he became certain that he would succeed in his ultimately goalless reign of terror. Everyone would suffer at his hands; they had made him to control an army of destruction and he would not disappoint them.

One Hundred Sixty-Four:
Implants

Daichi Yamada arrived at NOD Omaha very early the following day, and was personally greeted outside at the loading dock by Lieutenant Colonel Joshua Richardson, flanked by two guards. Yamada was a short, unimposing man with graying black hair, a thin mustache, and rectangular framed glasses. He shivered in the cold; he had worn only a light tan jacket over a shirt, a tie, and slacks.

Richardson smiled and held out his hand to shake, but Yamada harrumphed. "Let's skip the pleasantries, shall we?" He motioned to two very large metal-edged crates behind him. "I have all of my equipment. I'll need a lab set up and full details about what *exactly* I'm doing. Now, *where is my daughter?*" He stressed every word. The last he had seen was a picture Richardson had emailed him as proof. Her head was shaved and she looked catatonic, but it was definitely her.

"In due time. I want to make sure you don't go back on your word first."

"You're a monster."

You have no idea, Richardson thought. "Come this way." He motioned towards the freight elevator. The guards moved to the crates and pushed them on their dollies.

Later, when Yamada had his laboratory set up, Richardson introduced him to Jameson. "He'll help you with anything you need," Richardson said.

"Fine. When I leave, though, I'm taking my daughter."

"Now, now, doctor, don't get ahead of yourself. You're going to be with us for quite some time."

Yamada was very cross but Richardson was worried as well. Matthew—Angel's—commands were putting him in a more dangerous position than he was already—any day now, Kresge would surely arrive with an order to remove him from his position, or worse. Blackmailing Yamada would no doubt expedite that, and increase the chance of punishment. On the other hand, Angel was clearly mad and dangerous himself. But Richardson didn't have the power to resist him at all. Before—maybe, for short times, when Angel was distracted, he had moments to himself. Once Angel had started to draw power from Nod through Arty, though, his abilities had strengthened and Richardson didn't have a moment's thought to his own.

Richardson left and Jameson and Yamada shook hands. Yamada decided that the best thing for him to do was just to throw himself into his work, and keep his mind focused. "So, I understand I'm supposed to create a sedation delivery system that won't be rejected by a healer?"

"Yes," answered Jameson. "I can get you her genetics or any other information you need."

"That won't be necessary. It's all the same." He pulled a small object out of his pocket and held it up for Jameson to see. It was a clear, green crystal, tapered at both ends. A small ring of indeterminate color sat in the middle of the crystal, with tenuous strands like small hairs running off of it.

"This is an artificially produced composite crystal based upon both nephrite and jadeite jade. Jade is sympathetic to psionic activity."

"What's the ring in the middle?" Jameson asked.

"It's useless unless implanted with psi-active tissue. Once it's been properly formed, it can do all sorts of things—in this case, it can be used to contain an implant which will not be rejected by a healing psychic. We can create a drug delivery system to sedate or even control a test subject." Despite his concern for his daughter, he had been an employee of NOD for far too long to see the other test subjects as anything human. Calling Richardson a monster was a touch hypocritical, and Yamada knew it.

"Where do you get the tissue samples?" Jameson asked, his eyes narrowing.

"Usually from the prototype series." Yamada set down the crystal and tilted his head. "Do you know about the prototype series?" He supposed he should consider security clearance, but under the circumstances of his presence, it didn't seem that important, especially if this man was supposed to assist him.

"Yes. Like, Matthew, Andrew, Angel?" He didn't know much, but Emma had shared information with him here and there, and he had used his own security clearance to learn as much as he could.

"Yes. We usually use fetal matter grown from embryos of that series."

"Matthew's here," Jameson whispered. Hopefully, Yamada could be an ally in the ensuing madness. He had been here when all of this started, years ago. Maybe he would know something useful.

"What?" Yamada exclaimed, clear panic in his voice.

"It—its consciousness, it's come back again. It attacked a test subject a few weeks ago and now, I think it's here and *it's controlling Richardson.*"

"And I'm here to make an implant for a healer?" He walked over to a desk and sat down, logging into the computer. He used his old, original information, a back door he had tried to leave when he had been removed from this facility after the Andrew Incident.

It worked.

He went through a list of the contents of the cryo-bay. Jameson walked over and looked at the heading. "I was on the staff the other day repairing and cleaning the cryonics lab. There was some sort of explosion down there."

Yamada went through the list serial number by serial number, looking at the status next to each.

Deceased, deceased, frozen, frozen, frozen, deceased, frozen—finally, the one he was looking for. "Empty. Oh dear." He took his glasses off and buried his head in his hands. "I believe it's worse than that. This empty one—that's the Angel."

"I don't...really know any of the specifics."

"Okay. We designed a series of organisms. One as a "control unit," that should possess the power of psychic domination—the highest theoretical ability of intrusive telepathy. That was Matthew. We developed one, a mental simpleton, but with strong telekinetic abilities. That was Andrew. Finally, we had a third in slow development, a being that in theory had no conscious mind but very strong psychic powers. That was Angel."

Yamada continued after a brief pause. "The initial plan was to see if Matthew could control Andrew, with both under sedation, to keep the situation in check. Only then, if that was successful, was Angel to be completed and Matthew tested with him. Angel was intended to be biomorphic—a high form of healing—and we would not be able to sedate him. It would be risky, but we hoped by then we would have a fool-proof way to keep Matthew bound to our will."

"We never got the chance. Test after test, Matthew seemed to be a failure. We took him off of his medication—it was on purpose—to see if that had any affect. He immediately took control of Anna, the photokinetic subject."

Photokinetic? thought Jameson. *I thought she was a brain-damaged pyro.*

"We subdued her—after a lot of bloodshed—and found his body. He was alive, but a vegetable. Dr. Utsugi wanted him for her biomorphism research—she was basically responsible for R.T., you know? She succeeded in making a generator out of Matthew's body, with Dr. Hanin's help. I don't know how. He wasn't even a healer, I don't think. Maybe. It was so long ago. Andrew was kept on as his unique nature, post-pubescent and artificial, made him still worth studying. Follow so far?"

"Yes," answered Jameson.

Yamada had a point, of course, but it had been years since he had talked to anyone about this in depth. It felt good to get the words out, almost penitential.

"Dr. Hanin spoke with me quite a bit, in secret, after the 'Andrew Incident' and my departure to the Groom Lake location. He was certain—and he had the evidence—that Matthew had somehow survived, mentally, and had taken control of Andrew as well. The only vector we could determine he had used was his old body—the M Generator. As far as we know, though, he's been quiet since, at least until the events you mentioned."

"In the following years, Dr. Utsugi seemingly perfected the biomorphic processes she was working on, and had created a viable product—a 'super-soldier.' Not very long ago, I had succeeded in creating these implants, so a control unit like Matthew was no longer necessary. The test was brutally flawless, I'm told."

"So, this brings me back to Matthew," Dr. Yamada continued, getting to the point of his story. "If Matthew is indeed 'back,' and Angel is missing, it would be reasonable to assume that Matthew has taken control of Angel's body. If its body is developed fully, it's likely to be far stronger than Anna or Andrew was. And with no conscious mind, it has no defense against Matthew's control."

"So, what you're saying is?" asked Jameson, hoping for a summary after all of the information he had just taken in.

"What I'm saying is, we have much bigger concerns than your boss acting oddly. In fact, whatever these implants are going to be used for, I don't doubt that Matthew made the order, not that Richardson fellow."

"The implants are for the test subject Matthew attacked."

Yamada didn't reply; he just seemed deep in thought.

"So, what should we do?"

"Proceed as directed," Yamada calmly replied. "I must admit to being intrigued; but I have my own reasons for doing as I've been told." He didn't want to bring up his daughter; that was his problem to worry about, and he didn't want to risk the pain right now of possibly hearing what she had been through, assuming Dr. Jameson knew anything.

"So, let's begin, Dr. Jameson."

One Hundred Sixty-Five:
Together

Mina and Raven's second day at Steve's was much like the first, and Raven reveled in the lazy, peaceful downtime she had with her girlfriend. At one point, she walked over to Steve's window and looked out. His house was the only two-story one nearby so she had an unobstructed view across the rooftops and the length of the street below. She watched the wind whip grains of snow out of their resting places and against obstructions, where it piled up in gentle slopes.

After a minute or so of this, she felt an arm around her waist, and Mina rested her head on Raven's shoulder. "What's on your mind?" the blond girl asked.

"I was just thinking, every person out there has their own problems and concerns. Ours aren't even the worst, I bet, maybe just the weirdest."

"There's a lot of people in this world, aren't there?"

"Yes."

"A lot of them seem unhappy."

"I think you're right," Raven agreed. "How do you know?"

"When we were walking the other day. I watched their faces. We were happy just to be together. So many of them looked sad or lonely."

Raven put her arm around Mina. "I am happy."

"Me too."

One Hundred Sixty-Six:
Orders

That night, Yamada reported to Richardson that the implants were ready and again demanded to see his daughter. Richardson told him he had further work to do, and ordered him to his office.

Upon arriving, Yamada was greeted with a horrifying site: next to Richardson stood a being, more monster than human, with a smile of fangs and blue skin.

"Matthew," Yamada said, shock overwhelming any pretense of naïvety he might have shown.

"It's 'Angel' now. I've taken the name of this vessel."

"Lieutenant Colonel, with all due respect," Yamada said sarcastically, "what the fuck is going on?"

Richardson sighed. There was no way to keep things from moving forward. "The implants are for our test subject Mina. He—we—want to keep her subdued, while...."

Angel cut him off. "You are going to take this body's genetic material, cross it with hers, and implant it into her uterus. I will merge with my own child. You will override the coding that gave me this useless brain. I'll know at a touch if it's been done right, doctor." His tone of voice for the last sentence was very threatening.

Yamada looked at Richardson. "And then I get to see my daughter." It was a statement, not a question.

"I don't think that will be a problem. I think she'll come to us."

"You mean—she's not even here?" He was floored; he felt his stomach drop.

Angel spoke next. "Joshua tells me that the girl that escaped with Mina is your daughter, Raven. Did you know that I met her once? When I was...Andrew. I'm eager to meet her again, but not in this form. I understand she is quite strong."

Yamada was a maelstrom of emotions now—anger, fear, sadness, regret—and was doing his best not to let them show.

"Begin your preparations, doctor. I'm sending a team to recover Mina. Don't worry, we won't harm your daughter, just sedate her. We're—he's—not ready to have her here yet." Richardson wasn't sure what Angel's timescale was regarding his plan, but clearly, things were coming to a head.

"I have to ask," Yamada risked, addressing Angel, needing to know how much the creature actually knew. "What makes you think any of this will work? How do you intend to 'merge' with another organism?"

"The nature of this body—biomorphically, at least—was all based on Arty's creation, as I have read. Only, I can control it, rather than an outside force. We'll call it a well-educated hunch."

Yamada left the office a shell of the man he entered as. He had intended to chew Richardson out, to demand his daughter, to report him to General Kresge himself. His hunch—that Matthew was controlling the Angel's body—was far more unsettling and terrifying in person than it had been when he had merely thought of it.

And, of course, the creature was right. Its crude form had been developed from the knowledge gained from R.T.'s creation. It could certainly merge with an offshoot of itself. Yamada suspected that, without a properly formed brain, Matthew's consciousness was only tenuously grasping onto the creature. He needed a fully developed mind to imprint entirely, and a freshly born one wouldn't have a presence to fight him off with.

He also hadn't expected it to be fully grown. But, as the body was intended to be biomorphic, perhaps it had accelerated its growth. What worried him the most, however, was its apparent interest in his daughter, a girl he hadn't seen in years but had never stopped loving, a girl he wanted more than anything not to be involved in any of this, as he had tried so hard long ago to ensure never happened.

One Hundred Sixty-Seven:
Acquisition II

Marcus was glad to have something to do, finally, but it made him uneasy. "Acquisitions"—kidnappings, really—were Carlos' specialty and something he personally wasn't fond of. He had personally done, and was aware of, many unsavory things in his line of work, but this was one of a handful he really, *really* didn't like being a part of.

His partner on this mission was Tony Bradshaw, a capable man whose specialties also did not lend well to the mission at hand: he was an accomplished sniper. However, they were two of the best soldiers not currently assigned to NOD, and thus Dr. Graley had picked them.

"We're almost there," Tony said, motioning to the GPS display. "Looks like they're hiding in a residential neighborhood."

"Okay, you know the plan. Enter silently, tranq anyone we see before they can act. The dark-haired Asian is incredibly dangerous and needs to be handled first. The blond Caucasian is our target and she needs to be sedated constantly."

"Yeah, what's up with that?"

"Some psychic power mumbo-jumbo. She's nearly immune to toxins, I gather."

"Okay, 'tranq,' though? Your orders, or theirs?" Tony asked.

"I've been given discretion," Marcus answered bluntly.

"All righty then." Tony let out a sigh of relief. Killing civilians was not something he savored.

"Lock and load, man, we're here."

Raven slept well that night, but Mina woke once from a nightmare. It was one she hadn't had in a while, not since being with Raven. She could never remember it all when she awoke, but she was always cold and hungry, and remembered blood. If she knew yet of such things, she would have considered it a bad omen.

"Phillips residence. Mother works evenings but should be home by now. Son is in college. Daughter is a baby. Mother's boyfriend lives here—his car isn't here." Tony had put in a quick request for information about the target's household and read aloud what he had received.

"So, likely, three targets other than the girl. Home security?" Marcus asked.

"Checking...none."

"Let's go."

The fence gate made noise, but luckily the squeaking wasn't very loud. The door's locks were easily picked. They moved into the landing. Lights were off throughout the house from as far as they could tell. The night-vision goggles they wore let them see things in exquisite detail, however. They moved through the kitchen and the attached dining area. Marcus pointed at the couch in the next room; a teenage boy was sleeping on it. Tony leaned into the room: front door, closet, stairs. Marcus walked over and with a quiet *ffft* shot a tranquilizer dart into the boy's exposed neck.

Likely as not, the girls were upstairs, and it made sense to secure that before heading to the basement. This was the risky part; one bad stair could ruin their entire night. Luckily, only the gentlest of squeaks emanated from them.

At the top of the stairs were two bedrooms and a bathroom and a couple of closets. Tony checked the closest while Marcus took point in the middle of the hallway. It turned out to be the mother's room, and he tranquilized her easily.

They both proceeded to the next room and looked in. The bed was up against the right wall, and they could see the back of the dark-haired girl, spooning the light-haired girl. They couldn't get a completely clear shot from the doorway, so they slowly moved in, Tony aiming for one, Marcus ahead of him, aiming for the main target.

Marcus, eyes trained on target, had forgotten, just long enough for it to matter, to watch his step as well. He banged his toe against some manner of junk on the floor, and the dark-haired girl stirred, and looked over.

She strained her eyes in the darkness. "What? Who?" She gasped, suddenly aware that there was someone in the room, but by then, the dart had found its mark. With her out of commission, both men rushed over to the other side of the bed, both shot the light-haired girl, and Marcus pulled out a large syringe and quickly injected her with the entire thing.

"All right, let's get the fuck out of here," he said, pulling her out of the bed and cradling her in his arms. She looked 16, maybe 17, certainly no older than 18, and she was beautiful. She looked completely peaceful in her drug-assisted sleep. Guilt pangs attacked his heart.

Tony's voice was dour, giving away similar feelings. "Yeah, let's get out of here."

Mina woke up groggy, with a massive headache. All she could see was a glaring whiteness that hurt at first but slowly became bearable. She tried to get up, but couldn't. The confusion passed and she realized she was strapped down to a table. She lifted her head and tried to look around.

She was in the White Room.

She was wearing a hospital gown and was strapped down at the upper chest, waist, and ankles. Her arms were off to her sides, strapped down at the wrists. An IV was inserted into her left arm. She was aware of an odd pressure on the right side of her neck, and she looked off to the right and saw an odd electronic mechanism with a difficult to understand display screen, and a tube coming out of it that presumably led to her neck.

She looked in the direction of her feet and saw a man sitting at a desk some ways away, looking down as he wrote. He was surrounded in the rear with lab equipment.

She tried to use her telekinesis to break the straps, but it wasn't working. She concentrated and could feel the power like a spark in her mind, but it never manifested. She looked down again in panic, and the man noticed she was awake and got up.

"You'll find that your powers are subdued, I'm afraid. I'll explain in a moment." He walked over to her. "I'm Dr.—," He stopped. She had been staying with his daughter; he didn't want to give up his identity just yet. "You can call me Daichi."

Her mouth was dry and she was having trouble speaking.

"To your left is an IV. It will keep you nourished. To your right is a device that is steadily pumping a chemical into your bloodstream that is going to leave your mind in a foggy, painful state. I apologize for that. What it will also do is prevent you from focusing on your powers—that's why you can't break your bonds, as I'm sure you tried."

Daichi wasn't very tall, not much taller actually than she was, she surmised. Behind his glasses she saw eyes that looked weary. There was no malice in his voice, but no warmth, either.

"Why...why am I here? Where's Raven?" Mina finally managed to get out.

"She's fine. She's not here." She seemed a little relieved, an emotion he shared.

"You're here because..." he began.

"You're here because of me," a voice, ethereal and gravelly, interrupted. Mina looked over to her left, where the noise had come from, and recoiled in shock. An inhuman creature walked towards her. Benny stood behind him, further back in the room. "I came at just the right time."

She could feel the raw energy radiating off of it. She recognized the feel of it, the intense green of its eyes, and tensed up, horrified. "Matthew...." she said.

"It's 'Angel' now. That's the name of this body."

He put his hand on her abdomen. She instinctively tried to pull away, but of course she couldn't. "You're carrying our child. The doctor here made it and put it in you. He says it will grow very quickly."

"Why?"

"So I can merge with it and use my abilities to their full extent."

Mina struggled against the bindings.

"Stop it," he said. "There's no point." Mina watched as he walked back over to Benny, grapsed his hand, and they vanished into thin air. She looked over at the doctor. In spite of the insanity of the situation, one thing was very clear.

"You can't do this! He's a monster!"

"Believe me, I know," Yamada responded. "I doubt you know the half of what he's done. I know what he's done to you, and I'm sorry. The last thing I want to do is release a creature like that on the world, but my hands are tied." He turned around and started walking back to his desk.

Mina was at a complete loss and began silently sobbing. The last time she was awake, everything had been wonderful, and one way or another, things were going to be fine. Now, she was alone, violated, back in hell.

"Just try and rest."

Raven awoke first, scratching at her neck in confusion. She grabbed something sticking out of her and looked at it. It was a dart, like the tranquilizer darts she'd seen in movies and TV shows, complete with the red fuzz at the back end.

She suddenly sat with a start, remembering seeing someone in the room last night.

Mina wasn't in the bed.

She wanted desperately to believe that she had just gotten up already, that she was in the bathroom or downstairs, but she knew it couldn't be true. The dart was proof enough of that. She wanted to scream, she wanted to cry, but did neither. She would check on the Phillips, make sure they were okay, and then she was getting Mina back.

There was only one place she could be, only one organization that would have come after her. Two things needed to be figured out, though: how they had found her, and why they had only taken Mina. She remembered the number Emma had given her; she figured maybe, maybe she could help her.

"Ahem."

She looked over to the door, and a disheveled Steve was standing there, holding an identical dart, a puzzled look on his face.

"Do you know anything about this? Uh, where's Mina?"

"They came last night and took her. I think. I'm sure."

"Uh, my mom's gonna be pissed." He was still woozy from sleep and it took him a second to catch up. "Wait, what? They took her."

"Yes. And I'm going to get her back."

One Hundred Sixty-Eight:
Motel Surgery

After a couple days of anxious uncertainty, Emma had finally made up her mind to pack her things in her car and just leave town. She had brought two bags from home and hadn't done anything with them beyond taking out a change of clothes the previous day. She got up to grab them and was startled by an unfamiliar ring tone. It took her a moment to realize that it was her emergency phone, and she had only given the number to one person.

She considered not answering, even destroying the phone and leaving, but her conscience, which had been on a roller coaster for weeks, got the better of her.

"Hello?"

"Dr. Jacobson?"

"Raven."

"They took her. They took Mina." Raven sounded panicked. "I need to get in there. I need to know where she's being held."

"Just a moment." Emma took a deep breath. Going back could be suicide. Or...it could be business as usual, but she didn't think that to be likely.

"Fine. I'll help. Get something to write on. I need you to meet me somewhere."

"Okay. My friend Steve is going to bring me."

Emma gave her the address and told her to hurry. After they hung up, Raven looked around the table. Steve was sitting to her side, and Mrs. Phillips was across from her.

"Steve will take me to see Dr. Jacobson. After that, I'll be on my own. You won't see me again."

Mrs. Phillips looked apologetic, but worried. "I'm sorry. It's just..."

Raven cut her off. "You don't have to say anything. They broke into your house last night. It could have been a lot worse. I'm a danger to your family."

She tried to lighten the mood and looked over at Steve. "Stop brooding, butthead!"

He got up, refusing her eye contact. "Go get your coat. I'm gonna get the car started. I guess, this time, at least I get to say good-bye."

She heard the front door close and she sighed. "I shouldn't even have come here."

"He knows you're alive. At least there's that."

Steve looked over as Raven got in the passenger's side. "Not exactly going for subtle, huh?" She had on white pants and a black tank top with a large heart on it, and was wearing a neon pink winter coat with a fur-lined hood. It was on the warm side, but the snow was blinding and she had large sunglasses on.

"Well, you didn't get *all* my clothes."

"It's fine. It's cute. Just not what I'd wear to sneak into a military building."

"I doubt I'll be doing much sneaking."

"Just—," Steve began, not really sure what to say. "If—when—you get out, at least let me know you're okay, all right?"

"I promise."

"Now, where are we going?" She handed him the address. "Jeez, this is at the edge of town. Probably some crappy motel. Yeah—here's the room number."

"I'd die for a cigarette right now."

About twenty minutes later there was a knock at Emma's door. She opened it and a young man was standing there. "You Dr. Jacobson?"

"Yes. Are you Steve?"

"Yeah." He yelled over his shoulder. "Okay! C'mon." He walked inside.

"By all means," said Emma, mildly exasperated. She held the door open and Raven walked in afterwards, and took off her sunglasses.

"This isn't as bad as I thought it'd be. Dr. Jacobson—can you get me inside?"

"Slow down a second. Come here. And call me Emma. No point in formalities anymore."

Raven walked over to the couch and sat down. There was a tray on a small table, with a scalpel, scissors, surgical needle and thread, syringe, and alcohol wipes. There was also a gray, plastic rectangle with an LCD display.

"What's that for?" Raven asked suspiciously, pointing at the tray.

Emma sat down next to her while Steve walked around and checked out the fridge.

"It's how they found you. You have an RFID tag in your arm with a GPS locator. I'm going to remove it."

"So...it's my fault."

"No, it's my fault. I didn't think to warn you before you left. Give me your arm."

"Can I have a beer?" Steve asked from the other side of the room.

"How old are you?" Emma asked.

"Not old enough."

She sighed. "Yeah, and bring me one too."

The gray rectangle was an RFID reader, and Emma was using it to scan Raven's arm. She heard the top pop off of two beers, and Steve walked over and set one down on the table.

The machine beeped. "Found it." She set it down, opened one of the alcohol wipes, and cleaned the area. She grabbed the syringe. "Local anesthetic."

Steve sat down across from them and took a chug out of his beer. He saw Raven wince as Emma injected her with the syringe. "You're gonna cut her arm open? Gross."

"You're going to watch, aren't you?" asked Raven.

"Of course."

A few minutes later, Raven was staring at the stitches on her arm. Emma walked out of the bathroom. "I flushed it. We're clean. Let's go."

"I...." began Steve.

"Go home," Raven said, concern in her voice. "I'll call you." She walked over and hugged him tightly.

"Changed my mind. I'm not going to say good-bye," he said.

"That's fine, butthead," Raven responded. They laughed, and stepped apart. She wiped a tear out of her eye. Steve nodded to her, then to Emma, and left.

Neither Emma nor Raven spoke during most of the ride to the Gates Building. When they were a few blocks away, Raven finally questioned her. "So, do you have, like, a plan or anything?"

"I have an idea. You remember Benny? He can phase, possibly teleport. I'm going to try to get him to take you to Mina, and then get you both out."

"Hmm. Interesting. That might actually work."

They were quiet for another minute, and then Emma spoke up. "Look, I'm not doing this because I want forgiveness from you or Mina. I'm doing it because it's right. The last couple months I've gone down a dark path at my job and I've seen proof of how much deeper it can go. I can't stand it anymore, and I'm scared."

"Scared?"

"Did Mina tell you about Matthew?"

With her sunglasses on, Raven's surprise at this question was not evident to Emma. She nodded.

"He's in the building, somehow. I think he's controlling my boss. I know Mina's important to you. I'll do my best to make this work for you, but when it's done, I'm out."

"Damn right, she's important to me. She's my girlfriend," Raven said, matter-of-factly.

"Oh."

The silence resumed.

Emma let Raven out about a block away from the parking structure after handing her her cell phone. "Don't go too far. I'll text you when...when I've got something."

Raven nodded and stepped out of the car. She watched Emma drive off. At this point, she trusted her, but the Matthew angle was disturbing.

She decided to go get a coffee.

One Hundred Sixty-Nine:
In the Lion's Den

Emma parked her car and began her walk to work. Thinking of Raven, sitting next to her, her sunglasses hiding her eyes and her voice devoid of emotion, she couldn't help but be overcome by the surreal nature of it. Seeing her in the confines of NOD, as a test subject, she could (though not without difficulty) put aside certain...concerns. But, seeing her outside the building, having a conversation with her, meeting a friend of hers for Christ's sake...it was hard to believe that they were the same person. But, they were, and it only deepened Emma's guilt.

She reached her office without fanfare, passing only a few guards and scientists, none of whom seemed to pay her much attention. She pulled up a status report. Nearly half of the staff wasn't present; there were no on-going or scheduled experiments. Jameson was tasked with rounds. As for the building itself, the White Room on subbasement two and the SDF laboratory on forty-four listed as off-limits. Mina was probably in one of those rooms.

It suddenly occurred to Emma that it was strange that Mina had been taken but not Raven. What could be the purpose behind that?

The answer suddenly came to her. "Matthew," she said aloud. He wanted her back.

"He's busy right now," answered a voice in front of her. Startled, she looked around the side of her computer monitor. Benny was standing in front of her door.

"Did you...did you phase in?"

"No."

"So, you really can teleport."

"There's a lot we can do that we haven't showed you," Benny said. That one admission threw everything Emma thought she knew and had learned about the entire NOD project system into doubt.

"What can you tell me about Matthew?" she asked.

"There isn't much time. He's Angel now, anyway. Keiko and Johnny sent me. I'm supposed to get Raven, right?"

"Yes. Can you?"

"Where is she?"

Screw texting, Emma thought. She dialed her emergency phone using her regular cell. After a moment, Raven answered. "Emma?"

"Yes. Where are you?"

"The coffee shop. About two blocks away, near where you dropped me off."

Unfortunately, in this day and age, that didn't really help. "The one at the north side of the street, or the south?"

"Um, ...south," she answered.

"You sure?"

Raven thought for a moment. "Yeah."

"Okay. Wait there. Bye."

"Bye."

Emma hung up.

"I need you to think about exactly what it looks like," Benny said. "And how you get there."

She did her best to visualize the place. She felt a dull pressure on the front of her head.

"Got it," Benny said.

Emma narrowed her eyes. "You're an intrusive telepath, too?"

Benny held his finger up to his mouth as if to say "shh," and then he vanished.

Emma sat, shocked, for a moment. She decided then, that perhaps Benny knew, but if not, she needed to find out for sure where Mina was. She got up and left her office.

She hadn't walked for more than a minute when she ran into Jameson, who looked even more disheveled than he had when they last spoke.

"Emma? I wasn't expecting you...."

"Spencer. Uh...yeah, I was feeling better. Got some rest."

"Can we go talk in your office?"

She whispered, "everything's under surveillance."

"It doesn't matter anymore," he said, slowly shaking his head.

Moments later, they were in her office.

"Dr. Yamada is here," Jamesone said.

"Hanin and Utsugi's predecessor?"

"Yes."

"Why?" Emma asked.

"I'm not sure. But they have Mina. Yamada invented jade implants that aren't rejected by healers. He said you can use them to deliver drugs to them safely...I helped him make IV needles. They're sedating her for something."

"Okay," she said, taking everything in so far. It was standard procedure to keep test subjects drugged; a new method that would work on Mina didn't explain what they were doing to her. She was fairly certain the reason Mina had been re-acquired was because of Matthew, but hopefully Jameson knew more.

"Yamada told me about the prototype series—Matthew, Andrew, and Angel—and he checked the cryo-bay manifest. Angel is gone. He thinks that

Matthew has taken control of it, like he did with Mina. And this Angel is supposed to be designed to be very powerful."

"I saw Benny earlier," Emma admitted. "He told me Matthew was Angel now. Where's Yamada now?"

"I'm not sure. I can't get a hold of him via the intercom. We worked in the White Room on the implants, and subbasement two is completely off-limits. But, so is forty-four."

"Yeah, I noticed that." She felt it was best not to tell Jameson what she was actually up to, but she quickly texted Raven. *White Room or 44. Maybe Benny can check first?*

Jameson gave her an exasperated look.

"Sorry."

For a moment, Emma entertained a crazy thought: that they should just go straight to Richardson and just lay all their cards on the table. That could be suicidal, though. Then: "Have you thought, maybe, that Keiko and Johnny know exactly what's going on?"

"Their supposed precognition has been uncanny in the past, in the few instances when they were actually specific."

"I'm wondering if there's a bigger picture here they are aware of that we're not. Maybe we should go see them."

"I tried asking them for information," Jameson said, sounding depressed. "They said 'paths are shifting' and...." His voice trailed off. Emma's eyes widened, waiting for him to continue.

"They said I had no place in what was to come, whatever that means," he finally said. Emma tried not to look let down; it wasn't exactly the earth-shattering news she was hoping for.

She thought for a moment and decided she wasn't going to divulge any more information to Jameson. She wasn't one hundred percent sure he was trustworthy, and she didn't want him to know about Raven or that she was leaving town as soon as Raven was done. It was about time to end this conversation so she could monitor what was going to happen.

"Did you want to go see them?" Jameson asked.

"Who?" Emma responded, lost in thought.

"Keiko and Johnny."

"Oh. Maybe later. I have paperwork to catch up on."

Jameson shrugged. "There hasn't been anything much going on, but all right." He got up and left after Emma nodded and pretended to start looking through the papers on her desk. When her office door closed, she set them down and breathed deeply. She took her glasses off and nibbled nervously on one of the temple bars.

"Good luck, Raven," she muttered under her breath.

One Hundred Seventy:
Check, Please

The door opened to the coffee shop and what appeared to be, at first glance, a young boy came in. There were hushed gasps at his appearance from patron and staff alike. His skin was almost translucently pale; his eyes, colorless. The fact that he was alone, walking with confidence, added to everyone's surprise.

Of everyone who saw him, only one person wasn't surprised. She sat in the back corner table, eyes hidden behind sunglasses, watching him approach.

"Hi, Raven."

"Hi, Benny."

"Are you ready to go?"

"Can you take me to her?"

"Yes," he answered. "But Keiko and Johnny want you to see something first. They said it's very important."

"Benny...I don't really have time for side trips. Mina's in danger. I have no idea what they're doing to her."

"It's okay," Benny said. "You can take a path that will lead right back to about when you left. It's all circles and arcs."

"Where am I going?" she asked, puzzled.

"Nod," he said, simply. He held out his hand. She took it.

They vanished.

One Hundred Seventy-One:
Implications

Angel sat on his make-shift throne and surveyed the "court" he'd created: a debris-strewn room with "pillars" he'd made by mentally crushing and reshaping the SDF chambers and other objects. They formed a semi-circular line, cutting the almost-square room into two parts, with his throne in one corner, facing towards the center of the room (and the line of pillars.)

He smiled, a nefarious, toothy grin. Down, down below, over forty stories beneath him, a new life stirred in the womb of its unwilling mother. He would visit her later; he was tired now, the constant thrum of power he was drawing off of Arty was actually fatiguing his incomplete body. He dialed back the flow to allow himself time to recover.

Richardson was sitting in an unused office near the bottom floor; he was trying to stay as far from Angel as possible, without getting too close to the White Room, where Mina was. His nerves were shot, and both Angel and the thing growing in the White Room (inside Mina) filled him with dread. He was so on edge that he jumped when his cell phone rang. He almost dropped it trying to answer it.

"Nicholas?"

"Joshua, goddamit, what the hell were you thinking!?"

"Sir?" He had a lot on his mind; he honestly didn't know offhand what Kresge was referring to.

"Blackmailing Yamada. I just got a call from his director. She wanted to call you herself, but she doesn't need to know everything that's happened there. You've taken an already explosive, hell, an exploded, situation, and made it worse. The advisory committee is going to be out for blood after they hear about this."

"They...don't know yet?"

"Right now, they only know what I tell them, Joshua. You're damn lucky of that." He had no intention of protecting Richardson, but he wanted some answers.

"To be fair, sir, it was your idea."

Kresge was silent. Richardson continued after a bit. "I'm moving forward. I'm not going to sit around and do nothing while waiting to lose my job." It seemed a reasonable answer to his frazzled mind.

"Fine. Fair enough." Kresge didn't want to risk Richardson implicating him, so he was going to have to let this one go for now. "Just next time, run it by me first?" Not that there should be a next time, he hoped.

"Sure. Anything else?"

"No." Kresge hung up the phone before anything else could be said. Something was going on and he was damned if it was going to stand in his way.

One Hundred Seventy-Two:
East of Eden

Raven floated with Benny in the airless void they were phased into. She was oblivious to the vibrations that wracked the giant room they were in. They were nearing a large ring of hazy yellow light with dim rays extending outward from it. A black sphere sat at the center, above it an intimidating tentacle with three spikes sticking out of it.

They were approaching at a low angle to avoid getting too close to the tentacle. Despite the bizarre nature of what she was seeing, Raven was calm.

Benny brought her near to the ring. *I'll be right here, waiting. I'll grab you as soon as you come out. I'll put you on a path that comes back in moments. Don't worry. You have to learn something.*

She was apprehensive, but willing, now. *All right,* she answered.

He took her in to the sphere and touched her to it, and let go....

And light overwhelmed her, and she felt so full of energy she thought she was going to burst.

The next sensations were not as pleasant. They were completely undefinable by human standards, and they carried with them a multi-sensory vertigo so strong they surpassed any sense of nausea that a terrestrial human had ever experienced. The result was agony on a level so far beyond anything she ever knew as possible, that it threatened her very consciousness.

Sight, hearing, taste, smell, and touch combined in a way wholly alien to what her brain was used to. Full 360-degree sight left her unable to reconcile her normal viewpoint with her new ability to simultaneously experience not just what was in front of her, but also behind her, around her, within her, and without her; smell and taste overwhelmed her cortex with a blood-like, coppery sensation that felt like the bleeding of a lost tooth multiplied and extrapolated over her whole tongue and her whole surface. Hearing and touch combined into a distance-based perception of the vibrations and undercurrents of space/time itself. Proprioception inundated her, her limbs no longer defined by a static placement; it was as though she were a hecatonchire; she had no limbs, nay, a hundred limbs, in every perceivable orientation that could provide useful data to her brain, and many more that did not seem to.

Of the rest of her non-elementary senses, her sense of heat was neutralized, and the apparent void seemingly provided a comforting nature; pain was more than negated, filling her with a bodily experience of sub-conscious pleasure. Her sense of time became immediately, absurdly fluid, and greatly contributed to her vertigo. Reversal of time was still an obvious impossibility, but forward movement became alternately choppy and dreamy, and standstills seemed reasonable, at least as momentary lapses in any forward-moving process.

As immediately as she created the thought that she couldn't stand it, however, she found that she could. It may have been an eternity of anguish and scrambled thoughts and senses that brought her to that point but once she passed the crescendo, it seemed but an instant. There was no way to tell, and likely, no real meaning. As much as the human mind looks back on endured pain in a truncated way, so as not to harm the sanity of a being with the full remembrance, this was similar, yet, more real, as though the time span had literally shrunk in retrospect, and not just in the thought of it.

The whole ordeal was akin to a bright light momentarily ruining vision; slowly, it comes back, details sharpening, afterimages fading, until sight was fully restored. It was very much like that indeed, but multi- (and cross-) sensory.

Only then did she perceive her surroundings in anything resembling order.

Her surroundings were like what she had envisioned outer space to be, though alive in a way the gaps between planets and stars could not be. There was a *graying*, an uncertainty of time, location, and emptiness that seemed to roil and bubble at a scale just slightly beyond what she could see, yet close enough to perceive, only just.

She turned to herself, and the multiple states her body existed in seemed to create a rosette that constantly turned inward into itself and simultaneously spread outward. She was orange-yellow, the color of her aura.

She became aware of presences around her, like living wavelengths that flitted by in a multitude of colors and shapes.

She could see, at all distances and in all sizes, what looked like tears in space. Out of one came a being, more like her in appearance than the wavelengths she saw. It was a rosette like she, only green and gray.

There was something in a particular direction, at the very edge of her vision, that she couldn't quite make out. It was a long shape, and it gave the impression of a roiling, bubbling surface. The more she concentrated on it, the more it seemed to come into a more defined sense of reality and vision. It was suddenly aware to her that there were seven of them, not one.

They were mountains, no, continents, perhaps worlds—they sat on the exact edge of vision, and scale was impossible to tell, and it was certainly possible that scale was of no reliable meaning in regards to them. They were huge, for sure, and felt threatening—always at the exact edge of vision, but always feeling like they were coming closer, slowly, slowly, but surely. Their edges were indeterminate and always changing; they had an aura about them, like flies, and looking at them, she tasted *yellow*, and was afraid.

"They are Leviathan," the other being spoke to her. "Spoke" wasn't entirely accurate; she heard the words, but she also felt them, and each seemed to wriggle off in a myriad of directions of subtext and language. The voice *seemed* to be a man's.

"I'm scared," she said simply, but her words also seemed to lead to dozens of others each quieter than the previous. It was almost overwhelming.

"I'm going to hazard a guess that you're human," the being told her, "and thus your confusion is that you were born into a three-dimensional perception of space and that is how your mind is trying to explain everything to you. It's not entirely incorrect; you can move that way if you wish, but you need to learn to view things differently to see the pockets where structure are, as they are in higher forms. It is lucky the Wyrm sent you here, as we were told of your arrival, and I came to meet you. You aren't rooted in a pocket, and your arrival was quasi-random. If I was not here to meet you, you could have wandered forever without learning to turn your perceptions."

"I see...they're like tears."

"Maybe you're a natural, then."

"What is the 'Wyrm'?"

"Your 'Arty'. The Great Wyrm of Earth. He is an anachronism, born of a cosmically unlikely intersection of chances. He sent you here, with very specific instructions given by the two. I am to show you how to pull back the shroud, and root you in the light of glory. Oh, how rude of me! What shall I call you?"

"Raven. And you are?"

"Twilloughby, though you may call me 'Twill' if you prefer. I rather dislike 'Obie.' Come, hold my hand, and I'll take you to The City."

The way he said "The City," the meanings that dripped off, it was clearly with great meaning, it felt capitalized, no commonness about that noun in this regard. It held meaning of turmoil, of work that would have called the pyramids mere trinkets in comparison. It was both mental and physical, and in this multidimensional world, it gave both the reassuring embrace of normal physics as well as the chaos of unlimited, unchecked growth.

Not really having much other choice, Raven tried to move towards Twilloughby, but felt something innately weird about the geometry.

"I...I'm not sure how," she said.

"You're not accustomed to fourth-dimensional space. Time is a construct here; everything is movement. Concentrate on me and you will figure out how to move."

A fourth-dimensional space, where it seemed empty, wasn't that hard to look at. Empty was empty (at least, the perception of emptiness was similar.) Though Raven could feel it buzzing, this higher-dimensional space looked no different really than the 3D space she was used to.

She tried to concentrate on Twilloughby, and found in moments that she could perceive cross-sections, and these revealed three-dimensional cross-sections of him, but they roiled into one another and she could not maintain focus on any one for long. She had momentary, absurd visions of a giant cat.

Slowly, she began to move, and she took delight in it.

"What is 'The City?'" she asked.

"Gloria Incandessa, the Light Behind the Shroud, the Truth Behind the Veil, the Secret Behind the Curtain...it has many names. It is a construct that you will find more...bearable, if not usual."

Momentarily, she was near enough to reach out, and dozens of her perceived limbs seemed to grasp dozens of his. He pulled her towards a tear, and it opened inward, and the light that met her—a hundred of her eyes cried, it was so beautiful.

And then, she saw it as a whole, a city so vast, so indescribable, with architecture of every describable (and some indescribable) types, bathed in light, with tall, noble trees and a multitude of people walking its streets. Some of them were clearly more than people; others, a little less. Her mind was bursting with a hundred fantasy worlds she had read of. There was no longer any doubt in Raven's mind of Nod's power; that it reached into the psyche of every mortal was no longer a question; it was just a matter of how attuned one was to its secrets.

They set down on a grassy hill, clouds above and below in the endless sky. A single tree gave shade as a light breeze scattered dandelion seeds. A path led from the tree to the city proper.

Raven realized that she was herself again, a simple (not really so simple) girl. It was with great shock that she viewed Twilloughby in his true self. He was at least six feet tall, impeccably dressed in a black pin-stripe suit, with a matching fedora and a gold chain that probably led to a pocket watch. His hands, however, were covered in gray fur, his fingernails like claws. His head was immense; a gray and black tabby cat's with a wide, toothy grin, and brilliant yellow cat's eyes. His hat sat squarely between his ears. A tuft of light gray hair sat on each cheek, giving the impression of mutton chop sideburns.

"You're...not human," Raven said with trepidation. She found that here, her words didn't multiply and continue; speech was as she was used to it.

"I may have been once," he said. He took his hat off and bowed. "Twilloughby, at your service. I will be your guide and perhaps your friend."

One Hundred Seventy-Three:
Second Trimester

"I can't find Benny. Isn't that odd?"

Mina could feel the heat of his breath, he was standing so close to her, leaning over her. He placed a clawed hand on her swollen abdomen.

"See how quickly he grows? It's...convenient."

"What are you going to do with me when it's out?"

"I've been thinking about that," Angel answered. "I suppose I'll kill you. You won't serve any other purpose to me, and I don't want you and your friend trying anything funny. She'll be easier to confront without you helping her."

Mina had no doubt that he meant what he said, but she'd only just found life, only just found love. She refused to despair. "She'll come for me. I know it."

"That's funny that you say that." He ran his index finger in a circle around her stomach. "I could have sworn I sensed her earlier, but now I don't. How strange."

She could feel the energy crackling off of him as he touched her, sense the malice in his intentions. The power in him was very evident. The world was new to her, but she couldn't bear the thought of letting a monster like him out into it.

He stood up abruptly and turned around. "Joshua, where is the good doctor?"

"Sleeping. He hasn't rested since he arrived until now."

"Keep her company, will you? I'm going back upstairs." He quickly left the room.

Richardson was glad to be free of his presence, but not so much to be down in the White Room with Mina.

She looked at him desperately. "Please, let me out of here," she pleaded.

Richardson merely shook his head. "I couldn't if I wanted to."

Several minutes passed. Richardson leaned against a supply crate, smoking a cigarette. He avoided eye contact with Mina. He felt the presence in his mind wane, as it had before. Why, he wasn't sure. Perhaps Angel required rest like any person would, and this weakened his grasp. Maybe it was the deficiencies he complained about of the body he had. Whatever the case, he wasn't going to let this chance get away.

"I want to be clear of one thing," he said, looking at her now. "You are a thing to me. An object to study. But...the situation at hand...is out of control. I know he touched your mind, and you know how full of spite he is."

She merely looked at him, silently. He continued. "He's been in my head for...I'm not even sure anymore. Days? It feels like forever. You have no idea how empty his heart is. I don't understand his motivations, or if he even really has a plan, but I don't doubt whatever he does, it's going to kill a lot of people."

"There's a knife in that desk," Richardson said, pointing at Yamada's desk, off to his side. "A hunting knife." He walked over to her, cigarette still in hand. He touched a fingertip to her belly. "Right here. It's big enough; it'll be in the front. If your friend comes for you, if *anything* gives you the chance—*you cut that thing out of you and you kill it, do you understand me?*"

She nodded as best she could.

"Good." He flicked his cigarette off into the distance and, turning away, lit another.

One Hundred Seventy-Four:
One Foot In and Out

Raven walked with Twilloughby down a wide lane with colonial style houses on either side. Most of the trees were covered in green leaves, but here and there she saw a purple or blue tree. Those that they walked past seemed mostly human, and were dressed in all manner of outfits, from tee shirts and jeans to tweed suits to robes. She caught the eye of a man with a long, elliptical face, and four arms. He nodded to her in greeting. She heard chirping and looked up in time to see a flock of rainbow-patterned swallows fly past.

"I have a lot of questions to ask," she said bluntly.

"Good for you, then, as I have a lot of answers. Hopefully, they fit your questions."

"Okay, let's start with the basics. What is this place?"

"Well, the place where I found you—your scientists call it 'Nod.' It has a true name, a long name, that's very hard to remember. We usually just call it 'the sea.' It's a multi-dimensional, frothing fluid space with many pocket dimensions. Many of those are three-dimensional, like this one, and are easy to live and work in."

"So," asked Raven, "there are other places like this?"

"Yes, but this is the largest. It's kind of a capital, and our most well-guarded outpost," Twilloughby answered.

"What's it guarded from? Those things out there?"

"Yes, the Leviathan. And the occasional interloper."

A strange group of creatures passed them. Raven's best attempt at a mental description was that they looked like human-sized grasshoppers in wizard robes. She shook her head, dumbfounded.

"Those guys look like wizards," Raven said, after they had passed.

"They *are* wizards," Twilloughby said plainly.

"Like, magic-wizards?" she asked, surprised.

"You can move things with your mind, can't you?"

"Point taken, Twill."

Raven looked ahead. Far away, past the end of the lane, she could see what looked to be a castle of sorts, but with towers and parapets mirroring the different types of architecture she had seen when arriving. She would definitely have to ask about that. First, though—

"How did I get here? How do people get here at all?"

"That's a big question. You came here through a portal created by your scientists. That's one way. Some came here with magic, some had powers like yours, only stronger, or different. Some got lost and wound up here. Others were asked to come. There are nearly as many ways to reach the sea as there are inhabitants of it."

"And they're not all humans," Raven said. "Are they aliens?"

"I suppose so. They're not even all from your universe."

"This is...this is...." She struggled to find the right word. Amazing? Too small. Absurd? Yes, but useless.

"I suppose this seems a bit much this late in the game, yes?"

She had no idea what he meant. He continued.

"You're here to learn something very important. Do you know the two called 'Keiko' and 'Johnny' from the institute you were at?"

"I know who they are," Raven said.

"They sometimes communicate with us about important matters, usually, things that may affect both of our worlds. Since your scientists have impinged upon the sea, it's become a necessity. They can see everything, but the further away it gets the murkier and more uncertain it gets."

"Isn't that kind of how vision works?" she said, a slightly bratty tone in her voice.

"Oh. I meant in time."

"All right, then. So why am I here?"

"Ah, we're here!" Twilloughby pointed to a pleasant looking, small colonial. "Come in for some tea before we continue our journey? I know there's a lot on your mind. The tea will help."

Raven half-expected cat toys and the like, but the inside of the house was well-appointed, with antique looking furniture, several full bookshelves, and large, comfortable looking chairs. One thing caught her eye, though. It sat atop a pedestal in the corner of the living room. It was made of metal wire, and looked like a cube within a cube, and it seemed to continually rotate in on itself.

"What is that?" she asked, pointing at it.

"Oh, that. I made that," Twilloughby said. "It's a tesseract. A fourth-dimensional cube, more or less. Here, like in your realm, the fourth dimension is time, so it can only show us one face at once, which changes as time passes."

He led her into a combination kitchen/dining room. He had a small stove but normal, earthly amenities as well: a refrigerator, a microwave, even a dishwasher. He put a small kettle on the stove and turned the burner on. He bade Raven to have a sit and he sat as well.

"So, where were we? Yes! That's right. You wanted to know why you're here. We were talking about Keiko and Johnny."

"Yes. You said they can, what, see the future?"

"They see probable futures. Very little is certain until it gets very near to them, and even then, sudden changes can occur. But they're pretty sure about this. Do you know about a boy named Matthew?"

At the mention of this name, Raven's face dropped. She responded in a depressed tone. "My—girlfriend, Mina—she was...assaulted by him. Mentally, I think, but she said it seemed physical. He made her do horrible things."

"A long time ago, he came here with a girl called Anna." Raven wondered if it was the same Anna from the institute—clearly she had come back, if it was. "We invited them in. We didn't know what he'd done, yet. She accepted, but he declined."

It must be a different Anna, Raven thought.

"He said—I wasn't there, you know, so I'm not exactly sure—something about The City being fake. That the light hurt him. He didn't believe in a place that was just a construct. He lashed out at us, and left. But he couldn't go back to your realm; his path was cut off."

"So how did he attack Mina?"

Twilloughby looked deep in thought. At this pause in conversation, Raven reminded herself that she was speaking to a giant cat in a suit. In a floating city. In another dimension.

Her head hurt.

"It's easiest to say," Twilloughby finally continued, "that he moves in cycles. Every so often, he could go back. You know, we asked him back in now and then. I believe in forgiveness, as does much of the council that leads this City. But he always declined, and every time he left for your world he did terrible things. Which brings us back to Keiko and Johnny."

The kettle began to whistle and he got up and walked over to it. It was only now that Raven realized he did not have a tail.

He poured the water into two mugs, one, very large, one normal-sized. He placed several tea bags into the large one and a single bag into the small one, and then walked back over to the table, setting the small mug in front of Raven. Next to his enormous, furry head, the large mug looked normal. He sat back down.

"They told us that he had permanently entered your world, and a certain conflux of events would put you in the right place to aid in his defeat. And he must be defeated, they said. He's grown desperate and angry, and quite possibly a bit insane, not having his physical body for so long. Some beings don't do so well without one, you know."

"Of course," Raven agreed, shrugging. She sipped the tea; it was actually quite good, and she wasn't really a fan of the stuff. "So like what? I have to fight him? A psychic duel or something? I just want to save my girlfriend from those doctors and get the hell out of town. I don't have time to defeat some psychic madman with a chip on his shoulder."

"Apparently," said Twilloughby, pausing to take a large sip of his tea, "you're not going to have a choice. And, it changes your future."

"I don't get it. What do you mean, I don't have a choice? What about my future?"

"You're on a path that leads, very far down the line, to destruction. Whether now or later in life, you will fight him. Your paths intersect, no matter what. Keiko was very specific on that. But this new intersection, this one is better, they said. It happens specifically because Mina was captured. Matthew himself was the one who ordered it. All the right people are in the right place, but it has to be before nightfall."

Raven's heart dropped. *Okay, maybe I do want to fight this asshole after all,* she thought. "So why is this 'intersection' better?"

"Because, if you wait, he kills a lot of people, and when you finally do fight, it dramatically damages your world. That's what I think, anyway. Specifically, they said it 'tears the world apart.'"

"All right. Let's say I go along with this." She sipped her tea while choosing her next words. "How do I defeat him?" She chuckled. "I'm pretty sure I could crush him. I can move some really heavy stuff with my abilities."

"You're going to *help*. I'm supposed to show you something that finishes it. I'm supposed to introduce you to Anna."

"Benny—the boy that brought me here—said I can return not long after I left. How is that possible?"

Twilloughby thought how best to explain. "Time...it's kind of like a thick fluid. It flows differently in different places. You came here on an arc that rounds back almost to its point of origin. So, no matter how much time you spend here, you'll go back to a certain time in your world."

"That's...terribly convenient," Raven said, confused by the whole matter all the same. "Can I go back earlier?"

"Oh no, I'm afraid time travel is strictly impossible."

A bizarre thought came to Raven. "Can I meet someone from my world here, who's from a different time?"

"*That*," answered Twilloughby, emphasizing 'that,' "is an excellent question."

"Well? Can I?"

"I have no idea," he chuckled.

"All right, Twill, one last question. For now." She set down her mug, now empty. "Who exactly are you? What do you do here?"

"I have many duties. Among them, I serve as a guide, to help new arrivals adapt to life here." He took the final sip of his tea.

It didn't answer her questions entirely, but it was good enough to pique her interest. "All right then, you said I basically have as much time here as I want?" She was worried about Mina, but if staying here didn't put her in any further danger, she may as well take advantage of it. She'd read a dozen books about magic cities in other dimensions; she'd be damned before she'd find herself in one and leave immediately. Since her first experience with psychic powers, things were becoming more and more weird while she was finding it less and less shocking. Adaptation, perhaps. And, her anxiety had waned. The tea, maybe?

"All right then, Twill," Raven said, standing up. "Show me the sights!"

"As you wish."

One Hundred Seventy-Five:
The City

The central boulevard cut straight through the City from edge to edge, with the castle in the center surrounded by a lush garden and circular roadway. Twilloughby's street came directly off of this boulevard, near the edge of the City's landmass. He and Raven walked to the boulevard, which was bustling with activity.

Beings of all shapes and sizes, from the very tiny to nearly giant, from the human to the indescribably bizarre, walked, shuffled, and floated to and fro between whatever errands or business they had.

One made Raven stop dead in her tracks, and she couldn't help but stare. It was at least ten feet tall, with lengthy, spindly arms and legs. Its torso was a narrow, tight coil, like a spring, and its skin (presumably it was its skin, as it appeared to be unclothed) was jet black. Its head was entirely different, though. She watched as it walked by; it was like a man's head, with the face repeated at every eye, forming a ring of faces topped with a cone-shaped scalp that glittered in the light as though covered in infinitesimal jewels. It paused briefly behind a group of short, lizard-like beings in cloaks. Too engrossed in their conversation to notice the giant, it gave up on waiting for them to move and in one long stride, moved swiftly over them.

"Wow," she said under her breath.

The boulevard was very wide, and the median was covered in well-manicured grass with the occasional tree or flower garden. Most of the buildings on either side were grander than the ones on Twilloughby's street, and they showed off the variety of architecture she had seen when she arrived. Many of the buildings looked like older-style buildings she'd seen from pictures of Europe: wooden-edge with plaster facades and shingled roofs. But there was Greek architecture, Roman architecture, columned buildings, some open completely to the air, with people in the center having lively conversations. There was a building made entirely of windowed cubes, each the size of a small house, attached to each other with no apparent rhyme or reason as to where. There were stranger buildings, too; collections of spheres or geodesic domes. Here and there was a small building; most appeared to be shops, with dozens of languages on most of their signs.

They continued on and on down the street, becoming harder and harder to make out with distance and angle, until far away Raven saw trees where the boulevard terminated, and above that, the castle she had seen earlier. It seemed to be, from her point of view, two rings of towers, with smaller, shorter ones surrounding a ring of larger, taller ones, with a grand, medieval castle jutting up in the middle. The towers did not all match the castle in design.

Raven couldn't help but feel giddy, and for now, her worries had subsided. She believed Benny and Twilloughby; Mina was but a moment away, at any moment. She felt some guilt at not rushing to her side; despite knowing she technically still *was*, it wasn't a way she was used to thinking. But the glory of this City—this world—was too much for her to ignore.

Twilloughby flagged down an open-top carriage led by two perfectly normal horses and controlled by a perfectly normal human. He tipped his hat to Raven. "Good to you two. Where to?"

"Hillpoint, please," Twilloughby answered.

"Sure thing. Careful stepping up."

Twilloughby held Raven's hand as she stepped up into the carriage, and then got in himself. Settled in as the carriage took off, he explained to her where they where going.

"Hillpoint is...an unusual place. It will afford you a much better look at the City than the brief one you had when we arrived."

Conversation was a non-issue on the way, as Raven was enthralled in just seeing the sights, which was difficult as the carriage seemed to be moving abnormally fast compared to what she expected. It took them about twenty minutes to reach what seemed to be about the halfway point between Twilloughby's street and the castle.

They had traveled up the left side of the boulevard; they got out, carefully crossing to the right. An unexceptional cobblestone path led between two brick buildings. It led to a large hill in a walled-in courtyard. They began to climb it.

Raven quickly understood why Twilloughby had said it was unusual. The angle appeared steep, but didn't cause much discomfort, and the climb seemed to take far longer than expected: the top of the hill never seemed to get any closer, and looking behind herself, Raven saw the tops of the nearby buildings much further below than they seemed like they would have been.

"Try not to look down until we reach the top. If you get alarmed, it's quite a roll down from here."

The hill seemed to widen as they climbed further, until its breadth was all Raven could see ahead of her. Finally, after what felt like forever, they reached the top of the hill. It was larger than the courtyard it had been in, and there was a wooden door standing in the middle. A gentle wind fluttered the grass around.

Raven looked down and gasped. Vertigo took her for a moment, despite the fact that she knew she could fly if she fell.

She was (deciding that Twilloughby's house was at the south) at the west side of the hill. She could see off to the southwest the rows and rows of streets and houses, with a river further north of that they had crossed over, the area surrounded in the hustle and bustle of street markets. A lake was located halfway up that river as it led to the northwest area of the City, a mostly wild-looking area of lakes, mountains, and forests. She could see the castle in more clarity, and was right about its design: two concentric rings of bizarre towers, with an enormous structure in the middle, the entire thing surrounded in vast gardens.

There seemed to be another boulevard running east-west, and reaching south from it, almost to the castle, and south further to a second branch of the river, were what looked like mansions, but she wasn't sure as again the architecture varied wildly. Far, far off to the southwest, past the river and north of Twilloughby's neighborhood, reaching almost to the edge of the City, was a collection of large buildings and what appeared to be canopied sections in front of most.

"What's that, all the way over there?" Raven asked, pointing towards that area.

"That's the commerce district," Twilloughby answered. "There are shops throughout the City but that is where most goods move in and out, and where the main markets are."

He pointed to the large houses south of the castle. "That is where the heads of state and affluent citizens live. And that," he continued, pointing towards the mountains and forests, "is the Wild." He began walking towards the southeast side of the hilltop. "Come here."

Raven walked over until she could see most of the southeast part of the City. At the south end, the residential area continued across the boulevard a ways, until the edge of the river. Between that and a lake formed from the more northerly branch was something else entirely.

In a wide depression crisscrossed with streams was a multitude of stone objects, monuments of some sort or another: obelisks, statues, abstract objects, from sizes so small she couldn't make out their forms, to so large they rivaled small skyscrapers. In the center was an enormous stone ring, standing on its edge. It appeared to be covered in inscriptions, but at her distance she couldn't make them out, and doubted they were in any language she was familiar with, anyway.

Past the lake to the north was row after row of long buildings, like warehouses, and at the end of the easterly boulevard, there seemed to be a massive system of docks, with what looked like ships gliding to and from it, through the air.

"What's that?" Raven asked, pointing towards the docks.

"That," Twilloughby answered, "is the industries and imports of Gloria Incandessa. We are not entirely self-sustaining."

She nodded in understanding. That, at least, made sense.

They walked around to the northeast side of the hill to view the final quadrant of the City. Not far from the castle was a massive structure like a giant, many-faceted jewel, glowing intensely in all the colors of the rainbow. It was a wondrous sight, something she had glimpsed when she first looked into the pocket, something that had awed her with its beauty.

Twilloughby knew immediately what caught her eye. "That's the Sanctum Solarium. That's where we're going to go."

In the midst of her amazement, she was still able to giggle at the reference.

"What is it?" Twilloughby asked, his large eyes narrowed in confusion.

"I don't think you'd get it," she answered. "I doubt you get basic cable here."

"Well, around the sanctum is the academy, the large group of buildings and fields surrounding it." The structures of the academy, let alone the grounds they were on, absolutely dwarfed any earthly college Raven had ever seen or was even aware of.

An arc of what looked like fortresses spread along the edge of the academy, from the north-south boulevard to the east-west one. Almost the entire quadrant beyond looked like a wasteland, and it bothered Raven to look at it. It was overwhelmingly gray, and filled with crooked, bizarre structures, many of them huge in size. The entire area, the objects as well as the ground itself, seemed to be in a state of constant, dizzying motion. It gave her the impression of an optical illusion, the kind made of concentric rings that gave the impression of wiggling spirals. The entire thing made her sick to her stomach, and she looked away.

"Beyond the academy is the Final Fortification, and the rest is the Incursion Zone." The tone of his voice had become somber. "We fought a desperate battle there once, long before my time. There were many, many deaths. The land is scarred to this day."

Raven saw a tear wet the fur of Twilloughby's face. Whatever the loss had meant, it must have been great, as it apparently spanned generations. She decided not to ask about it.

The City was amazing; it lived up to its absurd, overblown name, and then some. "I want to explore all of it," Raven said, her voice subdued with awe.

"You will," said Twilloughby, chuckling. "I have no doubt of that. One day, at least. For now, we have an appointment, and then you have a lover to save, yes?"

"Yes," said Raven softly, as she was snapped back to reality.

"This way," Twilloughby said as he gestured with his clawed hand towards the free-standing door in the center of the hill. He opened it, and Raven looked through. She saw the alley they had taken to the hill, facing out towards the Boulevard. She tentatively stepped through, followed by Twilloughby.

She heard the door close, and spun around. All she saw was the rest of the alley, and the lonely, small hill in the courtyard.

"It's a one-way door," Twilloughby said, addressing Raven's obvious confusion.

"Okay.... Anyway, Nod...the sea... what exactly is it, really?"

"Have you heard the term 'astral plane?'" She nodded. "It's probably easier to understand as that. It's a place where the mind is free to express itself. It's in a constant state of energy flux. That's where the energy comes from to build in the pockets."

She wasn't really sure if that explanation helped her any.

"Anyway, let's get another carriage, yes?" he continued. "It's quite a ways to the sanctum."

One Hundred Seventy-Six:
The Sanctum

The second carriage seemed to move just as quickly as the first, up the boulevard, towards the center of the City. A large stone bridge led over the second river, leading into the area immediately surrounding the castle. Off to her left, Raven saw the large houses and mansions where Twilloughby had said the affluent lived. Apparently, wealth was an issue even here, but even though she couldn't be absolutely sure, Raven was glad that she had not seen anything from the hill that looked like slums. She didn't like the idea that anyone should be living in poverty in a place so fantastic and literally other-worldly.

Off to the right, in the distance, through wooded meadows, she could just make out the ends of the long row buildings that were the City's industrial center. Ahead, however, was the castle, glorious in its tiered majesty. She couldn't directly see the base, as a tree-filled garden surrounded it as far as she could see, and here many of the plants varied wildly from anything she'd ever seen. There were trees with leaves of all colors, some with thin, squiggly branches, others with branches that grew into other trees, connecting them in intricate webs.

The carriage moved onto a circular road surrounding the castle and turned right. They drove directly along next to the garden. Raven saw flowers of more kinds than she had ever imagined, some in small clusters, others the size of dinner plates. Their perfume hung in the air, a smell that normally would have made her sick, but she was too enthralled to notice. She looked up, past the trees, to the first circle of towers. They were tall enough that at this close angle they almost completely obscured the ones behind. Some were stone cylinders, built like ones she had seen in books and on TV, with pointed, conical wooden roofs. Others were square...others were colossal zigzags or built of stacked cubes like the building she had seen earlier. The variety was astounding, and she wondered what kind of creatures used them...how many sights had she yet to see?

They rounded the castle further, coming to the east-west boulevard. As they passed it, Raven could see the academy come into view, and surprisingly (at this point) it looked like an ivy league university of completely normal, terrestrial appearance.

A glow became apparent as they continued around the circular road. It became brighter the further they traveled, but it was soft and not difficult to look at. Finally, the source came into view, the Sanctum Solarium, a large, faceted dome, each facet shimmering with colored light.

"Here we are," Twilloughby stated. The carriage began to slow down as it moved up the lane towards the building. They got out and Raven stared at the building. Its glow was now tangible around her; she could feel warmth, she could see the brightness in the air, on the ground, on her own skin. "This is where Anna is. This is what I'm supposed to show you."

They entered through paired glass doors, and immediately Raven was shocked; the building was somehow bigger on the inside than the outside. It was completely open, but there were terraces held up around freestanding columns with gentle spiral staircases leading up to and between them. Scattered throughout the air and on the terraces were groups of people in conversation. Raven saw many of them manipulating odd objects without touching them. Was it magic? Psychic?

Was there a difference?

The glow inside the building seemed more subdued; it was still there, but it was as if it was moving out through the facets and most of its energy was there. Up on one of the terraces Raven could see a brighter light, and that seemed to be where Twilloughby was leading her. Up close, she could see that the terraces were made of thick, colored glass edged in dull brass, with railing around the edges to prevent falls. The columns appeared to be nothing more than concrete, but the staircases were also glass and brass.

As they scaled one, Raven noticed a being like Twilloughby walk by, a tall humanoid cat-person, only this one was calico and wearing a simple sky blue dress. Raven smiled.

At the top of the stairs, Raven was met by an odd sight. Standing in the center was a girl, with what appeared to be a ball of pure white light floating above her hand. But what was odd was that the girl *was* the Anna Raven had seen, but healthy looking with normal skin tone and a full head of strawberry blond hair.

"That's Anna?" Raven asked. "That's who I'm supposed to see?"

"Yes," Twilloughby responded.

"She *is* the same girl from where I was being held...I saw her there, but she was frail and sickly like the other children."

"My understanding," Twilloughby began, "is that, Matthew invaded Anna's mind. She expelled him, and he pulled a piece of her with him. Somehow, they wound up here. So yes, it is the same Anna, or rather, a part of her."

"She's...just a mind?"

"Oh no, she's very much skin and bone. They're still connected, tenuously, though." They walked closer. "Miss Anna, you have a visitor."

The girl stared intently at the ball of light, and then in a literal flash, it was gone. She turned slowly to face the giant cat-man. "Hello."

"This is Raven. She's met your other-self."

Anna looked over at Raven. "Hello," she said again. "Do you want to see a trick?"

"Sure," said Raven.

Anna was wearing jeans and a tee shirt. She reached into her front pocket and pulled out a coin. She let Raven see it, and then threw it up into the air.

What exactly happened next, Raven wasn't really sure. There was a brief glow in front of Anna, and the coin seemed to burn in midair for a brief moment, giving off sparks and smoke. When it landed, Anna picked it up and showed it to Raven. There was a hole burnt clean through the middle.

"That's really neat," she said, turning to look at Twilloughby with a confused look on her face.

"Anna is what your scientists called 'photokinetic.' She can manipulate light."

"I gathered the light and made a laser out of it," Anna said.

Anna showed Raven a few other tricks. She made dark spaces by not letting light enter them; she made bright spots by channeling more light into those spots. She could change the direction of groups of waves, hold them in place, make then coherent, creating laser beams. The latter was obviously dangerous, and she only showed them the one time, and had aimed only at that coin.

Is that how she's supposed to help defeat Matthew? Raven thought. *Am I supposed to have a little girl fire lasers at him?* It seemed absurd. Surely any conventional weapon would be better than a little girl, even one with magic lasers.

They stayed for a time, Anna showing Raven tricks of the light. It seemed to make her happy to be able to share. There was color in her cheeks when she smiled that the "other" Anna never had.

Twilloughby pulled out his pocket watch and opened the gold cover. "Well, it's time we were going. I have other matters to attend to." He put the watch away and addressed Anna. "Do you remember what we talked about?"

"Yes. I'll be ready."

"Good." He tipped his hat to her. "Come Raven, let's be off."

As they walked away, Raven asked him, "I'm confused; is this about her, or the one in my world?"

"Both," he said. "You'll need both."

"Shouldn't she be coming with us, then?"

"It's a bit more complicated than that. She'll be ready when the time is right."

"All right, then." *Puzzles and riddles, all of it!*

They left the sanctum and walked down the lane for a bit until they found a carriage and they boarded it.

"You said you had other business to attend to?" Raven asked.

"Yes. You are, of course, welcome to stay as long as you want. But I imagine your heart is pulling you back."

"Yes," she said, quietly. "Mina...." She spoke more loudly now. "There's so much I want to see here. I want to understand everything."

"And you will," Twilloughby said confidently. "In time."

"How will I come back?"

"You'll find a way. Fate will probably push you back here, most likely."

"Do you know something?" she asked, her eyes narrow.

"Perhaps," he answered, his wide, toothy maw in a grin.

Puzzles and Riddles.

Twilloughby looked around at their surroundings. "I actually have a bit of free time still and I'd wager you're quite hungry by now. There's a very nice bistro around here. Care to dine? My treat."

Raven smiled. "Yeah, I'd like that, Twill."

Sometime later, the pair stood on the same hill with the single tree at the edge of the City where they arrived. "I'll take you to the edge of the pocket. After that, just follow your arc. When, some day, you return, you will recognize the shroud. You have now been here and once in the sea, you will be always able to find your way back."

"Thank you," she said. She still wasn't sure exactly what Anna meant, but she trusted that the fates (or, more correctly, Keiko, Johnny, Benny, and Twilloughby) meant well. She threw her arms around Twilloughby in a big hug, this strange, polite, giant cat man having shown her sights she had only ever dreamed of. After a surprised moment, he returned the gesture.

"It was very nice meeting you, Raven. Best of luck to you."

"Thank you."

Presently, they were floating, more so than flying, towards the upper sky, hands held. Raven glimpsed back as the City fell beneath her, and smiled at its wonder. Then, the light inverted, and the grayness pervaded her, but this time she was not overwhelmed by the sensation. She moved under her own free will to where she had entered this place, grimacing at the Leviathan as she did so. Then, she felt as if her many hands where held, and...

...she was floating with Benny near the portal. They vanished, and almost instantaneously appeared in a small room with a vending machine and chairs; a waiting room, by all appearances.

"How long was I gone?" Raven asked.

Benny looked up at a clock on the wall. "About fifteen minutes."

"Good."

"Are you ready to see her?"

Raven nodded emphatically. "Yes." Benny held out his hand, and she grasped it, and they vanished once again.

One Hundred Seventy-Seven:
Leaving

When Raven materialized, she was horrified at what she saw. Mina was strapped down to a hospital bed, IV tubes coming out of her arm and neck. She was wearing a hospital gown, and the bulge underneath it gave every indication that she was several months pregnant.

"Raven!" Mina was choked up as she yelled.

"Oh God, hun, what did they do to you?" She started to step forward.

Click.

"Don't move."

Raven turned slowly towards the sound, coming from the direction Mina's feet were pointing. Richardson was there, pointing a handgun at her.

His hands were trembling. He had wanted to see this done, let the *thing* be out and killed, but his hands weren't his own.

"You're the guy that runs this place, right?" Raven asked.

Richardson nervously laughed. *Not anymore.* "Something like that," he said. There was a push against his hand and his gun flew across the room, skittering along the floor.

"What do you possibly think you could do to me now?" Raven asked defiantly.

Richardson put his hands to his temples as an intense pain made him wince. *She's here!* Angel screamed into his brain.

"I know!" Richardson yelled. "Get down here!" Choices were gone.

No! I can't fight her yet! I'm not strong enough!

Raven gestured with her hand, and Richardson flew backwards against the shipping containers in the room with enough force to knock himself out cold. She ran over to Mina and broke the straps holding her down with telekinesis.

"You have to take the needles out," Mina said.

Raven's vision followed the IV tubes to their point of insertion. At their ends were odd, green needles with a somewhat crystalline structure. She removed them and carefully pocketed them.

Mina stood up shakily, leaning against Raven and burying her head in her chest. Raven put her arms around her and kissed her on the head.

"Mina?" She was crying. "It's going to be okay. I'm going to get you out."

"There's...there's a knife in the drawer. You have to...cut this thing out of me. Matthew put it there...it's evil." She looked up into Raven's eyes, which were now wet as well.

"I can't cut you open...I can't hurt you."

"You have to. Please."

Raven walked slowly to the desk, every nerve in her body fighting her orders. She opened the drawer and clumsily fumbled around until she found it. It had a black handle and matching sheath; she removed it slowly, carefully, revealing a curved blade with serrations on the edge opposite the smooth cutting side.

She walked back over to Mina, who lifted her hospital gown above her swollen belly.

Raven, still several feet away, dropped the knife, defeated.

"Can't...can't I just take you somewhere?"

"This thing's connected to him. He'll follow us; he'll find it. We can't risk bringing it."

Raven put her hands to her face. "I'm sorry, hun, I just can't cut you. I just can't."

"Turn around," Mina said. "Don't watch."

Raven did as she was told.

Mina telekinetically lifted the knife off of the ground and pointed it at her abdomen.

Raven had never heard anyone scream that loudly. The only saving grace was that she couldn't hear the cutting. Finally, after what seemed like an eternity, Mina told her she was done in a weak voice.

Raven turned back around and gasped at the site. Mina's belly was no doubt already knitting itself back together, but the front of her gown, as well as the ground beneath her, was drenched in blood. On the floor just in front of her was a pile of gore: placenta and umbilical cord, and a pathetic, pale blue organism, about the size of a cat and roughly the shape of a featureless fish with fat fins. Purple veins crisscrossed its surface. It writhed in agony, the knife buried in its side.

Mina was trembling and Raven could tell she was about to falter. She rushed over and grabbed her before she could fall. She held her tight, muttering apology after apology as she cried.

A voice startled them from across the room. "What the hell is going...." it began.

Daichi Yamada stared, incredulously, at the woman who could only be his daughter.

She was beautiful. She was all grown up.

He had missed most of that growing.

"You need to get out of here," he said.

"No shit," Raven said. "Benny?" She looked around. He was gone.

The man pointed to a set of doors on the wall far behind him. "There's a freight elevator through there. It goes right up to the surface." He tossed a key and Raven caught it. "Hurry. The guards will probably be after you, and *he* is going to be livid."

Richardson stirred. "Angel's coming," he slurred.

Raven looked at Mina questioningly. "Matthew's permanent body," Mina said.

There wasn't another moment to waste. Hand-in-hand, the two young women booked it for the freight elevator. Whether or not Raven truly believed in what Twilloughby had told her, she wasn't going to stick around and fight with Mina in the shape she was in. The girl healed, of course, but she had lost a lot of blood and probably wasn't in the best frame of mind.

When they had left the room, Yamada walked over to the discarded fetus and knelt next to it. With a bit of work he pried the knife out and used it to cut the umbilical cord. He watched as the wound in its side closed up.

Just then he became aware of a pressure, a mental dynamo in the room. "Angel," he said, standing up.

Angel stood nearby, holding Benny's hand. He gave the boy an angry, threatening look. He was furious at the boy's disappearance, and would have snapped his neck if his powers weren't so useful. What was frustrating was that he couldn't get control of the child's mind; he wondered if perhaps full-fledged, autonomous psychics could only be controlled by his actually inhabiting their brains with his being. Regular mortals like Richardson and (hopefully) the incomplete brains of mass-production psychics seemed easy enough to affect from the outside, however.

Benny knew precisely why Angel was angry, but wasn't worried; he was confident that his time having to play helper to him was nearing an end. His survival, he had been told, was very important to keep the events flowing smoothly, so he did what he had to to stay alive. He did not doubt Angel would end his life if he no longer found him useful.

Angel released Benny's hand and walked over to Yamada, who, with no other real option, picked up the fetus and handed it to him. Angel looked incredibly pissed off but took the offering from him, and then with little more than a thought, he tossed Yamada like a rag doll across the room, where he landed painfully on the side of his pelvis and slid several feet.

"This pitiful excuse for a child will have to do, won't it?" Angel said. He grabbed the creature around where its neck would be, if it had had features as well defined as a head, and pulled. In one swift motion the creature's "head" was off, blood speckling the immediate area. Angel pushed the lump of flesh against his own head, where, to Yamada's scientific amazement and human fear and disgust, it melded in.

He then took the limp bodily remains of the creature and pushed it against his chest, where it too merged with his physical form.

A change came over him; he grew in size and stature, nearing the six foot mark as his head and body filled out, gaining the physique of a statuesque (but genital-less) man, and a handsome, if no less terrifying, face. For his fangs, claws, hairlessness, and blue and purple coloration remained. Yamada, fascinated despite his terror, hypothesized on the spot that Angel's mass gain was being pulled directly from the elements in the air around him.

Angel smiled, his teeth menacingly sharp. "It feels good to have a real brain again."

Richardson sat on the floor, awake now, looking bemused. "All right, then, what now?"

"Now, you send your guards to go kill those girls. I have an army of my own to awaken. First though...."

He began to walk over to Yamada, who was lifted off the floor and brought face to face with Angel.

Not that it mattered, not that anything fucking mattered anymore, but Richardson spoke up. "You probably shouldn't kill him. He could still be useful." He lit up a cigarette and wished he had some aspirin; his head was pounding.

"I'm not going to kill him. I'm just going to teach him a lesson, the old fashioned way."

"I did everything you asked!" Yamada pleaded.

"I wanted a child, not a half-grown abortion!" He pulled his arm back, and socked the levitating Yamada square in the stomach.

Richardson looked away, and noticed that Benny was gone.

Emma had received a text a short while ago from Raven saying that she had rescued Mina and that they were leaving. It appeared hastily typed and was garbled, but understandable. Truth be told fear had gotten the better of her and she was already almost to her car when she got the message.

She had just turned the ignition when a voice next to her surprised her. She looked to see none other than Benny, but it took her a second to recognize him. His skin was a healthy shade of brown, his hair, tight black curls. His face was free of wrinkles.

"Hi," she said back, the tone of confusion evident in her voice.

"Hello," came two voices from the back seat, startling her further. She turned around to see Keiko and Johnny, and they too looked like healthy young children. Johnny had freckles and a mop of red hair; Keiko had short, sleek black hair and a light complexion.

"It's beginning," Johnny said, smiling. "We're free now."

"How?" Emma asked.

"Some of us haven't been taking our medicine for days," Benny said. "Keiko's orders. I watch people put the pills in their mouths, then I teleport the pills into the trash."

"You can do that? Without touching it? Is that why you look...healthy? Did the pills do that too?"

"No. That's a mystery still," said Keiko.

"All right," said Emma, "So, what do you want with me?"

"You have to help her," said Keiko.

"You are part of what follows," said Johnny.

"What exactly is 'following?'" Emma said, exasperated.

"There is going to be a battle," Keiko answered. "You are supposed to help in that battle."

"Look," Emma said, defiantly, "I just want out. I'm done. I'll die if I go back there."

"That's possible, but not definite," Johnny said.

"You've come this far. You helped her in once. She's not ready to fight him yet, she needs your help again. She's coming to you." Keiko spoke in monotone. "You will have to help her in again."

"This is about Angel, I assume?"

"Yes," said Johnny. "There is a chance now to avoid a darker fate. By night time it will be too late. He will rampage across the earth, bringing death through conquest."

"Why?"

"It's what he was made to do, but now no one controls him save himself."

Emma put her hands on the steering wheel and bowed her head against her arms, mentally wrestling with her options.

"And if I refuse?"

"You won't," said Benny, cheerily. "Your conscious won't let you. You won't let her go in again alone."

"You peeked around a little, didn't you?" she asked. She had had a dream last night, of standing in a darkened room, surrounded by her coworkers as well as strangers, all of them dead. Their blood was on her hands, and it spread until it covered her entire body and violently entered her mouth. It was vivid, and she remembered it with full clarity. She didn't put much stock in dream analysis but she was certain it was a manifestation of her guilt all the same.

She couldn't help but feel responsible, at least in part, for Mina's massacre, for Carl's death, for whatever had brought Raven to NOD, for the years and years of human experimentation she had been a part of. For the longest time she had pushed it out of her mind and her heart but the most recent events had put it on a slow burn until now she was wracked with guilt. Running away would, in all honesty and probability, just make it feel worse. If she could save lives by putting hers at risk again, it might not even the scales, but it would give her a sense of closure and a release of her self-condemnation.

At least she hoped so.

"Fine," she said, giving in to fate, or whatever it was that seemed to be guiding her (or forcing her) to continue being a part of this madness. "What do I do now?"

"We need to regroup," said Benny. "Think of where Raven will know where to find you."

Emma did; she thought of the motel, and could feel Benny picking around in her head.

"Got it," he said, and the entire car vanished.

One Hundred Seventy-Eight:
Escape II

Raven and Mina burst out of the freight elevator into a long hallway, Raven in the lead. They could see light at the end; hopefully, it was the outside world. Three guards stood between them and their freedom; for a moment, Raven considered bringing the ceiling down on them, but she wasn't keen to become a murderer, especially after the experiences Mina had shared with her.

The two nearest fired their guns; Raven and Mina just barely managed to deflect the bullets with their shielding. Raven had never really grasped the speed at which bullets actually moved at, and she wasn't keen to give them a second shot. Without breaking stride, she ripped their guns from their hands telekinetically as she neared them, and then threw them at each other head first. They slumped to the ground, (hopefully) unconscious.

In the time it took her to do that, the third guard had lined up a shot with what was clearly a gun but looked clunky and unfinished, like a prototype of some sort. She wasn't yet close enough to reliably manipulate it, so she got ready to erect a shield, when a spot on the wall next to her sizzled, sending down a rain of sparks.

"What the hell?" She muttered. She could hear the guard at the other end of the hallway curse. He fiddled with his gun, and then aimed at her again. She threw a shield up immediately, but the gun literally burst into flames in his hands. He panicked, rolling around on the ground, clutching his blistereing fingers.

"Serves you right, asshole," she said as she and Mina ran by, now side-by-side.

The door was there, and then it was open, and....

It was a large, well-lit parking garage by the looks of it, a loading dock in usage. In the second it took Raven to survey her surroundings, (two guards ahead, at the far end, vehicles including trucks and tankers to the right, garage and regular doors to the left) a shot was fired, a rocket-propelled grenade, a small missile, maybe, but it was almost at them....

Mina solidified her aura until it was nearly opaque, and instinctively, she wrapped it around Raven rather than herself. Raven could hear the muted concussion of the explosion, see the fire and smoke; it seemed to happen in slow motion, her ears ringing even with the subdued sound. It was personal now, it was too much; the moment she could see clearly she willed one of the tankers to fly against the wall, crushing those *sons of bitches* in the process. It was majestic in its arced trajectory, from a complete standstill, through the air, diagonally across the empty space in the middle of the large room, smashing into the wall with enough force to crack the concrete and rupture and crumple the tank.

She didn't know what was in it, but feared for an explosion (that was how it always happened on TV, anyway,) and she looked to her side for Mina, to grasp her hand...and screamed in horror when she saw that what remained of her love was a burnt-out corpse slumped against the wall.

"No. No no no no. NO!" She knelt down, and grabbed one of Mina's skeletal hands, and stared into her eyeless, burnt face. "I can't lose you too!"

There was a sigh just as Raven's eyes began to well up. The body slumped forward and a layer of desiccated flesh fell off of the rib cage, revealing damaged bones and fresh muscle beneath. The limb Raven was holding fell away from the body, and a bright pink nub formed at the shoulder. The burnt sinew of the mouth seemed to knit itself back together and the mouth closed.

As Raven became aware that Mina was breathing, albeit shallowly and raggedly, she watched in wonder as her eyes re-grew, like white balloons filling up with air. The irises were pink and unfinished, but even in this half-formed state, Mina managed to turn and face Raven, and look her in the eyes.

Then, suddenly, the rib cage separated from the pelvis, sending flecks like charred wood to the ground, and the torso started to slide. Raven caught it, holding it to her, cradling Mina's now fleshy, wet head.

Raven heard the sound of flames behind her, from the direction of the crushed tanker, and turned to face the garage doors. It was at least three stories inside this room; she concentrated, and blew a hole out of the wall about fifteen feet up. At the sight of buildings and sky, she stood up, cradling the limbless torso of her beloved, and flew.

Conflicting thoughts plagued her on the trip. Rejoiced that Mina had survived that, but unsure what (if any) the limits of her healing were, she was afraid the girl still wouldn't live. She could only think to see Emma, and hoped that she was home already.

When she got there, she was happy to see Emma's car parked in the lot, but Steve's was there too.

There was a pounding on Emma's door. Steve went to answer it; he looked through the peephole and immediately threw it open.

"Holy shit!" he yelled.

A bizarre sight greeted Raven: Emma, sitting on the couch, was fine; Steve, shouldn't have been there, but that wasn't a big deal at the moment; but the three children sitting around on the floor, eating microwave dinners, was a bit confusing.

However, Raven was just as alarming to them, or rather, what she was carrying was. Emma got up immediately and Raven put Mina down on the couch. By now she had regrown most of the muscle and bone of her torso and head, and skin was starting to grow on her nose, ears, and around her eyes and mouth. The nubs at her shoulders had lengthened and were differentiating into tissue types; the bottom rear of her rib cage had sprouted vertebra.

"What...." Emma began, unsure what to say.

"She survived an explosion. She's been regrowing the whole way, but I think she needs more...matter, I guess?"

Emma watched her for a moment, seeing veins curl over her face, building into layers of skin. "I think she's absorbing elements from the air. That's not going to be enough." She pointed into the kitchen. "Steve, get the vitamins from that cupboard. Benny, go grab the milk from the fridge. You two, go get all the rest of the food and bring it all here. And water. *Lots* of water."

"Benny?" Raven asked.

"Yes, that's Benny, Keiko, and Johnny. Don't bother with questions, I don't have any answers."

They set the objects down next to her, food, an open milk jug, running back and forth filling everything they could with water. As ludicrous as Emma had thought her idea had been, it seemed to work. She could literally see the surfaces of vitamins and meat and vegetables slowly wear away; Mina was telekinetically breaking down their structure and absorbing their elements. She was glad she had prepared for an indeterminate stay.

"She's going to need a lot of calcium," Emma said. She grabbed her wallet from her purse and threw it to Steve. "Go to the store. Milk, chalk, whatever. Get lots. And protein. Get chicken. Lots and lots of chicken. And hurry!"

He ran out the door without a single word.

"I have some more supplies here. I could feed her intravenously if only she wouldn't reject the needles."

"Oh!" Raven exclaimed. She rummaged around in her pocket, nearly stabbing herself, and pulled out the two green, clear needles. "They were using these on her with IVs. I think whatever it's made of, she won't push it out."

"It's worth a shot."

A few minutes later and Mina was hooked up to two IVs. A while after that Steve showed up with groceries. They set everything out. Mina's face was now fully formed, and she was asleep. Emma motioned for Raven and Steve to come into the kitchen area. The children were sitting in a circle on the floor, their eyes closed.

Emma spoke quietly. "Back in the labs, when I was trying to figure out how her healing ability worked, I thought it might be strictly biological, but determined it was in fact psychic. My best guess is that her aura is seeking out the elements she needs to reform her body and taking those in."

"So she's going to be okay?" Raven asked.

"I don't see any reason why not. She's done nothing but improve since she got here, and based on the condition she was probably in, originally, she's well on her way to recovery. I don't know how she survived an explosion at all, though."

"I think I do," Raven said. "She used her shield on me, to save me. I think she only had enough left to cover her vital organs."

"It's possible. I've read about subjects who could manipulate their aurakinetic shields with high....sorry." Emma felt awful at using the term "subjects," but Raven let it go.

"Why are you here?" she asked Steve, a little aggravated, but still glad to see him.

"I couldn't leave it at that. I'm sorry. I came back here because I figured Emma would know what happened right away."

"I said I would call you, butthead," she said as she hugged him tightly.

"The best thing for you to do," Emma began, addressing Raven, "is, as soon as Mina's well enough, get as far from here as you can. I'd planned on doing the same." After seeing Mina in a state that would have killed any normal person, her resolve had wavered.

"Well, that's kind of the pickle we're in," Raven said. "That Matthew/Angel guy seems to be in charge of your building, and the weird ones —" she pointed to Keiko and Johnny "—are pretty sure I have to fight him. Apparently if I do it now, it saves a lot of lives further down the road."

"Wait, some kids want you to fight some guy?" Steve was confused.

"Not just any kids. Not just any guy, for that matter. They're all like me, Steve, they have powers, and those kids are supposed to be able to see into the future, and this Angel guy, he's really, really strong, and really, really crazy. So I guess I'm just here to regroup and go back."

"Okay, that's crazy, you know that? Your girlfriend almost died getting out, and you want to go back and pick a fight?"

"Trust me, I wouldn't, but I've seen things worth fighting for. *She's* worth fighting for." Raven looked over at the half-formed girl sleeping on the couch, and smiled. She turned to face Emma. "Emma, I went to Nod. I saw a city. It was beautiful. I can't even begin to describe the things I saw, the people. I believe I have to do this."

Emma was awestruck. "Honestly," she said, after a pause, "the children told me the same thing. They said you would be instrumental in destroying him, and they were adamant that you must."

"When did they say that?" asked Steve.

Emma tapped her forehead. "They said it in here. And, before I got back, they actually said we needed to 'regroup.'"

Steve put his face in his hands. "How did everything go from kind of crazy to bat-shit insane so fast? Well, if you're going, you're not going alone. I'm coming too."

Emma sighed. "I guess I owe it to you, to everyone, to see this through to the end. I'll come too." After telling Raven that they should all just run, she wasn't going to admit Keiko and Johnny had told her she had to go back to the building as well.

"You guys don't have to. I don't want anyone else to get hurt. This is a suicide mission."

Steve just declared, "I'm coming," and Emma responded with "I know the building pretty much top to bottom. It's huge. You'd be lost. You might need me. They said you would, actually." She looked around at the motel room. "Besides, it's not like I've got a lot going on, right?" She forced a chuckle.

"Fine. There's something else, too. Mina was pregnant when I found her. They put something in her. That's why they kidnapped her. She...cut it out, and it was this weird blue fish thing. She said it was connected to Matthew—Angel—whatever."

Emma was puzzled at first, and horrified, but then it dawned on her, and she spoke. "The body he's using—the Angel—it was made artificially. I don't know all of the details, only what little I've been allowed to read, but it wasn't supposed to have higher brain functions. Matthew may have been trying to create a more suitable body for himself." The words "control unit" flashed through her mind.

"Oh shit," Emma continued, realizing something. "There's a whole army worth of experimental human soldiers in cryo-freeze in the basement. I'll bet anything he's planning on releasing them. That's why this is such a big deal."

"Okay, you guys are seriously going to have to catch me up on the car ride over," Steve said.

"We might want to check the news before we go there," Raven said. "I kind of maybe blew up a tanker truck and I saw a lot of cop cars and fire trucks going there on my way here."

"Great," said Steve sarcastically.

They went into the living area and Emma turned on the TV. Sure enough, one of the local channels had a "breaking news" banner at the top of the screen, and a reporter was speaking over footage of the Gates Building. Other than the parking structure next to it, there was no buildings close in front, as it had a fairly large plaza with a terraced garden surrounding the main entrance. They could see thick black smoke billowing out of the side of the building, and a maze of police cars, fire engines, ambulances, and military vehicles in and around the plaza. Uniformed men ran around like crazed ants, back and forth between each other. On top of all that, a pale violet-red glow surrounded the building, which Emma and Raven recognized as looking like an aurakinetic shield.

A man's voice spoke. "To recap, just a short time ago in this early afternoon, yet another explosion rocked downtown Omaha with more unverified reports of *flying people* leaving the scene. The mayor and chief of police have both called for immediate, full investigations of the Gates Building. The mayor has personally demanded to speak with the head of the primary corporation there but so far has not been able to reach anyone. Now to our reporter in the field, Noelle Jones."

The view switched to that of a pair of people standing quite some distance from the Gates Building which was visible in the background. There was a young woman in a red blazer talking to an older man in an army dress uniform. The banner on the image identified them as "Noelle Jones" and "General Nicholas Kresge."

"Hey, I know who that guy is," Emma said. "He's my boss' boss."

"Can you confirm any reports that people were seen flying, unassisted, out of the building today after the explosion?" the reporter asked.

"I can neither confirm nor deny that at this time," Kresge answered. It was clear from his tone that he was irritated.

"What about the impassable barrier that has appeared around the Gates Building? What is it?"

"I can't comment on that other than that we're looking into it."

"Can you tell us what led to the explosion, and what the nature is of the corporation that uses the Gates Building?"

"I can't comment any further. This is a military matter now, and we need all civilians and non-emergency vehicles to clear the area."

"General Kresge," Noelle began, but he cut her off.

"That includes you," he said, and walked off-camera. The operator centered Noelle in the shot.

"Speculation runs wild as the military has become involved with this incident, the most recent in a series of unexplained events at the Gates Building in downtown Omaha. We have some amateur cell phone footage of what appears to be the alleged 'flying people.' We'll show you those after the break."

Emma turned the set off. She sighed deeply. "This just got a whole lot more complicated." She walked over to the circle of children. "Benny, can you teleport past a shield?"

He opened his eyes and looked at her. "I'm pretty sure I can. I'll have to get close though. It takes more effort the greater the distance AND the stronger the barriers in between."

"Well, at least there's that," said Emma. "Let's try and get a game plan figured out."

"Good," said Raven. "I'd like to talk to our pre-cogs before we do this."

One Hundred Seventy-Nine:
The Downward Spiral

Nicholas Kresge walked over to Amanda Graley. "Are the road blocks set up?"

"Marcus is seeing to it. Do we have any clue what's going on in there?"

"My guess is Richardson's staging a coup, or a final stand, at least. He was in horrible shape last time I saw him. I think after what's happened he's lost it. But we haven't had any communication with the inside since the explosion."

"And that barrier?"

"Hell if I know," Kresge said. "Either psychic or some black project I don't know about. In any case, I'm in a hell of a spot here if my non-NOD superiors start asking questions. Hopefully the advisory board will, ahem, pull the necessary strings."

He was pissed. What had seemed like the perfect chance for an easy transition had blown up in his face. What the hell was Richardson thinking?

Lieutenant Colonel Joshua Richardson stood in front of Angel's throne in his make-shift court. "Have Jameson speed up the thawing of the rejected test subjects," Angel said, his voice now deeper than it had been before his change. "I want Yamada to study the successful one, Tom. I want him cloned, eventually." He picked several sheets of paper up off of his lap.

"I have learned so many interesting things since you so politely gave me your security clearance, Joshua. I do hope I get another chance to meet little Miss Mina. I have some interesting things to tell her." He laughed.

Richardson left to go carry out his orders. Most of the staff were with Jameson in the cryonics bay, unfreezing those ghastly things. They had been taking positions in various points in the building; Angel assured Richardson that they were under his complete control, but he still freaked out a little whenever he turned a corner and saw one. They were inhuman monstrosities, deformed and reshaped into failed, but apparently still useful, instruments of war.

The children, however—rather, the test subjects—he had no idea what they were up to, and that genuinely worried him. Also bothering him was that he hadn't seen a single guard since not long after Raven and Mina had escaped. Where the hell were they?

Dillons did a head count. They were shy a couple, but nearly all of the soldiers under his command had made it to the surveillance room on his orders.

"We're missing two," he said.

"I think they're dead," a voice spoke up. "They were in the loading dock when the explosion happened."

"All right, then," Dillons said, unhappy at that announcement. "In any case, we have a big problem of what-the-fuck-is-going-on right now. All communication outside the building is cut off. There's some kind of purple force-field blocking anyone from getting in or out, and—those things, did you guys see those *things*?" Several heads nodded, including Carlos'. "I don't like whatever the fuck those are. They said we'd see some strange shit here, but I'll be damned if something big and *wrong* isn't going down right now."

"I want a team here on the surveillance videos scanning the building. Me and Carlos are going to lead the rest to gear up and then hopefully figure out this shit." He pointed at several soldiers, one-by-one. "You guys are on the video feed. Keep an eye on us; warn us if we're gonna walk into a bad situation and let us know if you see or hear ANYTHING usefull, all right?"

"Yes, sir!" came the replies.

Jameson was at his wit's end. Every tube that opened seemed to birth a creature less human than the last. They looked at him with empty eyes (those that had eyes) and then walked away."Walked" wasn't even entirely accurate; some where bipedal, but some were tripedal, some moved like slugs, some levitated, and some had a plethora of spindly legs like spiders; some, he wasn't even sure how they moved.

Each and every time he saw one he flinched, expecting it to attack him. He saw blades made of bones and arms that looked like rifle barrels, among other structures he could only guess at.

Had they been human once? Or were they completely artificial? The tiny bit of conscience he had hoped for the latter.

He glanced around at the other staff members helping him with the thawing and releasing cycles. As scared as they seemed to be, they didn't know as much as he did. The truth of things were far more terrifying than they knew.

Did they realize they were all prisoners? They must, he assumed. Nothing like this had ever happened while he had been an employee of NOD. Full communication blackout with the inside and the outside except for orders; a complete suspension of all normal duties including normal care of the test subjects; and then this, the awakening of an army of...

Things. A nearby tube opened. What came out made him gag. It looked like nothing so much as a collection of human heads, each face in an empty-eyed grimace. The overall shape was like that of an upside-down pear. The open mouths seemed to scream silent horrors. It floated away, dripping some green sludge on the ground in its wake.

He shook his head in dismay, not expecting to leave his prison alive.

Yamada sat at the damaged desk in the White Room, his face and body bruised and one of his eyes nearly swollen shut. Painkillers and a bottle of fine vodka he had brought with him were his only friends. He had consigned himself to his current predicament; perhaps it was just punishment for years of human experimentation. It had bothered him, once, but eventually, the people became faceless to him and his heart hardened. Proof that even the most terrible of tasks become mundane after repetition.

A door opened and he turned to face it.

"Ah, Mr. Richardson, care for a shot?"

Mr. Richardson? May as well be. Richardson shrugged and laughed quietly. "Sure. Make it a double."

"Good man. I brought plenty. I didn't expect *this*, but I knew that my 'invitation' here wasn't without worry."

Richardson pulled over a folding chair and sat opposite Yamada at the desk. Yamada placed a short glass in front of each of them and poured a small amount of the clear spirits in each.

Richardson picked up his glass.

"A toast, yes?" asked Yamada. "To our imminent deaths at the hands of runaway 'science.'"

Richardson shrugged and clinked his glass against Yamada's. Both downed their drinks in a single gulp; Richardson shuddered.

"Not a vodka man?"

"I prefer whiskey in its various incarnations."

"Ah. I like my drinks clear and authentically made. Now seems like as good a time as any to have one. But, I'm going to assume you aren't here for a social visit."

"No. Angel wants—" Richardson began.

Yamada cut him off. "Of course, Angel wants. That is what I started all of this, I'm guessing. That's why I'm sharing a drink with you, of all people. I don't blame you. Not any more, at least. Anyway, continue, please."

Richardson cleared his throat. "Angel wants you to figure out how to duplicate Tom."

"Well, as long as I'm useful, right?" He laughed loudly. He poured another drink for himself and Richardson.

Richardson pulled out his pack of cigarettes. "Do you want a smoke?"

"I quit years ago. I'd love one, thanks."

One Hundred Eighty:
Joining Forces

"I want to come with you. I can help."

"Sweetie, you're still hurt. Please, I don't want you to get injured anymore."

"Maybe, because I can heal, it's my fate to be hurt."

Raven was shocked that Mina could conceive of such a thought.

"What if you get hurt...or worse?" Mina pleaded.

"The children seem pretty sure this is what's supposed to happen. I never believed in fate and I was never one to blindly follow anything; but the last couple months have shown me things I could only imagine. You know them better then me, do you trust them?"

Mina communicated telepathically. *Yes, but they told me once you would "destroy the world." What if this is what they meant?*

This is supposed to prevent that. That's what the cat said. She had briefly described her visit to Nod to Mina once she had awoken, but it didn't make it sound any less silly to talk about what a *cat* told her. *That's what **they** said. It's what they showed me.* She was referring to Keiko and Johnny.

I have faith in myself, and in you, Raven thought.

I have faith in you too, Mina thought.

Raven leaned over the couch and kissed Mina. She whispered words into her ears. "You're my rock. I'll be fine all right as long as I know I have you."

Mina whispered back, "If I can, I'll come for you when I'm fully healed."

Raven smiled, and spoke aloud now. "I love you."

"I love you, too."

Raven got up and walked over to Steve, Benny, and Emma, who were standing by the door. "All right," she said. "I'm ready."

They got into Emma's car and she started driving. "I'm going to get us as close as we can get, and then it's up to you, all right, Benny?"

"Yes," he said.

"This is absolutely crazy," Steve said, his head in his hands. He was sitting in the passenger seat. Raven was behind him and tapped him on the shoulder.

"There's still time to back out. It's okay."

"No. I'm not going to let you do this without me. You're my best friend."

Raven put her arms around him in a tight hug.

"Is your seatbelt on?" Emma asked.

When Mina had been stabilized and was still asleep, Keiko and Johnny had communed with Raven. It had been more than telepathy; it was deeper, more connected.

What did you mean, I would 'destroy the world?' she asked.

We couldn't see clearly yet. It was Matthew, but you would be intrinsic to it. It's become much clearer as events progressed. They answered her in unison.

So how can you be sure now?

The paths are like waves in an ocean of possibility. They have collapsed into two lines. One ends before nightfall and is dripping in red; the other ends quite some time from now and is covered in swaths of red and black. When it ends, so does much of this world. Those are his lines. Your paths are varied, but everyone crosses at the end of his longer line; many, but not all, cross the shorter. You can only choose which to meet; you cannot avoid it.

I don't believe in fate like that. I believe in freedom of choice, of chance. Raven did not want to believe in predestination; it undermined how she hoped the world worked. She was grasping at straws though; she had already consigned herself to this.

You have freedom. But events will push you towards other events. Today is your choice. The future is not. If you make the choice to wait, the outcome will be far, far worse. Do you want to see?

Yes, she answered.

They shared their visions with her. She was glad she had experienced the sea of Nod, because this seemed quite similar in how it felt. She moved forward, drawn along a myriad of lifetimes simultaneously. Everything was smudged; she couldn't make out specifics, but she recognized herself.

Then, several of the paths crossed a dark line. It was Angel. There was blood on the ground, a bright light, a burned space. Angel's line stopped.

Now, she sped away from her paths and watched his. It crossed the earth, a cloud of darkness behind him, spreading death and destruction. It met her other paths, on a hill, in the middle of a ruined, ancient city. Her skin was black and her aura on fire. Three other beings stood with Angel, unclear smudges, with paths like his leading backwards across the earth. Whoever they were, they met with him to face her.

A little further in time, and it was like an implosion. She couldn't make out who survived and who didn't, but it hurt her emotionally in the deepest way, the pain of hundreds of thousands, if not millions, screaming in agony.

She opened her eyes, tears pouring out of them, a tight pain in her chest.

"Okay," she said. Where before she had believed, now she *knew*. "I get it."

When they were within sight of the Gates Building, it became evident that they weren't getting very close to it. There were roadblocks set up on every road they could see leading out of the plaza, and armed military men were everywhere. Emma pulled over to the side of the road and parked.

In person, the violet-red sheen of the barrier around the building did appear to be an aurakinetic shield.

"Good lord, if that's his own shield, his powers must be phenomenal," Emma said. "Are we close enough, Benny?"

"I think so. But I have to take us somewhere I'm very familiar with for it to work."

They got out of the car, a ragtag group: a scientist, a child, a teenage girl in a bright pink coat, and a teenage boy in a leather jacket.

"Ok. Let's go," Benny said.

A moment later they were standing in the dormitory halls on the forty-fifth floor. They seemed deserted. Benny and Raven both winced.

"What is it?" Steve asked, concerned.

"I can feel him," she said. "It hurts. His power is almost overwhelming."

"He was in the floor below," Benny said. "He isn't anymore."

"Yeah, I can feel him. He's far below."

"Can you take us there, Benny?" Emma asked.

"No. He's changed the building. It doesn't feel familiar on the way down there."

Emma looked at the expression on his face. "You look exhausted. This must take a lot out of you?"

He nodded.

"Well, let's see if the elevators are working," Emma decided.

"Hey hey hey, check this out." The soldier pointed to one of the monitors in front of him.

"What?" asked the soldier sitting next to him.

"These people just appeared out of nowhere. Like, literally."

"I'll radio Dillons and let him know. What floor are they on?"

"Forty-Five. They're heading for the elevators."

Dillons surveyed the damage. One of his men was down, one was severely injured. He was unlikely to make it. He'd lost his left arm below the elbow and they had stopped the blood flow, but he'd lost a lot and was unconscious.

They'd gotten to an equipment room with no altercations, to their surprise. They had gotten body armor and masked helmets, ammunition, and several of the various laser devices, three of which were now expended or damaged.

Three dead creatures lay in the hallway, a pool of blood spreading from one who'd split wide open when they fired on it. All three had laser shots straight through their heads, although in one case, Dillons hadn't been sure that it

HAD a head at first.

He knelt next to one to examine it. It had bluish-black skin and a somewhat human lower body, but its upper body was a mass of ropy tentacles with a head on top of the thickest. It was the reason one of the men was missing an arm; it had flailed its tentacles about, and when it grabbed the soldier, the end of the tentacle just *exploded.*

"Sir!" The voice in his helmet startled him, and he jumped.

"Yes, soldier?"

"There's four people who appeared on floor forty-five. We've identified two of them. One is a scientist here, Dr. Emma Jacobson; the other is Raven Yamada, a test subject from here. The other two are a young man and a boy."

"Is the boy a test subject?"

"I don't believe so, he has normal complexion."

Dillons addressed the soldiers near him. "Wasn't it that 'Raven' that killed Nelson and Daly?"

There were several nods.

Dillons talked into his radio again. "We're on thirty-three. We're going to try and cut them off at thirty-six where all of the elevators stop. Meanwhile, have you figured anything else out?"

"The creatures are coming up from the subbasements. All surveillance from there is out."

"Thanks. Keep me informed." Dillons stood up and addressed his men.

"All right, we're going to go to thirty-six and meet up with our new guests. The girl is extremely powerful and dangerous; we need to play this very carefully. We're better off with her as an ally than an enemy. Afterwards we're heading into the subbasements. Whoever's releasing these things, whoever's controlling this building and keeping us trapped in like rats, has to be down there. Any questions?"

"Robertson, sir?" One of the soldiers motioned towards his one-handed teammate.

The soldier kneeling next to him spoke up. "He's...already dead."

"All right, then," said Dillons, trying not to show fear or anger, "Let's get going!"

The elevator hummed as it descended. Emma spoke. "There's a central hallway at thirty-six where all of the main elevators meet. None of the elevators go directly past thirty-six. We'll switch over there to one that goes further down.

"What the hell!?" exclaimed Raven. A reddish-purple mist penetrated the bottom of the elevator and rose, as though the elevator was moving down through it. There were no ill effects to any of the group but they all felt tingles as the mist passed through them.

"It's him," said Benny. "That's how he's making it so I can't teleport down. He's using his aura to mask the path down."

"So that, too, was Angel's aura?" Emma asked, astonished. "Those must be everywhere, then." She was terrified now, trying to contemplate the psychic strength of a creature that could place a permanent shield around an entire building *and* maintain aurakinetic obstacles throughout. Raven and Benny understood the implications as well, but Steve was completely in the dark.

They passed through two more of these aural sheets before the elevator came to a stop and the doors opened. Emma sighed. Across the room she could see a plethora of armed guards, although they weren't pointing their weapons, which was hopefully a good sign. The group reluctantly stepped out into the large room, which was dimly lit with emergency lights and contained several large, ropy pillars of the purplish aura mist that reached from floor to ceiling (and probably further.)

Raven was ready to fight and was looking around the room for things to throw. The pickings were slim, mostly chairs and trash cans, although a couple vending machines on one wall were promising. Emma stepped directly in front of her and was about to address the guards when one near the center of the group stepped forward and took off his masked helmet, revealing himself to be a large, black man with stubble covering his head.

"Ms. Jacobson, Ms. Yamada—I'm Leonard Dillons. We're not here to oppose you. I don't think so, anyway."

"How much do you know about what's going on?" Emma asked.

"We're trying to get down to the lower floors. We think that's where—whatever is causing all of this—is at. The shield surrounding the building is preventing us from leaving or getting backup, communication is cut off." He pointed at one of the aural pillars. "These things are everywhere, and what I can only describe as monsters seem to be coming up from below. They've killed a few of my men already."

Emma narrowed her eyes. "What kind of 'monsters?'"

"They seem part-human, at least most do. They have bizarre features. I think they're...psychic. Some of them have telekinesis or something."

Great, Emma thought, *he's activated the rejected soldier subjects.*

"Well, yes, we're going down there too, to try and stop this."

"Do you know what's causing it?"

Emma thought carefully before she answered. "A rogue test subject," she finally said.

"Then we're both on the same side, after all."

Dillons put his helmet back on and walked over to his men, taking a pair of handguns from them. He walked back over and handed one to Emma, and one to Steve. Emma accepted it tentatively but Steve was visibly stoked. "Aim for the head, if you can figure out where it is. They seem to heal." He looked directly at Raven. "You don't need a gun, do you?"

"No," she coldly replied.

Dillons was doing his best not to let the fact that she had killed two of his men cloud his mind. They were only following orders; she had only been trying to survive. He looked back at Emma. "The child?"

"He is one of the...test subjects," she said.

Other than the older two, all of the test subjects Dillons had seen had looked pale and sickly, but he took the statement at face value, as he was well aware that he knew almost nothing of what work went on here.

"Let's get going, then," he said, turning back to his men. "The surveillance in the subbasements is out. We'll start there."

I don't trust them, Raven said to Emma with telepathy. Emma nodded, and shrugged.

The four of them followed the guards into the elevators, and proceeded downward.

One Hundred Eighty-One:
Motivation

The ride down to the lower floors was uneventful. Mina, Raven, Steve, and Benny were in an elevator with Dillons and several other guards. They passed through several more of Angel's aura filaments until the car abruptly stopped on the floor above the first subbasement. Warning lights and a siren came on. The door opened, and the entire room ahead of them was filled with the reddish-purple mist.

Dillons stepped out tentatively, and leapt back immediately as a glowing green blob flew past. He turned to the side to see one of the monsters, this one grey in color, armless, and covered in horny protrusions. He shouldered his rifle to fire, but hesitated as the creature erected a pale green shield in front of itself. Bumps began to appear on its surface.

In the brief time it took Raven to step out of the elevator behind Dillons, she recognized what was about to happen, and she jumped in front of him, raising her shield. Just as she did so, the lumps on the creature's shield shot out like bullets and dissipated harmlessly against her orange shield. Both of their auras temporarily spent, she ducked out of the way and Dillons fired, piercing the being's narrow forehead, dropping it instantly.

"Thanks," he said, looking over at Raven.

"Yeah. Remember that," she said.

The mist was thin but Dillons hadn't seen the creature at first glance in the dim lighting; he quickly scanned the room for more and found none. As he did so, the other elevators opened and the rest of the guards poured out.

The room mirrored the main elevator room on thirty-six, with several supporting columns being the only real difference. Doors led most likely to hallways and other facilities, with a large double door marked "Subbasement Elevators and Stairs. Have Access Cards Ready. No Unauthorized Visitors Allowed."

One of the men walked over to Dillons and spoke. "I thought the elevators went further down?"

"They do," he replied. He could hear the alarms from all of the open cars. "I got a feeling though that we're traveling the rest of the way on foot." He turned to Emma. "Normally this area is fairly restricted. What should we expect?"

"Sub one is just storage. Two is mostly taken up by a giant laboratory called the White Room. Beneath that is the, um, power generator, and at the bottom are the cryonics bays and main breaker room."

"I've been to the cryonics lab. After a certain someone," he turned to face

Raven as he said this, "caused a bit of damage down there." He didn't seem to be upset or irritated by it, but it seemed snide and pissed her off that he even mentioned it, after the hell *this building* had put her through.

She had had enough. It was time to say something.

"Considering that this company, or whatever the hell it is, is conducting experiments on human beings, is directly responsible for the *murder* of my family and previous girlfriend, and the kidnapping of my current girlfriend, which was probably carried about by one of you fucks, who also nearly killed her, it is by my good grace alone that I don't bring this entire building down on your heads. We have a bigger problem right now and that's the only reason I'm working with you. Do I make myself clear?"

During her speech, Raven's aura became visible, like orange flames dancing around her. The guards near her backed away and even Dillons took pause. "Yes, ma'am," he answered finally.

"Good." She realized her hands were tightly clenched and she relaxed them. Her aura vanished but the tension in the room was still almost palpable. She glanced over to the side and saw that one of the men was holding an odd looking weapon that she recognized from her earlier escape. "What's that?" she said, pointing at it.

"Laser rifle," Dillons said.

"Be careful with that," Raven said, facing the guard holding the weapon. "The last time I saw one of those, it exploded in the guy's hands. Let's go." She started walking towards the double doors. The soldiers rushed to form a ring around the civilians and Steve ran up next to Raven.

"You're terrifying, you know that?"

"When I have to be."

"You've been running on eleven since you escaped. You're going to burn yourself out."

"As soon as this is over, I'm taking Mina and going far, far away and I'm going to relax and try and put a life together for us," she replied.

"Why are you doing this?" Steve asked. "Really, why? Why not just run?"

"It's my fate. Or something like that."

"Really? Just fate. That's not like you."

Raven thought back until just after she had communed with Keiko and Johnny. She had noticed something when they showed her their visions. Angel's line seemed to be born from her, where almost immediately afterwards it met with Matthew's, creating the devil they were hoping to kill. She had asked them about it.

Angel was freed when you destroyed the cryonics equipment. He was held there. As soon as Matthew felt him, he escaped into him.

So...this is all because of me?
You set the motions. Now they play out.
No. Be honest. Is this my fault?
Yes.

"It's my fault," Raven admitted. "I found Crow's body, I destroyed equipment and it released Angel's body. Matthew would never have had this much power if I hadn't done that. The cat pretty much convinced me, but I was still ready to run until I found that out. It's my job to fix things, fate or not."

"Wow," was all Steve could muster.

Emma had been listening in and spoke softly to them, exposing her heart in a few short words.

"Guilt is a very strong motivator."

One Hundred Eighty-Two:
Family Reunion

The sounds of muffled gunfire came from the ceiling.

"It seems we will be having company soon," Yamada said. "Perhaps the cavalry has arrived."

It wasn't long before the sounds of marching neared the White Room, and a large group of soldiers burst in, weapons ready, followed by a woman, two teenagers, and a child.

"Stand down," said Dillons.

The vast, round room was empty save for several shipping crates, a desk, some medical equipment, and two men. Yamada was crouched over a body strapped to a medical bed. Richardson sat at the desk, his head in his hands, a half-empty bottle of vodka and his handgun in front of him. The stench of cigarette smoke was in the air.

Dillons walked over to Yamada and looked at the body. It was bizarre, but far more human than the things he'd seen so far. It appeared to be a man, naked but lacking genitals. He was quite tall, but the most remarkable thing about his appearance was his skin: his extremities were almost blue, but the rest of his body was a deep black, covered in red lines that crossed and appeared to glow and roil like a liquid.

"What's this?" Dillons asked. Yamada seemed completely unperturbed by his presence or his weapon.

"This is Tom. He's the perfect soldier." Yamada felt no need in concealing any information as he was pretty sure what was going to happen next. He was right.

Dillons pointed the barrel of his rifle at Tom's head and fired several times, spraying flesh, bone, blood and brain around and soaking the bed with gore at the exit wounds, beneath the head. The glow from the red skin faded.

"So you are here to stop them?"

"Yes. That's the plan."

Dillons stepped back from the bed and motioned towards Richardson. "Take him into custody." The two soldiers in the front of the group walked over to Richardson, who stood up, defeat on his face, and raised his arms. They padded him down, and then zip-tied his hands behind his back.

"I'm not important anymore, you know," he said, sounding slightly drunk. "I'm not even good enough to be his bitch anymore."

"What is he talking about?" Dillons asked Yamada.

"Do you know of Angel?" Yamada asked.

Dillons looked back at Emma, in the middle of the group. "The, uh, rogue test subject," she said, flustered.

Dillons turned back to Yamada. "Angel was using Richardson but seems to have no further use for him. He seems to have left his mind. As for deleterious effects, I can't say if that's from Angel, or from the liquor."

"And what happened to you?" Dillons asked, looking at the face of a man who had clearly lost a fight.

"Angel decided to punish me, the old fashioned way," Yamada answered calmly.

As Richardson was led over to the group of soldiers, he spotted Raven in their midst. "Hey, Yamada," he said, over his shoulder, "your daughter's back."

Raven's heart dropped and her stomach turned. She pushed her way to the front of the group and looked at the short, unimpressive, damaged man. She walked over to him. He bowed to her, an old custom he rarely used except when it seemed important. "Daichi Yamada...your father."

"My father? Works for these people!? I could kill you for what they've done to Mina, to my mother!" She had expected some tears but found only anger. She tried to calm herself. "It looks like you've already been punished," she said through clenched teeth.

"Your mother never told you? Please, let me explain. It's all I ask. Please."

Dillons, with one of his closest friends about to become a father, recognized this as an important moment. He pointed at each of the entrances to the room. "Secure the perimeter," he said, and several soldiers rushed to each doorway.

Raven nodded to Yamada, and he led her away from the others, towards the desk. She stared at the corpse on the bed, the same bed Mina had been strapped to, as they walked by it.

"I never stopped loving you, or your brother, or your mother," Yamada said.

"You cheated on her," Raven said, her tone accusatory.

"You remember that," Yamada sighed.

"I do now."

"Let me start at the beginning. I met your mother in college. I was a professor and she was an undergraduate student in genetics."

"Mom? A geneticist?"

"I'll explain. She was in a class of mine. We...liked each other. As soon as the term ended and she wasn't my student anymore, we started dating. About a year later she became pregnant with you and dropped out. We married soon after. Not long after you were born, I was approached by NOD, this facility, and asked if I wanted to work on black projects for the government. The pay was substantial; how could I say no? I was starting a family."

"You experimented on people."

He looked almost wistful as he responded. "You think, in the beginning, that you'll never get used to it. That you'll spend every night awake, wracked with guilt. It's not true. Eventually it just becomes mechanical. I have regret, but I don't think I'm capable of feeling guilt anymore."

"Anyway," he continued, "a few years after Jacob was born, the company announced a new program. It was a long shot; they knew it was unlikely to occur. But, they wanted to test a fully conscious, un-medicated psychic. They wanted to do this by testing the scientist's children for genetic markers, and if a candidate was found, the child's parent would oversee them. The idea was that it would keep the child in line without the need for sedation."

"That's...horrible."

"I sequenced your and your brother's DNA, secretly. You had the markers. That night I told your mother everything: the real work I did, every awful thing, and the program, and...you. We decided the only way to protect you was if we split up and I altered the records NOD had of my family status."

"So, the cheating?"

"You have to understand, your mother was a college drop-out and had no job. I had a very lucrative career. We had to make sure she got custody of you. It was staged: I never touched that woman. But her testimony that I *had* paid her for sex, and your mother's false claims that I was verbally abusive to her and ignored my children, got her custody and a nice alimony settlement. I requested a transfer to Nevada and altered my records with NOD to show that I had no family."

Raven felt defeated. All her remembered life she had hated him for leaving; when memories resurfaced she had hated him more. Now, what she felt was strange and confusing, a mix of regret, of sadness, of anger at herself and her mother for never telling her the truth. She held back tears.

"And yet, it happened anyway. Here I am," she said.

Yamada nodded, a sad look on his face. "Apparently I didn't do as good a job covering my tracks as I thought. They used you to get me here."

"They killed mom and Jake," Raven said, the tears beginning to push through. "And my girlfriend."

"I know. I'm sorry. In the end, it was worse this way." Yamada's eyes were wet as well.

Raven still felt like she had recently had the wind knocked out of her. There was still so much more to say, to ask.

Dillons walked over at this time. "I'm sorry to break up the family reunion, but this 'Angel' thing, where is it?"

"I'm not actually sure," Yamada answered.

Benny spoke up. "I could feel him down here before, but now I'm not sure. He's masking himself."

Yamada looked at Emma. "You're Dr. Jacobson, correct?" She nodded and walked over to him. "Angel is siphoning power from Nod through Arty. That's how he has the energy to keep this entire building shielded, how he has been able to suffuse the air with his aura."

"So if we deactivate Arty, he'll be weaker, and the aura will disappear."

"Well, yes, that's the idea, but there's an issue: Angel essentially made me remove the 'off' switch. There's no way to deactivate Arty."

Emma looked dejected. "So what do we do?"

"We release him," Yamada said, smiling. "What he didn't know is that Arty isn't here of his own accord. He's held captive. I know how to remove the docking clamps. It's a two-person job; I'll need your help."

"All right, so where do we go to do this?" Dillons asked.

"Further down," answered Emma.

"All right, men, we're moving," Dillons yelled. The entire group, now including Yamada and Richardson, started to head towards the stairways.

Steve slipped in line next to Raven. "I heard everything. You okay?"

She wiped a tear out of her eye. "Yeah. No. I will be."

He put an arm around her. "We'll get through this."

She faked a smile. "I know," she said, though she didn't completely believe it.

One Hundred Eighty-Three:
Berserk

Emma spoke to Yamada as the group moved down the stairs towards the third subbasement. "Will we actually be able to get to where the controls are? What about the vibrations?"

"Those are actually only dangerous inside the portal room and distortion chamber. We only need to go to subbasement four," he answered. "If you've noticed, the elevators and stairs to the cryonics labs go outward quite a bit and then come back in towards the center. That's because SB eight and nine are held in a giant gantry system that allows for movement, and that in turn is surrounded by a massive amount of sound-proofing. Any excess energy is focused upwards."

"Seems like it would make more sense for the cryonics bays to be above the rest, though, doesn't it?"

"Ah, that's because the distortion chamber and portal room were built later. We had the cryonics bays long before we had Arty."

"Oh."

Dillons peered into the door to subbasement three's main room, a large, mostly vacant place that branched out into hallways leading to smaller rooms. He didn't know it personally, but since the introduction of Arty under Hanin and Utsugi, the subbasements went mostly unused except for control rooms.

"Shit," he said, backing away from the door. "We have to cross this room to get to the next stairway, and there's at least fifteen of those *things* in there."

"Ha ha, good luck!" laughed Richardson.

Steve pulled out the pistol he had been given; Raven looked worried.

"Remember, everyone, they heal, so aim for vitals," Dillons said. *If you can figure out where they are,* he thought.

Benny tugged at Emma's sleeve. She looked down at him.

"They're calling for me. I'll be back soon. This place is easy to remember."

"Okay...." she began, but he had already vanished.

Dillons kicked open the door and ran in, firing immediately. The other guards poured in after him.

Gray-skinned aberrations swatted, clawed, and whipped at the soldiers; shields of various colors were erected and dissipated. Telekinetic projectiles were fired. One creature, a cylinder-shaped being with no arms and dozens of short, bug-like legs, burst open to reveal a massive vertical maw in its front, filled with large, tooth-like spikes. It launched itself forward towards one of the men, crushing his torso into a bloody pulp as he closed his mouth around him and pushed him to the floor.

Another of the men used the full power setting on his laser rifle to practically vaporize one of the monster's heads, only to have his own head severed seconds later by a bladed arm enforced with a telekinetic edge. The men were taking casualties quickly while outside of a couple good kills, the rejected psychic soldiers were bleeding everywhere but were in no real danger from their (rapidly closing) wounds.

Emma, Raven, and Steve were still in the hallway. Seeing the bloodshed inside, Raven steeled her resolve, threw her coat off, and went in, Steve slowly following her. She telekinetically threw several of the creatures at the walls and ceiling, stunning a couple, who were then easily picked off by the soldiers. She ripped out part of a support column, extracting its steel core. She mentally launched it at the head of one of the more human-looking creatures, but he erected a pale blue shield at the last moment. She pushed it with all her might, sparks flying, until the shield dimmed and it passed through, crushing her opponent's head against the wall behind him.

She heard a loud bang off to her side and spun around in time to see one of the creature's reeling backwards from a shot to the shoulder, standing just inches from herself, and Steve, standing there with his gun outstretched.

"Thanks," she said, and proceeded to telekinetically throw her assailant head first into the ground, where Steve unloaded several bullets into its face before it could react.

Raven had helped turn the tide of the battle: tossing the creatures around and throwing objects at them, when it didn't outright kill them, bought the guards enough time finish them off. A guard would go down, then two of the monsters; another guard, and three more monsters. It quickly became clear, however, that more were arriving to keep their numbers from depleting.

"How many are there!?" Dillons yelled, shoving a new clip into his gun. Nearby, a laser gun exploded, having reached its threshold.

"Dozens...hundreds, maybe," Emma mumbled, her voice completely inaudible over the din of gunfire and yelling.

One of the psychic beings with a collection of tubes for an upper body shot out a viscous glob of green goo at one of the soldier's faces. Raven grabbed a piece of rebar that had come loose during the destruction, and focused, crushing its edge into a make-shift blade. She enforced its energy with a kinetic edge, and swung with all her might, lopping off most of the tubes. As they fell to the ground, a head that had been hiding in the middle fell too. She jammed the rebar into it as the body slumped over.

Raven turned back in time to see the guard remove his face mask and throw it to the ground, the ooze having turned it into a sizzling, melting mess. She looked up into his face and her heart dropped.

"YOU!" she yelled. The Hispanic man looked at her nervously. Carlos had really hoped that his identity would not be revealed. "YOU MURDERER! YOU KILLED MY FAMILY!"

All bets were off. She ripped his weapon from his hand and threw it across the room. She was going to end his miserable existence. Her anger was intense and her aura was becoming visible again, heatless flames that licked the air around her. She made a fist and layered a kinetic edge over it, and pulled back....

A startled look appeared on Carlos' face, and he looked down. Raven followed his line of sight to his stomach, where a pair of bloody protrusions extended out from him. They quickly shot outwards to his sides, bisecting him and spilling his guts to the floor as the two halves of his body fell down. She could see the life drain from his face.

She looked up at the thing that had killed him. It was so dark in color it was almost black, and seemed to be watching her intently, even though it had no eyes, or really, any facial features. Its arms were like swords; it relaxed them, and they became pliable, like ribbons.

"HE WAS MINE!" she growled. Her anger had reached a threshold; her aura was hot now, and glowing red lines began to crisscross her skin. Steve could see it most easily on her naked arms, and became worried and scared.

The creature whipped its left arm-ribbon into a tight spiral, making a tube, and a glow began to shine at the base of it. Raven dove to the side, roaring, as the blast of energy it created whizzed by. It reconfigured its ribbons into skinny, atrophic arms, with long, sharp fingers at the end of both. It leaped towards her, its claws aimed at her throat. She returned the gesture, leaping at it. She grasped the animal's wrists, and using her kinesis to grant herself extra strength throughout her body, she pulled its arms violently sideways, kicking up at its faceless head with a blow so forceful that blood spattered on the ground behind it. Something cracked.

She fell down with it, onto it, pinning it down. Breathing deeply, her chest heaving, she roared at it and spit in its "face." It wrestled, its arms bending in strange directions as it tried to pull them free of her hands. Veins pulsing on her forehead, the redness on her arms grew brighter and with two sickening snaps she freed the creature's arms from its body and tossed them aside. Blood pooled freely from its wriggling shoulders.

It screamed directly into her mind, one part anguish, one part fury, and pushed upwards against her. It tried to buck her off of itself, lifting its head up and beginning to form a mouth.

She would not let it win. She ran a kinetic edge along her fingers, and strengthened the force of her arms to a higher level. Her sweat rained down on the beast as she reared up and pointed her fingers down, ready to strike.

The sickening crunch of a pulverized sternum was drowned out by the surrounding fighting, but Raven couldn't hear any of it. Steve and a few of the soldiers had seen what she was doing, what had happened to her, and were dumbstruck by it. Steve almost got killed due to his negligence, but Dillons himself stopped his attacker while watching Raven brutalize hers. He saw the two halves of Carlos' body on the ground and silently wept.

Raven's fingers were buried deep within the monster's chest; she could feel the warmth of its body, the beating of its heart, the rasping of its breath. She tightened her legs around its waist and projected a downward force against its legs as it renewed its escape attempts. She jammed her other arm into the creature.

Pressing through muscle and tissue, she bent her fingers beneath the monster's ribs. Her arms glowed as if on fire as she pulled sideways; ribs broke free and flew through the air as Raven tore the creature's chest completely open.

Looking down now, she saw the glisteningly bloody lungs of the creature, moving to an uneven beat as the diaphragm pushed against them. The heart was nestled in, tucked into the chest cavity, forcing its own juice out through the monster's wounds with every pulse.

The monster was physically weak, and at best had resisted ineffectually to Raven's capture of it. But here, looking inside of it, her true fury was unleashed. She roared again, her eyes green, her body blackening under the strength of her psionic psychosis, her polygonal lines bleeding as their power seared through her own veins. She screamed; was it pain, anger, rage, or some combination of all three? She tore, fist over fist, ripping and shredding vital organs, tissues, membranes, haphazardly tossing gore in every direction, splattering the floor, walls, ceilings, and bystanders. Every blow came with a grunt or a roar. She was dehydrating herself by sweating so much, but it only fueled her fervor. Every mitochondrion in her body cried out, working past its limit just to keep her body going. By the time she paused for even a second, nothing but the shattered shell of a spine and the skin of the monster's back connected its head to its abdomen.

The monster was not breathing, for it had no lungs. Its blood was not moving, for it had no heart. Its head was lying sideways at a crazy angle; its legs twitched, then stopped. But it was not enough. Like all of these monsters, it would heal in time.

Like her beloved.

It just wasn't enough.

She screamed again, tears pouring from her glowing eyes. She pulled back her right arm, as if to punch. She forced power into it, more than was necessary. The aura around it burned with living fire. Then she did it. She pushed into the monster's neck, causing it to expand as her punch traveled through it, crashing in through the base of its skull, cutting her own knuckles to ribbons on its bones as she tore through the emergency shielding of its brain and pulverized it from the inside of its own head.

Her hand stayed inside for a moment even after it was clear the creature was dead. She watched until its aura, visible to her in her state, faded and dispersed completely. What was left of its once-human soul had departed.

There was a suction noise as she pulled her arm out. She stood up. She looked down at the cuts on her knuckles and watched them bleed. Standing over the obliterated body of the monster, she smiled and looked at its kin.

She roared and leapt into the fray like a feral beast; she was all weapon: teeth, hands, and feet ripping and tearing and pulverizing flesh and bone in a fight that pureed her foes. She was in danger of exploding, of losing herself completely to the fight, in the fight. She knew her purpose but everything else was fading; her power was simple, but it was absolute.

She went from foe to foe, and killed every creature that the others could not. Finally, there seemed to be no more. She stood with her back to the door, facing the room, drenched in the blood of the fallen. The room was covered in the splattered remnants of Angel's troops. The soldiers were tending to their wounded. Steve and Emma were afraid to approach Raven; she was standing in an aggressive stance, expecting more monsters. She was breathing quickly, her pulse quick. The blackness had faded from her skin but the glowing lines and aura remained.

"Dear."

She felt a familiar touch on her hand. She turned.

It was Mina.

She smiled at the sight of her, and fainted.

"There's thirteen of us left."

"Shit."

Raven's eyes fluttered open. She sat up with a start and winced at the ensuing headache. She was on a couch in what looked like a waiting room. Mina brought her a bottle of water from a vending machine, which she happily accepted. She looked completely healed and was wearing an old dress of Raven's and a winter coat. She smiled.

"I'm fine now."

"I'm so glad, hun. How long was I out?"

"Just a few minutes. We still have time, but the sun's going down."

Raven remembered Twilloughby saying something about finishing everything before dark, so even though she didn't understand the meaning of it, she didn't ask Mina anything. It was probably something the little pre-cogs had told her, anyway, and they probably were maddeningly non-specific when they did so. She looked at her hands; the right one was bandaged. Her pants were ruined, the white fabric covered in red splotches.

She looked across the room and focused on a trash can with splotched paper towels poking out.

"I washed off as much of the blood as I could," Mina said.

"Thanks," said Raven weakly. She gently pulled Mina down next to her and threw her arms around her. "I need you," she said. "I'm glad you came."

The only other people in the room were Dillons, his face mask removed, and another soldier who still wore his.

"Listen," he said, facing Raven. "whatever the hell that was back there—and it was terrifying—thank you. I don't think there would be as many of us left if you hadn't done—that."

"You're welcome." She gulped the water. "That man—"

"Carlos," Dillons guessed.

"I was going to kill him."

"He was one of my best friends. Under the circumstances, though, I can't say I blame you."

She finished the water and started to get up. "C'mon, let's get moving." She held Mina's hand as she also stood up. "How did you get here, by the way?"

"Benny just showed up and said it was time. Keiko and Johnny are here, too."

The four of them walked out into the hallway. Emma and Steve were standing closest to the door. Steve handed Raven her coat.

"That was awesome. And scary as fuck."

"I hope you realize now how serious this is."

Steve blushed. "Ye-yeah," he stammered.

The entire group walked in silence to the next stairway, past the lifeless bodies of the dead.

One Hundred Eighty-Four:
Releasing the Beast

Subbasement four seemed curiously empty. Dillons stationed five guards at each staircase, while he and the remaining two went with Emma, Yamada, Raven, Steve, Benny, Keiko, and Johnny towards the control room. He left Richardson, who hadn't said a word since they left the White Room, by the up staircase.

Dillons opened the door and looked in; it was clear. "All right," he said. "Do your dirty work." Yamada and Emma went in and closed the door behind them.

"So...." said Raven, after several moments of silence. She pointed at one of the men who was carrying one of the laser devices. "Why lasers?"

Dillons smiled. "Even you psychics can't dodge at the speed of light."

"Noted," Raven said.

Mina leaned over and whispered into Raven's ear; she nodded. Raven held her hand out and Mina grasped it.

"Um, Steve, considering we might, you know, die, uh...me and Mina are going to go around the corner and make out. Come get us when it's time to go?"

"Uh...yeah. Sure."

"Thanks."

Yamada and Emma sat down in front of a bank of monitors and complex controls in the cramped room. Yamada flicked a switch and everything powered on. Lights lit up, computers hummed, screens buzzed.

"I never knew this was here, that Arty could be released," Emma said.

"No one knew, except me, Hanin, and Utsugi," Yamada explained. "It's not in the files, either."

Emma looked at the images that were appearing on the monitors. Most were security camera views of Arty. One was a wide-view shot looking down into the hallway of Arty itself; she could see the sinuous cords and flesh-covered far wall, the hanging sheets that served as lungs. Another was of the massive collection of eyes that hung in the high corner of the room. It repulsed her, but saddened her at the same time.

"So what do you mean exactly, 'release Arty?'" she asked.

"Arty's body spans three floors. His upper body is held on seven; the bulk of him is on eight, where he actually generates power. His tendril and maw are on nine, where he draws in energy from the portal. There are clamps holding him in place."

"What happens when the clamps are disengaged?"

"He will reform into his proper shape. After that, I'm not sure."

"Proper shape?" Emma asked, puzzled.

"You don't really think he's just an open collection of organs, do you? He's held that way to keep him immobile."

"That's—that's awful! He must be in such pain!"

"It is. And he is," Yamada agreed, emotionlessly.

The process of releasing Arty involved simultaneously activating levers placed far apart on the console, the idea being that one person alone could not sabotage the power system. Emma had seen the same trick countless times in movies, usually involving keys and weapons, but had never seen anything like it in person.

After the first levers were pulled, Emma watched on the wideview monitor as the room seemed to shrink; she realized that it was Arty himself contracting into a worm-like shape. His outer skin was colored a light tan, and she could see the bruises and cuts from where the clamps held him. They healed in moments. On the far, now exposed wall, she could see the line of retracted clamps. large, metal, bloodied hinged hooks.

She jumped as the mossy-looking mass of eyes suddenly fell on the floor in front of the body, connected to it by unknown cords and tubes. It pulled into the end of the worm and was sealed over by skin. Bulges appeared, opening as eyes, and a face formed. It was covered in those eyes and they were arranged bilaterally symmetrical, with the lower half of the face split by a large vertical mouth. It was simultaneously terrifying and amazing.

"Once the distortion room's clamps are released, we'll stop receiving electricity from Arty," Yamada explained. "The building will switch to the city's power grid but we might lose power for a moment. Angel will probably realize something's wrong as soon as that happens. Once Arty is free from the portal, Angel will no longer be able to draw energy off from him and he should be unable to maintain the aurakinetic abilities he's currently using."

"Should?" Emma asked.

"It's my belief that he's formed a mental conduit and is directly absorbing some of the psionic energy Arty is drawing from Nod. He doesn't have the necessary organs to do it himself and shouldn't be aware of how to form them if he wanted to."

"So...you're not really sure."

"He's drawing energy off of Arty one way or another," Yamada said. "I haven't seen him plug himself into a wall so I doubt it's the electricity. If it is, we're screwed."

Yamada flicked a small toggle switch and pulled over a microphone that was sticking out of the console. "Arty, I'm going to release your tendril next. It's imperative that you keep it in place and continue to draw power until you're fully released. I don't want Angel knowing what we're doing until it's done."

A thousand almost simultaneous voices spoke through a speaker. "UNDERSTOOD."

Yamada directed Emma to skip the middle lever and proceed to the third. Upon pulling them, they watched on the monitor as a metal shaft surrounding part of the tendril's upper segment split in two and pulled away on robotic armatures. The maw remained in place, above the portal.

"All right; this is it." Yamada pointed to the middle lever by Emma. They both grabbed theirs and pulled. There seemed to be a subtle rumble in the building and the lights in the room flickered and then shut off, although the monitors and console remained on. After a few seconds the lights came back on.

Emma's eyes were glued to the portal room monitor. Arty had pushed his entire bulk into the room; pieces of the ceiling were scattered about. He floated in mid-air, a vast, pinkish worm with a horrifying face; his rear end tapered down to a thin extension that was apparently the tendril, as his three-toothed maw was at the end of it.

He spoke into Emma's and Yamada's minds, saying only "Thanks," before disappearing into the portal. Emma could swear that at the moment he vanished, he appeared to be a gigantic baby, with his tendril as an umbilical cord, the end a hungry mouth. She wasn't totally sure though, and it wouldn't have been the first time Arty had caused her to hallucinate.

"Well," said Yamada, getting up, out of his chair. "We're done here. Angel is likely to be very ticked off."

Outside the building, Kresge watched as the shield around the building wavered and vanished. He spoke to Dr. Graley who was next to him. "Try and get a hold of your men now and see what the hell is going on. I'm going to try to call Richardson." He shivered; the sun was low in the sky and the temperature was dropping.

Emma and Yamada stepped out of the control room. "It's done," Yamada said.

"The interference is gone," Benny said. "I can tell where he is, too. He's back up top."

"Of course he is," Emma sighed.

"I'll go get Raven and Mina," Steve said. He walked around the corner they had rounded earlier, fully expecting to see them locked in a passionate embrace, something he didn't want to see, despite his wishes for his best friend's happiness, and the fact that, if he was honest with himself, it would be pretty hot.

Instead he found them silent on a bench, Raven sitting up, Mina laying down with her head in Raven's lap, Raven gently stroking her hair.

"We're good to go," he said. Raven nodded and the two of them got up. They followed him back to the rest of the group, hand-in-hand.

Dillons had his face mask on and was talking to someone on his com, though they all could only hear him.

"Yes, ma'am. We're working on the situation. There's a—," he glanced at Emma, "—rogue test subject causing this incident. We're going to take him out." A pause. "We have Richardson in custody." Another pause. He looked at the children; the scientists; the teenagers. "We have a couple of the scientists with us. They're helping us proceed through the building." A final pause. "Understood."

"That was my commanding officer," Dillons said to those around him. "Also, we have full surveillance again and the report is that most of the remaining NOD staff is a few floors below. I'm sending most of my team to get them out. Anyone who wants to see this ended, let's go."

"I'm ready," Raven said. Yamada walked over to her and placed a piece of paper in her hand.

"This is a safe number. Call me sometime when this is over. I have more to tell you. I love you, daughter. I don't expect you to return that emotion, but I'm glad I got to clear the air with you."

"Me too," Raven said. He bowed to her, then turned to address Dillons. "This is where we part, then. I'll accompany your men below. If the staff are still attempting to release more of those creatures, I can probably sabotage the cryonics system." He turned to Emma. "It's been a pleasure working with you, doctor."

Before she could reply, he turned and walked towards the guards standing by the down staircase.

"You two are with me," Dillons said, pointing at the other two soldiers nearby. "I'm going to go get Richardson and give everyone else their orders." He walked off.

Keiko spoke to Raven. "Everything is proceeding well, but time is running out."

"I've got this," she said, confidently. She squeezed Mina's hand. "We got this."

Presently Dillons arrived, Richardson behind him.

Emma spoke. "Benny, can you take all of us right to him now?"

"Yes." He nodded.

"Them too?" Dillons asked, pointing at Keiko and Johnny.

"Of all of us," Emma replied, "I'm worried about them the least, honestly. They'll be fine."

"All right, then. Everyone who's packing heat, lock and load. Let's try and get the drop on him."

Keiko and Johnny held hands with Benny, and the three of them vanished, along with Steve, Emma, Raven, Mina, Richardson, Dillons, and the two soldiers he'd picked.

One Hundred Eighty-Five:
The Final Confrontation, Part One

Dillons had never experienced teleportation before. It left him feeling tingly. He immediately raised his gun and assessed his surroundings.

They were in a square room with a semi-circle of pillars made out of what looked like crushed machines behind them. On a make-shift throne sat what must be the Angel: a hairless, genital-less man, with grayish blue skin that changed to purple near its hands and feet. The ends of its toes and fingers were red and clawed. Its eyes were green, almost glowing. It opened its mouth to laugh, revealing fangs.

Dillons fired, but his shot bounced off of a reddish purple shield that quickly appeared. It reached from ceiling to floor and cut across the room, blockading all of his group away from Angel.

Angel stood up and walked over, sneering at Dillons. The shield did not fall.

"You may have cut off my supply," Angel said, in a voice that sounded like wind chimes and gravel, "but I have enough energy stored to keep this shield up, long enough, I expect, to share some interesting facts...before I kill you all."

His ego was overwhelming. "You were expecting an angel, yes? Angels have wings." He grunted, and grew from his back six large, lacy wings like a dragonfly's, three on each side. The veining was deep purple, like his hands and feet, and the membranes between scintillated.

Dillons sighed. "Is this the part where you tell us your evil plan?"

"No," Angel said, lacking the pop cultural knowledge to understand why Dillons had said that.

"It's a shame that Dr. Yamada isn't here. Maybe he could have answered a few questions." He addressed Emma. "You know they made me? When I was Matthew. I was a *prototype*. Completely artificial. I never had parents, just a DNA sequencer and an embryo."

"I was supposed to be a 'control unit' over weaponized psychics. The instinct to do so is *in my genetic code!* They drugged me into submission. Told me if I was good, I could meet my brother, Andrew. I asked about him all the time, about my parents. They just kept stringing me along." He laughed, a disagreeable, piercing noise.

"Did you know that the entire time I was here, I never actually met Andrew? They always told me 'soon.' Soon never came. They even had the gall to tell me I would have a *second* brother eventually...this 'thing' they called 'Angel'...I wouldn't even have known this previously pathetic excuse for a being *was* Angel except for the writing on the tube I crawled it out of...that pathetic meat-sack with its slimy, useless brain. But I've improved it." He smiled at Mina, and then laughed manically, finding the lies he had been subjected to incredulous.

He turned to face both Richardson and Emma, who were standing near each other. "Do you know why I took control of Anna? She was a kinetic dynamo. I could have gone *anywhere*...I just wanted to see my brother. Of course, that didn't really matter, did it? We weren't 'real,' just brothers in math. I didn't even intend to kill anyone, but they got in my way."

"But I met Andrew. It took *years*. He was an uninteresting telekinetic with no knowledge of me and no will to resist. He knew nothing of our supposed parents, either. So I left. And then I met *you*." He pointed at Raven. She stepped back, alarmed.

Angel smiled. "I met you in the street, with your mother, during my one day of freedom. You were a child. I crushed men in front of you with slabs of the street. I threw their blood up in fountains. I was celebrating you; I could feel the strength in you. And here you are."

Raven shook her head in disbelief.

Johnny spoke up now. "They made us alter everyone's memories. It was awful. So many were broken by it. She doesn't remember."

"No," Raven admitted. "I remember bits and pieces. I thought they were nightmares."

"I have nightmares, too," admitted Mina. "Nightmares where I'm a child, and I...I eat people." She didn't know why she chose now to admit this. Maybe, it was to stand in horrified solidarity with her beloved.

Angel laughed again. "This is too perfect! Those aren't nightmares, either!" He held his hand up and a few pieces of paper flew over from his throne to his grasp. "I have your history files, too. We're both lies, you know that?"

He read from the paper. "Wilhelmina Ingraham. That's you. Daughter of Wilhelm and Olga Ingraham, of British, German, and Nordic stock. The best part? You were born *seven years ago.*"

Mina was shocked and confused. Surely that was a lie? She looked over at Emma, who nodded, looking ashamed of herself.

Angel continued. "We were both artificially aged and educated subliminally. Inside the tubes I built my throne room out of." He raised his hands and his wings fluttered. "But that's not the best part. I'll get to that. Your parents were *terrified* of you. See, you had powers since birth. They thought you were possessed. You could move objects with your mind, and when you got hurt, you healed instantly."

"They abandoned you in the woods in the dead of winter. You had nothing to eat. You would have died. They couldn't get over their guilt, though, and told the police everything. When they found you, days later, you were covered in frostbite and the blood of a couple hikers that had been killed by a fallen tree."

"You had been *eating* them to stay alive." He got right up to the shield, as close as he could get to Mina. "I think *you* killed them with that tree." He smiled, an ugly, sinister grin.

Mina gasped, her hands at her mouth.

"You were going to be a new experiment: a teenage, natural psychic. But, they did their 'process' on you anyway, and it backfired. You were almost powerless. I fixed you."

"So, you see, we're both monsters. Actually, I'd bet, except maybe for little Benny there, we're all monsters. We've all done terrible, awful things."

The shield started to waver. Guns were raised.

"Time's almost up, I guess. I'm ready for this. You know, Mina, I thought when I combined with this body, I'd have the same powers I had with you. I don't. But I can still kill you all." He looked again at Raven. "*Especially* you. I've been waiting most of my life to see what you can do."

One Hundred Eighty-Six:
The Final Confrontation, Part Two

The shield dissipated but before anyone had time to react, Angel pulled every gun in the room towards himself where he telekinetically mangled them into a ball, which he launched at Raven. She stopped it in midair and threw it to the side.

The three soldiers found themselves thrown violently against the ceiling. Dillons fell painfully on his back; one landed on his head, knocking him out, or worse; and the third fell on his legs. There was a sickening "pop," and Dillons could see a lump in the man's outfit that indicated a compound fracture. The man screamed before going into shock.

Raven tossed one of the pillars at Angel, but he resisted, holding it in mid-air with his telekinesis. She pushed back, but she could tell he was strong, and she would lose her mental grasp on it sooner rather than later. He raised a hand and a reddish ball of aura energy shot at Raven. She didn't have time to react, but the amber glow of Mina's shield appeared in front of her and saved her.

She redirected her push on the pillar to the side and it flew diagonally across the room, crashing into the wall. Steve ducked out of the way, and he and Emma herded the children into the far corner of the room. Richardson had cut his zip-tie off on a sharp edge of one of the metal pillars; he was now standing, smoking a cigarette, a neutral expression on his face. Dillons had checked on his men; one was dead of a broken neck, and the other, unconscious. He dragged him towards the back wall of the room, near everyone else.

Raven threw *three* of the pillars at Angel. He knocked two aside and the third impacted his shield, which he erected mere moments before he would have taken the blow.

"I don't think you're really that strong," Raven said, smirking.

"A general is only as strong as his army. And *I will have my army.*" He pushed aside the pillar in front of him as his shield disappeared.

"I've killed your army."

He smiled. "There's plenty more."

Raven flung two more pillars across the room. Angel dodged one but got clipped on the shoulder by the other, knocking him back. The one he dodged traveled straight through the wall, revealing the open sky beyond.

It was getting dark.

Raven ran right up to Angel and the red glow started to crisscross her skin again. It would give her strength, but she couldn't let it get as far as last time. She was afraid of it, and rightly so.

Angel smiled. "*Now* you're getting serious!" His wings fluttered eagerly.

She was devoting every ounce of her power to offense. Mina, having realized on their escape the true potential of her aurakinesis, provided Raven's defense.

Angel and Raven traded blows; he was physically weaker than she, but he continually fired energy shots at her, which Mina flawlessly shielded her from. He lifted one of the pillars behind Raven and threw it at her. Mina established a shield in mid-air and the pillar hit it and fell to the ground, pieces shattering off. Raven heard it and looked over her shoulder; she raised a hand in the air and a long, sharp piece of twisted metal flew into her grasp.

Angel raised a hand to her face and it started to glow; she grabbed his forearm and pulled it to the side so hard his elbow popped, and in the second he took to process that, she screamed and jammed the metal shaft straight through his chest, her glow burning almost white.

He staggered backwards, looking at the bleeding wound in his chest. He smiled, his elbow already healed. He pulled the bloody shaft out of his chest, and the wound started to close up.

"See..." he began, looking up. The next thing he knew, he was pushed out the hole in the building, and was falling. He landed with a sickening thud, hundreds of feet below.

"I guess he can't fly," Raven said, looking down at his mangled body. "I bought us some time," she continued, looking back at everyone else. "Benny, get everyone to safety, okay?" He nodded. She pulled Mina close and gave her a quick kiss. "Let's go," she said.

"Yes," said Mina.

Raven levitated them out the hole in the wall, and then slowly descended to the earth below. Just then, the door to the room burst open and more of the psychic monsters poured in.

"I guess his backup was a little late, huh?" Richardson said, lighting another cigarette. He looked over at Benny, who smiled at him. The next thing he knew, he was standing near the building's entrance with the rest of the group.

The courtyard lights had come on and the area was well-illuminated. The sun was still up, but it was hidden behind buildings and night was coming soon. Raven and Mina stood in the middle of the courtyard, near an abandoned semi truck. Raven continued to fight physically against the already-healed Angel, her skin glowing brightly.

Richardson looked around; there were military vehicles at the edges of the large courtyard and blockades set up at every road leading out; he wasn't likely to sneak his way out of this one. Military personnel were everywhere, staring at the brutal fight going on. He heard helicopters and looked up.

They were news choppers. He could only imagine the nightmare this incident would cause for NOD, for the military, for Kresge.

Richardson spotted Kresge standing near one of the vehicles. He was staring at the fight as well; he was quite a ways away, but Richardson thought the look on his face was one of dread and panic. He heard a loud snap and turned to see the semi's trailer lurch into the air, the trailer's pin broken off in the cab's hitch.

Angel leaped away from Raven, his wings flapping likely for show more than use, and brought the trailer into the air between them. It lunged at her and she pushed back, feeling its weight in her mind. She was going to lose the battle, so rather than try and keep pushing back at him, she exploded it, rupturing it from the inside and trusting Mina to protect her from the rain of debris. She did, and it was a good things she did so, as it was more than just the metal and wood of the trailer that scattered throughout the courtyard. Transport crates spewed violently outward, carving craters into the ground all around them. Some shattered, littering glass, metal, and plastic pieces of unknown devices across the courtyard.

Angel shielded as well, delighted that the ground was now strewn with weapons of opportunity. He threw piece after piece of the refuse at Raven, and the attacks were coming so fast she had to assist Mina's protection of her by redirecting some pieces and shielding against others. Despite Mina's abilities, there was only so much she could do in such a short period of time.

His local area cleared of waste, Angel ripped out a chunk of concrete and tossed that at Raven. She weakly shielded, rebounding it, but she fell down in the process. A second chunk of concrete hung in the air, but then there was a loud "bang," and Angel dropped it harmlessly.

He touched a hand to the side of his head, which he found to be warm and wet. He looked at his fingertips.

It was blood.

HIS blood.

He turned around, and saw two soldiers within yards of him, one panicking as he tried to aim his rifle more exactly, the other aiming a strange, unfinished looking gun at him while something on his back seemed to be emitting smoke. In mere moments the men found themselves dozens of feet in the air; they did not survive the impact when they landed.

Richardson saw this and looked back at Kresge, who seemed to be screaming into a walkie-talkie, anger and defeat commingling on his face. He scanned the courtyard and spotted several soldiers in ones and twos backing away towards the roadblocks.

Angel turned back around to see Raven lunging at him with a piece of metal from the wreckage in her hand.

He wasn't going to fall for this trick twice, but this time, she went straight for his head.

The attack merely deflected to the side.

Raven repeatedly tried to stab Angel through the head with the object, but every time she failed. Her glow was fading and her reaction time was worsening.

If I can't kill him, why am I fighting him?

If I'm not supposed to kill him, why does it matter if I fight him?

She glanced over at the Gates building, glad to see Emma and Steve were safely out of it. All of the children had come out from wherever it was they had been hiding. There were at least two dozen of them, and they all looked healthy and vibrant...except for Anna, whom she noticed standing near Danny.

It has to be before nightfall.

Even you psychics can't dodge at the speed of light.

Raven had her epiphany.

Keiko, Johnny, can you tell Twill to bring her to the entrance immediately?

Yes, came the reply.

She looked around hurriedly until she spotted Benny.

Benny, grab Anna and come to me. We need to go to Nod, and we need to come back almost immediately. Within seconds.

All right, he replied.

Raven turned to Mina. "I'll be right back. Just keep him here, okay? Protect yourself."

Mina nodded with a look of resolve on her face. Raven turned and ran to meet Benny and Anna, who were crossing the courtyard towards her.

"I guess I'll have to settle for killing you first," Angel said.

"Good luck with that," Mina replied.

Benny, Raven, and Anna floated above the portal. He released them, and they entered it. The vertigo came and passed. She navigated towards the light, and the blue sky opened before her....

One Hundred Eighty-Seven:
A Brief Sojourn

They stood on the hill, near the tree, the a gentle wind rustling through the leaves and grass. Raven stood with her Anna, damaged and mute, across from Twilloughby with his Anna, healthy and alert.

"So, you've figured it out?" Twilloughby asked, a grin on his huge face.

"Yes. I believe so."

Twilloughby knelt down, and addressed Anna. "Anna, are you ready to reunite with yourself? You'll be whole again."

"Yes, but, I don't want to leave."

"It's okay. You'll be back very soon. And, I imagine, you'll have others with you as well."

"If you're sure."

She walked over to the other Anna and held her hand out. "Hi," she said.

The other Anna held her hand out, and when they touched, there was a blinding flash of light. When it had faded, only one Anna remained, a composite of the two, but healthy, with a full head of hair.

"It wasn't very nice there," she said. "I had almost forgotten about it." She winced as the memories of two people merged back into one."

"I need you to help me. We have to defeat Angel—Matthew. The one who hurt you."

Anna breathed deeply. "I'd like that. I don't want him to hurt anyone else."

"Well, I have a plan...."

One Hundred Eighty-Eight:
The Final Confrontation, Part Three

Benny grabbed Raven's hand as she and Anna fell from the portal. He teleported them back to the courtyard outside. Angel was attacking Mina, who was dodging and shielding defensively.

"I can't see the sun," Anna said.

"Can you still do your thing?" Raven asked.

"Yes. I can sense it. It's a lot better if it's direct, though."

"I can do that," Raven responded.

She ran to the center of the courtyard. "I'll take over," she said to Mina. Mina nodded and backed off.

"Ready to die?" Angel asked. "I have things to attend to." Both of his hands started glowing.

"Not quite yet," she said. She grabbed both of his arms and snapped them outward so his shots missed her completely, and she took off to the sky, carrying him with her.

"What are you going to do, drop me again?" Angel asked sarcastically, the air whipping past them.

"Yes," Raven answered.

They flew up and up, until the sun came into view. It was large and orange and just touching the horizon. Raven tossed Angel up, and then rocketed away, back down to earth.

On the ground, Anna concentrated. It was so much energy to manage, it was incredibly draining on her, but it had to be done.

The sky darkened. The sun's rays became coherent by the force of Anna's will. The beam was visible simply due to the sheer volume of rays, with enough scattering off of random bits of dust that the people in the courtyard could see it.

Anna turned the sun's light into a laser beam, and aimed it at Angel.

It felt like an eternity to him, the intense heat, the utter disintegration of his body. In truth, it was over in an instant. His mind was free again, but here was not like Nod; it would die on its own. He fled, his thoughts screaming as they, too, began to disintegrate. The last thing he was aware of before his ego was stripped away was Richardson's terrified face.

All of the children had gathered around Richardson. They were glowing, bright white-blue light.

"No...what are you doing?" His almost-finished cigarette fell from his lip.

They were so bright, he could no longer discriminate between them, and then a tower of light illuminated the sky, and they were all gone, Richardson included, leaving only a smoldering cigarette behind.

One Hundred Eighty-Nine:
Loose Ends

Raven and Mina walked, exhausted, over to Steve and Emma, their arms around each other.

"It's over," Raven said. Steve hugged them both as Emma smiled, a little of her guilt finally lifting.

"So, what do we do now?" Steve asked.

"I suggest," came a voice from behind them, "that you get out of here before everything calms down and the investigation starts." They turned around to see Dillons, followed by the rest of the staff coming out of the building.

"He's dead, isn't he?"

"Yes," Raven said, smiling.

"The rest of the guys are clearing out the building floor-by-floor. Ever since you started fighting him, I think he's been distracted because those monsters became easy pickings. I expect now they won't even put up a resistance. Anyway, as soon as that building's clear, they're going to go in there, and you are all over the surveillance tapes. I really, really doubt it will be safe for any of you to stay in town."

Raven, Mina, and Emma were already prepared mentally and emotionally to leave, but Steve had never honestly contemplated that he'd have to. "Shit," was all he could muster, suddenly depressed.

"Come on, I'll get you past the checkpoints," Dillons said. "It's the least I owe you."

"My car's that way," said Emma, pointing.

"Follow me," said Dillons, and they headed out.

Yamada and Jameson spotted Kresge and walked over to him. He was standing with Dr. Graley.

"I'm sorry you got involved in this mess, Dr. Yamada," Kresge said. He motioned for one of the soldiers to come over. "Get this man out of here and on a plane back to Nevada."

"Yes, sir!" The soldier led Yamada away, while Jameson stood nervously in silence.

When Yamada was sufficiently distant not to hear any conversation, Kresge spoke. "And what have you been up to?"

"Hiding, of course! It was madness in there!"

Kresge harrumphed. "You're just as useless as Richardson said you'd be." He turned to Dr. Graley. "Gather the staff. As soon as the building's clear, get them in there and have them prepare *everything* of value for a full transfer to the

Nevada facility."

She looked at him skeptically. "Beg pardon?"

"Well, after the grand scale of this fuck-up, the shit's gonna land on us all. I might make it out unscathed, but if you want to have any chance of staying out of a federal prison, you better stay on my good side and work strictly for me."

She was at a loss for words, a situation she wasn't well prepared for. "Uh, understood."

Kresge turned to see Jameson was quietly walking away. Wordlessly, he pulled his handgun out and shot Jameson in the back of the head. There were no last words, no closure, as his body slumped to the ground, dead.

Dr. Graley jumped, both surprised, and shocked to see how cold Nicholas Kresge really was.

"Once everything's gathered up, have your men kill the staff. Every one of them. Then we're going to torch the building. I'm not leaving any loose ends. At least Richardson's already taken care of, whatever the hell that was."

Emma looked over her shoulder when she heard the gunshot, but she didn't see anything and she assumed it was just more fighting between the soldiers and the creatures.

They had arrived at the checkpoint, and Dillons was happy to see that Marcus was one of the two people stationed at it.

"God, Dillons, it's so good to see you." He held his arm out; it was Predator time.

Dillons just shook his head. He sighed. "Carlos is dead."

Marcus' arm slowly dropped as he processed this information. "That...sucks," was all he could manage to say.

"Yeah. Well, without these people, a lot more of us would have died. I want to let them pass."

Marcus stepped to the side and held his arm out.

Steve, Emma, Raven, and Mina walked by. Emma looked at Dillons as they passed him. "Thank you," she said.

He nodded, and smiled.

They piled into Emma's car, Steve in the passenger seat, and Raven and Mina in the back. As they began to drive away, Emma spoke.

"I figure we have some time before they sort any of this out. I want to pick up some of my stuff. I...have a place to stay. If...we want to stay together. I think that's safer for now."

"Yeah...." Steve said, forlornly. "I'd like to say good bye to my family, and do the same. And I'm sure Raven would like to get some of her things as well. He turned around to look in the back seat.

Mina had her arm around Raven, who had fallen asleep against her. There was a smile on her face.

Epilogue

Steve, Mina, and Raven sat uncomfortably, as every spare bit of room in the car (and some that wasn't really spare) was filled with boxes and bags of clothing and other belongings, as was the trunk. Luckily for them, it was a large car.

They turned down a long dirt road. The snow had mostly melted, leaving it a muddy, gravelly mess.

Emma turned on the radio and found a station that came in. It was fuzzy, but bearable.

"With no explanation of the events in downtown Omaha two days ago, the public is understandably quite vocal in their anxiety. Multiple protests and demonstrations, some anti-military, some led by conspiracy theorists, have overwhelmed local police. The government is considering imposing martial law after rampant property destruction and several homicides have been reported."

"The Gates Building, the center of the incident and once a shining example of human progress and good-will, lies in ruin after a fire apparently gutted the building, collapsing it to the ground. Reports of explosions are unsubstantiated at this time. The military is blocking investigation, citing the possibility of sensitive materials that may have survived the destruction. The exact nature of the goings-on inside the Gates Building are still not publicly known."

"More on this story as it develops."

Emma switched off the radio. "Well, that's...something."

As they continued onward down the road, they began seeing fences, farmhouses and barns some distance away. After awhile, they seemed to hit the center of town, a half-mile strip of businesses and restaurants. The few vehicles they saw looked ancient, the oldest clearly being from the 1940's.

After a bit more driving, the buildings became fewer and far between, and dirt roads led off, ostensibly, to other houses. Emma turned down a wooded road and after a few turns it opened up to an overgrown clearing, with a large house in front of a field.

The house was two stories tall with a large, covered porch, two chimneys, and a tall, triangular roof that probably contained a sizable attic.

"Holy shit, is this the house from *Ninja Turtles*?" Raven asked.

"What?" asked Steve.

"*Teenage Mutant Ninja Turtles*? The one from the nineties? When they have to leave and they go to April's farmhouse?"

"Yeah, I never saw that one."

"Wow. Okay."

"Yeah, this house has been in my family for forever," Emma said. "No one's lived here in years, though, so it's going to take a lot to make it a home."

Raven turned to face Mina.

"We'll make it a home," she said, smiling.

~END~

ABOUT THE AUTHOR

Jason Chmielewski was raised in Detroit, Michigan until middle school, when his family moved to Saint Clair Shores, where he's lived since. Brought up on a study diet of video games, cartoons (both foreign and domestic,) fantasy, and science fiction, he now writes horror, sci-fi, and weird fiction. He is the co-author of *Secrets Best Kept*, a collection of short horror stories available on Amazon and through www.StefaniManard.com. His first major project, *Nothing Sacred, Nothing Harmed* is the first novel in a series exploring interpersonal relationships against a back drop of science fiction and the possible end of the world.

Jason Chmielewski